Greig Beck grew up across the
Sydney, Australia. His early
sunbaking, and reading science .... then
went on to study computer science, immerse himself in the
financial software industry, and later received an MBA.
Today, Greig spends his days writing, but still finds time to
surf at his beloved Bondi Beach. He lives in Sydney, with his
wife, son, and an enormous German shepherd.

If you would like to contact Greig, his email address is
greig@greigbeck.com and you can find him on the web at
www.greigbeck.com.

Also by Greig Beck

The Alex Hunter series
Arcadian Genesis
Beneath the Dark Ice
Dark Rising
This Green Hell
Black Mountain
Gorgon
Hammer of God
Kraken Rising
The Void
From Hell
The Dark Side

The Matt Kearns series
The First Bird
Book of the Dead
The Immortality Curse
Extinction Plague

The Fathomless series
Fathomless
Abyss – Fathomless II

The Valkeryn Chronicles
Return of the Ancients
The Dark Lands

THE WELL OF HELL

GREIG BECK

momentum

Pan Macmillan acknowledges the Traditional Custodians of country throughout Australia and their connections to lands, waters and communities. We pay our respect to Elders past and present and extend that respect to all Aboriginal and Torres Strait Islander peoples today. We honour more than sixty thousand years of storytelling, art and culture.

First published 2022 in Momentum by Pan Macmillan Australia Pty Ltd
1 Market Street, Sydney, New South Wales, Australia, 2000
Copyright © Greig Beck 2022

A CIP record for this book is available at the National Library of Australia

The Well of Hell: Alex Hunter 10

EPUB format: 9781761263934
Print on Demand format: 9781761263941
Original cover design: AJ Swarthout

Proofread by Laura Cook

Macmillan Digital Australia: www.macmillandigital.com.au
To report a typographical error, please visit www.panmacmillan.com.au/contact-us/

Visit www.panmacmillan.com.au/ to read more about all our books and to buy books online. You will also find features, author interviews and news of any author events.

Eventually, all things that were hidden will be found.

Time does that for us, whether we want it to or not.

— Greig Beck

The Well of Hell (aka the Well of Barhout) is a giant sinkhole in Yemen's Al-Mahara desert. It has a circular entrance that measures around 100 feet across at the surface and drops to nearly 400 feet deep.

Local folklore says the cave was created as a prison for demons, and superstition has it that objects near the hole can be sucked toward it. To this day, locals never visit there, and some think that it's bad luck to even talk about it.

PROLOGUE

5021 BC – City of Allonia, in what will one day be
Yemen

An abomination.

The king stared at the huge cage as if in a trance. It was
covered over now so none could see the horrifying thing that
his beautiful son had become.

He barely heard his advisors, wise men, and spiritual
leaders all talking at once. Because he didn't want to.

He was the first great king of Allonia and had united
most of the land under his single centralized monarchy. His
kingdom was a land at peace, bountiful, and was at the
crossroads of many civilizations so he grew rich on trade and
taxes. And Akmezdah was the first leader to be called a living
god by his people.

But the title of god did not sit well with him because it was
the time of the eighteenth season, the moon was hidden once
again, and the *real* gods had returned.

The first time he had laid eyes on them he felt the blood
freeze in his veins – the horror of them – nearly twice as
tall as a man and with faces that belonged on the reptiles

1

that hunted the waterways. And with them were their vile servants; crawling abominations that tore at a man's sanity.

When they first appeared they called for tribute – but not of gold, or food, spices, or fine cloth, but instead it was the youth they wanted, young, strong men and women, who were taken and never came home to their families again. Every eighteen years it was the same.

In return they shared secrets of fantastic machines that could count time, or follow the lights in the heavens, or show them advancements in architecture that had enabled them to make huge buildings like their own pyramids that reached up to the sky. The visitors' gifts had made the city of Allonia wealthy, safe, and strong, and he thought if he just looked away, just for a week once every eighteen years, his city would be safe.

But then they had taken his only son, Zadahsen, in just his twelfth year. Akmezdah was in agony and knew he should have stayed silent like the rest. But he could not. After all, who were these so-called gods to demand one of royal blood?

The king knew the old gods had once again made their home in the great pit beyond the first desert. And he had set out with his army to make war on them.

For days they had battled and eventually fought their way into the pit, and there found the hidden pyramid. Of his ten-thousand-strong army, the mightiest in the land, there were just a few hundred remaining with the rest burned to ash, or captured to be taken to a fate that, he now knew, was far worse than death.

A war-weary Akmezdah had succeeded and retrieved his son, but he felt no elation from the deed because he knew the war had doomed his city.

The king turned again to the covered cage. Tears streamed down his face and his stomach roiled as he remembered what his beautiful son had been, and he refused to even attempt to look at him again.

His last act would be to give little Zadahsen a grand burial, in his son's own pyramid – even though the king knew that somewhere in that obscene thing the boy had become, he somehow still lived.

INCIDENT 01

Eventually, all things that were hidden will be found.
Time does that for us, whether we want it to or not.

CHAPTER 01

June 7, 1925 – The great desert beyond Harbarut – Yemen–Oman border

"They've found something, hurry." Iraqi archeologist Atafi An Omar turned, his grin showing through a face covered in yellow dust. "They say it is a wall."

His colleagues, Mohammad Marboosh, a Saudi, and the English dig leader, Phillip Saunders, hurried along the freshly excavated trench to join him in the passageway beneath the arid desert.

At the end of the tunnel, Omar stood aside. "See here."

Saunders stepped forward and lightly, almost reverently, touched the flat stones with his fingertips. "Carved granite, and it's old, so very old." He slid his fingers along the hard surface, finding some areas of unusual smoothness. "This was once polished to a glassy sheen but has been exposed to the elements for perhaps thousands of years."

Marboosh lifted his lantern. "Then buried and forgotten for thousands more."

Saunders turned to smile. "Until now."

"The legends are true then?" Marboosh whispered. "A great civilization *was* here, one that might have even rivalled the Egyptians."

"The ancient Egyptians rose to greatness 5000 years ago. But if the legends are true, these people were here thousands of years before them." Saunders continued to explore the stone with his fingertips. "All we know has come from a shard of ancient pottery, and some oblique references from tomb wall carvings – a mighty race existed here around 7000 years ago, and then they vanished, almost overnight. Wiped out by some catastrophe."

"But who were they?" Omar asked.

Saunders leaned forward to blow dust from an area of the wall. "Yemen has long been at a crossroads of cultures and civilizations, but this might be an entire race of people that we have never come across." The Englishman turned and smiled. "We could be meeting them for the first time."

Omar cleared away a little more sand. "We need to get the men to excavate further."

"Agreed." Saunders looked up. "We're only about twenty feet down. We'll bring in a larger team and take the layers off, come down at it from above so we miss nothing."

Marboosh grinned. "I feel we are on the precipice of finding something truly magnificent. Let's begin immediately."

* * *

Hundreds of workers toiled like an army of ants over the site, removing thousands upon thousands of bucketloads of sand, soil, and dust every hour. Working in continual shifts right around the clock, three weeks later they had excavated down another forty feet.

The three archeologists now stood looking into the massive crater, but it wasn't empty, because at its center was an apex structure, like a pyramid.

"It's only got three sides," Saunders said. "Unlike the Egyptian structures that have four."

"It's unique." Omar turned. "Maybe this is a prototype pyramid as it was constructed long before even the Pyramid of Djoser that dates back to around 2630 BC." He turned back to the excavation. "It's perfect, but who had the technology back then to build it?" he asked.

"Indeed, that is the question." Saunders looked around at the hills surrounding their site, and then back at the debris that had been excavated. "And one more thing. The heavy stones that were laid up against the structure were not from around here. They were brought in. That tells me that the elements alone didn't bury this site. I think this pyramid was covered over on purpose."

"Why would they do that?" Marboosh asked.

"Royal tombs were hidden, but it was only the accursed that were weighted down to stop their souls ascending to the afterlife," Omar replied. "But in this culture, we can only guess."

A cry came from the excavation pit, and the three men stared down at the commotion. Omar was first to decipher the yells.

"They've found an opening – a door."

Saunders smiled. "Bring the equipment."

The workers were pulled back from the pit, and the three men made their way down to stand before the huge doorway – it was bricked in as was standard with sealed tombs.

Saunders ran a finger down between two stones and then used a knife to scrape at the line. "Gypsum mortar – soft, but effective. It should be easy to make a hole in between them."

Saunders called for the long auger drill that would create an opening just an inch in diameter. It had a crank handle that could be operated by two men, and Omar and Marboosh turned it slowly, grinding and sinking in between the hard stones.

At around the eleven-inch insertion mark, the drill suddenly sunk in fast. "*Through*," Omar exclaimed.

He removed it slowly, and then waved a hand in front of the hole toward his face, sniffing deeply. "Breathable." He sniffed again. "Strange odor, musky; it's dead air, but not toxic," he said.

"Good, we won't need gas masks." Saunders pointed to a place a foot lower than their first hole. "Sink the sight-hole here."

The two junior archeologists drilled another hole below the first, and when done, they held a lantern up to the first hole while Omar crouched and placed his eye to the lower opening.

"What do you see?" Marboosh asked.

"Wonderful things." Omar looked up and grinned at his Howard Carter joke. "Kidding, nothing so far; just an empty space."

Saunders helped him up. "Alright, let's get the men to take out several stones and make a larger opening. We're going in."

It took the workers another two hours to remove around a dozen of the two-foot blocks to create an opening big enough for them to enter. Marboosh was chosen to go first.

"History will remember me." Marboosh smiled and turned back to the impenetrably dark hole. He paused to draw in a deep breath. "And may all the gods and prophets hold back their curses on this day." He held his lantern up and stepped through.

Saunders and Omar waited a moment and then followed. They found that the *empty space* was actually a long corridor and high enough for them to be able to stand upright.

"It is the only path forward," Marboosh observed.

"Then …" Saunders motioned forward, and the trio followed it for around a hundred feet.

Omar consulted a small compass, but then frowned. "I can feel we're tracking downward, maybe at an angle of fifteen degrees. But the compass is going mad, spinning."

"Maybe because there's ..." After a moment Marboosh shrugged. "I have no idea."

"Leave chalk marks," Saunders suggested.

After another half-hour Saunders exhaled in a *whoosh*. "Getting thick down here. I'm betting the stale air is heavy and settling in the lower passages. It'll be more toxic the deeper we go. Any thicker and we'll need breathing equipment."

"Stale, but I smell cloves and salt; embalmer's tools." Marboosh tied a scarf around his lower face and the others did the same. "We can go a little further, I think." He made another chalk arrow on the wall. "It opens up just ahead."

In a few minutes more the trio entered a large room, and around the walls were fresco-style art that, even after all the millennia, was still richly colored in ochre, black, reds, and white.

"This is magnificent." Saunders held his arms wide. "This is who they were, here, it's all here in their story." He pulled out his notebook.

"I can't understand it," Marboosh said. "Some symbols are familiar, but not quite like anything I've ever seen before."

"Or anything anyone has seen for many millennia." Saunders paced around the room, trying to find the beginning of the pictorial sequence. "This here ..." He indicated an image of the night sky with what could be the sun, Earth, and moon all in a direct line. He turned. "Is this an image of an eclipse? But if it is, how did this race even know about the planets in the solar system?"

His men just shrugged.

"Amazing." Saunders blew air through pressed lips. "This looks a little like ancient Sabaean, or maybe a proto version of it. I think I can read it, or at least some of it." He found the start. "Here their story begins."

He cleared his throat. "*The city of Allonia, the greatest city in the world.*" He smiled over his shoulder at his colleagues.

"So now we know who they were, Allonians; in the kingdom of Allonia." He turned back to continue reading. "*The gods have returned to heaven once again*," he intoned. "*And their pitiful slaves left behind will sleep and await their return*." He held up his lantern. "Yes, look here."

There were images of tall beings that bore a resemblance to some forms they had seen before. Saunders quickly sketched the familiar figures before glancing up at them again.

"Recognize them?" Saunders asked.

"*Sobek* – the alligator-headed god – but how could it be?" Omar asked. "He was the ancient Egyptian god who was supposed to bring life to the land of the Nile – and he wasn't worshiped for thousands more years."

"True. And yet here he is. Or something like him." Saunders moved his light closer to the images. "Oh my god," he whispered.

Up close, the alligator-headed creature was grotesque and not like a normal reptile. It had six eyes up a long tooth-studded face, and each eye was blood-red. Even after all this time it was clear the artist had managed to capture a glint of intelligence and malevolence in them.

"Maybe not such a benign god then," Saunders mused.

"And what do you think these represent?" Marboosh asked.

The others joined him and looked up at the pictures. The men were silent for a moment, but Saunders felt a chill on his neck.

"Are they supposed to be giant spiders?" he asked.

There were creatures that looked to be helping the people build a pyramid-type structure.

"Or are they the slaves they mentioned?" Omar whispered.

"Maybe it is just meant to be allegorical, like a representation of action or desire," Saunders replied and held his lantern closer – its light showed a strange entity that had multiple arms and legs, ten of them, but they were human limbs.

"Here's another," Marboosh breathed. "*Ach*, even worse."

This one was a four-legged figure that had human arms all the way up its sides and a long torso like a centipede. Each hand was holding a tool of some kind. There was a head end, of sorts, but there were no features discernable – or even an actual head, as the neck seemed to end in a stump.

"I've never seen anything like this." Omar turned to the tall Englishman. "Perhaps, as you say, they are just meant to represent hard work, or something like it. We don't know enough about this culture and its deities yet." He smiled, but it seemed fragile.

"Many hands make light work, as they say." Saunders turned and grinned but noted that his companions didn't share his humor that day.

He sketched a few of the images in his leather-bound notebook and then turned to another part of the wall. He soon found more writing. He began to translate, but the messages made no sense to him, and he questioned if he was interpreting them correctly. But how could he know if he was, he asked of himself, seeing he might be the first in 7000 years to read it?

Saunders picked up the translation again. "*Every ten plus eight seasons we must give up our sons and daughters so the others may not be merged*, or, hmm, *joined*, or something like that." He shook his head. "That doesn't make a lot of sense. But many of the symbols are new to me."

Saunders moved a little bit further along the wall and saw images of an army approaching what looked like a massive hole in the ground. Its size dwarfed the approaching soldiers. "Omar, Marboosh, do you know what this is?" He held his light a little higher.

The men looked for a moment, conferred, and then Omar turned. "We believe it might be the Well of Barhout. It is far out in the harshest part of the desert." He shrugged. "There is nothing there but sand, heat, and scorpions. The area is said to be cursed."

"Cursed, hmm?" Saunders raised his eyebrows. "To an archeologist, a curse is an open invitation. It usually means there is something there the ancients did not want us to find."

Saunders turned back to the image, studying it for a few seconds more, making plans. He made more notes as his two colleagues walked around the room.

"Look here." Omar wiped the flat of his hand across a wall. "Another doorway, sealed. There might be a room or passageway beyond." He held his lantern up close to a wall decorated with more images of the strange many-limbed beings. There was also a single line of the unique language.

"*The waiting place of Zadahsen, son of the mighty King Akmezdah.*" Saunders stared at the words. "Waiting place? Strange reference for a tomb."

"But maybe the tomb of a prince," Marboosh whispered.

"A royal tomb. We must get inside." Omar began to press along the wall.

"And we will." Saunders joined him and ran his fingers over the stone. As usual there were no hinges or clues as to how the door opened. "There must be a pivot point. Look for it."

The three men held their lights closer and almost had their noses to the stone as they examined the ancient wall, looking for the key to opening the heavy door.

Soon Saunders found an almost imperceptible line running from his head height to the floor. "Eventually, all things hidden will be found." He took a step back, a small smile lifting his lips as he looked over the ancient wall. "Time does that for us, whether we want it to or not."

He stepped forward and pushed. Nothing happened.

"Omar, give me a hand here." He pushed again, and this time Omar also put his hands against the wall and shoved.

With a sound of grating stone, a six-foot-high and four-foot-wide door pivoted and revealed a space beyond that showed nothing but impenetrable blackness.

"*Oh* ..." Omar pressed his scarf closer to his face. "... bad air."

"Very bad. And more of the cloves smell." Saunders waved a hand in front of his face, trying to dissipate the gases. "We check this out and head back." He held up his lantern, and the small flame flared a little. "Careful, there might also be methane," he remarked. "Odd; usually only found if there is something recently decomposing."

Inside they found a room about fifty feet square that contained several large stone boxes like sarcophagi.

The Englishman turned slowly, taking in the austere room. "This doesn't seem like a place of royalty or even nobility."

"Then this must be the slave interment room," Marboosh added.

Saunders noticed that the stone boxes were all different sizes and only the central one, the largest, bore more ornate carving. The others just had simple markings carved into their lids. Saunders looked down at one of them.

He brushed at a layer of dust, and then leaned forward to blow away the rest. "It says: *sleep*, or *slumber*." He turned and raised an eyebrow. "Short and to the point, I guess." He shone his light on the other smaller boxes. "The same on all."

Marboosh stood beside the large middle one that was square rather than long. Its sides were easily ten feet long. "We should open this one."

Saunders turned slowly. "This is like no tomb–vault I have ever been in or seen in my life." As he turned about, he saw that there were no paintings decorating the walls, and no life story of what or whoever was in the sarcophagi.

He approached the larger stone box. Unlike the others, this one was heavily carved with rose-like flowers, and the workmanship was magnificent as each petal, leaf, stem, and stamen was perfect. There was just a small inscription on the top, nestled in among more carvings of boats, and horses, and a bow and arrow – all things that might have been a child's favorites.

"*My beautiful son and heir*," Saunders read. And then: "*Forgive me*."

"Forgive me? Why is he asking that?" Omar asked.

The Englishman looked up. "It seems the son died before the father. Maybe he couldn't prevent it."

Omar looked back at the huge stone box. "It refers to the 'heir' – that means this could be the 'waiting place' of Zadahsen, son of the mighty King Akmezdah."

"'Waiting place'." Saunders walked around the huge stone sarcophagi, his brows coming together. "This is interesting."

Around the edges of the box were holes cut in the stone lid, and pegs sticking out from the side of the base – at one time there had been stout rope tied to each peg, which would have sealed the box closed.

"Do you know what these are?" Saunders pointed.

Both men shook their heads.

"Locks. Crude but effective locks." He stared, perplexed.

"The rope has rotted away," Omar noted. "But it's hardly secure, as the smallest of knives could have cut through them. They would not have stopped the box being opened by robbers."

Saunders lifted the remains of one of the ropes and crumbled it between his fingers. "They were designed to keep the lid closed, and would have made it very difficult to open." He turned to his colleagues and half-smiled as he dropped the rope dust. "If you were inside."

Saunders' fellow archeologists looked up at the Englishman, their eyes suddenly as round as moons.

"I'm not sure I want to disturb it now," Marboosh said softly.

"Yes, you do." Saunders went around the sarcophagus, sweeping away all the remnants of the rope locks. Then he placed his lantern on top. "What say we meet a prince?"

Omar propped his lantern on another close sarcophagus, so it was pointed at them, and Marboosh did the same on one opposite, casting a field of light on the huge central stone coffin.

"We slide the lid to the side. But be careful; it'll be heavy and we must try and avoid it breaking." Saunders tested the three-inch-thick lid. It must have weighed at least 250 pounds, so even with three of them they would struggle to shift it. "Very heavy."

He braced his hands on the edge. "Ready?"

The other two men did the same either side of him.

"One, two, three, he-*eeaaave*." He pushed.

The lid held tight, and held, and then with the sound of grinding stone, it finally slid a few inches.

"We've got it moving now. One more push." Saunders braced his legs. "And ... he-*eeaaave*."

This time the sarcophagus lid slid at an angle about a foot and a half, revealing a dark void within. Saunders turned his face and momentarily held his breath. "*Phew*, that smell again, cloves and something else, sour, like old sweat."

He picked up his lantern and the small tongue of light flared again – perhaps he had found the source of the methane. He carefully held the light over the gap. He frowned and craned forward. "Something in there. But I can't make it out." He put his lantern on the ground this time. "Let's push it all the way off; we need to see. And be careful, I want this lid in one piece."

Omar and Marboosh glanced at him and hesitated for a moment, but then placed their hands on the edge of the capping stone.

"One, two, three-*eee*." Saunders heaved and his two colleagues did the same.

The stone slab slid and then teetered on the edge of the sarcophagus for a moment before sliding off and thumping to the ground. Saunders snatched up his lantern, and all three men peered inside.

Marboosh shrieked, threw his hands up in front of his face and quickly backed out of the room. Omar covered his mouth with one hand, either stifling a scream or his nausea, and took one step away, perhaps not wanting to leave his friend and mentor.

But Saunders was rooted to the spot. He felt a shot of revulsion threaten to void his stomach, a cardinal sin in an uncontaminated archeological site like this. But the thing in the large box-like coffin was not just leathery skin over bones. It was still plump and full. It seemed to have at least half a dozen legs, all human, and all attached to a central body that was like a large pillow of muscle. At one end there was what looked like a short spinal cord, a pipe of dried flesh, but no skull on the end.

"This can't be real. It can't have been alive," he whispered. He couldn't tear his eyes away.

Though his scientific brain told him the abomination of flesh and bone was some sort of fake, his primitive brain whispered that *yes*, this was real and had been alive. And worse, that this *thing* was somehow once Zadahsen, the beautiful son of the mighty King Akmezdah.

He remembered the glyphic images in the other room of those multi-legged and -armed slaves that had toiled in the dark caverns, perhaps building the pyramid, or somehow serving their masters in some other way. But who were the masters, or what?

The image of the Egyptian god Sobek came rushing back, and Saunders glanced at the other odd-shaped sarcophagi in the room. He wondered what other physical atrocities lay hidden within them.

Right now, he didn't have the stomach to find out.

"Let's, *ah* ..." He wiped his hands on his pants. "... leave this to the medical experts." Saunders grabbed his lantern and headed for the doorway. As he did he looked up and saw the words carved above their heads on the lintel.

He read them: *Made to serve.*

Made. He wondered at the word. And then the words in the other room suddenly made horrifying sense: *We must give up our sons and daughters. So the others may not be merged.*

Merged. Somehow these poor souls had been merged, *physically* merged. And it had also happened to the king's son. It was why Akmezdah begged for forgiveness. Perhaps because he let it happen? Saunders wondered. Or maybe he had no choice.

Suddenly he desperately wanted, needed, to be out in the sunlight. He backed up, bumping into Omar.

The man pointed. "Look, there."

It was an alcove about head height that was little more than an open box. Inside there were what looked like jars, and something else – a scroll tube.

Saunders went to grab the scroll when from behind them there came the sound of movement, shifting. The men spun, but in the dancing light of their now shaking lanterns nothing seemed out of place. However, Saunders was sure the noise had come from the open sarcophagus and the hair on his neck stood up straight. He remembered the locks on the huge coffin.

Saunders glanced again at the scroll. "We'll get it when we return." They backed out, but once outside Saunders stopped. "Wait; help me here."

He grabbed the edge of the heavy door and dragged on it. Omar reluctantly helped him. But it began to swing and then its momentum pulled it fully shut in a grinding shower of dust.

Phillip Saunders coughed as the stink of cloves and sweat began to coat the back of his throat. "Yes, we can come back later." He turned and began to walk fast back up to the light with Omar and Marboosh jostling to keep up.

At the surface the men sucked in air as though rising from below deep water, and Saunders drank deeply from his canteen. He finally felt his heartbeat returning to normal.

He turned to his ashen-faced colleagues. "And now, I think we need to visit this Well of Barhout and see what else there is that the Allonians did not want us to see."

CHAPTER 02

2002 – The Saunders Estate, Covington,
Cambridgeshire, United Kingdom

At twenty-five, and following the death of his father, Bradley
Phillip Saunders as the sole heir inherited the entire Saunders
estate. Or what was left of it.

The tall, thin young man with blond hair and a long,
straight nose with flaring nostrils walked the halls, noting the
faded beauty of the magnificent reception room and taking
in the artworks, gilding, massive chandeliers, teak floors, and
rugs that were handmade in Persia and each a good fifty
square feet.

He paused at the tasseled end of one rug to appreciate
the weaved artwork – it was the typical Mina Khani design,
the distinctive pattern made up of repeated daisies interlinked
by curving diamond shapes and in rich blues, greens, and
burgundy. It was over 150 years old and he bet it had seen all
manner of gentrified foot traffic in its life.

He sniffed, detecting hints of cigar smoke, old brandy,
and dust. The rugs probably hadn't been professionally
cleaned in decades and he knew why – each cost around

£5000 to carefully clean – well beyond the budget of a bankrupt estate.

He turned to look up at the plaster ceilings and saw the faces of plump, flying cherubs and burgundy florets, all with a dusting of mold. Everywhere was in decay.

He sighed; the grand house had seen better days and it was true what they said, at least in the circles he was brought up within, that owning a grand estate was one thing, but paying for its upkeep was another.

He knew the estate was a money pit, but he didn't care. Bradley Saunders had established a company that had created an internet search engine while he was still at university. Within a year he had paid off his student loan and bought a Mercedes. Then in two years he had become a millionaire. In five he had branched out into other areas of technology and was soon a billionaire, then a multibillionaire, so owning a castle-like house and estate just seemed fitting now.

Then one day he'd simply lost interest in the business and had cashed out. Some said the tech wunderkind had burned out. And they might have been right.

He knew he had become one of the idle rich – idle and bored. His view was that he, and the world, was out of ideas, and needed some fresh thinking, fresh ideas, and fresh leaders. But where to get them? He decided he needed to either buy them or create them.

He looked up at the magnificent ceiling again – the massive grand house sported three stories and 152 rooms: most of which he'd never even seen inside.

Lately, he'd looked over a few of the rooms and he'd noted that the several staff he had retained had done well to keep the place looking comfortable. But it was well beyond their meagre efforts.

But money solved everything, and once he'd injected a few million more dollars into it, it would be brought back to a level that would satisfy royalty. That thought brought a smile to his face; he bet he'd even get the heir to the monarchy to pay a visit if he played his environmental cards just right.

He just needed one thing to be accepted into the stratospheric social set: an impressive, and squeaky clean, backstory.

He had many interesting ancestors and relatives, and he was told their personal effects were stored in the huge attic. Anything he found by way of pictures of hunting, or owning slaves, or even shaking hands with German generals, would be erased from his history. And that job would start now.

Young Saunders began to climb the stairs to the attic storerooms.

* * *

Three hours he'd spent already, and so far, he'd found evidence that some of his forebears had been big game hunters, with images of them beside dead rhinos, elephants, lions, and even a damn giraffe. He'd have the pictures burned before the day was out.

There was a grainy image from 1938 of one of his ancestors smiling broadly somewhere in Bavaria and lifting frothy beers with a short man with a toothbrush mustache and side-slicked hair. "Seriously?" Saunders chuckled and put this, too, in the growing *to-be-burned* pile.

He sighed as he turned to a set of sealed crates that had belonged to his great-grandfather, Phillip Bradley Saunders, who had been his namesake. Apparently, Phillip was a keen archeologist, and had many artefacts stored in the house.

Bradley opened the first crate and right on top there were two, single middle pages from a yellowing newspaper but from different dates. He lifted them out and carefully unfolded them.

The first was from *The Times* of London, 9 August 1925, and toward the bottom right-side corner there was a picture of a young man, similar in looks to Bradley himself, with slicked-down hair and stiff, high-buttoned collar and tie.

Bradley read the article: *Eminent archaeologist Phillip Bradley Saunders has vanished while on a field trip at some undisclosed location near the small town of Harbarut on the Yemen–Oman border.*

After an unsuccessful search, the local police fear he may have become lost in one of the most inhospitable areas of the desert and succumbed to the elements.

His work in the Middle East was shut down following news of his disappearance and his personal effects will be returned to his estate.

"So that's why the old boy has no headstone in the family cemetery." Saunders turned the page over but saw nothing else of interest so lay it down and lifted the second sheet. It was from just a week later.

Saturday, 11 am, 16 August 1925, a service will be held for Phillip Bradley Saunders at Covington Cathedral and will be attended by close friends and family.

Death notices then, young Saunders thought. *Hmm, guess I'm starting at the end of his life and working backwards.* He put the papers aside and quickly sorted through dusty-smelling shawls, hats, some carved statues that looked as old as time, and various notebooks. He then lifted free an ornately carved teak box and shook it – there was something in it, something heavy. The box was locked, but a quick twist with a screwdriver and the locking hinge popped open.

He looked inside. "Well, well, what have we here?" It was a leather-bound journal. *At last, something interesting*, he thought.

The leather was a little dry but well preserved and on the front was an embossed and stylized 'P.S.'

"Phillip Saunders." Bradley Saunders smiled. "Hello, Great-Granddad." He unwrapped the leather string binding that held the book closed and flipped it open.

He saw it was the man's journal – a dig journal – from his time in Yemen. He wasn't all that clear on dates but given the notations at the start of each new entry, it seemed to be the last project he was working on before his demise. Or at least his disappearance.

Young Saunders read quickly. And then slowed to read some parts twice. He sat down and the hours flew by, his brow creased as he adjusted to his great-grandfather's writing style and took in the details of what he had been doing nearly a hundred years ago.

His great-grandfather wrote for many pages of something called the 'Saros cycle' of the moon, whereby every eighteen years the sun, Earth, and the moon all arranged themselves in a straight line, creating an eclipse and a heavy gravitational effect on the tides. He seemed obsessed with it being some sort of key to a puzzle.

Saunders read on, but when he came to the section on the discovery his great-grandfather had made in the Yemeni desert, he stopped, reread it, and then began again.

He stopped reading. "You found something strange out there, didn't you, old boy?" he whispered into the gloom of the old attic.

He wasn't an expert, but one thing was for sure; there had been no announcement anywhere or at any time he could remember of anyone finding a buried pyramid in the Yemeni desert – especially one that predated the Egyptians by several thousand years. That would have been huge news all around the world.

There were maps, detailed coordinates, and Phillip Saunders described briefly what he had seen after they had entered the pyramid structure. However, about some things he was vague, only hinting at both wonders and horrors. But one thing was for sure: the man vowed to go back, and this time with a team of scientists.

That wasn't all; just before the journal ended, Phillip had been making plans to travel to a remote area called the Well of Barhout. But then the journal abruptly ended. And the man had vanished. So, he obviously never went back to complete his work.

"A royal tomb. In a hidden, 7000-year-old pyramid." Bradley Saunders sat back and closed his eyes, the hint of a smile just lifting his lips. "Which means it's still there." His eyes flicked open. "Waiting for me."

INCIDENT 02

While the lambs sleep, the dogs of war never do.

CHAPTER 03

Six months ago – Jungle village of El Guanito, Venezuela

The boats sped down the Río Apure, six of them, each loaded with five men. All were dressed in dark clothing, armored vests, and, oddly, face shields that looked like black hockey masks.

Over their shoulders were automatic rifles, plus they had sidearms, knives, ammunition, and grenades hung from their belts. One of them even carried a small flamethrower – outlawed internationally as a weapon of war, but those laws didn't matter here, because here *they* were the law, and they had come for violence and death.

As the boats sped in to the shore a youth who had been cleaning fish on the riverbank stood to watch them. The first man to alight lifted his left hand in greeting.

The youth just stared back.

With his right hand the black-clad man pulled his sidearm and put a bullet in the center of the kid's chest, blowing him back into the foliage.

Within seconds the thirty-strong team had assembled. They were some of the Manudro Government's wolf packs, the death squads sent out to eradicate the supporters of Juan Gualdino, leader of the opposition government-in-waiting.

Rumor had it that Gualdino was sending out spokespeople to spread misinformation and gain supporters. As far as Manudro was concerned, if you weren't 100 percent for him, you were the enemy, a terrorist, or potential member of a rebel army, and therefore you were a cancer, and surgical removal was the only solution.

The death squad had been moving down the Río Apure, village to village, rounding up the young men and older boys from La Florena, Los Matias, Bruzual, and now at El Guanito, their latest stop.

Sousa, their leader, checked his GPS, grunted his approval, and then motioned his men forward – the town was ahead, and they would approach from the west. There had been little movement out from the other side of the town, meaning they were not expected.

Their modus operandi was the same as with all the previous villages – once they had rounded up the young men, they marched them into the jungle to be executed, and then dropped their bodies into a sinkhole or simply left them to the jungle scavengers. There would be no rebellion this summer, or the next.

Sousa split his team into two columns and they spread out. His census data told him there were around thirty males between the ages of twelve and fifty. He expected to round up every one of them in the next few hours.

* * *

Saqueo lived in El Samin and had heard the frightened rumors that the Manudro death squads would soon arrive in El Guanito, just a dozen miles down the river from him. Perhaps they were already there.

The young man had no family, none left now, anyway, after his small brother, Chaco, had been killed by some demon in the jungle of Paraguay just on ten years ago. The only reason Saqueo was still alive was because he had been saved by the American soldiers – a strange band of giants called HAWCs.

He had helped them and perhaps saved many of them with his knowledge of the jungle and its dangers. They had called the jungle *a green hell*, but he called it home.

Saqueo closed his eyes for a moment as fear made his heart race in his chest and caused him to feel light-headed – he had heard the whispers of the first mass grave found a few miles outside Bruzual. All the vanished ones, the men young and old, were found there, and all had been shot in the head, or stabbed, or bludgeoned, perhaps when the killers had run out of ammunition. Then more were found in the jungle around the other villages.

And, he was sure, the killers would come for his adopted village of El Samin as soon as they were done with El Guanito. It was clear that Manudro's death squads were cleansing the area of anyone who might even think of rising against him.

He thought again of the HAWCs. There was also a pretty science woman with them, Miss Aimee Weir. And the big man, Captain Alex, had told him that they owed him their lives. In return he had promised to be there if ever Saqueo needed him. If anyone could defeat the death squads it would be Captain Alex, Saqueo decided.

The HAWC man had left him with one thing: a phone that had a contact number already within it, which he always kept charged. The soldier had told him to always keep the phone with him, as they might not be able to find *him*, but they could always find the phone.

He sat in the darkness of his small hut and typed in a message: *The death squads are coming for us. They are killing everyone. Help me. Urgent. Saqueo.*

He sent it and then simply sat staring at the tiny screen of the ten-year-old satellite phone for several seconds. He had no idea what to do. Should he run into the jungle? The monsters were still at El Guanito and would soon be finished their killing there. Then it would take them a day to reach El Samin. He had time to warn people. But if he did, would not the wolves follow them into the jungle?

He sighed and lowered the phone to his leg, feeling helpless and confused.

And then it pinged.

He snatched it back up and looked at the screen.

Message received. We're coming. Keep the phone with you.

His mouth dropped open for a moment. Then he tilted his head back and stared heavenward. *Thank you*, he thought.

Saqueo sat forward. Now, he just had to stay alive until then. He looked again at the phone and the time displayed on it.

He made up his mind. He would do one more thing: try to get as many of the young men and boys as possible to follow him out of the village. He could save them too.

* * *

Twenty-three hours later, the boats pulled in at the El Samin shoreline and Sousa had his men do a quick ammunition check. They had enough, but not enough to be spraying bullets into the jungle. He'd have them use knives when possible. Or even tie several villagers together and place a grenade in among them.

Allesandro was left behind to mind the boats, but the rest filed into the jungle – all of them knew what to do and had done it many times over the past few weeks. But even after all those times Sousa still felt a thrill run through his body. He had been a poacher in his younger days and loved to hunt.

This was little different, except the quarry begged and cried when they were cornered.

Sousa knew that they could also fight back. But to date, none ever had. He snorted with contempt; one day he wished they would, because he'd love his expert team to be really tested.

He waved his wolf pack onward. He wasn't sure exactly why his superiors wanted the villagers eradicated as they didn't seem a threat. But the money was good, and while much of the country starved, he and his men lived a good life. They'd make their peace with God one day. But just not yet.

In another hour, they had surrounded the village and on Sousa's signal, charged in, kicking down doors and dragging people from their hiding places. But there was something wrong – there were very few young men.

It took a few more beatings but eventually one kneeling woman confessed that a young man named Saqueo had come and warned them. But she said she didn't know anything more than that. Or she wouldn't tell him.

"It's alright, *shush*, it's all fine," he cooed as he cupped her cheek for a moment. Then he pulled his gun and shot her in the face. He holstered his weapon and turned to the next kneeling woman. "How is your memory, mama?"

Sousa then quickly learned that this Saqueo had taken the young men and led them from the village. "Find the tracks. I want to be after them in the next five minutes."

The group circled the village and eventually found a trail into the jungle. There were the tracks of many men, and, like their namesakes, the wolf pack took off after them at a jog.

After another twenty minutes Sousa's scouts came back to the group and reported their findings. "There's a cave a half-mile up ahead. All the tracks lead toward it. They must be hiding inside."

"Good." Sousa organized his team into three groups, sent one out to the left, one right, and the third up the middle.

He wanted to ensure no one escaped – he was angry now, so would take great pleasure in killing them all. But he would save a special death for the one who organized their escape; the one called Saqueo.

The men crept forward, maintaining complete silence as they expected there were lookouts. They didn't want to panic them and *stampede the horses* as the saying went.

When they were about 100 feet from the entrance, Sousa signaled for them to spread wide and create a barrier that none would slip through. Then the three teams squatted and waited for the signal.

Sousa smiled and inhaled the scents of the jungle. He liked this bit; the anticipation before the hunt concluded. Around him the jungle had grown as silent as a tomb; perhaps the creatures of the night had been frightened away by his wolf packs, or at least sensed what was about to happen.

He lifted his radio and whispered: "Kill them all, but the one named Saqueo, leave for me. He needs to be a lesson to all others."

* * *

The two black parachutes glided silently toward the jungle canopy. They maneuvered past large spreading treetops until they found the tiniest open area, then the pair released their chutes while they were still fifty feet in the air so they wouldn't get hooked in the branches.

Alex Hunter and Casey Franks landed not forty feet apart and stayed down on one knee as they assessed their surroundings. The pair wore night-dark uniforms, with non-reflective, shell-like armor plating on the chest, thighs, and biceps, and also banded ribbing over the areas that needed high mobility.

Over their heads they wore retractable helmets, giving their faces an eerie, matt-black, featureless appearance. But internally, the wearer had multi-vision spectrums – to them, the jungle at night was as light as day.

On each of their forearms were gauntlet devices. One acted as a range of sensors and a communication system and the other was a retractable shield that could even stop a fifty-caliber round. Over their shoulders were long, dark skeletal weapons.

Alex Hunter rose to his feet and Casey joined him. Around her waist were ten black blades, all honed to scalpel sharpness and weighted for precision – one of her night-fighting preferences.

Alex quickly checked a panel on his left gauntlet – they were less than half a mile away from the phone, but it had taken them longer to arrive than expected. A knot tightened in his gut – in this brutal game, seconds mattered, and minutes meant the difference between life or death.

Alex targeted the youth's device, found the direction and then he and Casey began to sprint. As he did, he remembered the pair of cheeky kids, Saqueo and his little brother, Chaco, who had led them through the jungle on the Paraguayan mission. Chaco hadn't made it, and Alex was determined they wouldn't lose Saqueo, too.

He moved fast, and Casey pushed herself to her limits to keep up. She was always one of his first picks for backup – the female HAWC had been stabbed, shot, burned, and blown up too many times to count. And she always got back up, stronger than ever.

Stripped down, the five-ten woman was a mass of muscle, flaring tattoos, and scar tissue, and the scar that ran down the side of her face pulled her mouth and cheek up into a permanent sneer. She probably could have had it fixed, but he guessed she kinda liked it. And with her white crew cut she looked as fearsome as they came.

Alex stopped and held up a hand. He turned slowly. The four-lens quad systems built into his helmet gave almost

180-degree vision that could be switched between a number of different spectrums, and right now he moved it from night vision, thermal, and then to distance amplification. Satisfied, he waved her on.

When Alex was about 200 feet from his target he slowed. This allowed Casey to catch up. From there the pair moved cautiously – black wraiths in a dark jungle.

Alex retracted his face plate, and Casey did the same. In the dark Alex's eyes shone silver like those of a wolf and he noted that around them the jungle was tomb silent. And there was something else.

"Smell it?" he asked.

"Blood," Casey replied.

"Lots of it," Alex said, and the knot wound a little tighter.

The pair crouched at the jungle's edge outside the mouth of a large cave draped with vines – it was a good hiding spot.

"Reconnoiter," Alex said.

Casey immediately vanished off into the jungle to scout around the entrance. There were three likely scenarios: the death squad was lurking outside, they were inside, or they were gone.

A small part of him hoped Casey would find them, as that might mean they hadn't entered the cave yet. And then Saqueo and the other villagers might still be alive. But the smell of blood told him otherwise.

In a few minutes she was back.

"Big group, maybe forty, mostly in bare feet. The villagers, I'm betting. They were followed by men in military boots, around thirty of them – they came in from the west and then only the guys in the boots evac'd."

"And the villagers never left." Alex's heart sunk. "Let's go."

They crept toward the cave entrance, paused a moment, and then entered. They didn't need to go too far.

"We're too late," Casey said.

The bodies were everywhere. Most had open wounds, like gaping second mouths on their necks that had spilled their lives to the cave floor. There was so much blood the HAWCs stood at the edge of what seemed like a rapidly cooling lake. Already the jungle flies were taking their fill.

Alex lifted his gauntlet and used the tracker to find Saqueo's contact phone. He found the signal and followed it to a cave wall. There was a youth's body there, nailed to the bare rock.

The young man was only about five-six in height. It had to be Saqueo, but it was hard to tell as the features of his face had been obliterated. Alex slowly looked down to see the young man's nose, lips, and ears had all been cut away and lay at his feet. It had been a slow and grotesque torture.

"Fucking inhuman," Casey growled.

Alex felt the blood surging in his ears and something inside him began to coil and burn. He reached out and lay a hand on the youth's bloody face – and then he saw it – the torture, and the sneering face of the torturer.

"He was still bleeding out. He was alive when they did this, and he was alive when they left. They wanted him to die slowly in his world of agony."

"Why? Why this brutal?" Casey seethed.

"Because this was a message." Alex took his hand away and closed his eyes for a moment as he felt a storm of pain begin in his head.

And then the whisper began: *Yes, it was a message, a message for you. And now they're laughing.*

Stay cool, stay clear, he prayed. *Not now.* He reached up and dragged the metal spikes from the rock with his bare hands, and then gently lowered the body to the ground.

"Bury him?" Casey asked.

Alex shook his head. "He's already gone. They all are." He walked to the mouth of the cave and looked at his bloody hands – in the darkness the blood looked like glistening oil.

The throbbing in his head became a drumbeat. It urged him on, called for war, and then a rasping voice in the ether whispered again: *Their souls cry out to be avenged. Run them down.*

Alex exhaled long and slow. He nodded.

They'll move to the next village now.

"They'll move to the next village now," Alex repeated.

"We can't let them keep doing this," Casey replied.

Then we kill them all.

"Then we kill them all," Alex said like an automaton.

Casey glanced at him. "Hell yeah."

* * *

Sousa and his team were just a mile or so from their boats. The slaughtering, the torturing, and degradation they had inflicted on the villagers meant nothing to him. In fact, the only thing on his mind was the new car he would be able to buy from the bonus payments he would receive on his return.

In his mind, he knew his job was dirty, hard, and high risk. But someone had to do it, and it might as well be someone like him who would do it well.

His thirty-strong pack of mercenaries had coalesced, and now laughed and talked loudly as there was no need for haste or silence anymore. Before heading to the next village, they would return to base and restock on stores and ammunition. Their eradication mission would go on for as long as the dry season held, which might be only two weeks or up to four if luck was with them. Sousa hoped four, as he was paid by the head, so the longer the mission, the more heads he would take.

"This way." He remembered the landmarks and already heard the river in the distance. But when they stepped from the jungle, he stopped, his eyes widening. Their inflatable boats had been destroyed. All six of them had been shredded from bow to stern. Sousa immediately went onto high alert and motioned for his men to take cover.

"*Allesandro*," he hissed.

There was no reply from the man he had left behind to mind the boats.

"There." One of his men pointed to a man slumped against a tree, forearms on knees and hat pulled forward as though he was sleeping.

Sousa bared his teeth for a moment and cursed and then motioned for two of his men to go forward. The pair crept toward Allesandro, calling his name, but it looked like their man slept deeply.

When they were just a few feet in front of him, one of the men leaned forward and grabbed his hat, lifting it.

To their horror they saw that the man's head was twisted all the way around and faced backwards. And worse, the man who held the hat saw that there was a thin, metal wire running from the hat to a dark curved metal box attached to the tree. It detonated – with enough force to shred the top halves of the two men into blood and bone fragments no bigger than a fist.

Sousa and his pack of killers threw themselves flat, and when the blast was over they jumped up and began to let loose hundreds of rounds into the jungle all around them. Leaves were shredded, bark splintered, and sparks flew from any exposed rocks.

After a moment Sousa screamed for them to cease fire as they were burning through the last of their ammunition. Silence returned and he just let his eyes move over the clearing now opaque with a haze of cordite smoke. They stayed like this for a full minute as the fog of gunfire cleared.

"Maybe there's no one there now," the mercenary closest to him whispered.

Sousa nodded. "We must have hit them or scared them off." He looked again at the shredded boats. "We will need to go back to the village and take their boats."

"Who would have done this?" another of his men asked.

Sousa hadn't even asked himself that. The villagers certainly had reasons to want them all dead. But they did not have the courage, skills, or equipment to set a booby trap like this, let alone the ability to take down a trained soldier like Allesandro.

"I think we need to ask the villagers a few more questions." Sousa got to his feet, and the men around him did the same. It was then that the knives came out of the jungle, two of them, both scoring hits into the throats of the men on either side of him.

Sousa dived to the ground. "*Fire, fire.*"

The men began to empty their clips into the jungle once again.

"I'm out," one mercenary called.

"Out," came another.

"*Stop, cease fire, cease fire.*" Sousa knew what was happening – they were being goaded into burning through their remaining ammunition.

The smoke dissipated again, but this time when it did there was a black-clad figure standing at the opposite side of the clearing. It stood stock-still and there were no features on its dark, flat face. But Sousa could tell it was staring at them.

"Who the hell is that?" he whispered as he quickly reloaded his last few rounds.

From its belt the black armored figure drew another blade into each hand.

"*Bastardo,*" Sousa hissed through clenched teeth. Whoever it was seemed to be alone, but for some reason he felt a chill on his neck, and didn't want to confront them.

"*Uh*, I think we'll go around," he said, and, still in a crouch, turned away. But then froze. Not fifty paces behind him was another of the frightening figures, this one enormous, powerful looking, and at least a head taller than any of his men.

Automatically, Sousa's soldiers raised their guns at the apparition and began to fire. Even Eduardo with the flamethrower raised the nozzle of his weapon, preparing to bathe the giant in a gout of liquid fire.

But the huge man didn't try and dodge the bullets but instead just lifted one arm, from which a swirling vortex appeared, like a shield, and none of their last bullets could penetrate it. Their firing began to die down, and then the figure attacked.

He was in among them in seconds, smashing, crushing, and decimating his mercenaries. From behind, the other smaller, armored soldier joined the attack and with a blade in each hand it danced, twirled, and spun, each time opening throats, or heart-stabbing his soldiers.

But this was nothing compared to the giant in their midst whose speed and ferocity was like a creature possessed, and he unleashed a level of savagery Sousa had never witnessed even in his own brutal experience.

The man's strength was unbelievable, and he was an unstoppable force as he twisted heads, ripped one man's arm from his body, and punched another in the chest so hard the rib cage staved in on itself and the heart was undoubtedly stabbed by the bones.

For a while, their last bullets still flew and a brief tongue of fire from the flamethrower lashed the foliage, and Sousa ducked under the friendly fire from his own panicked mercenaries. But it soon ebbed as all their ammunition expired, and Sousa's wolf pack was destroyed one by one. In another few seconds the gunfire ceased entirely, and Sousa knew he was alone.

The smoke cleared. He was standing in the midst of a killing field of shattered and bloody bodies. The smallest of the strange soldiers, or demon, or whatever it was, still held a blade in each hand. Thick blood dripped from the dark steel, and the figure flicked it onto the ground and then sheathed the weapons. Once again, the being became statue-still as it simply watched Sousa.

"*What are you?*" he screamed.

The smaller dark warrior never moved, so Sousa carefully eased down to the body of Eduardo lying at his feet and unclipped the flamethrower from his torso.

"I have money," Sousa yelled as he pulled the tanks over one shoulder and held the nozzle in one hand, sliding his finger onto the trigger. "Plenty of money. You can have it all."

Now we will see, Sousa thought, and raised the flamethrower's nozzle. The smaller shadow soldier still never moved a muscle, instead simply stared. But then Sousa noticed the blank face of the thing wasn't pointing at him, but just past him. He spun quickly and his heart leapt to his throat. The other demon was not more than six paces behind him.

Perhaps it was fear, but without even thinking his finger tightened on the flamethrower's trigger, sending a boiling gout of fiery death toward the other man. The explosion of super-heated gases bathed the figure, and Sousa smiled knowing that he would be cooked to cinders no matter what armor he wore.

After a moment more he shut it off, as the weapon's barrel was becoming too hot to hold in his hands. But when the smoke cleared and his eyes adjusted to the night's darkness once again, he saw that the demon man was still there, smoke rising from the black suit.

The giant then reached up to touch something on his neck and his dark face mask slid up into the helmet. The face was burned and scalded but from it his eyes shone silver from the ruined flesh.

"How can …?" Sousa's mouth couldn't finish the question, because as he watched the blisters popped, dried, and then vanished. The red, ruined flesh flaked away, new skin formed and what remained was a face so devoid of pity and humanity that it could have been carved from stone. He knew then he was right; these things were demons.

"For Saqueo," the monster said as those twin pools of mercury bored into Sousa. In a blink he was on top of Sousa and grabbed his head in each of his large hands.

Sousa scrabbled at the man's hands, and in a last effort he reached down to snatch up a dagger from his belt and swiped it across the demon's face, cutting the cheek, deep. Sousa grinned through his pain as he saw blood flow.

He is just a man after all, he thought. But then it stopped, and there was a hissing noise as the wound closed and in seconds was just a line.

"Forgive me. I didn't …" Sousa begged.

The pressure began, harder and harder, until there came a noise like a green branch beginning to splinter. The agony was like nothing Sousa had experienced in his life, and he knew there would be no forgiveness this day.

* * *

Alex's hands came together, and Sousa's head flattened to explode bone fragments and cranial matter over the clearing.

Casey whistled in appreciation. "Harsh."

"We failed." Alex ripped the shirt from the dead man before letting the body drop. He then wiped his gloved hands on the rag. He straightened. "But they'll be back. These regimes have no shortage of killers."

"Then they'll do it again. And again." Casey looked over the bloody clearing. "This would be a full-time job for us."

"Unless the head of the snake is removed," Alex replied. "I'll talk to the Hammer." He looked around one last time. "We're done here."

He called in the chopper.

* * *

A week later, hovering in the Venezuelan air was a drone no larger than a hummingbird. It was a simple device and had few functions; basically, the tiny machine was a floating eye. It also carried a miniaturized form of a laser pointer.

Right now, it was 1000 feet over President Manudro's palace in the capital, Caracas. It watched the party below – 200 of the country's elite gathered with military generals, secret service personnel, and like-minded politicians for a party celebrating Manudro's birthday. And right now, the birthday boy had just taken the stage to sing.

As the crowd stood and erupted into applause as he was handed the microphone, the laser came online and fired its invisible beam down onto the ground at the man's feet – no one noticed the matchhead-sized dot among the carpet of confetti.

Just outside of the exosphere, 12,500 miles up, the THOR military satellite was awaiting its signal. The barrel-shaped satellite was a bus-sized object covered in sensors, with a flat front turned to face the Earth. Silently that flat front split down the middle and two doors swung wide.

Inside there were twenty long and pointed rods. One slid out, and small vapor jets helped it on its way. Inside the nose of the rod were multiple sensors that controlled small wings on its side that would help align the device as it focused on its single objective – hitting that red dot.

The space-to-Earth kinetic arrow – or SEKA – weapon was constructed of a dense ceramic composite that was heat resistant and heavier than solid granite. The rod did not use rockets on its descent and, coupled with no significant iron signature, it was invisible to detection and impossible to stop. However, the resultant impact was not able to be differentiated from a meteor strike.

The SEKA soon punched through the lower atmosphere and then slowed to a mere 500 miles per hour. The red dot drew it ever closer just as President Manudro's eyes closed as if in rapture, as he reached the crescendo of his song.

The Venezuelan leader threw his arms wide and belted out the very last lines. He opened his eyes, holding the note in a long warble, and looked skyward. He noticed the speck above him. But by the time he noticed it, it went from a dot, to filling his world.

The impact was magnificent, and the resultant molten crater was fifty feet wide. Manudro ceased to exist, along with seven generals, the head of his secret service, and several politicians.

* * *

Colonel Jack "the Hammer" Hammerson, the commander of the elite Special Forces group known as the HAWCs, grunted and recalled a saying by Machiavelli: *If an injury has to be done to a man, it should be so severe that his vengeance need not be feared.*

And so it was.

He hummed as he sent a brief message to Alex Hunter: *The head of the snake has been severed.*

He sat back and lifted his half-glass of bourbon in a toast. "And another speck of shit is sent back to hell."

He sipped, and then downed the entire drink; a few more assets like the Arcadian and they could make the entire world a safer place. But right now, he only had one more like him.

Jack Hammerson put the glass down on the desktop and checked in on his other major asset. This one with far greater potential.

CHAPTER 04

Today – Buchanan Road, Boston, Massachusetts

Twelve-year-old Joshua Hunter sat cross-legged staring at the wall. Beside him the wolf-like 250-pound dog, his guardian called Torben, or Tor for short, also sat like stone.

The eyes of both were totally white as they traveled with Alex Hunter, seeing everything through the man's own eyes. They saw the joy of a mission successfully concluded. They also saw Casey Franks kick, punch, and stab her adversaries. And the pair watched as Alex Hunter obliterated the men with a hate bordering on volcanic.

Joshua knew this both was and wasn't his father. It was 'the Other', that demented being of pure hate that resided deep in his father's mind. He had to keep telling himself that.

Joshua pulled back, back through the void of time and space, and then blinked a few times as he reoccupied his own body.

Beside him Tor whimpered and placed one large paw on his shoulder. The boy patted it, and then got to his feet and crossed to his door, opening it a crack. His mother, Aimee, had gone to bed early and was already asleep – *good*. He turned and smiled at Tor.

"Don't worry, boy, we can control it."

He then turned to look out of the dark window; it was 10 pm and he should also be asleep. But he couldn't, and instead was wide awake, energized, and felt he needed to do *something*. He wouldn't even admit it to himself but watching his father tear people to pieces was exhilarating.

Alex Hunter was a hero, a savior, and only hurt bad people. His father was different to everyone else, better. Joshua paused as a thought came to him – so was he.

He walked to the window and stared out at the dark street, still wet from rain earlier in the evening.

He could help people too. His mind worked furiously for a moment, planning, and calculating the risks. And then he decided. He quickly crossed to his large chest of drawers to drag out a dark pullover, and also pull on sneakers.

Tor went and stood beside the door, waiting. Joshua shook his head. "No, you stay here; I won't be long."

He then turned, lifted the window, and leaped the two stories to the ground. Joshua looked back and pointed at the huge dog now staring down at him. He sent a forceful command to him: *You stay.*

The dog sat, still watching him, and Joshua turned to walk down the night-dark street toward the shopping district.

* * *

Hammerson's wrist messenger pinged and he lifted it to read the communication: *High order asset on the move – follow or intervene?*

The colonel quickly opened the space bird plotter for the local VELA satellite fleet with a complementary orbit. He found one, sent the commands to shift the aspect and then amplified the perspective.

In seconds more, he saw the figure in the dark sweat top walking toward the shopping district.

He typed out a message: *Neither – pull back*. He narrowed his eyes and craned closer to the screen for a moment. Hammerson began to chuckle. *He's already got backup*, he finished typing.

Hammerson saw the massive form of the dog moving through the backstreets, staying in laneways, between cars, and always in the shadows. For an animal so freaking huge, it was a master at becoming invisible as it tracked Joshua.

The dog was a military experiment from a special breed of animals they called guardians. And guarding was what he was doing now.

Hammerson went and poured himself another drink. He'd give the kid some space to let off some steam. What could it hurt?

Colonel Jack "the Hammer" Hammerson laughed out loud; he already knew.

* * *

Joshua was fascinated by people. By their actions and their thoughts. He could feel good humor, and joy, and love, and he could also sense anger, hate, and fear, as well as the very darkest of thoughts.

That's what he sought out that night; those violent thoughts – those people wanting or hoping to do damage to their fellow citizens.

Some of them simply conjured angry thought bubbles that were never acted upon. But others had hearts that were blackened by years of aggression, violence, and abuse, and would never be redeemed. And others seemed to just be born bad.

Innocence was becoming a rarer commodity by the day. And it wasn't fair that innocence was punished by those who brought nothing but pain and anger. He could be like his father. He could be the one saving the innocent ... and doing the punishing.

Joshua picked up a trail and followed it like a shark following the scent of blood on a warm current. He left the main strip and saw the small convenience store up ahead. And he also saw the two young men look furtively one way then the other, and then slip inside.

He had glimpsed inside their minds, and already knew what they had planned. He smiled as he sped up; he could be a savior too.

* * *

Kylie Leung was working the register that night when the two men came in. As soon as she saw them, she knew there was going to be trouble. Hoodies up over their heads, a brief glance at her, then faces down at the ground as they quickly moved into the food aisles.

Here it comes, she thought, and quickly pulled out her phone to dial her cousin.

There was one other person in the shop, a guy who looked like a trucker who pulled a sixpack of beer and headed to the counter. The two guys hung back, watched, and waited.

The trucker placed the beer on the counter along with a twenty, and Kylie stared, frozen.

He frowned. "There a problem?"

She nodded, her eyes going from him to the two guys. She tried to speak without moving her lips as if the hoodie guys could lip-read.

"I think I'm going to be robbed," she whispered.

The trucker snorted and then shrugged. "Welcome to the big city." He pointed at his twenty. "Just give me my change."

"Thank you very much." She slammed his money down, and he grabbed it and the beer and shuffled out without a second look.

And then the doorbell became the dinner bell, because the two hoodie guys were suddenly hard up at the counter. And the gun appeared. She stared into the muzzle, and that black hole became the biggest thing in the world.

They were screaming, but she was like a deer in headlights. One leaned forward and grabbed the front of her shirt to pull her closer and screamed again. This time the gun was pressed into her cheek.

She blinked and saw that the other guy had a long knife in his hands that might have been a machete.

"The register, you dumb bitch. Open it." The scream was so loud it hurt her ears.

And then she heard the bell over the door again, and turned to see the kid standing there, young, angelic looking, and just staring.

Go home, she mentally pleaded.

But the look on his face wasn't one of fear or even surprise, but instead was of excitement or exhilaration. And there was something wrong with his eyes; they looked silver, like mercury.

A thought came into her head: *I'll save you.*

She blinked, wondering where that idea came from. Kylie continued to watch him. Instead of leaving when he saw the gun and blade, he came closer.

The gun was still jammed in her face, but machete guy looked panicked and swung to the boy, pointing the large, flat blade at him, and holding it not more than a foot away from his face.

"Stay out of this, kid," he screeched.

"Too late, he's seen our faces up close now," gun guy said, almost in a monotone. "You know what to do."

"The kid too?" Machete guy half-turned.

"Yeah, the kid." Gun guy cocked the hammer on the gun and stretched his arm out, his eyes never leaving Kylie's face. "Money, now."

Kylie went for the register and hit the no sale cash drawer ejection.

"You were going to kill her anyway," the boy said.

"Maybe you too," machete guy replied.

"I don't think so." The kid spoke so softly Kylie barely heard it. He smiled, and then said: "Hey, cut his arm off."

For a split-second machete guy looked like he had seen a ghost. Then in a blur he spun around, the huge blade going in an arc so fast it was up and down, and across the gun arm of his friend before you could blink.

The force was phenomenal, and the arm separated cleanly at the forearm. The gun with the man's hand still clinging to it spun once in the air and landed on the countertop.

The nerves in the hand flexed causing the fingers to contract, and the gun fired. The bullet pierced the wall beside Kylie, and she flattened herself against the cigarette shelves, sucking in air at the shock of what she had just seen.

Machete guy screamed and screamed at what he had done. Even louder than his friend who clutched the spurting stump of his arm, his eyes wide in shock.

"Good." The boy was still smiling. "Now cut off his head," he said, soft and calm as ever.

Machete guy's eyes streamed with tears, but once again he went rigid. Then he drew the blade back behind his shoulder, getting the angle right.

He swung the blade so hard and fast it was a blur. But Kylie never saw it land as she collapsed to the ground unconscious.

* * *

Detectives Markowitz and Holston came into the shop to see several uniforms standing around the body. Another guy was in cuffs and sobbing as he sat on the ground. The stink of blood hung heavy in the air.

Markowitz recognized the sergeant. "Danials." He nodded. "What have we got? Besides a freakin' mess."

"Detectives." Danials nodded in return and opened his notepad. "Okay, we got one Miss Kylie Leung, young lady on duty this fine night, said this guy did it no question – the pair of perps came in together. And the corpse in three pieces was robbing Miss Leung with a gun. At that point we just had a normal Friday night stick-up. Then it gets weird, because the guy with the knife suddenly swings around and cuts the other guy's gun arm off. But he ain't done, because, get this, then he beheads him."

"Holy shit," Holston replied.

"It gets better." The sergeant flipped a page. "A kid came into the shop, maybe eleven or twelve years old. The girl said he had silver eyes." He chuckled. "Then the kid whispered to sword guy, told him to do it. The arm and then the head." He looked up. "And guess what? The perp did."

"That's nuts." Markowitz frowned. "She's in shock."

"Yeah." The sergeant bobbed his head. "That's what I thought, until we checked the security camera feed."

"We got it on tape. Good." Markowitz nodded.

The sergeant clicked his fingers to one of the police guys out back. "Henry, show the detectives the feed." He turned. "You bet we got it on tape. But not sure it's gonna help." He touched his cap. "Have a nice night, gentleman."

The detectives stepped over the blood and headed down between the food aisles to the rear of the shop. Through a doorway was a back room that doubled as washroom, storeroom, and work desk, complete with computer as well as a small screen that displayed the security camera feed.

"Rewind it," Markowitz said.

The cop nodded and brought it back to the two offenders first entering the shop. Both detectives bent forward to watch.

They stood in silence watching as the young woman noticed them and tried to engage some guy buying beer. He paid and left, and then the two perps rushed the counter – one with a gun, one with a machete.

Markowitz folded his arms as he watched. The woman seemed to freeze, and the gun holder pressed the weapon into her face. It looked about to go real bad for her. Then the kid walked in and that was the first weird part – his face was all blurred.

"Hey, did someone fuck with this tape?" Holston asked.

"Nope, you're seeing it exactly as we saw it," the uniformed officer declared. "And the girl claims she hasn't touched it either."

The knife guy looked at the youth for a few seconds, as though listening. And then in an almost graceful arc, he swung the long blade back and then down with all his strength across his accomplice's gun arm.

The hand holding the gun spun off, cleanly severed.

"Ho-*leeey* shit," Holston whispered.

Detective Markowitz whistled. "Make a fucking samurai proud."

Then, the kid seemed to whisper again, and knife guy grimaced for a split second as though straining against something. But then he gave in and finished the job by beheading his partner. Then knife guy simply sank down to the floor.

The kid turned and paused to look up at the camera. But there were no features where his face should have been, except for two dots of silver staring through a blur.

"She said he had silver eyes," Holston said.

Markowitz straightened, not taking his eyes off the image.

"So, who's the kid?" Holston also stood back from the small screen.

Markowitz folded his arms. "My money is on the girl knowing him. Maybe a cousin or friend. And she screwed with the tape to hide his identity and cover for him."

"Maybe," Holston replied and looked across at the still visibly shaking girl.

"Bring her in." Markowitz turned away. "We'll squeeze her a little and see what happens."

* * *

Hammerson hummed an old tune as he navigated MUSE, the military computer system that could invade and interrogate any other system and technology on the planet. He had accessed the application that allowed him to reach into the convenience store's network so he could watch the camera feed of Joshua's activities inside.

He sipped his bourbon as he saw the boy invade the guy's mind and turn him on his buddy. "Impressive," Hammerson said softly as the gun guy's hand and then head were severed.

It was everything he had hoped for. One day he expected the kid would be able to do that remotely. The end goal was for Joshua to reach out during armed conflict to take control of an adversary general's mind. And then have him turn their missiles back on their own launch bases. It could end a war before it started.

Hammerson was also impressed that the kid knew to hide his appearance and not to touch anything; even the door was opened by itself. *Good* – no mess for his team to clean up and he bet the cops wouldn't have noticed.

One thing bothered him, though. He had the programs rebuild Joshua's face from the original files, and there it was, the only thing that concerned him: the boy had a smile on his face. He had enjoyed it.

* * *

Joshua headed home, moving quickly because he was late. He knew a few shortcuts and after a moment he turned off the main strip, but then he slowed, stopped, and turned.

He put his hands on his hips. "I know you're there."

Tor slowly emerged from the shadows, his head down, and approached the boy. Joshua was tall for a twelve-year-old, but Torben's head reached his waist. He came right up to Joshua and bumped his head into him. Joshua grabbed the head and scratched it, ruffling the fur.

"I know you worry about me, but you don't need to." He smiled as he stroked the huge animal, who looked up at him with eyes silver in the dark.

"I can look after myself," he said softly, his eyes shining back, just as silver.

CHAPTER 05

2002 – The great desert beyond Harbarut –
Yemen–Oman border

Young Bradley Saunders had already spent millions and knew
he had little time left. The situation in Yemen was deteri-
orating and fragmented anti-Western groups were patrolling
the deserts and were now within the cities.

Months before he set foot in the desert, he had used his
wealth to begin a dig at the coordinates his grandfather had
left him. It was a gamble as he had no idea if what his
forebear had written about was real or just the ramblings of a
sun-addled mind.

But then he received word that they'd found it, the
pyramid, and he had then needed to bribe, bully, and trick his
way into the country. Now he was on his way.

In the chopper with him were six mercenaries, all armed
to the teeth. They too were expensive, as this was bordering
on a suicide mission – if they were captured by hostiles,
the likelihood of them surviving was around zero, with or
without weapons.

As soon as the helicopter touched down the group leaped out and scurried in a crouch-run through the swirling sand and grit toward the dig leader, a Yemeni excavator by the name of Harmoud Barboudi.

The man waved at Saunders and then shielded his eyes against the flying grit to reach out and shake his hand. He then quickly led them down into an excavated hole in a hillside.

The mercenaries stayed outside, all except David 'Winter' Winterson, Bradley's lead man and personal bodyguard; he was around the same age as Saunders, young, ruthless, but highly skilled, and not afraid to get his hands dirty. He was the only man Saunders trusted and he kept him by his side.

Dust rained down on them as Barboudi led them along a hastily excavated tunnel with dubious wooden struts holding back the dirt above and beside them. It was no better or worse than Saunders had expected – the people left behind in the city were not craftsmen but handymen willing to give any job a go if the money was right.

As the saying goes, he thought, *beggars can't be choosers*, especially when time was the priority. Saunders just hoped the tunnel didn't cave in on them, as he suspected no one was going to dig them out if it did.

They came to the wall, already open, just as his grandfather, Phillip Saunders, had left it in 1925, obviously expecting he would soon return.

Bradley Saunders saw that the dig teams had removed all the sand that had spilled in over the last century as the desert tried to reclaim another of its secrets.

Winterson went in first, gun up, scouting the first few dozen yards. He returned and nodded, and Saunders entered next. He followed his grandfather's steps, reading off the diary entries and quickly navigating the labyrinths below the desert surface. With a guide and moving quickly it wasn't long before they entered the antechamber, which was still adorned with the magnificent frescoes, but sadly, they seemed faded now, and not the vivid colors that his grandfather had described.

Saunders pointed. "See; it shows the masters, the tall beings, like the alligator-headed Egyptian god, Sobek. And their servants, these, *ah*, other things."

"Fucking horrible," Winterson muttered.

Saunders stood back to examine the painted frescoes and wondered how long it had been exposed to the air before the desert covered it back over. Or perhaps even the slight exhalations of the people back in 1925 had been caustic enough to start degrading the 7000-year-old dyes that had been used.

"Here," Saunders said and walked toward an area that was supposed to be a pivot-wall leading to the prince's tomb. He pressed along the wall until he found the faint line. He half-turned. "The son of a king is in here," he said. "And according to my grandfather's translations, this ancient race met gods. Living gods." He turned back. "Give me a hand here." He put his shoulder to the door.

Winter put his rifle on the ground and put both hands against the wall.

"On my three, two, one ... *push*." The two men pushed while Harmoud Barboudi stood back with a large flashlight pointed at the wall and a face that seemed drained of color.

There was a grinding sound and then the wall, or massive door, swung inward on its pivot point. Sand and dust covered their heads and shoulders.

"Fuck me, that's nasty." Winterson coughed and put an arm over his lower face.

"It's just dead air," Saunders said, but he held his breath against the stench and waved a hand to dissipate the gas.

"Dead air? Dead something," Winterson replied. "Is it dangerous?"

"No." Saunders had no real idea but lifted his flashlight into the totally lightless room, and then went in anyway.

He panned the beam around; just as his grandfather had described, there were several sarcophagi and the large central one had its stone lid pushed to the floor.

As the men entered, Barboudi hung back and edged to the side. Saunders half-turned to see the man furtively reach up into an alcove and pull something out.

"Give me that." Saunders held out his hand.

"Of course, sir." Barboudi nodded and smiled obsequiously as he held out the item.

Saunders snatched it from him and glared for a moment. He looked down and saw the object was a wooden scroll tube sealed at each end with beeswax. He broke away some of the seal at one end and let the ancient wax fall to the ground. Then he shook the tube and a roll of papyrus, a scroll on wood, slid out. He tried to carefully unroll it, but even as he managed to straighten just a foot of it, the ancient parchment crinkled and some broke away. He lifted it in front of his light and stared at the strange writing and pictures.

He only examined it briefly but he knew it was priceless for the secrets it contained alone. The two other men silently watched him. And then from behind them there came a small sliding sound.

Saunders paused to listen, and sure enough, the sound came again. He frowned as he let the scroll slide back into its tube, and then pushed it into the front of his shirt. This time he could pinpoint the origin of the noise – it came from the open coffin box. He remembered the confused writing from his ancestor about what he thought it contained.

"In there," he said, pointing, but no one moved an inch.

Barboudi turned to him, his eyes like saucers, and Saunders frowned deeply. "Go on, man."

Winterson cursed, perhaps remembering that his rifle was outside, and instead unclipped his sidearm and approached the box from the left side, while Barboudi went straight for it.

Saunders saw that Barboudi's flashlight was wobbling in the man's visibly shaking hand – he knew how he felt, as his own heart raced in his chest as he watched intently and tried to hold his light steady on the stone casket.

Winterson was closest. He held his gun in one hand and the flashlight over the top of it and raised his hands so he could shine the light down into the sarcophagus.

His brows snapped together, and his mouth turned down. "What the fuck?"

Barboudi joined him to also peer inside. The Yemeni squinted and leant closer, just as an arm shot out and the hand grabbed the excavator. He shrieked, and tried to yank himself backwards, but as he did another and then another arm came out to reach for him. Then from within the sarcophagus a body rose, or rather less a body and more an obscenity made flesh.

"Get down," Winter yelled to the man, and he pointed his gun at the grotesque mass of limbs and muscles.

Saunders stood with his mouth hanging open. He felt frozen to the spot. The flashlight beams in the pitch black, airless room swung about chaotically, adding to the nightmarish scene.

Winterson couldn't get a shot off while Barboudi was in the way and the small man danced and smacked at the hands that held him tight.

Finally, Barboudi broke free and ran screaming from the room. Winterson let off round after round into the thing and punctured its body several times, but no blood flowed, and it didn't seem to even notice the wounds.

The mercenary moved in front of Saunders with one arm out and was backing them both toward the door. But

Saunders looked over Winterson's shoulder, transfixed by the thing as it lifted itself fully from the large stone sarcophagus. It was many-limbed, muscular, like a spider made with human limbs; exactly as his grandfather had described when he'd encountered it nearly a century ago.

"Gods," Saunders said as he backed up. "Only gods could do this."

In the wavering light, Saunders saw that the creature's flesh was dried and more like corded leather now, but it still functioned after all the millennia it had been entombed.

How was that possible? he wondered. It wasn't, he concluded.

At the door, Winterson holstered his gun and fumbled for one of the grenades on his belt. He ripped one free and pulled the pin. "Fire in the hole." He tossed it and turned to shove Saunders out through the doorway and then grabbed the edge and used all his strength to shut the heavy stone wall.

He dragged Saunders with him out of the antechamber and up toward the entrance, and then in seconds there came a muffled thump from behind them. Followed by more thumps of falling stone blocks.

The pair arrived back at the surface, and they threw themselves to the ground next to Barboudi, who was still shaking with fear.

Saunders rubbed his face, and Winterson turned to grab his arm. "What the hell was that thing?"

Saunders just blinked for a moment more, his mind whirling. "In the Book of Job, 10:9 …" he babbled, "… it is said: '*Remember Lord, that you molded me like clay*'." He swallowed noisily and then looked across to the men. "We just saw a servant of the gods."

He rested his head back, staring at nothing as his mind galloped. If the servants were real, then that meant the masters, the gods, were real. Saunders stood and felt the scroll in his shirtfront. His entire life he had wanted to find some sort of meaning. Now he had found proof of a divine being or even proof of a cosmic intervention – either one made him feel giddy with the possibilities.

"They were here," he whispered. "Really here."

He knew that if these visitors had been here once, they would come again. He must learn more. He must learn more about the Saros cycle of the moon and when its next perfect line eclipse was due. And he must learn to communicate with the beings so that when they returned, he would be there waiting for them.

* * *

It had taken Saunders weeks to obtain a full translation of the ancient writing. To begin with he had photographed the scroll and divided the images into three sections, and then sent a section to three different translators who specialized in ancient Middle Eastern languages. He did this because there was something about the scroll that made him want to avoid having any other *one* person knowing all its contents – call it intuition, he thought. But he knew that if it did contain something of unique interest or referenced something of value, he had no doubt at least one of the translators, all of whom barely had two pennies to rub together, would try and sell it or seek out any secrets it contained.

Now, the translations complete, he had the ancient papyrus scroll spread before him on the long dining room table, and in front he had the translation notes. This way he could line up the translated words and meanings with the diagrams on the original scroll.

His eyes moved between the ancient and the modern as he tried to understand what he was looking at. His translation of the Allonian language still contained strange words, but in brackets there was an English substitute. When he'd started, he had thought it would be difficult to discern if what the scroll referred to was history or myth. But after seeing the monstrosity in the tomb, he was ready to believe any explanation. He began to read.

"*They have come, and they will come again.*" He moved on. "*They merge us so we may serve them better.*"

He shrugged and moved again. "*Every* (symbols = eighteen years) *they descend from Nizral* (heaven? The stars?) *to demand the strongest among us. We are their insla* (meaning = wood, stone, or other raw material).

Raw material – after what he had seen in the tomb, Saunders now understood what that meant. And *eighteen years* – his great-grandfather had been obsessed with that number.

On the papyrus there was the image he recognized as an Egyptian god that the translator had referred to as *Sobek*. But the specialist had queried it as this was clearly so much older than the Egyptian race and their deities. And the creature depicted looked far more grotesque than the alligator-headed Egyptian god.

Saunders poured himself a glass of red wine from a decanter on the table and walked back to the last piece of the scroll. He sipped as he stared down at it.

The translator had made extensive notes on one section and had even brought in a different specialist to confirm what he had assumed was depicted there – constellation maps – star charts.

And there was something else that would not have made sense to anyone without the necessary expertise – there were rows of numbers. And using the star chart as a reference point, the astral physicist who had been brought in to consult had said that they were probably coordinates, referencing places on Earth.

Saunders' brows knitted; but how could that be possible some 7000 years ago? And if that wasn't mind-blowing enough, a few of the illustrated map images on the ancient papyrus, when viewed with that in mind, seemed to show places on the planet, geographically accurate continents, but impossibly, viewed from high above the Earth.

There was no explanation.

Or there was *one* explanation.

"They were looking down at us. Because they came from the stars," Saunders whispered, almost reverently.

"But are they still coming?" He sipped his wine. "Or ... are they *still* here now? Somewhere."

The young billionaire turned away to walk toward the large window that looked out over the expansive, manicured grounds. His great-grandfather had been on the trail of something and had vanished before he could fully explore it.

Was there a race of beings visiting Earth? Or was this proof that some old gods were real – perhaps guiding and helping the human race? The notes said they strengthened us, and merged us – perhaps he had gotten it wrong originally, and maybe it meant they found us hopelessly divided and wanted to bring us together?

Saunders sighed. Or did it mean something far darker? He thought again of the 'merged' creature in the tomb.

Bradley Saunders held up his hand and saw that it was shaking. He felt like there was electricity running right throughout his body. Pure excitement, he knew. The possibilities suggested by this find were both terrifying and exhilarating.

He refused to believe a race this advanced would have malign designs, and figured they probably had more to fear from humans than humans did from them. His mind worked a mile a minute. This was something he could get his teeth into.

Imagine if he could meet this race. Help them. And together they could bring everyone on the planet together – every country, every race, every religion – and show them all that humans were not alone in this vast, cold universe. He couldn't help his commercial mind working, too, as it sped ahead, thinking of potential advanced technologies he could be the first to control – what marvels could he command?

He paced as he wondered how to use what he had found, then moved quickly back down the table and looked again at the charts and notes from the astrophysicist. She had indicated that the locations identified by the charts were used only occasionally but repeatedly. So the creatures were returning to Earth again and again, and always to the same places on the globe.

Saunders wasn't clear if there was one set of visitors or several, but it seemed they turned up for a while, a few days or a week, and then moved off for around eighteen years.

He banged a hand flat on the tabletop; this was the Saros cycle, a period of 223 synodic months, or just on eighteen years, that he now knew could be used to predict eclipses of the sun and moon. One Saros period after an eclipse, the sun, Earth, and moon returned to approximately the same relative geometry – a near straight line – and then a nearly identical eclipse would occur again. In this time, extreme tidal effects and other gravitational effects were observed. But only for a few days.

Saunders' focus turned inward. Could those gravitational effects provide a focused corridor for the visitors to open some sort of gateway? And come through.

He quickly traced the numbers and coordinates – he just needed to anticipate exactly where and when they indicated, and then he needed to be there.

He ran a finger down the lines of numbers and calculated dates. *Damn*, he thought. The extrapolation calendar indicated the beings would be here again in a matter of months, and somewhere close to the Russian border this time. He straightened and let his mind work.

He needed to be there but keep himself at arm's length as he certainly wasn't ready to meet these visitors. But perhaps he could at least influence what happened there; urge the local authorities in the right direction and learn everything he could. He had the money, and he had the contacts.

"I can do it," he whispered.

Saunders snatched up the phone and dialed his personal bodyguard.

"Winterson, I have another job for you."

"Yes sir. Same rates?" the man replied sleepily.

"Of course. I need a bodyguard in the Russian Caucasus." Saunders grinned to himself. "We're going hunting."

He ended the call and Saunders felt his boredom drain away just as he drained his wine. He held up the empty crystal glass. "I think I have finally found my life's true purpose."

CHAPTER 06

Joshua Hunter was nearly home; it was 11.30pm now, and he'd been gone far too long. But he felt wide awake and exhilarated – he'd really saved someone tonight, and it felt great.

He couldn't help the grin splitting his face as he crossed Colbert Street. But then he slowed and stopped. His grin fell away as he stared. There was something like a storm cloud hovering over the entrance to the train station – but the cloud wasn't full of rain, it was heavy with dark thoughts. It began to move into the station, and Joshua felt his stomach flip as he watched it.

Tor grabbed his arm, the teeth not penetrating the skin but the jaws clamped. Joshua grabbed the snout and levered the jaws open. "Wait here; I'll just be a minute." He stared hard, his silver eyes flaring. "I mean it this time."

He then walked quickly across the street to follow the cloud. He jumped the turnstile and headed down the escalator and saw at the bottom that there were only a few people on the platform, maybe no more than half a dozen.

He stood back, watching them, and noticed that most had simple thoughts of eating, getting home, seeing loved ones, worrying about jobs, or just wanting to get some sleep. But then he spotted the cloud again – now it was smaller but darker, as if it was coalescing. It roiled now and coiled in on itself, and he could imagine it rumbling with thunder, and forked lightning spiking the ground beneath it.

Joshua focused on the man directly beneath the cloud – his thoughts were far different from the rest. The young man was in turmoil and saw conspiracies everywhere. He believed the government was invading his dreams, watching him, controlling him, and he needed to strike back to teach them a lesson. He saw their agents everywhere, and as he leaned against a tiled pylon, he looked along the row of people waiting for the train.

But it wasn't people he saw, but instead the agents who he believed had been ruining his life. And tonight was the night he would strike back. Joshua knew then what he planned – he was choosing someone to die.

The man dismissed anyone heavier than he was. He then discarded anyone in the wrong position on the platform. That left two people – a young guy listing to something on headphones, and a woman, perhaps mid-forties, holding a bag – she was smaller, and closer to the platform edge – her, then.

His addled brain conjured up thoughts of her watching him, informing on him with a camera in her lapel brooch, transmitter in her bag, and taking her orders via a small receiver in her ear.

The man's bloodshot eyes narrowed as the whoosh of dank, warm air filled the tunnel, announcing the coming of the train. He coiled his muscles, ready to strike back at the machine that he believed was destroying his life.

A few seconds passed and the sound of the train was clear now. The passengers readied themselves, and each moved closer to the platform edge, all eyes on the tunnel where the train approached. All but the dark mind. He moved furtively to stand directly behind the woman.

As the train lights illuminated the tunnel, he sprang forward and lowered his shoulder, aiming his body at the center of the woman's back. In his mind he saw himself collide with her, her shooting forward, and him being stopped or bouncing back from the impact.

At the last second, when he was at full speed, the oblivious woman was yanked out of the way and the young man flew forward onto the tracks.

Joshua's eyes went wide, and he felt a warm feeling in his stomach as he knew the man's body would be mangled into several separate grizzly balls of bone and meat. Already people were helping the middle-aged woman to her feet.

He looked up; the dark cloud was gone. Joshua smiled and turned away. *Now* he could go home.

* * *

It was near midnight when Detectives Markowitz and Holston got the call about the train station suicide. It wasn't normally an incident that required the homicide police, except for a comment one of the first responding officers had mentioned about the platform CCTV of the incident – it seemed the victim had taken a run at one of the passengers standing on the edge of the platform. A woman. But somehow, she'd got out of the way.

So, it might have been a potential homicide attempt. And suddenly it fell into their laps.

They were only ten minutes away, and on arrival the first thing they did was head to the station control room. By now the victim, or potential perp, was being scraped up and bagged. The other witnesses on the station platform had made statements and been released.

On entering the control room, the bored and burstingly overweight station surveillance officer nodded to them.

"Evening, officers." He waved them closer.

"Evening. How's your night been?" Holston asked.

"Uneventful. Until this," the big guy replied.

"Okay, let it roll," Markowitz said, and folded his arms.

The detectives watched and the controller paused the footage at the moment the woman was yanked out of the way. "See it?" He turned to them. "How did she do that? How did she even know he was coming at her with her back turned to the asshole?"

"It didn't look like she knew he was coming. Looked more like she was pulled out of the way by something," Holston said softly.

"What?" the big man asked.

"Nothing. Keep rolling," Markowitz ordered. A prickle of suspicion ran down his spine. "I wanna see what happens next."

The film rolled on, showing the seconds after the man's death.

And there he was – the kid walking away while everyone else rushed to aid the woman or looked to be screaming in horror. But not the kid, he walked away as calm as you please.

And his face was blurred except for the silver dots where his eyes should be.

Holston narrowed his eyes. "Oh, you gotta be shitting me."

Markowitz let out a long breath through pressed lips. "I think we got a serial."

CHAPTER 07

2002 – Mountain village of Mazeri, border of Georgia and Russia, the Caucasus

The two trucks jerked and bounced along the rutted path toward the mountain village. In the back of the open vehicles was a joint military team that was a mix of Georgian local army and Russian soldiers, and all sat stony-faced in the freezing air.

Tanya Kolsov, also a Russian, was the only woman and she sat up front in one of the cabins next to the driver. There was no heater, but at least being so close to the engine afforded a little warmth against her legs.

She was a physician and had worked with the police and military before, assisting with everything from bomb victims to children suffering from trauma – a jill-of-all-trades – as good with a scalpel as with her soothing words.

As they crested a hill, she spotted the picturesque village of Mazeri, all single-story clay-fired tile roofs, barns, and pens for animals close by, and all with the backdrop of a towering pine forest so thick the sunlight barely reached the ground. Then, behind them, the colossal, jagged ridges of the Caucasus mountains. The scenery was breathtaking.

Their joint objective was to investigate complaints of disappearances from this village and others. To begin with, Georgia and Russia blamed each other – both inferring that people, mostly fit young men and women, were being kidnapped and force-conscripted into various militias. But then after some superficial investigation into local records, they found it had been going on for years, or rather going on in bursts every eighteen years, for as long as the records went back. With the last time being exactly eighteen years ago, almost to the day.

Even then, villages this far out were not a priority. But something had changed – and very recently. It was rumored that some other person or group was financing this investigation and money had changed hands at a higher level. Then had come word that in one of the villages the locals had captured one of the suspects. Or what they thought was a suspect – and the Mazeri mission was miraculously escalated. So now, here they were.

The trucks pulled up on the outskirts of the village and the Georgian and Russian group leaders ordered their crews out. Tanya jumped down and hugged her jacket tighter – it was as cold as she expected, but bearable as at least the wind chill was down.

Tanya slowly turned, taking it all in – the Caucasus region was an enormous area thousands of miles wide, spanning Europe and Asia – it was wild, remote, and a place of mystery and legend.

Uri Churnov, a captain in the Russian army, called to Andrev Beridze, his Georgian counterpart, and the two conferred for a moment before organizing the men into a single group. Tanya was at least happy that there didn't seem to be any rivalry that would complicate their mission and lead to faulty results and in the worst case, as had happened previously, outright violence between the two teams.

Though it wasn't common knowledge, Uri Churnov's son from his broken marriage was also in attendance, a young private by the name of Nikolas, or Nik, Belakov – Uri's wife had even given him her maiden name. Uri often took time out to talk to him, chide him, or offer advice, without trying to show overt favoritism.

Tanya had spoken to Uri on the flight down, and he professed that his ex-wife wasn't talking to him, believing he had influenced the boy's decision to join the army. Maybe that was true, but not through any pressure he had applied. Nikolas had hero-worshipped Uri as a kid, and now wanted to emulate him – just like a lot of boys want to do with their fathers.

Uri had told his ex-wife that he would never dissuade his son from his own chosen path, but he'd look out for him. And besides, this trip to Georgia was safe and would be interesting. Whatever path the young man chose, Tanya thought Uri was a good man, a good father, and a good role model for the youth.

She continued to watch the Russian captain from the corner of her eye. She wondered why his wife had left him, as he seemed strong, clever, and well balanced. If he were her husband, she would not have let him go. Perhaps there were other issues, she thought. And perhaps she might have time find out while they worked together.

Churnov raised his hand as their group was met by a small delegation of bearded Mazeri elders who were all swaddled in thick coats, their broad grins showing few teeth between them.

The Georgian officer spoke to them in the local Kartvelian language, and he had his men hand over food packages, some farming tools, and a little cash, as compensation to those who had lost their loved ones.

Though the elders tried to persuade them to come for a gathering in which the local fermented alcoholic milk beverage would have been consumed, Uri Churnov's group simply wanted to get on with their mission.

Churnov requested that they see the captured suspect as a priority. So, instead of drinks and a few local songs they were taken to a large barn on the edge of the village. Churnov observed there was a large and heavy plank of wood propped against the door to stop it being pushed open – from the inside.

"You said you shot it, yes?" Churnov asked, mimicking a rifle with his hands.

The men nodded but seemed uncertain.

The Russian ordered the doors opened, and the plank was removed and the doors dragged wide. The men entered cautiously with Tanya following. They turned on their flashlights, but there was good light coming in from the open doors.

Tanya inhaled the odd smell of cloves, salt, and something like bad body odor. She could see that at the back of the barn there was a rusting tractor and a tarpaulin covering a large lump in the center of the straw-covered room. Even though the village elders had said that their hunters had shot the suspect, Churnov had two men train their weapons on the covered mass.

He ordered the tarpaulin dragged away and two of the soldiers complied. And then they saw it.

Men cursed and some turned away. Tanya frowned in confusion – at first, she thought she was looking at several bodies knotted together, but on closer inspection she saw that it was one, with all the limbs, all the arms and legs, attached to a central large pad of bone and muscle. At one end was a sagging pipe of flesh or cartilage, that could have been a short spinal cord, with what looked like a rubbery mouth at one end.

The thing revolted her, and she blinked several times as she struggled hard to try and see it only from a professional viewpoint. She saw then that pressed into the base of the spinal cord where it attached to the body was a dark glassine-looking orb that was sunk into the flesh. At first, she thought it was an eye, but then she discounted this as it looked artificial.

Churnov's mouth was turned down and he turned to the village elders. "Tell me about it."

Andrev Beridze translated back and forth, and the head villager's brows were deeply knitted as he replied. "It was very strong. At first it wouldn't die, no matter how many bullets we put in it." He continued to stare at the thing. "It is the first time I have seen one."

Churnov grunted. "I'll wager it's the first time *anyone* has seen one."

The old man shook his head. "There are stories. They have been here before. Many times."

Churnov looked back at the thing and just stared, his eyes half-lidded. "This is an abomination." Finally, he turned to the villagers. "Where was it captured?"

"In the high mountain valley, where the forest is darkest," the elder replied and his answer was translated. "My son shot it first." He pointed to several punctures in the thing, and one that had grazed the orb. "But no blood came."

Churnov looked up. "Take us there."

"No, no, no, we will not go to that place again. I forbid it." The elder waved a hand vigorously in front of himself. "We must wait a few more days. Then they will be gone."

"That's no good to us." Churnov would not be put off. "Then bring your son. That is an order." He looked hard at the small man, who looked at the other elders. After a moment, they nodded.

The old man sighed. "As you wish."

Churnov looked back at the strange body. "Doctor, your opinion please."

Tanya was still trying to detach herself from the nausea that roiled in her stomach. With an effort, she forced her focus to her scientific background. She walked around the thing for a moment, before reaching into her pocket and drawing out a pair of rubber gloves.

She snapped them on and crouched. She prodded the creature. It was stiff now but definitely of real flesh and bone. But the skin was tough, like leather. She put a finger in one of the bullet holes and felt that the dermal layer of skin was incredibly thick. When she withdrew her finger, she looked at it in the flashlight's glare, and saw it was dry – no blood or any other body fluids.

She then examined where the limbs joined with the body to see if there were stitch marks that would indicate some sort of fraud. But there were none.

She hovered her hands over the creature, not really wanting to touch it again. Tanya looked up. "They said this thing was alive? Moving?"

Beridze translated the question, and the small village elder nodded firmly. He spoke rapidly and Beridze grunted his understanding. "He said, yes, alive, strong, and it moved very fast."

She shook her head. "I don't see how this thing could have survived. Or even what its purpose was."

There was silence in the barn for several seconds before Churnov spoke softly.

"Doctor Kolsov."

She turned to the Russian leader.

He spoke without taking his eyes off the thing. "Could it be a mutation?" His eyes shifted to her. "Like the fish in the Chernobyl pond?"

She immediately pulled her hands back from the thing. She had also heard the stories of the giant mutated catfish in the cooling pond of the Chernobyl reactor. Rumor or not, it scared her.

Tanya pointed to her bag. "Please."

One of the soldiers brought her bag closer, and she quickly retrieved a small Geiger counter. She turned it on and pointed it at the creature.

Tanya exhaled with relief as the needle didn't move much past background normal and cursed herself for not checking that immediately. She, and everyone in the barn, could have been seriously contaminated by now if the entity had been radioactive.

She folded the machine away. "All clear."

"Good, that's good," Churnov said. And then: "Please continue."

She nodded and leaned closer to the appendage that looked like a feeding tube, noting that there were no teeth in the fleshy pipe. But ribbed muscles inside indicated an ability to use a peristaltic motion probably for swallowing.

She proceeded to run a hand over one of the limbs, a leg, and then moved to the next limb. "Look here," she said. "This is clearly a masculine leg, covered in dark hair. But here, next to it, this one is slenderer and has a lot less hair. It's a youth's leg, or maybe even that of an adult female."

Churnov's expression was one of distaste. "I don't understand what that means."

"Me either, yet." Tanya then shone her light on the glassy orb. It was the only thing on the creature that wasn't natural. It seemed attached, but slightly embedded into the thing's flesh. There was a bullet wound right beside it, and a corner of the object was chipped.

Tanya leaned closer. There was something inside it that might have been glowing, or perhaps was just the reflection of her own light. She had no idea what it could be for. Identification, maybe? She placed her fingers on it and tugged but it was stuck fast. She made a mental note to remove it and examine it later.

"How did it move?" She continued to examine the limbs.

Once again Beridze translated for the elders, listening to their answers, and the old man turned his hand over as he responded, making the fingers move.

Beridze turned back to her. "Like a spider. All the legs moved at once."

The old man spoke again. Churnov frowned as he listened to the translation and then asked another question. The elder replied and then turned away.

Beridze turned to Tanya, his face grim. "He said that it attacked them. Tried to grab one of their men. Also, he thought there were more of them."

"Attacked them and tried to grab one of their men," Tanya repeated, then looked up to stare at Churnov for a moment. "Is that how the people went missing?" she asked softly, and then had a thought. "Hey, ask him whether he thought these things were here eighteen years ago too, and whether people went missing then?"

"Good question." Churnov asked the men via the Georgian. Their response was quick. "Yes." And then the old man added something. Churnov nodded. "Every time. Every eighteen years they come, and they always take people. The youngest and strongest."

"So. it's been happening for a long time?" She frowned.

The old man said a single word, and Beridze grunted and turned back to Tanya, his eyebrows raised. "*Forever.*"

"This is getting weirder by the minute," she said.

The elder pointed, and everyone understood his words this time. "*Burn demon.*"

Churnov understood the sentiment and felt the same sense of revulsion looking at the thing. A cleansing fire would send it back to hell. But it was critical evidence and needed to be examined.

"Leave it." He turned to the older villagers and raised a warning finger. "This is not to be touched, no burning, understood?"

The old men started for a moment and then, reluctantly, nodded.

"We have work to do." Churnov glanced at the mass of limbs and muscle one more time before turning away. "Cover this horror but leave it here. The cold will preserve it. We'll take it back when we go."

Captain Churnov then turned to the group of elders, his face grim. "Now take us to where you caught this creature."

* * *

The twenty-strong squad headed up into the mountains with one of the village elder's sons as a guide. The young man had needed to be ordered by the elders first, and Churnov next, and Tanya could see he was clearly fearful of going back to the dark forest. She heard that he was one of the few youths that hadn't been 'taken', due to being away hunting at the time, and apparently also being a swift runner. But right now, she bet it wouldn't take much for him to simply vanish if he got spooked.

And she could understand why. The forest was so dense with towering trees whose branches interwove so completely overhead that the daytime shadows turned it to twilight. Even as they dropped down into the valley the ground was rocky and steep, and it was a blessing when they finally reached the bottom and found a partially frozen stream running down its center which they now followed.

It was several hours before the young man looked around and announced they had arrived. He pointed to a large flat rock.

"There. It was watching us from there." He stared at the spot as though expecting the thing to appear again. "Then when it saw us, it vanished very fast."

"But it had no eyes," Tanya replied.

"But I know it saw us." The young man just shrugged.

"Then it came back?" Churnov asked.

The youth nodded. "It came out of the forest, there …" He pointed. "… and tried to grab my friend, Vallech."

"Tell us," Churnov pressed.

"One minute we were facing the rock where it was, and then it must have got behind us. It came out of the forest and grabbed Vallech. He screamed loudly." The youth paled. "It made no sound, just held him with all its hands. So many hands. Vallech was a strong man, but this thing was much stronger and could easily drag him."

"You shot it then?" Tanya asked.

"Not right away as we were frightened we would hit our friend," he replied. "Vallech still held his axe and swung it. The beast dropped him, but I don't think it was hurt, as it just wanted to get a better grip." He looked up. "That was our chance. Then we shot it."

"You hit it many times," Churnov prompted.

He nodded. "Our people are good shots. We hit it lots of times, but it didn't seem to feel pain. And it lost no blood. Until one more shot, and it simply dropped dead."

"When you hit the small object on its back," Tanya added.

Churnov selected half a dozen men to scout their surroundings and in ten more minutes a trail had been picked up.

"Where does that lead?" Churnov pointed along a small side trail.

The young man faced where Churnov indicated. "I don't know. I've never known anyone to go that far. They say it is a bad place."

Churnov nodded. "Then that's where we must go." He then held out a hand to their young guide. "Your job is over. You can return to your village with our thanks."

"Thank you." The young man bowed and gripped the captain's hand, but then his face grew grim. "I would not go in there." He held Churnov's eyes for a moment and then turned to sprint back the way they had come.

Churnov watched him go for a moment more and then sighed, turned away, and began to organize his men. This time he purposely placed his son at the center and close to one of the more seasoned soldiers. He also had them move in pairs now, no matter how narrow the trail got. All would carry their firearms at the ready.

He glanced at the guns – all were new, and still shone with oil. Their mysterious benefactor had supplied all their weapons, ammunition, and supplies. He wished more rich people would assist national security this way.

Their path took them up a slope, and then an hour later began to lead them down into an even steeper, darker gorge. From their vantage point it was hard to see the ground at the bottom, such was the density of the canopy cover of the trees. The group wound their way along what seemed an animal track as they slowly descended.

It was the leader of the Georgian team, Captain Beridze, who lifted his field glasses to his eyes for a moment before then handing them to Churnov. "What do you think that is?"

Uri took them and glanced down into the heart of the gorge. He saw it. "It's a structure, I think." He focused the lenses a little more. "To me, it looks like the top of a pyramid." He lowered the glasses.

"A pyramid?" The Georgian nodded slowly. "Maybe. This area of the Caucasus is a very ancient place. Even older than the pyramids."

Tanya had climbed up to join them, and Churnov turned and held the glasses out to her. She took them from him and for the first time she noticed that under the Russian captain's rolled-up sleeve he had an armed forces snarling wolf tattoo on his forearm.

Churnov leaned closer as she focused on the structure below. "My Georgian friend tells me this land is very ancient. Older than the pyramids."

She lowered the glasses. "It's true; people, or proto humans, have been in this area for hundreds of thousands of years."

"And I'm sure there are plenty of ancient legends of monsters and ghosts." He winked at her as he took back the field glasses. "Let us take a closer look at what this valley has been hiding."

The group headed down into the valley. As they descended the freezing air became noticeably warmer. Tanya put it down to some sort of dropping thermals in the valley and being in the weather shadow of the huge mountains rising on either side of them.

But there were other differences, too – the birdsong stopped, and even the insects had either learned to be silent, or just didn't exist down in this gorge. There was nothing but silence – at least for a while.

Churnov held a hand up and the group stopped. He just let his eyes move over the forest for a long moment.

"Did you hear that?" he whispered.

Captain Beridze nodded almost imperceptibly. "And for the last five minutes; we are being followed."

"On both sides," Churnov replied.

"I think we should prepare," the Georgian said.

"Agreed." Churnov turned to call up two of his lieutenants. He then pointed to a couple of large trees just to their west.

"We need to get to those trees, weapons on ready. We're about to be attacked. Await my orders."

The men went back to relay the instructions and organize the group into two lines. Churnov scanned the forest for a moment more, his mind working. He then made a decision. He called to his son.

The young soldier's face was nervous but eager and Churnov grabbed his shoulders in both hands and stared deep into his son's eyes. "I have an important job for you."

Nikolas Belakov came to attention. "Yes sir. I stand ready."

Churnov stood tall before his son. "You are to head back to our camp. You are to wait twenty-four hours, and if we do not return, you are to immediately report back to headquarters and await their instructions. Make sure the ... *creature* ... is taken back for examination. Do you understand?"

Nikolas blinked as he tried to comprehend. "But – but I want to stay and fight. With you."

Churnov gave him his sternest look. "You are the swiftest among us. This is an order, and one I trust you and you alone with. Understand?"

Nikolas snapped to attention and saluted. "Yes sir."

"Go. Fast," Uri ordered.

His son stood there for a moment longer, looking like he wanted to say something more. But then he turned and ran back along the trail as if the devil was after him.

Churnov sighed. "Goodbye, my son," he whispered. But it was at least one less thing he needed to worry about. He then turned back toward the mighty tree trunks. He spent a few moments observing the dark forest. It was so silent now; all he could hear was his own breathing. He felt the woman doctor's eyes on him, watching him as he watched the forest.

He knew they weren't alone. And his gut instinct told him they were surrounded. "On my word, double time ..." He raised an arm and then waved the group on. "*Forward.*"

He and the men charged, heading for the large tree trunks, but before they even made it halfway, the forest around them exploded into life. And it was if the gates of Hell had been opened and all its demons were pouring forth.

* * *

Tanya ran in a crouch as gunfire burst around her. Men shouted and screamed, and things that moved like giant spiders but were instead obscenities from a madman's nightmare came at them from the dark of the forest.

The creatures moved blisteringly fast on multiple legs – no, that wasn't right – they weren't moving on just legs, but some of them had only arms all working together below them, or some legs and some arms, which had fingers grasping in the air, eager to grab onto them.

The beings seemed immune to the bullets, but oddly, after all the shooting she didn't see any damage or holes in the muscular bodies, or even a drop of blood spilt. But the soldiers couldn't have missed them.

She knew now what had been happening to the villagers as she watched her squad members being leaped upon and grabbed by a wrist, ankle, or neck and dragged off into the forest still fighting and screaming.

In seconds more she had her back to one of the trees and the remaining men formed a ring around them.

She, Churnov, and the Georgian captain stood firing handguns while the men were down on one knee with rifles.

Churnov screamed brutal Russian curses as he fired, and then frowned deeply as he looked at his weapon. He then fired it into the ground at his feet – nothing. He grabbed his rifle and did the same, and then slammed the weapon into the earth.

"Blanks," he roared.

"What?" Tanya didn't understand what that meant.

Captain Beridze confirmed it, and then tossed his own rifle to the side. He drew his longest blade. "We have been sold out, my friend – the poison gift of the new rifles and ammunition from our mystery benefactor has sealed our fate."

"We weren't meant to win," Churnov said as he backed up. "We have been delivered up on a plate."

There seemed dozens of the powerful things all around them, darting in and grabbing at an individual and drawing them away. It reminded Tanya of the stories of sailors cast into the sea and forming themselves into rings, and where the unfortunate souls on the outside were snatched away by sharks.

But Churnov had one last trick – he hadn't fully relied on the new weaponry, and he unclipped a single grenade that he had brought from his own stores from his belt.

He threw it into the mass of thrashing limbs and the explosion seemed deafening in the forest valley. But it did blow one of the beings apart and its pieces finally stopped moving. Oddly, many of the creatures raced to the grisly debris, scooping up the separated arms and legs and taking off with them into the trees. But others stayed and continued their attack.

In seconds more, the men were down to just a half-dozen of their ranks, and they were forced to fight with knives and tree branches. For the first time Tanya wished she had a gun, a *real* gun. She had no desire to be taken to whatever fate these beasts had in store and would even have preferred to have the option to end it herself.

One of the huge creatures landed among them, men yelled, and then she was grabbed and being transported through the forest, dragged by an arm. Someone called her name, but already it seemed from far away. Her body bounced over fallen branches, rocks, and her clothing became torn, her skin abraded.

The thing moved swiftly, and she managed to look up at its body but could not see any eyes or sensory organs on it anywhere. She wondered how it knew where it was going.

A few minutes later they entered the deepest and darkest part of the gorge, and groggy now, she looked up to see a cliff and over its rim something at its center – it was the apex of the huge pyramid.

The thing never stopped or even slowed. They went over the edge, and into an abyss of darkness.

* * *

Tanya opened her swollen eyes and blinked with difficulty. Her head was pounding. Then she realized it was because she was upside down. Her feet were stuck on the ceiling, but her hands were free.

She felt her face and touched dried cuts and abrasions. Probably the result of their brutal dash through the forest.

She turned slowly and saw a few others from her group all hanging upside down around her, and all still unconscious. How long had she been there? she wondered. Some of her wounds had crusted over so it was a certainty that more than just a few hours had passed. Maybe even days.

She knew she needed to free herself and tried to lift her upper body to her feet, but the pain in her stomach muscles was excruciating and she wished she was fitter. But she got close enough to her feet to see that it was some sort of resin holding her boots in place.

From outside the doorway or opening to the chamber she was in, one of the many-legged things went past, and she froze for a moment. Another of the hideous creatures went past the same way, but thankfully none came into the room.

She decided that if she couldn't free her feet, then maybe she could pull her feet from the boots. She sucked in a breath and strained. Her hiking boots were oversized because they were new – all part of the kit supplied by their mysterious benefactor who had turned out to be their betrayer.

After several minutes, one of her feet came free. She then used this foot to push against the other boot and then it too popped out and she dropped the few feet to the floor. She lay there for a moment, eyes closed and panting. Her head spun but she was determined to free some of the others and escape.

Tanya sensed movement close by and opened her eyes. One of the many-limbed creatures had come into the room and was right behind her. It had no eyes or ears, but she knew it heard and saw her somehow. She looked up at the thing and saw that all its limbs were arms ending in hands, maybe a dozen of them.

Her eyes widened when she saw the brawny arm closest to her – it had an armed forces snarling wolf tattoo on it. Suddenly she knew what had really happened to the missing villagers. And also what was in store for her.

She screamed as the creature fell upon her.

* * *

Nicholas Belakov had an agonizing stitch in his side and was puffing heavily when he finally arrived back at the village. The cold and lonely trucks waited for him, but there was something new: a large, unmarked, black helicopter and two men only a few years older than he was. One looked military, maybe a bodyguard, the other a civilian, and neither looked Russian or Georgian.

Another group of men came from the barn carrying something in a large bag to the waiting helicopter, and he saw that even though they were big men they strained under its weight. It was the strange beast, he bet.

"Where are you taking that?" Belakov asked.

"Where is your team?" the non-military man asked, ignoring his question.

Belakov thought the man sounded like an Englishman, but he understood very little of the language and knew how to speak it even less. He just shook his head.

"Try Russian," the military person said, and then turned to keep his eyes trained on the forest again.

The Englishman cleared his throat and came closer. "My name is Bradley Saunders," he said in broken Russian as he stared hard into Belakov's eyes. "Did you see them? The visitors?"

"The things with many legs?" Belakov frowned.

"No, their masters," Saunders pressed.

"I don't understand your words. What master?" Belakov's frown deepened. "I was sent back to bring reinforcements."

"This is hopeless." Saunders turned away.

The young Russian pointed to the chopper that was just finishing loading the creature. "That must go back for examination."

"Oh, it will be examined, I assure you," Saunders replied.

The bodyguard waved in response to a call from the helicopter. "They're ready. We're done here."

"We need help ..." Belakov begged.

"Of course you do." Saunders turned back to the Russian soldier. "We'll be back."

"Wait ... my father." Belakov followed for a moment.

The pair ran to the helicopter and once inside it lifted off and quickly vanished over the treetops.

Belakov blinked several times, confused. He finally turned back to the forest. "My father," he whispered to the dark wall of trees.

CHAPTER 08

2002 – The Saunders Estate, Covington, Cambridgeshire, United Kingdom

Just days later, Bradley Saunders came down in the huge industrial elevator with the workmen guiding the massive, refrigerated crate.

Money made things happen. Money made them happen ahead of schedule. Money changed lives and could end lives. And Saunders had plenty of money.

He had spent close to three hundred million dollars creating a full research laboratory beneath his sprawling estate. He had staffed it with some of the best minds he could find in areas as diverse as evolutionary biology, genetics, astral physics, chemistry, and behavioral science. Money bought them, and money kept their mouths shut.

"This way." He guided the huge crate to one of the laboratories where the surgical team was on standby. He wanted a fast analysis of what they had flown in at enormous expense from the Caucasus mountains.

He needed to know if it was the same *species* as the thing he had seen from inside the Yemen pyramid. And he also needed to know how they were created.

There was something else in his great-grandfather's diary that had perplexed him – the mysterious reference to some place out in the desert called the Well of Barhout. His initial investigations had determined that there was nothing of particular interest there despite the superstitious locals considering it a forbidden place. But that view in itself told him there could definitely be something worthwhile hidden there.

Maybe his great-grandfather went here, and his tale ended before he could write about what he saw. Saunders paused as the idea came to him – did his ancestor meet the visitors? Did he go with them?

He needed to know. And one final thing that gnawed at him – he needed more information on the alligator-headed creatures he thought of as the masters of these many-legged things.

He smiled dreamily; if he met them, what would he say to them? What would they say to *him*? And if they could give primitive humans advanced technology 7000 years ago, what secrets could they bestow on him, a modern man?

He had to make the first move and give them a sign that he was on their side – that he was worthy of their trust and friendship.

Saunders was already beginning to get an idea of what they wanted, and he knew he could help them get it.

He pulled out his phone and put a call through to Winterson. It was time for a good faith gift, he thought.

2012 – The Well of Barhout, Yemeni desert

David 'Winter' Winterson jumped from the huge helicopter, looked around briefly, and then walked backwards as he called all the young men from the rear.

"That's it, sunshine, out you get." He smiled and nodded as they piled out, patting a few on the back.

Phillip Saunders had found out a while back that these visitor things only performed their major harvesting every eighteen years during some sort of special eclipse cycle. But between those times at certain sites, they still had a presence. So basically, Winterson's job was to 'feed the beast', and, according to Saunders, 'work to build trust', whatever that meant.

After ten years serving Saunders, he was getting used to his strange requests. Like rounding up remote people with offers of things they desperately needed, whether that was money, work, or even offers of citizenship to other countries.

The group of young Yemeni men he had collected from the local village were promised a week's construction work out in the desert – they weren't told where, as they would certainly have baulked if they knew their destination was the Well. Instead, all they were told was that there was to be food, lodging, free clothing, and high rates of pay. It was irresistible to a villager living in poverty and where the unemployment rate was running at about ninety percent.

Winterson's interpreter formed them into two lines. The mercenary then held up the Handycam recorder in one hand that allowed Saunders to watch the proceedings. He bet the rich bastard was sitting there, sipping wine, and comfortable as all hell while he did the hot, dirty, and dangerous work. Didn't matter, as the guy paid well, and there were worse jobs than being some rich prick's bodyguard.

Winterson grimaced and remembered now what to expect from the area as he began to feel the force of attraction pulling on him. He surreptitiously turned to check that his harness and rope were secured to the chopper. Assured, he turned to the interpreter.

"Proceed."

The man urged the men forward and in a double line the dozen ragged-looking young men walked forward toward the massive hole in the ground.

Winterson walked beside them, and he saw a few glancing at him. He bet they were wondering why he was the only one tethered to the huge and heavy chopper.

He nodded and smiled back innocently. *You'll get your answer soon, lads*, he thought.

As they approached, he felt the dragging feeling become a pull, then it was like they were on a steep slope, and none could stop themselves beginning to run.

Holy shit, he thought. *This is worse than the other sites.*

When just a few dozen feet from the rim of the hole, the men saw what it was they were heading toward and panicked. But oddly, they began to sprint forward, or fell, and slid along the ground as though they were within hurricane winds. All of them screamed now, and Winterson struggled to hold up the Handycam while he kept one hand wrapped tight on the harness rope.

In seconds more he watched as the men, lemming-like, went over the edge; even the interpreter, who looked back with a mix of abject terror and betrayal.

The rope pulled Winterson up short, but he felt his entire frame being dragged forward as his muscles and bones strained against the pull. Even his teeth ached from the strange force being exerted on his body.

"Go further; I want to see," Saunders said into his ear.

"No chance," Winterson replied.

"I must see. Do it," Saunders commanded.

Winterson cursed but spoke into his mic to the chopper. "Give me another three feet. Slowly," he growled.

The extra rope was eased out, letting Winterson get right to the edge of the massive sinkhole. He looked down and felt his stomach flip. It was like staring into the nothingness of space. But it wasn't the darkness, or the force pulling at him, that made him feel nauseous with fear, but instead a feeling of dread emanating up for the pit. He held up the camera, but there was nothing to see in what seemed a bottomless void.

"Light it up," Saunders ordered.

With great difficulty he reached into a pouch pocket, withdrew a flare, lit it, and tossed it in. It plummeted into the inky blackness, creating a red ball of illumination as it dropped.

At about 400 feet down the light stopped – it didn't hit the bottom but seemed suspended in the air. Winterson could then just make out the men, like sides of beef hanging in a butcher shop.

And just before the flare burned out, he saw a towering figure with a long reptilian head approaching them.

"Oh shit," he whispered.

"*Speak to it, speak to it,*" Saunders urged. "Like we agreed. Hurry up."

Winterson cleared his dry throat and held up a hand. "Hello. We brought them for you. We are your friends."

The huge grotesque being looked up, right back into his eyes, and Winterson felt his knees go weak. And then the flare went out. Or maybe was put out.

"They didn't understand you." Saunders hissed.

Winterson felt the rope beginning to pop and creak and his back felt like it was breaking.

"Can't hold on much longer," he said in a strained voice.

"Throw the camera down; leave it on," Saunders said.

Winterson did as asked. Then with great strain he slowly turned to the chopper. "Pull. Me. In."

He was winched back, and once inside he ordered immediate lift off. He watched the massive sinkhole get smaller as they banked away.

One thing he had learned over the years was that this Saunders guy was as callous as fuck. While the money was good, Winterson would hang around. But he'd never trust the

The Well of Hell

guy, because he knew that in a blink, he could be the next one thrown into a pit.

I guarantee it'll be him before me, the mercenary thought grimly.

CHAPTER 09

Buchanan Road, Boston, Massachusetts

"Ready for the big trip?" Alex Hunter came in, wiping his hands on a rag after chopping wood, and with his t-shirt thrown over one shoulder. He looked at his son with bursting pride. At twelve, Josh was already around five-eight, whip smart and had a mix of his father's and mother's looks.

He headed for the refrigerator, but Aimee pointed at him. "Wash those hands."

"I was just going to." Alex winked at Joshua and then crossed to the sink where he let water run over his fingers for two seconds.

Joshua laughed and watched his father. Josh had seen his father's enormous physique before, marked by dozens of old scars. There was also the tattoo insignia on his shoulder of an eagle grasping a sword in one claw, a lightning bolt in the other, and some Latin words underneath; it was the insignia of the Special Forces unit Alex worked for called the HAWCs, or Hotzone All Warfare Commandos.

Alex pulled on the shirt. Even though he never really talked about it, Alex was aware that Josh knew what he did for a living. Because the kid had sometimes been there in his father's mind, and knew his missions were the hardest, bloodiest, and most dangerous, and he had seen for himself some of the things Alex had been called upon to do – because when he had been experiencing them, Josh had been there with him the whole way.

Alex had initially tried to block the boy, but even at his young age his mind was growing more powerful than Alex's and he had easily forced his way back in. He tried to be secretive about it, but Alex always knew he was there, watching, and though he hated the kid seeing the brutality of his missions, he kinda liked the company sometimes when he was enduring his darkest moments.

Josh grinned up at his dad. "You bet I'm ready. Can't wait to see those pyramids, and eat … what do they eat in Egypt?" Josh asked.

"Dates," Alex shot back.

Aimee scoffed. "Shawarma, kofta, kebab, all sorts of wonderful things."

"And dates." Alex winked. "Lotsa dates."

"Nice." Josh laughed and then raised his eyebrows. "Hey, did you know that the Great Pyramid of Giza has around 2,300,000 stone blocks in it?"

"I did." Aimee folded her arms. "And did you know that for 3800 years it was the tallest building in the entire world?"

Alex held up a finger. "But, it's over twenty feet shorter than it could be because the capstone is missing." He raised an eyebrow. "Which was said to be made of solid gold."

"*Whoa.*" Joshua's grin widened. "Can't wait to see it. And I just hope the hotel has a swimming pool."

"Priorities of a teenager." Alex chuckled, but then his face grew serious. "Hey, Josh, one thing … how are you going to survive without seeing your girlfriend for a week?"

Joshua's face reddened. "Aw, Dad, Armina is not my girlfriend." He looked away. "Anyway, gotta get ready."

Alex watched Josh race up the stairs to his room. Aimee looked up at Alex. "I'm not sure I like him traveling to the Middle East. Even if it is just a school trip to Egypt and staying at a safe hotel."

"Don't worry, Jack is sending a silent escort." He turned to her. "Whatever you think of Jack, he regards Josh as family and would never let anything happen to him."

Aimee made a small sound in her throat. "I don't trust him. He thinks of Josh like he thinks of you – as a military asset. Just another missile or bomb." She turned away. "And that's the only reason I let him go; because of this bodyguard Jack is sending."

"Jack's okay." Alex said.

Aimee turned back. "Alex, you don't see him the way I do. He is not some sort of kindly uncle. He's as hard and cold as they come."

Alex tried to laugh it off. "I disagree, he's always—"

"He's always thinking of how to use you," she cut across him, her blue eyes now turning dark. "And I'm betting Joshua too. Like I said, I don't trust him. And neither should you." She stared at him.

Alex straightened and their eyes met, but she broke it off. "Jack would lay down his life for us, especially Josh. The boy can take care of himself; you know that. He'll be fine," he replied.

"Will he? How would you really know?" She held his gaze this time for several seconds before turning to head up the stairs.

Alex watched her go.

"I would know," he said softly. But then he questioned himself – *would he?* He wasn't home enough, and it was beginning to impact his relationship with Aimee. They weren't as close as they used to be or as he wanted. And that was on him.

But was she right? Did he really know enough about what Joshua was doing, or liked, or anything other than what he was told by his son?

Nope, he thought. He's a good kid. I just need to tell Jack I must pull back on some missions. Maybe take some time off. A year should do it.

He hoped.

INCIDENT 03

The ghosts of the past speak.

CHAPTER 10

5 December 1945 – Routine US Navy bomber
training mission out of Florida base

Flight leader Lieutenant Charles Taylor looked from his port
to his starboard windows and noted the other four craft flying
in good formation. His training run today had comprised five
US Navy torpedo bombers with a total of fourteen airmen
under his command. The group's formal designation was
known as Flight 19.

It had taken them several hours, things had gone smoothly,
and it wasn't long before one of the pilots requested and was
given permission to drop his last bomb. As he flew, Taylor
made notes on his clipboard about the performance of his
crew – all had done well – as he expected.

They continued onward for another few dozen miles
without incident, but then Taylor felt a wave of nausea wash
over him and he had to blink several times to clear a feeling of
pressure in his head. *That's odd*, he thought. But it seemed the
oddness hadn't ended, as then Taylor heard one of the trainees
ask one of the other pilots, Powers, he thought, for a compass
reading – which was strange as they all had those instruments.

But the really alarming thing was the reply from Powers, probably one of the most experienced pilots they had with them: *"I don't know where we are. We must have got lost after that last turn."*

"Jesus, you guys." Taylor looked at his equipment, and then craned forward. Both his compasses spun madly as if confused about where true north was. In that instant, he looked up, and the blue sky was gone, everything was gone, and there was nothing outside but roiling smoke or mist.

Almost as if his hands had a will of their own, he pushed the wheel forward, taking the plane lower, telling himself it was to try and catch visual landmarks or even sight the ocean.

Suddenly, there were too many voices in his head. Some were those of the pilots, some from the command base, and all getting louder with confusion, unease, and panic. Taylor blinked and tried to find a landmark, any landmark, but the world had gone mad outside his windows.

"I can't see, I can't see anything," he said into the mic as perspiration stung his eyes. "Does any pilot have visuals?"

He got a reply, but it didn't help.

"We are entering white water, nothing seems right. We don't know where we are, the water is green, no white, no ..." The other pilots' voices were shrill. Though trainees, these men were still professionals, and the naked fear he heard in their voices scared the shit out of him.

Taylor pushed the stick forward again – why was he doing that? He must already be too low. He saw out the windows that his other pilots were following suit. He took one last look outside as his instruments still spun madly, and there was now nothing but the crackle of white noise in his ears.

Nothing, nothing, nothing, he repeated in his head. And then he seemed to break through the layer of fog and saw the ocean. But strangely, the water seemed to be parting, opening in a giant whirlpool, and at its center something began to become visible.

Taylor frowned in confusion. "Is that ... is that a pyramid in there?"

He couldn't help it. Almost in a dream-like state he nosed the bomber down directly into the vortex. His other pilots followed him in.

CHAPTER 11

Two days ago – South Beach, Miami

Walt Sommers stood at the water's edge as the sun was just peeking over the horizon. His long sand rod trailed a line well out past the small breakers, and he held the rod with one hand while resting a finger of the other gently on the line as it bumped along the edge of the sandbank where he knew the bigger fish liked to patrol.

The thing he loved about beach fishing was the unknown – you never knew what it was you were going to catch until you saw its shadow and color as you brought it in. He had caught redfish, cobia, king mackerel, flounder, sheepshead, and even spotted sea trout from right here.

Fishing was his greatest pleasure in life and sunny or cloudy, windy or still, cold or warm, he loved every second of it.

Today was a little quieter, but the conditions were good, the water warm, and the next person fishing was a good 200 feet further down the sand. He felt confident he was in the right spot out past the bank and close to the channel. When it came to fishing, patience was king.

As the sun came up, the light improved, and though the wind gently blew into his face, the water just a few feet from shore was only slightly ruffled by tiny wind ripples. And that was why he was able to spot the bobbing mass almost immediately.

It was still about 100 feet out from the shore, but his trained eye told him it looked like something organic, maybe a shark or dolphin carcass. That wasn't a bad thing, he thought, as the smell of the decomposing meat might bring feeder fish in after it. But it'd be bad news if it brought a shark or two because then he could kiss goodbye to any decent-sized fish hanging around until the predators headed out again.

As the tide brought the mass closer, he saw a couple of paddleboarders coming along the shoreline, and when they approached the object, one of them stopped to stare. He called his friend over and the pair looked at the thing, conversed for a moment, and then prodded it with their paddles.

It caused the thing to roll in the water. Walt squinted at the fleshy mass; one side seemed all ragged and looked to have been worried at by some sea scavenger. But as the other side tilted further, he saw what looked like a stiff human arm rise in the air. Then another.

Shit, that's a damn body, he thought. But it was all weird-shaped, and frankly he thought there were more limbs there than belonged to one person. Could it be multiple people? he wondered. He remembered reading once about some gangland execution where they tied two guys together and tossed them in the bay. A week later they washed up all bloated and the skin softened so much they almost looked melted together.

He looked up to see the paddleboarders waving to him. The man pointed at the thing, then made a cutting motion across his throat and then pointed back.

Walt nodded – *Yeah, I was right, a body. Okay, I get it* – then he waved back and reeled his line in. He sighed; fishing for the day was over. He took out his phone and dialed 911.

CHAPTER 12

US Army Garrison, USSOUTHCOM, Miami, Florida

Colonel Jack Hammerson knocked once, entered the room, and stared at the group of people gathered around a large mass covered by a sheet on the double-sized medical table.

"Why am I here?"

Hammerson had a million things to do, and he was thinking that every damn one of them was more important than looking at something weird that was pulled from the water at a Miami beach.

One of the people scoffed, pulled the mask down from over her mouth and nose and turned – it was General Lana K. Richardson, the twenty-fifth commander of SOUTHCOM. "Perpetually pissed off and blunt as all hell, as usual." She half-smiled. "Good to see you again, Jack."

Hammerson came to attention and snapped off a salute. "General."

"At ease." She walked over and shook his hand. "We've known each other too long for those formalities." She quickly appraised him. "Still looking good. For an old guy."

"Early rising, push-ups, and bourbon." Hammerson smiled back at the woman. "Good to see you too, Lana."

She nodded. "Sorry to call you in on this with zero notice, Jack, but when I heard you were close by, General Chilton and I thought you were the guy to talk to." She lifted her chin. "And get your unique perspective."

"Always happy to help," Hammerson replied.

She turned back to the room where the three medical specialists stood around the object on the medical table. All now watched him. The general pulled the mask up over her lower face again and handed one to him, but he just hung on to it. Hammerson figured if they really thought the thing was infectious, they'd all be in HAZMAT suits.

General Richardson nodded to one of the white-coated men. "Proceed."

The tall man drew the sheet back, and paused.

Hammerson's brows came together, and he walked forward. Then the smell hit him, and he decided he'd use the mask after all.

For several seconds his brain refused to organize what he was seeing into any sort of logical order. It seemed like a chaos of flesh, or a madman's play at creating a being from leftover body parts, and then crushing them all together into a mess.

"What the hell is this?" he asked.

"We've been wondering the same thing." The general looked up at one of the men in white. "Captain Evans, take us through what we know so far."

"Yes, ma'am." The tall man at the center of the trio placed gloved hands on the edge of the table. "This – *ah* – biological mass was pulled from a Miami beach at 0600 hours yesterday morning." He indicated a place on one side of the thing. "As you can see, it's been savaged by something and has obviously been in the water for several days."

Evans walked slowly around the table indicating different areas. "We believe this is a feeding tube at what we think is the front end but might not be. There is also a single excretory hole, like a cloaca, at the rear."

"A what?" Hammerson asked.

"A cloaca is usually found on lower-order creatures like reptiles, birds, and bugs. It is a single exit for excreting both solid and liquid waste." He looked up. "It's quite efficient, really."

"I'm sure. Carry on," Hammerson replied.

Evans turned back to the thing covering the double-sized operating table. "There are also five remaining limbs, but we believe it was probably symmetrical, so at least five more were torn away by whatever scavenger had worked at it."

"Wait a minute, those look like human limbs. They're arms and legs." Hammerson craned forward. "And they don't even goddamn match."

"Well spotted, Jack, and you're correct," General Richardson replied, and then nodded for Evans to continue.

Evans faced the thing again. "That's right, Colonel. There are several people's body parts included in this thing. We have run DNA tests on the different limbs and they are definitely human, but none of the samples match. But there are no surgical marks, no signs of healing; they are *welded* together, somehow. Undoubtedly by some sort of technique that is beyond us."

"Beyond us? Who do you mean, the USA? We have the most advanced medical professionals, techniques, and equipment, in the world," Hammerson said.

"Beyond all of us, Jack." Lana Richardson's brows went up. "*All* of us."

"I see." Hammerson got the drift, but then exhaled. "But why? What the hell is its purpose?'

"My questions exactly, Jack. What is it for?" Lana asked. "It's an abomination, something that wasn't born but created for a reason. But just hold your fire for a moment, as there are more answers to come in the autopsy. Although some just leave us with more questions." She nodded to the army surgeon again. "Evans."

The armed forces doctor reached forward to lift a sheet of skin from the back of the mass that had previously been sliced open. He then lifted away a section of ribs that were like the spokes on a wheel, but each as thick as a man's wrist.

"This thing was tough to get into – these are human ribs but they have been thickened somehow, or they might be several that have been merged into one. Regardless, they were extremely hard to cut through." Evans looked at them for a moment. "It's still bone and made up of a framework of a protein called collagen, with a mineral called calcium phosphate. But this has somehow been supercharged and the minerals accreted to make it more like armor plating."

He put the ribs aside and began to point out different things in the open body. "Simplified digestive system, bunched multiple hearts, all working together, and a lung grouping."

Bunched multiple hearts was right; Hammerson's swallowed down some bile as he saw that the hearts, half a dozen of them, were like a bunch of grapes all stuck together. The same with the lungs, in that there seemed to be two rows of four lung pairings in each side of the central organ bed.

Evans pulled the lungs aside to reveal more organs that were only barely recognizable, but all looked modified to be larger than a normal human's. He pulled his hands back but held on to the edge of the flesh wall that had been the skin.

"Notice the dermal skin layer – thickened. Like leather armor." He squeezed it and rubbed it between his thumb and forefinger, and then looked up at Hammerson. "When this thing was alive it must have been extremely formidable and enormously powerful."

"A freaking nightmare," Hammerson said.

"Oh, it gets better, Jack." Lana exhaled. "We examined the contents of its stomach and found traces of protein. The DNA of that protein suggests it was liquified human flesh."

"Whoa there." Hammerson's eyes locked on the man. "These things are made from people. And now you're telling me they ate – or were fed – people as well."

"Looks like it," Evans replied. "And being *fed* is an appropriate assessment as well. The feeding pipe has no teeth, so it could not bite off or chew food. But it had longitudinal pharyngeal muscles so it could swallow. The protein would have had to be liquefied first. So yes, they were fed by someone or something else."

"Jesus H. Christ." Hammerson felt his gorge rise. "Is there anything else?"

"As a medical professional, even I find this both astounding and revolting. But the thing that might give us a hint as to what this creature's purpose was or where it came from, was what we found internally. I examined the interior of one set of lungs, particularly the alveoli, the minute structures responsible for taking in gases."

He sighed behind his mask, more from exhaustion, Hammerson thought, and he wondered how long the man had been working on the strange cadaver.

Evans continued. "Just like everything on the exterior of this creature, the interior of the lungs is courser, stronger, and more robust than those of a human being. This lung was designed for extracting air from a different atmosphere, perhaps with a different pressure. Also, the gases would be heavier, perhaps with methane as the most abundant composition. One more thing, there were dust particles lodged in there." The doctor looked up. "Colonel, do you know how many elements there are?"

"On the periodic table? One hundred and eighteen, sorted by atomic number," Hammerson shot back.

"Correct. But we found an element lodged in the lung tissue that did not correspond to any of those known elements." Evans straightened. "For now, we'll call it element 119."

"Are you saying this thing is not of our world?" Hammerson asked.

"Yes, and no." Evans shook his head and exhaled through his nose.

Jack Hammerson's eyes narrowed as he saw that the man had something on the tip of his tongue. "Doctor Evans, I can tell you have a theory. Anything, no matter how far out, might be helpful now."

Evans looked to the general, who nodded. The doctor faced Hammerson again.

"Yes, I do have a theory." He half-smiled. "And yes, it's right out there."

"Give it to me," Hammerson ordered.

Evans began to pace and rubbed at his masked chin with the back of his hand. "If we wanted to go somewhere that was toxic, either due to the gases or water, we would wear a protective suit, and take our own gas to breathe and water to drink, right?"

Hammerson nodded.

"But, if we didn't have a protective suit, there are things that we can do to our body, or *for* our body, that can make it adapt to different environments. A good example is deep diving. When a diver wants to go deep, they need to have a special gas mixture, is that right?"

"Hydrox or hydreliox," Hammerson replied. "Usually around 500 feet the pressure on the diver's body squeezes different gases out of the cells and into the bloodstream. If you didn't change the breathing mixture, it would cause disorientation and confusion. The deeper you go, the more normal oxygen can become toxic."

"As I thought," Evans replied. "So, we've been able to adapt to deeper water just by breathing a different gas." He pointed at the creature. "Now, imagine you were going to a place where the gravity was enormous, or the light harsh, or the heat or cold was extreme, and you did not have suits." He looked up. "But you *did* have the ability to somehow modify your base material so it could survive there."

"Base material." Hammerson snorted softly. "Us."

"Yes, I mean us. You might toughen the skin, make the bones denser, lengthen the muscles, improve heart and lung function ..." Evans nodded slowly. "That's what I think we're seeing here. Extreme body modification for off-world existence."

"Jesus," Hammerson whispered.

Evans shrugged. "You asked for my theory."

The general blew air between her lips in a rush. "It's some theory, alright."

Hammerson continued to stare at the huge lump of chaotic flesh on the table. The horrible theory was insane, but it made sense. "Does it have a brain?" Hammerson asked.

Evans shook his head. "No, or at least not as we know it." He reached across to a small indentation on the top. "We think there was something grafted here that has come away. But beneath it, there is a collection of non-coalesced brain cells in a flattened sheet. Not really a central brain, but just enough to create a functional intelligence, and maybe some memory to capture and hold commands."

"It was created to take commands; that's what you believe?" Hammerson asked.

Evans shrugged. "I'm only guessing, but yes, like a drone worker ant, a beast of burden, maybe."

"A worker ant, or a soldier ant?" Hammerson folded his arms. "So why is it here ... on the army base? How come it's our problem?"

Lana sighed. "Because it *is* our problem, and that's why you're here." She walked around until she got to one of the thing's arms and laid her hand on it. "As you know, we took DNA samples from all the limbs, and the torso. Like I said, the DNA was human and seemed to come from different people, so we also ran the samples through our databases. And we got a hit. Just one." She looked up with a humorless smile. "Ready for the insane part?"

Hammerson's brows shot up. "You mean what I've just seen and heard was the sane part?"

"Hang on to your hat, Jack." General Lana Richardson went on, "If there's one thing the armed forces does well, it's that it stores the DNA of our missing soldiers, past and present. If they're pre-1960s, then we use the DNA of existing relatives to provide a match if ever we find remains in some dank jungle or mountaintop."

"I know all this," Hammerson said.

General Richardson stopped at another limb. "This leg here – just this one – had functioning cells only a week ago and it belonged to flight leader Lieutenant Charles Taylor." She looked up at Hammerson. "He was a pilot, one of ours, and he vanished on 5 December 1945, in the Bermuda Triangle."

"Good god," Hammerson said. "Flight 19."

"Did you hear me, Jack?" Lana held his gaze. "The cells were functioning *a week ago*, meaning Lieutenant Charles Taylor, or this part of him, was alive a week ago."

Hammerson's eyes went back to the mass on the table and he felt a knot tighten in his gut. "He was alive. In that thing."

CHAPTER 13

Colonel Jack Hammerson's office, USSTRATCOM,
Nebraska

Hammerson sat at his desk with his fingers steepled. He
had reviewed all the available material from the mysterious
Flight 19 that was commanded by Lieutenant Charles Taylor
and vanished in 1945 somewhere within the Bermuda
Triangle.

He had listened to the audio and read the transcripts of
the pilots' last messages. Several times. And even though the
sound recordings had been cleaned up, there were still parts
where the interference made them mostly unintelligible.

The fourteen airmen of Flight 19, plus thirteen crew
members of a Martin PBM Mariner flying boat that launched
from Naval Air Station Banana River to search for them, all
vanished without a trace.

Perhaps until now.

Hammerson looked at the images of the twenty-seven
missing airmen, all their bright, young, eager faces. And
then to the pictures taken of the abomination that had
washed up – was that them? he wondered. Was that all that

remained of flight leader Lieutenant Charles Taylor and his crew? God, he hoped not.

He shut his eyes for a moment to rest them. He had no good answers as there were none to be found. He'd certainly not be reporting anything to the family. As far as he was concerned the heroes would stay as they were remembered – heroes that were missing, but in their families' memories, intact.

Nothing made sense here, but there was one thing that gnawed at him. He'd read in the transcripts that the airmen talked about the white or green water, read about the horizon disappearing, and knew all about the effects of disorientation in bad weather or in failing light. But there was one reference that was jarring in its weirdness. Hammerson opened his eyes.

"Is that a pyramid down there?"

It didn't make sense. Nothing about this did. But something nagged at him from the deep recesses of his memory. Something he'd read, but about an event that had happened a few decades back. The more he thought about it the more he thought it might have been in Georgia, or Russia, or was it Chechnya?

Hammerson quickly searched his files and then narrowed his search to Russia. He got a hit then and found what he was looking for – a two decades old report, or rather a rambling account, from a junior officer by the name of Private Nikolas Belakov back in 2002.

The soldier had been on a mission into the Caucasus mountains to investigate missing villagers. He claimed his squad was attacked, and he was the only survivor. While he never saw who it was who attacked them, he did talk of something the villagers had captured. Something with too many limbs. Human limbs.

That was coincidence number one. But coincidence number two was what he claimed to have seen down in a mountain valley – a pyramid.

Jack Hammerson sat, drumming his fingers on the desk for several moments as his mind worked. He felt he had several pieces of a complex puzzle before him, but as yet didn't even know what the puzzle was supposed to look like.

He sprang forward to his computer and began to enter information into his search matrix that would explore everything in the published global news services, before diving down into their databases to look for the stories that never made it to publication. He was seeking other reports of similar anomalies.

The strike he had on the now missing Russian–Georgian mission in the Caucasus led him to believe that what was occurring was more widespread than he'd first imagined. He made a note to get the science division to do a deeper dive on historical anomalies.

He then searched data on pyramids where there weren't supposed to be any. Also, groups of missing people that were inexplicable, and finally, any sightings of anomalous creatures with the signature of *too many limbs.*

His search criteria and parameters sorted them by an approximation match, and he sighted each of the high-percentage match results. If they looked worthy of more investigation, he entered the location coordinates into his computer to quickly build up a model of similar anomalies around the globe.

In minutes he had five high-probability areas. The first was the incident in the Caucasus mountains. He had expected the Russians to have been all over that, but strangely, they hadn't. In fact, even the news stories had been quickly pushed into the unpublished section – which meant either that the media or military authorities didn't think there was anything to the story, or that someone had quashed it. The Russians could do that. But why would they?

After what Hammerson had seen, he knew there was probably more to the story, so maybe he'd swing one of their satellites overhead and peer down through that dense forest canopy with thermal imaging.

The next was the location of their own trigger event – the Bermuda Triangle. So far, they had never found the actual crash site of Flight 19. When they did, they might find the wreckage of the missing planes, and also the mysterious pyramid. Until then, they just had the abnormality in the lab.

Then came some historic events in the Borneo jungle, plus stories from remote communities in the Australian outback. The pattern was familiar: villages would vanish, or a large proportion of their people would. There were also sightings of many-legged demons, often associated with places in these remote areas that the locals had for generations designated as taboo and no-go zones.

The final location of this type that Hammerson read about was a sinkhole in the Yemeni desert that was also supposed to be the home of demons. It was called the Well of Barhout, and perhaps appropriately also named the Well of Hell. This one had a long and strange history dating back even before Roman times. Entire armies had supposedly vanished into the hole. Some historical reports said they had simply marched into the well and disappeared.

The colonel sat back and mulled over the information he had gleaned. Something was happening right under their noses, and had been going on for decades, centuries, and perhaps even millennia.

If that was the case, then it wasn't any sort of modern foreign power interference. He sat back. At least not an Earthly one.

Hammerson rubbed his chin. Russia was a no-go. The navy was already investigating the Bermuda Triangle, for the hundredth time, and Yemen was a war zone that would need an army if he wanted to investigate there right now. That left Borneo and Australia.

Colonel Jack Hammerson knew he needed eyes on the ground. Alex Hunter was still decompressing after Venezuela, but he already had a small team of his best finishing up a mission in the southern Pacific region that he could divert right now.

Then he could have Hunter assemble a team for Australia when he was out of the box – the fortified and sound-proof room the Arcadian used to decompress, and hopefully, *re-chain* the beast.

Hammerson's gut told him there was a global threat. He needed up-to-date intel and he needed it now. Best way to get it was to put reliable eyes on the ground.

Jack "the Hammer" Hammerson initiated the call-up.

CHAPTER 14

Outskirts of Kuala Belang, Terengganu, Malaysia

"Finished yet?" Casey Franks asked.

"Just takin' a piss," Sam replied.

"I can tell, it's makin' my eyes sting." She chuckled as she leaned against the rear of the truck and flipped through a magazine she had found under the seat inside the rusted cabin. All of it was written in Malay, the local language, and was totally indecipherable to her.

Sam zipped up and then walked toward the repaired truck engine on the ground and lifted it with both hands. Even though it was a small one, the V6 still weighed in at close to 600 pounds, and Sam used his MECH-assisted internal structure to give him all the power he needed.

Sam had had his back broken in combat about eight years before. At first, they had used an external framework to get him up on his feet and then fully mobile again. It was termed a MECH suit – the Military External Combat Harness – and it worked, but was cumbersome and heavy.

Then came the new MECH technology, the next-generation experimental model that was 'Endo' – internal.

It gave Sam the mobility of a normal soldier, but with the strength of a draft horse. It had taken fourteen doctors thirty-six hours to perform the surgery. They had needed to insert the hydraulics, and weave the nano-mesh over every bone, integrate them into the muscle fibers to act like nerve endings, and finally link them to each other – it all needed over a million micro-stitches to button up. But it had been a success and had made Sam Reid a human battering ram.

Casey looked up at her team leader and friend as Sam grunted and dropped the huge piece of machinery into the truck's engine bed.

"Need a hand?" she asked.

"Nah, you just take it easy there. Just yell out if you need a cup of coffee or a cookie," he said dryly and began to wire the engine into the frame of the chassis.

"Good idea. Like I've always said: wear the old guys out first." She looked up and grinned at the huge man.

"I'm only a few years older than you, Franks. And that's 'sir' to you." He finished and wiped his hands. "And next time you drive over a land mine, make sure it destroys something a little lighter."

"I seem to remember some big lug giving me directions." She smiled. "Sir."

"Jump in and turn it over." Sam slammed the hood, but the bent steel wouldn't fully close. He tried again without success, and then ripped the hood free and tossed it into the jungle. "Okay."

He waited while the female HAWC climbed into the cabin and slowly looked around at the tangled jungle surrounding them. It was dripping with humidity and alive with a million squeaks, squarks, chirrups, and croaks, from all manner of flying, hopping, and slithering creatures.

Sam and Casey had completed their mission to free some hostages from a terrorist splinter group that had been beheading its captors online. All the captives were now free, and all the terrorists were dead – it had been a good day's work.

The only problem was that when trying to make it to their extraction point, they found that the group had mined most of the tracks. Their truck took a hit, blowing up the front half. They'd needed to do urgent repairs – the truck really needed a week in the shop, to be put up on a hoist and have the parts winched out – but instead, all they had was Sam and his technical know-how. Thankfully it was enough.

Casey started up the engine, and the truck screeched, coughed, and then began to run while retaining a loud death rattle.

"*Yes.* And we are out of here." She banged the wheel. "Two days of R & R, maybe in Singapore, and I'll be good as new."

"Sign me up." Sam grinned. But then his wrist communication device pinged, and he glanced at it and then held up one large hand. "We aren't there yet – hold the phone." Sam read the message, and his eyes narrowed. "Singapore R & R just got deep-sixed."

"*Aww.*' Casey slumped in the cabin for a moment. Then she sat forward. "Where to? And don't say somewhere hot and humid."

Sam looked up. "Borneo."

"Borneo. Of course." She closed her eyes. "*Ah,* fuck."

* * *

Sam and Casey rope-dropped into the dense Borneo jungle. They unclipped and Casey immediately used her forearm scanner to check their surroundings.

"Anything?" Sam asked.

"Hot, wet jungle. Lots of it," Casey replied and shut it off.

Sam looked up and scoffed. "Remind me again how you became a HAWC?"

She turned to him. "Speed, agility, fearlessness, high threshold to pain, and topped my squad in hand-to-hand combat."

"Fair enough." Sam smiled as he checked their coordinates and then plotted a path to their destination.

"What are we looking for again?" Casey asked.

"Did you not read the briefing report?" Sam shouldered his weapons kit.

Casey did the same. "I did. But it didn't make much sense – pyramids and things with lots of arms and legs. Sounds like someone went on a bender before they wrote that."

"The Hammer will be very interested in that feedback." Sam grinned.

Casey pointed. "Don't even think about it."

"This way," Sam said. "This is as close as we could be dropped. So, we've got five klicks to cover, and there ain't no roads."

Casey pulled a long machete-style blade. "Just another day in paradise."

* * *

Sam and Casey crouched at the jungle edge. The eight wooden huts in the village were large and probably accommodated several families. The village had been carved out of the dense jungle and by the look of the hard-packed ground, it had been in use for many years, perhaps generations.

But now there was silence and a gauze-like mist hanging in the air that gave the entire compound an eerie, desolate atmosphere.

"Nothing," Casey said softly. "No people, no kids walking around, or even dogs. But a lot of footprints in the mud; something went down here."

Sam used a motion tracker on the village and then raised it to scan the surrounding jungle. "Gets weirder than that – notice something? No bird call, and I can't even hear any insects. This place is sterile."

"Missing villagers, like all the other locations – just like the report said," Casey replied.

"So, you did read it." Sam turned.

She grinned. "Skim, don't skip – just like they told us to do at school."

"You went to school?" Sam winked and then turned back to the village. "We go in, eyes on. Take the left flank. Meet at the large central hut."

"On it." Casey stayed within the jungle cover and edged along the tree and palm line. Sam did the same on the other flank.

Sam brought the visor down over his face and used its different vision spectrums to analyze his surroundings, going from magnification, motion detect, and then to thermal. However, as it was ninety degrees and eighty percent humidity, he didn't expect to pick up much. But it confirmed what he already knew; everyone and everything was just gone.

Sam weaved his huge frame along the tree line and then paused for a moment. He lifted his gun to his shoulder and then broke cover to cross the clearing in a crouch. His destination was the largest structure, the communal hut.

He approached the large doorway from the right side and saw Casey silently coming in from the left. She shook her head; *nothing.*

Sam nodded, and at the doorframe he paused to look to the female HAWC and counted down from three – two, one. On zero they both went in fast, Sam aiming high and Casey low.

The room was empty. Both HAWCs quickly scoured the space, looking over and under everything. They went into any partitioned rooms, and even looked up into the pitched ceiling.

"Must have been some party," Casey said.

Sam grunted his response, knowing what she meant – while empty of people, the room was a scene of chaos. Furniture that wasn't tipped over was splintered, and there were splashes of dark blood everywhere.

"They fought back," Casey said. "Good on them."

"Against who or what?" Sam replied, and took one last look around before lowering his weapon.

"Against something big." Casey said and motioned to one of the wooden doorframes – it had been smashed wider as if something bigger than a human had forced its way in.

Sam nodded and then after another moment straightened. "This party has gone elsewhere. Let's try and find out where."

The pair headed back out, but then froze. Standing stock still in the center of the clearing was a kid, a boy no more than six or seven years old and covered in dirt and scratches.

Without taking his eyes from the kid, Sam spoke out the side of his mouth. "Don't suppose you can speak Bahasa?"

"I know a few curse words in German and Russian," Casey replied.

"In different areas they also speak Cantonese, Mandarin, Tamil, and English," Sam said. "I know a little of each of those."

"Try English first, so I can buy in," Casey suggested.

Sam held up his hand. "*Hello.*"

The kid just stared.

"Friends." Sam tapped his chest and pointed at Casey. "Friends."

Still nothing.

He switched to Tamil. "*Vaṇakkam. Nām naṇparkaḷ.*"

After another moment, the boy nodded.

"My name is Sam." He used Tamil and pointed at Casey. "This is Casey. What is your name?"

"Sam, Casey." The boy pointed at each of them, and then at himself. "Nemja."

Sam approached and then went down on one knee. "Nice to meet you, Nemja." He reached into his kit for the only food he had – a protein bar. The boy's eyes never left it as Sam tore the foil and rolled it down. He handed it over.

The kid grabbed it and immediately stuffed half into his mouth. His eyes closed momentarily in ecstasy. The other half also went down the hatch in a blink.

Sam smiled. "Nemja." He cast a hand around. "Where is everyone? What happened?"

The boy stared and his eyes began to well up. "They came. They took my older brother, Utta." His mouth turned down. "And everyone else."

"They took everyone, and his brother," Sam translated for Casey. He turned back to the boy. "Who came?" he asked.

Nemja squatted and used a finger to quickly draw on the ground. The thing was round and had several arms or legs on each side. "Crab people," he said.

Sam turned to Casey. "Crab people."

"Just like in the report again," she replied.

"Yep." Sam turned back and pulled on his best calming smile. "Nemja, do you know where they went?"

"Where they always go," he replied.

"They've done this before?" Sam asked.

Nemja nodded and held up his hands, fingers spread. "The elders say every twice this many years." He flared his fingers, closed his hands, and then opened the fingers again.

Sam got it. "Every eighteen years."

Nemja nodded. "Yes, they take a few of our people, young, old …" He shrugged. "But this time …" He pointed at all the huts and then hiked his bony shoulders.

"Jesus. This time they took everyone," Sam translated for Casey again.

"I'm betting this has been going on for years," Casey replied. "But looks like this is the first time they, or whatever, decided to take the whole box and dice."

"And the first time we came looking. So now we know about it." Sam turned back to the boy. "Where?"

Nemja pointed. "To the river."

* * *

Sam had questioned Nemja a little more, and the boy had told them he survived because his mother had told him and his brother, Utta, to run into the jungle and climb the highest tree they could find. He did as she asked and stayed up there the entire night. But Utta wanted to see what was going on and just hid behind some palms to watch. When Nemja finally came down, he found he was alone. Everyone, even his brother, was gone.

When asked if he knew where his friends and family were taken, he had repeated that they went to the river valley. But that scared him, because no one was allowed to go there – it was taboo.

Casey gave him her protein bar and the promise of evacuation if he wanted. He took the food but declined everything else and said he would try and cross into the next village's territory over fifty miles away.

He looked up at Sam with eyes that were dark pools of fear, "I will be safe there. Until maybe the next eighteen years are up."

The pair of HAWCs had then watched the boy disappear into the jungle. Casey had exhaled. "I ain't ever going to complain my life is hard again."

"Yeah, tough kid." Sam turned away and then the pair checked their maps and the satellite overlays. There was a river gorge close by, and Nemja had pointed them in the direction of a track. This time they didn't need it, as the marks in the soft earth were clear – a lot of foot and handprints, and also signs of something being dragged – a lot of things being dragged.

The pair of HAWCs trekked down into the ever-thickening jungle. Near the bottom they were in a twilight darkness, and the heat and humidity meant water was dripping from the plant fronds, squelching underfoot, and literally hanging in the air as steam. It dragged at the super-fit soldiers, but they'd endured worse, so they ignored it. They kept up their speed and heading.

"No metallic signatures," Casey said as she examined her gauntlet scanner.

Sam looked up. "Canopy has got to be over 200 feet. Could hide a city down here."

They came to the river, which was little more than a twenty-foot-wide stream and only looked to be a few feet deep. But the banks were broad, and some of the rock walls climbed almost vertically into the mountainsides.

"In heavy rain, this would flood." Sam turned about. "Not sure you could build something permanent down here as it'd get washed away. Next rains, and all evidence would be gone."

Casey examined the ground. "River sand and rocky ground now, but the tracks of our crab people keep going."

Sam looked overhead. "So, what are we missing?"

"About forty to fifty villagers." Casey walked out and along the riverbank.

Sam scanned the jungle, turning slowly. Just like up at the village there was the absence of sound.

"Dead zone," he said.

Casey continued along the bank for another fifty feet until she came to a large, cleared area. "Tracks go all the way to here. Right here. And then nothing." She paused and looked down. Then she crouched.

"Got something?" Sam headed toward her.

Casey used one gloved hand to brush away some of the loose rocks. "Check this out.

Sam looked down and over her shoulder.

"You know what happens when you expose sand to extreme heat?" She looked up.

Sam nodded. "Turns to glass."

She punched down. Just below the surface rocks, the ground shattered into a web of cracks. She then brushed more of the top-layer gravel away. She picked up a shard of the melted sand and turned it over, examining it.

"There was something really hot here." She threw the piece back down as she got to her feet.

"A red-hot fire can get up to about 2000 degrees," Sam said. "But to melt sand, and turn it to glass, that's a whole different ball game. It's gotta be around 3000 degrees."

"This was no campfire, boss. Something else was here, and recently," Casey replied.

The pair of HAWCs turned slowly.

"So where is it now?" Casey said.

"And where are all the villagers? Around fifty people were marched or dragged to this point here. And then they just vanished." Sam looked up, and then squinted. "Hey, about 180 feet up, broken branches."

Casey followed his gaze. "Something big went up or came down." She pulled the visor down over her eyes and used vision amplification. And then further magnified something she spotted. "Got something hooked up there in the canopy."

"Well spotted, soldier. Up you go," Sam said.

"Thank you." Casey grinned.

"You're welcome. And don't worry, I'll catch you if you fall." Sam chuckled and then walked backward a few paces to give himself a better angle.

Casey walked to the tree trunk and rolled her shoulders once, then leaped up to the first branch.

The female HAWC was a battle-hardened professional and trained for several hours each and every day. Though the HAWC kit was an extra fifty pounds of weight, she went up the tree easily, and in moments was closing in on the thing that was hanging from one of the boughs.

Sam pressed his ear stud. "What have you got?"

"Tree branch is too narrow for me to get out to it. I'm going to cut through the branch and let it drop," she replied.

"So not a villager?" Sam said.

"Unlikely. But not sure what it is just yet, but looks weird," she added, and began to use her knife to saw through the bark. "Here goes."

The branch began to snap and then tipped, and whatever the pillow-sized thing was, it was released and dropped down, bouncing from branch to branch before hitting the shallow water on the edge of the stream with a soft thump.

Sam crossed to it as Casey scaled down with the agility of a monkey. In seconds she joined Sam who was crouching beside the object.

"What the hell?" Sam frowned down at it.

"A freaking torso," she said. "Two hundred feet up in the treetops."

"Male, young adult," Sam observed.

"Arms, legs, head, all gone." Casey looked up. "And I'm betting whatever it was that went up and over the trees dropped it there."

"After they took the limbs." Sam exhaled in a whoosh. "What the hell for?"

"Maybe they're just taking the tasty bits." Casey's mouth turned down.

"Well, that's fucked up." Sam rose to his feet.

"*Movement.*" Casey spun and went into a crouch as she brought her gun up.

Sam turned side-on to make himself a smaller target but with his bulk, that didn't help much. Both HAWCs engaged their helmets' face armor. They waited.

A man almost as big as Sam stepped out of the jungle, dressed in a heavily armored uniform not unlike the HAWCs'. He was fully armed, but his weapons were over his shoulder or hanging from his belt. He held his hands up at shoulder height and walked forward. He got within fifty feet of the pair.

"That's far enough. Identify yourself," Casey demanded.

He stopped. "Major Nikolas Belakov, Russian Special Forces." He lowered his hands. "Your turn."

"Who said you could drop your hands, Boris?" Casey spat.

Belakov just smiled.

"At ease, Franks," Sam said as he watched the man closely. "US, HAWC Special Forces. What are you doing here?"

"HAWCs?" Belakov grunted as if recognizing the name. He then pointed at the torso. "Same thing as you, I think."

Sam looked down at the mutilated body. "Party has gone elsewhere. What do you know about it?"

Belakov looked up at the treetops. "I know they'll be back." He looked down at Sam again. "But not for another eighteen years."

"You're aware of what's going on?" Sam said. "Who are they?"

"Not who, what," Belakov replied. "They come, they harvest the crops, then they go." He smiled grimly. "Then they wait until their game park has restocked, and they come back to harvest again."

"Who the hell are you talking about?" Casey growled.

Belakov snorted. "That is the question, isn't it?" He reached into his pocket. "There's something else." He retrieved something and threw it toward Sam and Casey. It was a crumpled tube made of silver foil.

"Food bar, military issue," Sam said.

Belakov nodded. "British; either military or mercenary." He smiled grimly. "Seems someone else knows what is going on, and was here before us – at about the same time the villagers were being rounded up. Or maybe they were *helping* round them up." He turned and gave a bird whistle. About half a dozen soldiers appeared out of the jungle, all dressed like the Russian.

Casey went into a full crouch and moved her armor to combat mode. Extra shielding came down over the front of her torso and face.

"Be cool," Sam said, and waited to see what would happen. Belakov turned back to the HAWCs.

"Next time, we must get here sooner." He gave them a small salute. "I think we will meet again, Sam Reid and Casey Franks."

"You know us?" Sam asked.

"I know of the HAWC unit. And the profiles of their senior warriors." He made a small twirling motion in the air to his men, half-turning away before pausing. "I have one question. A personal one." He turned back. "Is the Arcadian a real person or just a made-up bogeyman to try and scare people?"

Casey and Sam just stared.

After a moment, Belakov smiled ruefully. "I understand. We all have our secrets." He called to his men and then he and his soldiers melted back into the jungle.

The pair of HAWCs watched them go and then held their position for a full minute.

"Seems these things are on more than just our radars." Casey pulled back on her shielding and lowered her gun.

"And they knew us. We're not exactly in the phone book, so not sure if that's a good or bad thing yet." Sam turned away. "We're done here."

Casey looked up at the few patches of open sky above her. "Think they can get a chopper in here?"

"They damn well better. I'm sick of hacking through jungle," Sam replied. He thumbed over his shoulder. "Bag that; we'll take it with us and let the nerds check it out."

"On it." Casey pulled a rolled plastic bag and set about collecting the pillow-like torso.

In minutes they were gone.

CHAPTER 15

Jack Hammerson sat down heavily, and his face became like carved stone as he stared for a full minute at the image on the screen of the torso his HAWCs had recovered from the Borneo jungle. He finally exhaled, long and slow through his nose, and began to read the notes from the dissection analysis.

He cursed under his breath; if he hadn't seen the thing that was pulled from the water off Miami, this report would have been the strangest thing he had ever read in his life. But now, it was just one more insane and revolting piece of the growing puzzle.

It seemed the Borneo body had been dismembered and the head removed at the sixth cervical vertebra. He'd seen graphic images of torture before, and he knew that especially during war, human beings' treatment of other human beings could be beyond inhuman.

But the report made it clear that the limbs had been removed with great care, and all the corresponding muscles that wrapped up and around the shoulder, groin, and hips, had also been taken. In the case of the shoulder, he would have expected the bicep and triceps to be gone, but the deltoid, the teres minor, supraspinatus, and even some parts of the pectoralis were also missing.

That was strange, but it was the way they had been removed that caused him to reread the document. They were somehow detached with a precision that was beyond surgical – or at least surgical practices as they understood them. There was no evidence of tearing, cutting, or twisting the muscles free. Instead, it seemed they had been slipped out of the torso so completely, it was as though whoever the young man was, he had never been born with them in the first place.

Hammerson remembered General Lana Richardson's words during the examination of the Miami cadaver – she had said the surgical techniques used were 'beyond all of us'. And here they were being used again.

He flipped to the next images which were different in that they focused on the neck where the head had been removed. The portion of the neck remaining, and the resultant wounds, were somehow sealed over so completely that it looked like it had perfectly healed, and the effect was to fully retain the circulating blood supply.

But then came the kicker; the body had only been dead for a few hours, and that was where sanity left the room, because the skin surface told their medical analysts that the torso had been in that state and exposed to the elements for over twenty-four hours. That meant the torso had been hanging up in the tree all that time, but this mutilated bag of flesh had still been alive, and the suggestion was that its heart had only stopped beating when Casey dropped it from the tree.

Hammerson rubbed one hand up though his iron-gray crew cut and closed his eyes for a full ten seconds. His HAWCs had returned with few clues that were going to advance their understanding of who, when, and where. And that meant at this time he couldn't confront these monsters.

And without a confrontation, it was more than likely to happen again.

He needed to clear his head. He pushed his chair back and walked to the large double window to stare out over the grassy lawns leading to the parade and training grounds. He folded his arms, thinking. Maybe these creatures weren't hiding at all? Just like the Russian had said to Sam.

Sam's report on the Russian interaction told him they knew something, and by the sound of it, a lot more than the US. The Russians were playing catch-up with these beings, and it seemed the US was currently playing catch-up with the Russians. That was unacceptable.

Hammerson paused – that name: Major Nikolas Belakov, Russian Special Forces. He recognized it and crossed to his computer to quickly go back through his files.

He snorted softly. "And more pieces get added to the puzzle."

The only survivor of the joint Georgian-Russian mission into the Caucasus mountains to investigate missing villagers in 2002 was a young soldier by the name of Private Nikolas Belakov. It had to be the same guy.

Hammerson rubbed his chin. And added to that, Belakov had provided evidence of a group of English mercenaries on the ground.

Hammerson reached out to his counterpart in the UK's Special Forces, who had no idea what he was talking about. He sat down, his jaw clenched – this was turning out to be a dog's breakfast.

They weren't exactly on friendly terms with the Russians right now, but the old saying that "the enemy of my enemy is my friend" never rang truer. This Belakov was obviously still invested in these anomalies and could turn out to be an ally.

Hammerson remembered a quote from Sun Tzu – *Attack him where he is unprepared, appear where you are not expected – to know your enemy, you must become your enemy.*

"Become your enemy," he repeated, knowing what that meant. "Think like your enemy."

Who or whatever these things were, they hid in the remotest of places, but only for a while. So, he and his people needed to be there first.

He quickly crossed back to his desk and picked up the report on the potential abduction sites, looking again at the stories of the vanishings in the remote Australian outback communities. Whole groups had gone missing seventeen years, eleven months and three weeks back. But nothing since.

He stared for a moment and then began to nod. "Yeah, that's where you'll be next."

Colonel Jack Hammerson threw the report down and snatched up the phone. "Send a general call-up to all HAWCs not currently on mission. And get Alex Hunter out of the box; we're going in hot on this one."

CHAPTER 16

Yamatjeera community, Cape York Peninsula, Far North Queensland, Australia

Jojo kicked the stone across the ground and watched it bounce and skitter along the hard-packed red dust until it vanished into a clump of spinifex grass.

The community he lived in was situated where the rainforest met the great desert. It meant though they were a desert community whose territory was the great eucalyptus-wooded savannahs, which were mostly flat for as far as they eye could see, they could also hunt the tropical rainforests. Nana Bess, the last remaining elder, said they had the best of both worlds.

"We live in an old land, and we are an old people, the first people," Nana Bess had said by the fire one night. He liked that.

Jojo moved his large brown eyes over the landscape. Nothing ever happened here, he thought, and bent to pick up a handful of gravel and tested his aim by trying to hit gnarled tree trunks, keeping an eye out for anything that scampered from the clumps of spiky reed-like grasses.

Nothing, and he wiped his dusty hand on his fading yellow
Donald Duck t-shirt.

His community, the Yamatjeera, moved about, but had
been here now for many years. There were other communities
like his dotted around the place. Once every few years they
all got together for a big gathering which was fun, and there
were always relatives to catch up with that he hadn't seen in
like forever.

He knew that they'd need to move soon, as he had been
told that staying in one place attracted the attention of the
croc-head people. Those stories frightened him. The creatures
were supposed to call to you, make you come to them, and
you couldn't resist them. Then you were never seen again.

Apparently, it had happened to the Dyagaraji clan long
before Jojo was born. One day they were there, and the next
they were all gone. The police said they had probably moved
camp and would turn up again when they felt like it. But the
other clans knew better. The Dyagaraji were taken by the croc-
heads, and no one would see them again. And no one ever had.

Jojo was about to turn back when a glint in the sky caught
his eye. Something was coming down in the river gorge, and
he frowned as it descended. It wasn't like a helicopter or
an airplane as it floated straight down, silent like a balloon,
except it was pointed like a triangle.

It kept coming down until it vanished over the horizon.
Jojo felt his chest well up with fear – had the croc people
returned? He had to tell Nana Bess.

He turned, about to run, but behind him there were six
men, tall and all in some sort of army uniform. The one in
front raised his hand in greeting.

"Hello there." The man crouched in front of him. "My
name is Winterson, but my friends call me Winter."

His voice reminded Jojo of one of those English actors he'd
seen on telly once.

"We have to be quick. There's a carnival setting up in the gorge, and they have free food, drinks, and prizes. But they won't be there for long."

Jojo had only been to a carnival once, and he'd really liked it. "Do they have rides?" he asked, already forgetting what it was he was supposed to be alarmed about.

"They sure do, sunshine. They have a merry-go-round, ferris wheel, bumper cars, and even candy floss." The man grinned and placed a hand on Jojo's arm. "Now, where are all your people? We'll help them all get to the carnival as we've got to be quick."

Jojo turned to point back along the track. "That way."

"Good boy." The man stood. "Let's go, then."

CHAPTER 17

Six hours later – Cape York Peninsula, Far North Queensland, Australia

"Satellite position plotting tells us this is where the bogey came down," Captain Alex Hunter said as he read the information from his gauntlet data system.

He was heading up two dozen HAWCs, and they were on the peninsula in four teams where they suspected there might be an interaction with who or whatever had been abducting the local Indigenous communities. He was the overall group leader but was also running Alpha Team One.

"Converge on my signal," he said softly.

"Hold position until other teams are assembled," Jack Hammerson replied into his earpiece.

"Permission to send in spotters," Alex requested.

"Permission granted," Hammerson replied. "I want their comms open the whole time as we've lost satellite vision over the area. I have your camera feeds, but they're breaking up. I want continual commentary on what they see."

"Yes sir." Alex checked his wrist gauntlet again and saw that he still had camera feeds from the helmet cams of each of his team members. "I still have local feed on the ground so guess it must be some sort of altitude interference. Like a blackout net thrown over the area."

"That's what I think. They must have established an interference bubble over the areas they operate within. Keep us blind and dumb – Incursion 101 – cut the enemy's communications," Hammerson growled. "Keep your eyes open. Their tech is undoubtedly more advanced than ours. Over."

"On it." Alex selected two of his soldiers. "Bugs, Halo, you're up," he said into his comm.

Ben 'Bugs' McKinney and Jane 'Halo' Brent moved up and performed a quick and professional weapons check. Bugs then turned and nodded to Alex's position, and Alex bet he was grinning that oversized toothy grin – hence his name – behind his face shield.

Halo, so named because she seemed to be protected by angels and had survived more close calls than any other HAWC, followed him.

Alex's teams were in heavy combat suits and were armored to the teeth. Plus, they had formidable weapons tech from rifles, grenade launchers, mini-drones, and force shields. They could take down a city block if they felt like it.

"Low and fast. Eyes open," Alex ordered.

His two spotters nodded once and then set out fast across the landscape. The gorge was just on half a mile from their position, and Alex estimated it should only take the pair of HAWCs a few minutes to arrive. He watched the small screen showing the vision from their helmets as they approached the ridge of the gorge.

"Keep talking, people," Alex ordered. Jane 'Halo' Brent was in the lead, and she switched to her feed.

"Coming up on the gorge," she said.

He saw the beginning of treetops beyond the ridge leading down into the steep ravine, and then saw the pair of HAWCs pause behind a boulder as they got to the edge.

"Oh yeah, there's definitely something weird down there," Halo said.

Alex could just make out the top of something white-silver and pointed in among the trees down at the bottom. The vegetation was too thick to yet make it out clearly.

"I see it," Alex replied. "Hold you position and observe."

The HAWC leader then checked the position of the other teams and saw that they were only a few klicks out and converging fast. Once they arrived, they'd approach the gorge from several different angles and attempt to gain entry to whatever the structure was.

In the report Hammerson had given them in their briefing analysis Alex had seen the autopsy images of the many-legged, or -armed, creatures, and it was stated that these could not be the sentient beings who were running this freak show. If that was what the structure was.

His orders were to seek out the controllers – they'd be given one chance to peacefully respond, or he was to take them down. He was also ordered to bring one in, dead or alive.

As he watched the tiny screen displaying the situation from Halo's helmet camera, he heard the man beside her beginning to grunt as if under effort. He switched to Bugs' camera and saw him moving toward the ravine edge.

"Bugs, hold your position." Alex frowned.

"I'm ... *trying*," McKinney replied as if through gritted teeth.

"Dammit, something weird," Halo Brent grunted as she also began to shift forward.

"Report in; do not exit your position." Alex saw the pair continue to slowly move forward. "What the hell are you doing?" he demanded, feeling the tension grow in his belly.

"*Can't ... help ... it.*" Halo sounded like she was in pain. "Something pulling ... us ... in." She grunted. "It's getting ... *stronger.*"

Two things happened very quickly – Bugs McKinney went over the edge as if he had been thrown. Halo Brent spun and fired her cable dart into the rocky outcrop. The thin, high-tensile cable was attached to a three-inch expanding spike that smacked into the rock they had been behind, and stuck. It was connected to her gauntlet, so she was held tight.

Alex sent a rapid message to both Hammerson and the other approaching teams that his Alpha team was under attack, and he was going in.

The response he got back from Hammerson almost set fire to his eardrums. "Negative, Arcadian. You will goddamn hold your position and wait for reinforcements. That is an order."

"Sir, I must—" Alex began.

"*That is an order,*" Hammerson yelled back.

"Yes, sir." Alex cursed through bared teeth and went straight back to watching the camera images.

McKinney's feed was now showing him moving at speed through the forest, and he wasn't alone. Something had hold of him, Alex was sure of it. A few seconds later his body was violently shaken, and then his feed cut out.

"*Shit.*" Alex quickly switched back to Jane Brent's. "How you doin', Halo? Talk to me."

There was the crackle of white noise for a moment, and then: "Goddamn hurts, boss."

He saw the female HAWC look back toward the hand that the wire extended from and saw that it was strung tight, as if a truck was on the other end ... and moving away.

He heard her groan.

"Gotta cut it loose. Gonna lose my paw," she said through what sounded like clenched teeth. She began to reach out with her other hand to eject the cable from her gauntlet.

But he saw now that her tethered arm was already much longer than normal, and he guessed that the shoulder had dislocated – she could never hope to reach it. Alex couldn't imagine what sort of force the woman was being subjected to.

He heard her groan again. And then it turned into a long animal moan of pain before she screamed.

There was a popping-ripping sound, and Brent was then dragged down into the gorge like McKinney had been. The last thing Alex saw on the camera feed was the female HAWC's arm still cabled to the rock at the top of the slope.

Alex shut his eyes, feeling helpless. "Fuck you, Hammer."

* * *

Hammerson paced. One of his hands was curled into a fist so tight, the knuckles were white and beginning to ache.

He had seen the two HAWCs be taken, and had needed to use every order, threat, and vocal cord he had to ensure Alex had stood his ground. He fully understood what the man was going through, but Alex needed backup or he and his Alpha Team of six, now four, could all be taken. It was a command call. His call.

Hammerson's base protocol was to attempt to make contact first, because for all anyone knew, these beings had no idea they were causing damage. But now, as far as Hammerson was concerned, they'd just thrown the first stone, and peaceful negotiations were over.

He opened the mic to the field.

"All teams, state your positions."

"Team Two now in sight of team leader. Now in position."

"Team Three in position."

"Team Four in position."

Hammerson nodded. "Alex, take 'em in. Find out what the hell is going on down there. And I want one of those bastards, dead or alive, for the science guys to cut into tiny pieces."

"Order confirmed. Out," Alex replied impatiently.

Hammerson punched a fist down hard on his desktop and growled as he watched the large screen in his office that was segmented into Alex's and the various team leaders' helmet-cam feeds.

He sat down, his eyes like gun barrels. "Our turn."

CHAPTER 18

Captain Alex Hunter organized the remaining twenty-two-strong team of HAWCs. As far as he was concerned, it was damned war.

If they were going to capture one of the occupants of the silver-white structure down in the gorge alive, it would only be if they lay down and surrendered. Otherwise, as far as he was concerned, the creatures were already dead.

"Listen up, people; they are using some sort of force that pulls you in. Then they attack. We go full suit combat mode." He pointed. "Ginny, send up the swarm."

"On it." Lieutenant Gin Alcorn opened a dark case that had slots for a dozen small devices. He pulled out the controller, switched it on, and small lights came on in each of the objects.

He stood back and let each of them lift off from the case – the drones were no bigger than a sparrow, and each was basically a flying eye – except these had been modified to carry a condensed pellet of C4 with enough kick to blow a hole two feet wide in an oak door. They hovered above them in a perfect 'V' formation.

"Ready, boss," Gin said.

"Good." Alex turned. "We go in fast, take down anything non-human. We go with the attraction, don't fight it, run with it, use it. In three teams, spread a hundred feet apart." He turned to Gin. "Release the swarm."

The dozen micro-drones zoomed ahead through the eucalyptus trees and on into the ravine. Alex turned to the assembled HAWCs. "HAWCs, payback time."

"*HUA*," his HAWCs responded as one. All had fire in their eyes.

"Muscle up, people," he said.

All the HAWCs' visors slid over their faces as their suits went into combat mode. Alex Hunter, the Arcadian, took the lead.

Ahead as he ran was a gnarled tree stump about six feet high. Rather than swerve around it, he dropped his shoulder and crashed into it, exploding the ancient wood into splinters. His fury rose another notch when he thought again of Halo and Bugs. He knew he needed to burn some off, accelerate into the fight, but he also knew he needed to be cautious as this adversary was unknown.

* * *

The four groups of HAWCs were soon approaching the rim of the ravine. Alex held his hand up and slowed them down.

They were near the rock that Halo had tried to attach herself to. And had her arm ripped off. He saw the bloody and ragged stump still attached to the cable, and a molten-hot fury rushed through his system like a river of hate.

Alex waved his soldiers into a crouch as he waited for the other teams to move into place. Above them the swarm of drones hovered like glistening black hornets.

There was little of the force that had dragged his HAWCs away, and Alex guessed it had been focused like a beam on

Buggs and Halo. He had no doubt it would be applied when they advanced.

He turned back to the steep gorge and stared down into its impenetrable depths for a moment more.

"Ginny, send 'em in," he said.

Gin nodded and worked the controls. The small, intelligent machines had software that automatically stabilized them and kept them from crashing into each other, and they also had the ability to self-determine threats and avoid them.

Gin only had to control one, and like a general in the field, it then controlled the others. If this leader drone was destroyed, then the next down the command list would take over. They were part of the next generation of future battlefield dynamics.

The tiny fleet lifted and dived into the ravine like hunting raptors.

"Flock is away," Gin replied while working the command drone.

Alex watched the camera feed as the dozen drones weaved around tree trunks, over rocks, and under fallen logs, all maintaining top speed. And so far, no force field or anything else seemed to be affecting their mission.

"There," Alex said.

Through the forest they could make out the outline of the silver-white object. They could see now that it was some sort of narrow pyramid, about eighty feet high and with a triangular base with edges about the same size.

"That's it?" He squinted at the tiny screen – it wasn't as big as he expected. "Gin, take them in closer."

Gin did as ordered and brought a few of the drones right in close to the structure while the others hovered nearby. It only took them a few seconds to find what could be a closed doorway, in front of which were drag marks and a blood trail that led toward the entrance and obviously kept going inside.

"That's where they took our HAWCs. And that's where we're going." Alex lifted his head. "Armor up, and we go full automatic on explosive rounds." He turned about slowly, and then added: "Let's make 'em pay." He and his team headed down the rocky slope.

As the twenty-two HAWCs ran, Alex began to feel the force Bugs and Halo had described working on him – it was like having a hurricane-strength tailwind at your back. If he stopped now, he might be okay. But he knew his team would probably be swept along by it.

"Feeling it, boss," came the word from one of his squad leaders.

"Use it, nearly there," Alex replied. "Keep it tight, people."

One of his HAWCs was pulled forward and off his feet. The huge soldier fell, rolled and came back to his feet to continue running.

As they approached the pyramid, one thing perplexed Alex: this structure was supposed to have been responsible for mass vanishings. Some of the abductions were reported to have been up to hundreds of people. But how? It just wasn't damn big enough. There had to be more, or there was more to the structure than met the eye.

Just two hundred feet out now and he could fully see the alienness of the pyramid's composition – it could have been metal, but it had the look of veined glass. However, in no way did he get the impression of fragility.

Suddenly he felt the attraction force field vanish. And then—

Alex pulled his gun in tight to his shoulder. "Heads up, we got a response."

The eight-foot-high door opened – not wide, or by sliding to the side or up, it just seemed to vanish. And what came out tore at the HAWCs' sanity.

Like a mass of giant brown-and-pink spiders, multiple-legged creatures boiled out toward them, tumbling over each other as their limbs pounded the ground.

Even though the HAWCs had all read the briefing papers and viewed the dissection images, seeing the abominable creatures in motion was stomach turning – they had no eyes, or even discernible heads, just rounded, muscular, pad-like bodies ringed with limbs – and not only legs but arms as well, and a feeding pipe that was pulled in tight for now.

The creatures probably weighed about 500 pounds each but were fast and nimble and came at the HAWCs in a silent wave.

"*Engage!*" Alex yelled, and began to fire.

The HAWCs had above-average accuracy and nearly every round struck their targets. But the pillow-like bodies absorbed the red-tipped explosive rounds even though fist-sized holes were being opened all over them.

The high-velocity rate of fire meant chunks of flesh and limbs were blown from the figures, and many were flipped over onto their backs, their limbs still working furiously in the air as if they weren't even aware they were upside down.

One leaped from forty feet out to land right in front of Alex and then reared up like a spider to envelop him. He saw that the horrific creature had half a dozen legs at the rear and four arms at the front – which all grabbed at him.

Alex strained against it – the thing was strong, unbelievably strong, and he understood now how they were able to snatch even full-grown men so easily. Alex fired around a dozen high-impact rounds into its underside, each punching holes the size of his fist right through and letting in the daylight, but the thing still didn't stop or go down.

It tried to drag him then, its sheer mass outweighing him by more than twice as much, and he began to slide. Next, several hands grabbed at his helmet, trying to wrench it off.

End this, his mind yelled at him, and Alex grabbed two of the arms, strained hard, and then ripped them away. The flesh tore, but no blood spurted. It was like it had already been drained as just a few drops of clear fluid spattered out.

He tore away two more limbs and the thing turned and scuttled back toward the open door of the pyramid. He looked about; his team was being pushed back while even more of the horrifying creatures boiled from the doorway. One soldier was grabbed, and Hondo, a HAWC who was about six-eight and had been a linebacker at college dived on the thing's back, spearing a long blade into its flesh. He dragged the blade backward, opening a valley in the meat, until he got to a glassy-looking bulb embedded in its center.

He struck it, and like a switch had been flicked, the creature fell to the ground, dead or deactivated. Hondo pulled the captured HAWC free and shouted into his comms system.

"Boss, the marble things on their backs … take 'em out."

Alex immediately saw what he meant. "You heard the man, aim for the dark bulb on their backs."

Hitting something roughly the size of your thumb on a grotesque, fast-moving target was no easy feat, but with the firepower they'd brought, they began hitting their bullseyes one by one.

A few minutes later, the weird bodies had all been dropped. Alex turned to the door and saw that it was still open. But what caused him to freeze momentarily was what was standing there. Framed by the inner glow and staring back at him was something that had to close to eight feet tall, its skin a leathery greenish hue, and with a head that would give him nightmares for months – it had multiple red eyes on a long and muscular face that could have been a mix of lizard or alligator. It immediately reminded him of some of the images he had seen of ancient Egyptian gods from Joshua's pre-reading for his upcoming school field trip to Egypt.

This was something different, though, and he knew immediately it was no mindless brute, for in its malevolent gaze he saw intelligence.

"There you are," he whispered. It was the thing that had commanded his soldiers be torn apart. "*HAWCs*," he yelled. "On me."

Alex fired a stream of explosive rounds at the alligator-creature, but before any could actually strike, the solid door reappeared in front of it.

Alex half-turned as he ran. "Ginny, kamikaze on that door."

"*Banzai*," Gin yelled, and like a line of deadly hornets, the HAWC controller directed six of the drones to crash and detonate against the door.

As they exploded like continual hammer blows, Alex jacked a plug into his undercarriage RPG launcher.

"Fire in the hole." He fired.

The soldiers went to ground, and the rocket-propelled grenade exploded, big time. When Alex looked up, the door was gone.

Alex called half a dozen HAWC names to follow him in, and the others to stay on watch. He went in fast and moved to the side to go to one knee with gun up.

It was dark inside the structure now, and not at all as he expected. There were no futuristic spaceship rooms. No gleaming control panels, or glass tubes, or flashing buttons and lights. Instead, it was dim and dank, and just a few feet in front of Alex were what looked like a lot of animal pens. There were also corridors, and he waved his soldiers toward them. Gin was with him, and the man still had six drones hovering at his shoulders like a small flock of pet birds.

"Go," Alex said, and then stood up and took the team in further.

Scattered about the floor were shoes and torn clothing, some old, some new. Alex noticed a small, yellow Donald Duck t-shirt that must have belonged to a child. The HAWCs had their helmet visors engaged so they couldn't detect odors, and Alex was glad of that as he peered into one of the side rooms and saw the results of the creatures' handiwork – body parts, skulls, all scooped clean, and literally tubs full of organs, all seemingly separated by type – vats of hearts, lungs, and ropey blue-gray intestines.

"Fucking monsters," he heard one of his soldiers say in a choked voice.

"Stay cool, people," Alex said.

Then they found Halo Brent. The female HAWC was crumpled against a wall. She was chalk white, and though still intact apart from her severed arm, Alex doubted she'd survive her blood loss.

Alex crouched beside her, and her eyes slid to him.

"Sorry, boss. Got the jump on us." She slumped forward.

"You did good, soldier," he said softly, and then turned. "Get her out," he yelled, and one of the HAWCs lifted her and turned to the exit.

There was a strange hum coming from the end of the corridor. A large doorway beckoned, and Alex went in fast. He saw the tall reptilian creature standing before a dark oval shape – some sort of door? Alex wondered – that seemed oddly depthless.

The creature looked back at him, and Alex bet if the thing was capable of smiling, that's what it was doing. It then stepped into the dark center of the door or portal and vanished.

Several of the soldiers rushed it, but Alex yelled for them to hold their position. Above the door was a circle of lights, and as he watched one of them blinked out.

"Gin, send in the drones."

The HAWC controller did as asked, and the remaining tiny flying machines headed toward the dark void. As soon as they penetrated past the surface of the door-portal, they simply vanished.

On the screen from the camera feeds, Alex saw a rushing, as if the drones had been plunged into turbulent water. Then in a blink the camera images cleared. Sort of.

It was red, blood red. And it looked dust-dry and reminded him of the desert in some Middle Eastern countries, but everything was wrong and could only be described as alien.

One of the drones tilted to the sky, where a huge ball hanging above looked like a low sun that was a hellish red and the source of the world's hue. It also seemed to be easily three times larger than their own star.

Suddenly all the drones began to slowly drop to the ground.

"What's happening?" Alex asked. "Did we lose power?"

"No, fully charged. They're working, but just can't get height. It's like the rotors haven't got the power to keep them in the air," Gin replied as he furiously worked the sticks. "They're all still online but I can't get lift."

"Something is affecting the power," Alex said. "It's different there."

Gin looked up. "Yeah, but where is *there*?"

"All drone cameras up," Alex ordered.

Immediately, all six drone feeds came on at once. Alex then saw there was a path or road and, in the distance, he saw what might have been a city with pyramids that touched the sky. But then one by one the cameras began to short out.

"What now?" he asked.

"All electronics are overheating – it's gotta be hot – way above 200 degrees at least," Gin said. "Melting the machinery."

"Magnify, quick," Alex ordered.

The last drones also began to blink out. Only two remained, and Alex could just make out what looked like a procession of moving beings in the distance. Gin focused on them and used maximum magnification to bring the scene a little closer.

Alex could see it was probably the reptilian creature that had just abandoned its ship. But what was with them made his stomach turn. The mutated or altered many-limbed bodies were working like beasts of burden. They carried equipment and the tall lizard-like things rode on their backs. There were also dozens more following behind, their brown and pink–skinned limbs moving like giant spiders toward a future of eternal servitude.

Then this image too blinked out, leaving just one drone camera remaining. And this one had fallen facing back to where it had entered the strange world.

Alex narrowed his eyes, trying to make out what he was seeing. It looked like some sort of machine, or box, and at its center was another dark oval portal, just like the one the creature had escaped through. But around its outside there were different panels with dots on them.

"Boss." Big Hondo nodded up toward the lights above the portal doorway in front of them. More had blinked out, leaving just three lights left on. He tilted his head. "You think that might be a countdown?"

Alex nodded. "Yep, I bet it was that slimy bastard's parting gift to us. He turned. "Alright people, we've done all we can; we are out of here."

The HAWCs turned and ran back down the corridor and then piled out of the entrance. As Alex exited, he yelled to all his team members in the field.

"Pull back, double time, we got a probable detonation event coming fast."

The HAWCs scrambled up the steep ravine, and just as they neared the top, the pyramid below them began to glow.

"*Zero*," Hondo yelled.

As the HAWCs went over the rim, the glow became all-consuming.

"Get down," Alex ordered.

The soldiers threw themselves to the dirt and covered their heads. But even from up over the rim of the ravine the light and heat reached them – searing, and the light even penetrated helmet shields and closed eyelids.

But in seconds it was over.

Alex rose and quickly checked his gauntlet sensors. Thankfully, there was zero radiation above background normal.

"Hold." He alone walked back to the edge and stared down. He half-turned. "Clear."

The remaining HAWCs joined him.

"Ho-*leeey* shit." One of the soldiers whistled.

"Got that right," Alex said.

Below them the entire ravine valley was empty. It wasn't just burned away leaving blackened stumps, scorched rocks, and smoldering dead animals. Instead, it looked like every atom had been vaporized, leaving bare rock and shiny patches that must have been melted rock and sand.

"These guys are playing for keeps," Hondo said.

Alex dusted himself down. "Yeah, so are we. We'll get 'em next time."

CHAPTER 19

Colonel Jack Hammerson opened the file sent to him by the science division containing all reports of strange appearances of oddities with too many limbs. They had already filtered out the freaks of nature and scientific frauds. What remained were occurrences of plausible extraterrestrial intervention.

He flipped to a section of the file headed *1880s* that contained a set of old, grainy, black and white images labeled the *Longgupo Shales monster*. In 1889, the remains of the giant extinct ape, called Gigantopithecus, had been found in sixteen different sites across southern China. The fossils there had been dated to around 400,000 years ago, and paleontologists suggested that the once plentiful species had vanished completely in that region around that time. And, inexplicably, all at exactly the same time.

However, in Longgupo, just south of the Yangtze River, they had found something even more perplexing. And disturbing.

At the time it had been dismissed as a hoax, just like the fake mermaids glued together from human children's skeletons and dried fish to give leathery tails, or even rabbits that had had wings sewn to their backs.

But this find was both alarming and confusing as it seemed to be several parts of multiple Gigantopithecus somehow stuck together. There was only one massive set of ribs, with no head attached. However, there were many arms and legs joined to the central mass. It was assumed by the Chinese scientists that geological pressure had somehow welded the bones together.

But this was implausible on too many levels and after a while, such was the criticism and outright professional sneering, that the fossils were removed from display and probably now resided in the basement of some Chinese museum.

Hammerson sat back and folded his arms, his eyes remaining on the images. He now knew differently. He had no interest in trying to get access to the fossils as they would tell him nothing he didn't already know.

However, what it did suggest was that the vanishings of humans and then appearance of these multi-limbed abominations had been going on for a lot longer than anyone could have imagined. For all he knew, it had been happening since the dawn of time.

His computer pinged as Alex's report came in from the Australian mission, and he dived straight in.

He sighed. Jane 'Halo' Brent hadn't made it. Bled out before they even got her on the chopper home. And Ben McKinney was MIA, presumed dead. But it was less than a ten percent mission force loss, and he had factored in at least forty percent. On balance, he was in front.

Hammerson focused on the report and after reading for twenty minutes he was satisfied; the teams had gathered good intel. The creatures' exit strategy told him why there was rarely any trace of them found – you got too close, they vaporized everything.

Hammerson put the field report aside and sat with a neat bourbon in one hand and the artist's rendition of the lizard-like creature that seemed to be one of the controllers in the other. He sipped and eyed the beast – nearly eight feet tall, four hundred pounds easy, and either wearing armor or naturally armored – formidable, he thought.

Not just as a physical adversary, but because they had tech well beyond what humans had; things his teams might not even be able to contemplate. But his HAWCs had breached the pyramid and sent them packing. At least for now.

Hammerson reached forward to commence the footage from the drones after they had followed the things through the portal.

He played it again. And then he played it again, this time stopping it at various places for closer inspection of the procession of creatures – the controllers, and the things that had once been human. Each time he did his jaw jutted a little further and his hand curled into a fist.

"You bastards," he hissed between gritted teeth.

When he had been in the military laboratory down in Miami, they had wondered why human bodies would be altered in the way they seemed to have been to create the many-limbed things – with low centers of gravity, multiple arms and legs, increased strength, toughened skin, and simplified metabolism, plus low intelligence. Now he knew. It was all that was required of beasts of burden.

"Slavers," he spat. "That's why you're taking us. To turn us into monstrous worker ants."

That was why they had been taking people and modifying their bodies to be able to live on whatever godforsaken place they came from, and it seemed they had been doing it for perhaps for as long as humans had existed.

"I bet as soon as we humans evolved, you began to use us as your raw material." He shook his head in disgust. Never in his life had he wanted to wipe something out so badly.

Hammerson sat back and sipped his bourbon, thinking. But they'd encountered a problem now. Humans had evolved.

Got smarter. Perhaps that was why they had started taking people from remote communities, people who were less likely to be missed.

Hammerson looked at the last few seconds of footage one more time and paused it at the point where the camera looked back at the doorway or portal. There were banks of lights that formed into patterns beside it.

He sat forward. "Hello, what are you supposed to be, coordinates?"

This could be promising, he thought. He'd send the images down to the pointy heads and see if they could decipher what they were.

There was one other anomaly that their satellites had picked up – a stealth chopper had been seen leaving the remote Australian area just two hours before his teams got there. When he'd sent one of the teams in to investigate, they'd found military-style boot prints entering the community village, and then leaving it again along with what looked like the entire tribe to head back to the valley gorge. But they never entered the pyramid or the gorge themselves. It looked like they had been simply acting as shepherds.

From Alex's report, the limbs and body parts of the things that had attacked him and his HAWCs were mostly brown, and that made him think they might have come from the altered Indigenous villagers.

Did some group lead them to that horrible fate? Had they supplied the monsters with their raw materials? And if so, who, and why? Hammerson knew human beings could be just as monstrous when offered the right incentive. But what was the motivation here?

Jack Hammerson called up the image of the helicopter and sent it down to the surveillance teams. His call to them was curt and to the point: *Find me that chopper.*

Whoever was on that craft had some answers to give him. And right now, he was in the mood to beat it out of them.

Jack Hammerson turned his attention back to the drone footage one last time. He started the film again, and this time stopped it at the view of the procession and homed in on the large figure riding on the back of the things that had once been human beings.

He enlarged and clarified the reptilian head and slowly sat forward. "As far as I'm concerned, you're already fucking dead."

CHAPTER 20

Today – Wayland High School, Boston,
Massachusetts

"I can carry that, *ah*, I mean, if you want."

Twelve-year-old Joshua Hunter's face felt red hot as
Armina handed her pack to him.

"Of course, you can carry it." She smiled that smile that
made him tingle from his toes to his ears.

He took the pack and looped it over his other shoulder.
He'd liked Armina from the moment he saw her, and he was
pretty sure she felt the same about him. They'd almost held
hands once and she had even passed him a note in class that
had a red heart drawn on it – and that had been that; he was
in love. He was sure of it, because nothing else could make
you feel like this, he told himself.

Armina stopped at her class door. She had geography and
he had math. She took the pack from him and put it down.
Then she just stood there looking at him with those brown
eyes that were as big as a world. The electricity ran right
through him all over again.

"I'll miss you, Joshua Hunter," she whispered.

"I'll Armina you too miss ..." He blushed furiously as his words jumbled. "I mean, I'll miss you too, Armina," he quickly corrected.

She giggled. "You're very funny."

He nodded, not trusting himself to speak again. Josh and his class had the biggest school excursion of the year coming up – they were all going to Egypt to see the Sphinx and the pyramids. A once-in-a-lifetime chance, and all signed off by his parents.

At first, he had been thrilled at the thought of the freedom of being away from his parents, and Armina being there as well was just too cool. But then she had dropped the bombshell that she wasn't going.

Her father, a senator, was to visit Yemen to encourage some sort of peace deal between the Yemeni government and the Houthi rebels. It had to be him, because they were Yemeni, and her father was related to the Prime Minster, so they had family there. Armina was going to be introduced to the extended family for the first time.

Joshua was to depart next Monday morning, and Armina was due to fly out that day as well, but at a different time. They were due to arrive back around the same day, so it was just all washing up as bad luck.

Armina lifted her pack and then lightly punched him in the stomach, and then laughed, too loudly. She turned to enter her class.

Joshua sighed and turned away. *Bummer*, he thought. He actually didn't feel like going on his grand trip now.

As he walked slowly down the corridor, he glanced out the window down to the square and saw two suited men coming in to talk to some of the teachers.

One of them held several photographs which he handed to them – Joshua focused on them, and then concentrated harder, his eyes glinting silver. Even from hundreds of yards away he saw what they were – pictures of him from the convenience store and the train station. They had been cleaned up significantly. Not enough to clearly identify him, but if you knew him, you might recognize the clothes, the posture, and then the shoes – the same ones he was wearing now.

Oh crap, they're detectives, he thought, and backed up.

His mind whirled. They were onto him. He couldn't let them speak to him. Or even see him. He panicked, betting that they would track him all the way to the airport because they'd soon know that all the kids his age were going to Egypt. One look at him, and they'd guess it was him.

Think, he commanded himself.

Then he lifted his head. If they couldn't find him, they'd give up. What if he didn't go to Egypt, but went somewhere else instead?

A plan had begun to form in twelve-year-old Joshua's mind – one he bet only he could pull off.

He'd lie low until the flight – to Yemen.

* * *

At the airport, Joshua Hunter had spotted the military woman almost immediately. She was tall, dressed in civilian clothes, but he noticed things about her that set her apart – for one thing, the clothing was tight across her shoulders and biceps, indicating formidable muscle power there. Also, her knuckles were raised, undoubtedly because of constant bombardment against hard objects. He bet she was a HAWC.

His father had told him not to intrude on other people's thoughts, but he couldn't help peeking inside her mind. He found it tough, focused – and focused on him. He wasn't frustrated or annoyed by them watching over him. He kinda expected it.

His plan was simple; his school excursion flight was Egypt Air, EG12 direct to Cairo out of Gate 5, leaving at 5.25 pm. But Armina's flight with Felix Airways to Sanaa in Yemen left an hour earlier, from Gate 2, on the other side of the airport.

Armina, her father, and his secret service bodyguards, would all be in first class. He had already heard from Armina that her father had told her that the planes were usually only half full, so he needed to get on board, then by the time his own flight was supposed to be boarding, he would already be in the air and on his way to Yemen.

No one from his school would miss him, because when he was supposed to hand in his final permission note, he had changed it to read that he could no longer go on the trip and would be home-schooled until his class returned. Therefore, there was no longer a booking or seat reserved for him.

He had one last task, and this would require a little more mental heavy lifting. He had worn a NY baseball cap with a hoodie up and over it to the airport, and had convinced one of his school friends to wear the same outfit. Then, when the female HAWC was checking in, he had changed his clothes and imprinted on her mind that his school buddy was him. Josh had then created a mental shield around himself that rendered him in a blind spot for the HAWC woman – even if she looked directly at him, she wouldn't see him.

But for now, she saw someone that looked like him who was with the school group, and so she followed.

His next task was to get on the Felix Airways flight. When it opened for boarding, he approached the gate and handed the attendant a fake pass. Once again, he imprinted on the young man's mind a seat number, and a fake name. He was waved through – *easy*.

Josh smiled as he walked through the cabin, and when Armina saw him, her eyes widened and her mouth curved up into a smile. Josh winked and put his finger to his lips – *our secret*, it meant. She nodded and he headed past her to find an empty seat.

For several minutes as they boarded the last few passengers, his heart was in his mouth and beating a mile a minute. But the door was closed, and the crew began their last checks before takeoff.

"Come on, come on, come on," he whispered.

He kept expecting the flight attendant to detect him, or the police to arrive, or ... and then the engines whined up to full power and they began to move.

He sat back and smiled. With any luck the imprinting of the HAWC would hold up for the entire week. He bet her job was to observe him and not speak to him, so all he needed to do was arrive back when or before his school friends did, and he could take over once again. She'd think he'd never been out of her sight when he had never really been in it.

The plane began to pick up speed and then lifted off. Joshua sat back with a huge smile on his face.

CHAPTER 21

General Marcus Chilton sat down behind his desk and pointed to the chair in front of Hammerson. "Good information from the Australian mission. Answers questions we didn't even know we had to ask. But raises more complex ones." He smiled flatly. "So, what are you thinking, Jack?"

Hammerson sat down opposite his superior. "We believe they've been coming and going before human beings had even invented fire. I ran a quick search before I came; there are paleolithic cave drawings of pyramids dating back nearly a million years. But now they know we're too sophisticated and would find them if they set up shop near a modern city, so have been undertaking their abductions in remote communities."

"I got that." Chilton raised his eyebrows. "That tells me they're worried about us, and add to that the fact that we destroyed one of their pyramids, it means they're vulnerable."

Hammerson shook his head. "They blew it up, not us. But we had them on the run, so yeah, we find them and get close to them, we can give them a black eye," he replied. "But those pyramid-shaped objects seemed to be little more than mobile doorways. They arrive, they take a bunch of people, and then they move to their next destination. But I don't think destroying the door at our end will disrupt their operations."

"The pyramids are just a door?" Chilton frowned. "Then you're thinking we need to destroy the doorway at their end?"

Hammerson nodded.

Chilton sighed. "And we already know that they can close the doors from their end." He looked up. "If one of our teams went through and attempted to disrupt or close the portal at their end, and the doorway was closed on them or by them, then—"

"Yes sir, our people would be stuck there." Hammerson sat back.

Chilton groaned softly. "Being a soldier means sacrificing yourself, for something greater than yourself."

"The eternal truth," Hammerson replied.

Chilton ruminated for a moment before looking up from under his thick brows. "Question." His brows went up a little. "Do you think the people who were taken, and changed, can be saved?"

"No sir, not a chance." Hammerson recalled the autopsy of one of the things. There was no way anyone or anything was coming back from that. "If we came across any of those merged beings, I think the merciful thing would be to end their suffering."

"Okay." Chilton exhaled through his nose and shut his eyes for a moment. "Bad stuff." He stood, his huge frame dominating the room. "Make a plan, Jack. I don't want these parasites feeding off our people anymore. We're not cattle for the taking." He stuck out his hand.

"Already on it, sir." Hammerson shook the big man's hand, saluted, and headed for the door.

"Jack …"

Hammerson turned.

"Anything you need, you ask. And one more thing…" Chilton's gaze was cold as Hell. "… you burn them all to hell. The scientists can study the corpses. If you leave any." The general saluted again, and Hammerson exited the room.

Hammerson also wanted complete eradication. Or at a minimum, destroying the portal on the creatures' home world. He already had the mission clear in his mind; he just needed to work out how to get there.

CHAPTER 22

Armina had snuck back to join Joshua in the coach section of the plane, and they shared nuts and sodas even though in first class she had a choice of much finer foods.

"Three days." She giggled. "You're mad. Where are you going to stay?"

Joshua shrugged. "I'll find somewhere. Don't worry about me."

Thing was, he hadn't quite thought through that part of his plan – at all. Perhaps he hadn't thought he'd actually be able to pull it off.

So, where exactly was he going to stay? What was he going to eat? Plus, he'd need to call home, and hoped he could convince his parents he was in Egypt. He'd better just speak to his mom as his dad would see right through him.

The plane rattled in some turbulence – it was a Boeing 737–400, a twin-engine, short-to-medium-range airliner that could take up to 188 passengers. But today there must have been barely forty people on board, including about six crew and staff.

The front end where the first class cabin was situated was fitted out for space and luxury. But back where Josh was, it was the standard crush rows. He was just glad he wasn't as tall as his father.

They had already refueled and were now over Yemen, so it wouldn't be long until they touched down, and he felt the sensation of dropping as they began to descend. He also felt a flipping in his stomach as he began to wonder what the hell he was actually going to do when they landed.

He glanced out the window and saw that below them was miles and miles of yellow-brown land with a geology that was eerily moonlike in its lifelessness.

"Miss Armina."

Joshua turned away from the window to see one of the family security people, undoubtedly secret service, standing beside them. He gave Joshua the once-over before leaning forward.

"Miss Armina, your father wants you back up front as we'll be landing soon."

"Okay, thank you, Wilson," Armina said, and turned back to Joshua. "See you on the ground, mad boy."

She squeezed his hand and Joshua suddenly felt a shock run from his toes to his scalp. But not from her touch; it was the same sensation he got when there was danger. Somewhere. But where?

As she was about to unbuckle her seatbelt, he shot a hand out to grab her wrist. "*Wait.*"

She looked at him, and the bodyguard frowned.

Outside. Coming fast, something in his mind screamed.

He mouthed the word without even thinking: *missile*.

His head snapped around to the window. In one blink it was invisible to the naked eye; in the next it was on them. When it came, the detonation filled their world – first was the explosion and spray of high-speed fragments, then, when huge sheets of the aircraft's skin were shredded away, came the destabilization, and the scream of rushing air.

The plane was still high enough to create a decompression effect, and unfortunately for Wilson, he was the only one on his feet and not strapped in. His huge body was sucked out the hole faster than anyone could react.

Armina screamed, and Joshua kept hold of her wrist. The plane's pilot did what he was supposed to, and dived, fast. They needed to get down into a thicker atmosphere and pray there would not be a second missile.

Behind Joshua an older couple's seatbelts popped open, and the maelstrom lifted the man and woman from their seats. The older man clung to his headrest, while his wife held on to his waist – both had their mouths open, undoubtedly screaming, but the sound of the furious wind in the cabin drowned it out. The couple's legs were arrow-straight as they were sucked toward the gaping ten-foot hole in the fuselage.

Joshua felt his chair rattling beneath him and knew that's what would happen to all of them soon. So, he concentrated. And then harder.

In his mind, he saw the fuselage whole again – and then over the hole on the plane's skin a swirling mass of air coalesced and compressed, and immediately the hurricane inside the plane settled as the invisible barrier kept the normal air pressure in, and the sky out. Plastic bottles, papers, and the two airborne passengers dropped to the carpet.

"Missile," Josh said again, and let go of Armina's hand, but she continued to hold on to him.

"How did you know?" she asked in a small voice.

He shook his head and then chanced a look out of the window again and saw something that scared him even more – the engine was smoking and there was a line of tattered holes running across the wing. As he watched, the metal began to tear from one hole to the next, like ripping perforated paper.

"*Oh no*," he breathed.

Then the wing was completely torn away, flung backwards, and on its way also smashing away one of the rear stabilizer wings. And with it all control over the plane was lost.

The huge craft went into its death spiral as overhead the monotonic words: *brace, brace, brace*, did nothing to calm Joshua's fear. Or Armina's, whose fingers dug into his arm like claws.

Joshua saw there was nothing below them but an orange-yellow claypan landscape and only a few rocky hills looking like the backs of dark and scaly whales breaching in a desert sea. He grimaced; the ground looked impenetrably hard and like death coming at them fast.

Brace. Brace. Brace – that voice was driving him mad, disorientating him when he needed to think clearly.

"*Shut up*," he yelled, and immediately the speaker overhead stove in as if it had been punched.

The plane dipped further, nose down, and then accelerated into a long corkscrew dive. Things in the plane began to slide toward the cockpit door. Then, behind them, a few seats ripped free and tumbled toward the front.

Armina screamed, and her fearful voice was like a jagged knife to his heart. The field of energy he had created still covered the hole in the fuselage. It gave him an idea. He had no choice but to try, because if he didn't, then they were all dead anyway.

Joshua relaxed his mind, then concentrated on creating a massive energy buildup inside himself. *Now*, he thought, and flexed with more strength than he had ever drawn on before. A faint bubble of blue light surrounded him, and he flexed even harder, and harder, and harder. The bubble pushed out from him as the wave of energy moved, firstly over himself and Armina, then down along the plane cabin, enveloping the inside, moving forward to capture the first class and most of the coach section.

It wasn't enough. He gritted his teeth and flexed again, but try as he might he could not capture the pilots in the cockpit or the passengers who sat at the far rear of the plane, and he knew he had reached the extent of the field's power.

But there was one more job to do. With the last of his energy, he used one last flex to try to bring up the plane's nose, just a little, just enough so they didn't strike the hard-packed ground like a spear.

Joshua screamed as blood shot from his nose and ears, and even his eyes turned a bloody red as he strained to lift the massive machine against the g-forces acting on it, while continuing to surround the cabin with a force strong enough to shield them from the colossal impact that was coming.

And in the next few seconds their time was up – the 119-foot, 150,000-pound Boeing 737–400 hit the ground at around 400 miles per hour. The explosive impact sent a shockwave across the desert, carved a crater fifty feet deep and showered the debris for hundreds of yards in every direction.

In the center of the impact crater, the only thing still recognizable was about fifty feet of fuselage, and a shimmering glow still rippled over its skin. After a few seconds, this, too, vanished.

It only took seconds for the ghostly silence to return to the desert. Nothing moved. There wasn't even a breeze.

CHAPTER 23

Klara Müller glanced around uneasily in her seat aboard Egypt Air, flight EG12 – something had changed. They had been flying for twelve hours and had just begun their descent into Cairo. She hadn't slept and would never have even contemplated it.

The throbbing pain in her head that had started to come on at the airport, and which she'd suffered the entire flight, had abruptly vanished a few minutes back. But in its place was a feeling of disquiet. And that put her soldier's sixth sense on edge.

She was several rows back from Joshua Hunter and his school group, and the students were becoming boisterous and excited to be nearing the end of their long flight.

Klara didn't buckle up even though the seatbelt sign had come on. During the flight she had walked past Alex Hunter's son several times, seeing him in his familiar hat and hoodie, but it occurred to her that for some reason, she could never remember actually seeing his face. It was as if those memories had been corrupted in her brain, and no matter how hard she tried to access them, her memory refused to clearly show her what the kid's face looked like – it was all just a blur.

She sat tall in her seat and noticed that Joshua was still wearing his red cap, but he now seemed smaller than she remembered. Alarm bells rang in her head and she got to her feet and then stepped out into the aisle.

A flight crew member came rushing toward her; the man was tall, but so was Klara, and she was built from solid muscle. She calmly pushed past him despite his protests.

"It's okay, I'm a doctor," Klara said, and strode to the row in which Joshua was seated.

Joshua and the kid next to him stopped talking and looked up. When they saw the blonde with almost colorless eyes staring at them with an intensity that could have stopped a clock, both boys just sat mute.

Klara lunged forward and flipped Joshua's hat up. This time there was no distortion over the face, concealing it. This time she saw ... that it wasn't Joshua.

Klara's eyes widened, and her expression must have frightened the kid who had been wearing the hat so much that he looked about to panic.

"He made me," he said quickly, but then frowned. "I think."

Klara turned away. The female HAWC had been beaten up in fights before. Been shot and stabbed. But she had never felt like she had failed the way she did right then. She let the flight crew member lead her back to her seat as she tried to think through what had happened.

Right then, she guessed that the kid had never got on the plane. And then she remembered hearing a rumor a while back that Joshua Hunter was different. That he could make you "see things".

She was on a commercial Middle Eastern flight and even she had needed to surrender all her comms devices – it'd be another hour before she could inform home base what had happened, and she could already hear the Hammer's volcanic voice in her head.

Klara sat back and shut her eyes. "I fucked up," she whispered as she thumped her head back against the headrest.

* * *

In the kitchen of his home, Alex dropped his coffee cup and clutched at his head as an agonizing pain tore through it. At first, he thought it was the Other struggling to reemerge, but then realized this didn't have the usual underlying sensation of fury and aggression but was instead a feeling of fear and panic.

He barely heard Aimee calling his name as he crushed his eyes shut against the intense pain – and then the visions began. He felt dizzy and saw a flash of ground a long way down, brown, brick-red, mustard-yellow, hard, dry earth, and he was heading toward it at a dizzying speed.

"*Sto-ooop!*" he yelled.

But he couldn't stop it. Couldn't slow it. They were going to crash.

Blood burst from his nose and ears, and then came a fear-filled scream that tore at his heart: *Dad, help.*

Alex Hunter went down like a falling tree and was unconscious before he hit the ground.

CHAPTER 24

Following his meeting with the general, Colonel Jack Hammerson strode down the hallway knowing he needed one more vital piece of information. He entered the physics research center's meeting room in basement level three's underground research and technology division of the United States Strategic Command.

Four of their top physicists, covering several specialty fields, were waiting for him. But the one who looked most excited was their senior engineer and astrophysicist.

Doctor Alfred Linley stood and walked quickly toward Hammerson, hand outstretched. He then seemed to remember where he was and stopped to salute, before holding out his hand again.

Hammerson smiled, sort of. He'd worked with the guy before and liked him. He was early fifties, but tall, fit, and good-humored. Plus, he was one of the smartest scientists Hammerson had ever met, without being an arrogant asshole about it.

"Colonel, good to see you again and great that you could come down." Linley led Hammerson to a seat, and the colonel nodded to the other scientists already seated, who in turn introduced themselves.

Most of the group smiled and nodded, except for the one other man at the table. Doctor Lee Huang was short, overweight, supposedly brilliant, but with darting eyes that made him look evasive. With him were two women, Doctors Alice Benning, an evolutionary biologist, and Letitia Farrow, who specialized in theoretical astral physics.

"I'm going to begin immediately," Linley said as he darkened the room and rubbed his hands together. He started the drone footage Hammerson had supplied to them, and Hammerson saw that they'd managed to clean it up considerably. The other scientists sat forward again, and the screen's glow was reflected against their shiny faces.

"This film is unbelievable," Linley said. "Proof of intelligent life aside, this is truly amazing, life-changing. I'd love to see it, and them, myself."

Hammerson's gaze was deadpan. "They're disassembling human beings and using them as slaves. They are an existential threat to the human race. Don't get too excited about them, Doc. They're parasites and I intend to wipe them out."

"Oh." Linley cleared his throat. "But I would like to meet them. Under different circumstances."

"I agree," Huang added. "We now have concrete proof we have been visited by intelligent life. This is world-changing. We should try and—"

"It's not your call," Hammerson cut in flatly. "Time is expensive, move on."

Linley sighed. "I, *ah*, understand."

Hammerson grunted and turned back to the screen. The screen had been stopped at the tall being he thought of as the controller. The image had been cleaned up and he saw now that it looked like an intelligent gator with too many eyes up each side of its greasy, armor-plated face. But the face wasn't long like a gator's, but shorter and more powerful looking.

He wondered at the evolution it took to get there. Perhaps if dinosaurs had never been wiped out and humans had never evolved, then this might have been who would have ended up ruling our world, he thought.

"That's one ugly bastard," Hammerson remarked.

Doctor Huang snorted. "I'm sure they might think the same thing about us."

Linley progressed the film, pausing to amplify shots of the caravan and what they thought might have been a city in the distance, but instead of towers, the structures were pyramidal. In another paused scene, they simply focused on the landscape.

"Not unlike our deserts. But I see no vegetation or even remnants of vegetation at all," Linley remarked.

"Maybe there's nothing left. Maybe it's a dying world and that's why they need to plunder ours, as they've consumed everything else on their planet," Hammerson said.

"That's a long bow. Besides, we have cities in our deserts. Vegas, anyone?" Huang frowned, but only at the screen and not at Hammerson.

"These creatures look reptilian to me," Doctor Alice Benning, the evolutionary biologist, said. "So, a hot climate would be a necessity for something that may be cold-blooded. To them it might be a paradise."

The film then reached its end, where the drone camera was pointing back at the dark doorway it had passed through.

"Do you see? That's a portal." Linley bounced in his seat. "That's the door from their world to ours."

"I got that," Hammerson replied. "We think they've been coming through for hundreds of thousands or possibly millions of years."

"That is astounding. And to think we never knew." Letitia Farrow's eyes were glistening with awe.

"Maybe we did. Originally." Hammerson smiled grimly. "There is cave art depicting pyramids dating back nearly a million years. Plus, anyone here ever seen an image of Sobek?"

Huang nodded. "The ancient Egyptian god who was supposed to bring life to the land of Egypt."

Linley began to nod. "Yes, I am familiar with that image, and it's astounding – a high-order bipedal reptilian form. It begs the question; did the ancient Egyptians know about these beings?" He looked back to the screen. "And did they meet them?"

Hammerson went on. "Possibly. This might well be the original Sobek. And perhaps it, or they, visited Egypt thousands of years ago. And many other places around the globe."

"The fossil evidence we've seen indicates they were here before humans, and the Egyptian mythology says this Sobek was supposed to have been a creator." Alice Benning turned to Hammerson. "Did they create us, or have a hand in steering our evolution?"

Hammerson stared back. "If they did, it wasn't out of any benign plan. They just needed more raw materials to create their beasts of burden."

"Do we know that? Or do we know if they are even aware that we object to it?" Lee Huang asked. "I mean, I agree it's a terrible concept, but they've somehow perfected interdimensional or spatial–astral travel. This is a significantly advanced race; we must make an effort to communicate with them."

"They'll get the first hint that we object to what they're doing when I'm burning them all to ash." Hammerson folded his arms. "They can take that as my first and only communication."

Huang muttered something that sounded to Hammerson liked a string of curses, but he looked away when the HAWC commander turned to glare at him.

Alice Benning made a sound deep in her throat. "I just hope … I just hope those things that were once people, have no consciousness or sense of… self."

"So do I. Because they'd be trapped in those twisted bodies. And the scientific feedback I've received is that they could live for hundreds of years." Hammerson sat back and nodded at the screen. "Back it up to the landscape."

Linley did as asked and clarified the image. He then let it stay on the reddish dunes and barren rock.

"Hostile environment," the scientist said. "We estimate the temperature was around 300 to 355 degrees, based on the time it took for the electronics in the drones to melt and short out."

"And we believe the atmosphere is a different pressure and also methane-heavy," Hammerson added.

"How do you know that?" Linley turned to him. "And for that matter, how do you know they might live so long?"

"We autopsied one of the multi-limbed creatures that washed up in Miami. Told us a lot," Hammerson replied.

"I'd love to see it," Linley almost begged.

"All in good time," Hammerson said. "Anything else you can tell me?"

"Yes." Linley clasped his hands together and smiled. "Judging by the part of the footage where the drones fall to the ground on the red world, I agreed with the assumption that they were brought down by an unusually high gravitational force. So I conducted tests with that specific drone model and, based on the speed with which the fully functioning devices were brought to the ground, I was able to derive an answer." Linley leaned froward on the table. "How much do you weigh, Colonel?"

"About 195 pounds, give or take," Hammerson replied.

Linley nodded. "On that planet, or dimension, or wherever it is, you'd weigh more like 588 pounds – around three times your Earth weight. You'd barely be able to move, if at all."

Hammerson nodded slowly. "Yeah, hostile environment is an understatement. Be hard to fight them there."

"Why would you want to?" Huang's eyes blazed.

Hammerson ignored him.

"It's hostile, but ..." Linley shrugged. "... we've walked on the moon, remember?"

"More recently than you know." Hammerson half-smiled. "You and Quartermain finished the new suits?"

Linley smiled. "We have. They'll do everything you'll need."

Huang turned.

"Good," Hammerson replied, and sat forward. He placed his elbows on the desk and clasped one fist in his other hand. "So, they've been coming forever. And still are, but now they're hiding. Because we've evolved and we're smart and powerful enough to resist them. Plus, we know they only arrive in the most remote places in the world to do their abductions."

Hammerson looked at each of the scientists. "But our eyes are open now and we see them." He smiled grimly. "What I want to know today is, how do I find them?"

"If that's all you want to know, then I think you're in luck." Linley moved the film on to the last few frames. "Around the portal, you see this collection of small lights here?" He pointed again.

Hammerson nodded and Linley went on. "They're star charts, with the one at the top being our solar system."

Hammerson had already guessed that, so it was no real help. "What else?"

Linley looked up. "Doctor Farrow, why don't you take it from here?"

Letitia Farrow moved a laser pointer down the side of the image and stopped at another grouping of lights. "I think that's our Earth, or at least a destination *on* Earth. And we've been able to decipher some of the other chart references."

Hammerson sat forward. "Go on."

Farrow nodded and picked up the thread again. "They reference zones in the Caucasus mountains, Egypt, Borneo, Florida, Australia, and Yemen. We can pinpoint them from those coordinates."

"Every eighteen years they come and seem to stay for a few days or a week, as if they're grazing, or harvesting. And then when they either have enough people, or they have run out of local stock, they move on. They have some sort of natural progression, moving down their list, as it were." Linley straightened. "We think we might be able to predict where they'll be next."

He looked back to the star chart. "And based on that progression, next up they should arrive in—"

"Yemen," Hammerson finished.

* * *

After Hammerson departed, three of the scientists, doctors Alice Benning, Letitia Farrow, and Alfred Linley, stood at the front of the room and continued their discussion.

Only Doctor Lee Huang remained at the table, twirling a ballpoint pen, his eyes fixed on it. "We shouldn't be helping them, you know?" He stopped its spin and looked up. "Because they're all wrong, dead wrong."

The three doctors turned, and Linley smiled. "Who? Who is wrong, Lee?"

"The colonel. The military ... you," Huang replied. "How can anyone truly know the visitors' motives? Their thinking might be so different from ours that we can't even comprehend how they see us."

"But we know what they are doing is wrong. They are harming people," Linley replied. "They either need to stop or be made to stop."

Huang sighed theatrically. "Imagine landing from the stars among a field of animals, say horses, and using some of them to do your laborious work. Our early settlers have done exactly that in many countries."

"But not through irreversible body modification," Doctor Farrow said, her brows knitted.

"If we had their technology three hundred years ago, I'm betting we would have used it," Huang replied, and then held out a hand. "Look, all I'm saying is that we have a race of beings that have perfected interplanetary or interdimensional travel, have medical procedures we can't even fathom, and probably have a hundred other things that would greatly benefit our entire species. If only we could speak to them. Show them who we really are."

"Unfortunately, they've already shown us who *they* are." Linley shrugged. "The military are involved and it's out of our hands now."

Huang stared at them for a moment, his eyes half-lidded in thought. "Not quite yet," he said softly.

INCIDENT 04

A child has no greater shield than the strong arm of a parent.

CHAPTER 25

Alex came awake and was immediately on his feet. "Joshua?"

Aimee had been leaning over him and bathing the blood from his face. When he said their son's name she also shot to her feet and grabbed his arm. "What is it? What's happened?"

In the house there was an unholy noise that it took Alex a few seconds to identify – the huge dog, Tor, was howling as if it had been severely wounded. He tried to blank out the sound and concentrate as he faced Aimee.

"Where's Josh? Right now, where is he?" Alex stared off into the distance and reached out for more sensations, but there was nothing but blankness, and emptiness.

"Their plane is due to land in Cairo ..." Aimee quickly glanced at her watch. "... any time now."

"No ... he's ... not on that plane," Alex whispered.

"*What?*" Aimee's eyes went wide, and her fingers dug into his arm.

Alex crushed his eyes shut and pushed aside his consciousness, trying to reach out and find some trace of his son. But nothing came back. It was odd, as usually no matter where he and Joshua were in the world, they could find each other, sleeping or awake. But not now. "I can't see him."

Greig Beck

"If he's not on the plane, where is he? Where did he go?" Aimee's voice was high with tension. "I know he went to the airport – I dropped him there."

That was right, Alex thought. *But* ... "Oh no. His friend, Armina Saeed, the daughter of the senator – *ah* – Mahdi Saeed. She was accompanying her father to Yemen." Alex turned. "He wouldn't dare."

Aimee gritted her teeth. "Of course he would. If there's one thing he inherited from you it was a foolish desire for risk-taking." She pushed her dark hair back. "Where are they now?"

Alex spun on his heel and raced to the computer. He signed in to the secure HAWC database and entered the section on aircraft flight paths. From there he had access to every flight that lifted off, its flight time, destination, and even current point-in-time global location.

He quickly found that a Felix Airways flight to Sanaa in Yemen had taken off from the same airport from which Joshua was supposed to have departed to Egypt. Alex felt a sense of rising trepidation – Aimee was right; you bet Joshua would have found a way to sneak on board. Everything was a game and an adventure when you were twelve.

He then followed the flight path toward its current location. The line on the map traced toward Yemen, but then suddenly ended in a red flashing dot. He clicked on it and the words '*unplanned incident*' appeared.

Alex felt like his blood was freezing in his veins as he searched for more data, but the next screen told him there was no further flight path data – the plane had gone no further. He rose shakily to his feet, his eyes almost bulging. "*It's gone down.*"

Aimee wailed. "*No, no, please no!*"

Alex turned and hugged her. "He might not be ..." He couldn't bring himself to say the word. "If anyone could survive it'd be Josh."

192

"Go get him." Aimee pushed him back from her. "Get a team, and go there, today, right now!"

"I'm the only HAWC not currently deployed – it'll take hours to call others in and prep them." Alex thought for a moment. If he called Jack Hammerson, his boss, he would want to help, but he'd also want to organize a team, and although the colonel could act fast, that would still cost him many valuable hours.

Aimee looked at him, her gaze dead level. "Go find him, Alex. Get our son back."

He hugged Aimee close to him, and then kissed her forehead. "If he's there I'll find him no matter what, no matter where." He headed for the door, grabbed the handle and then turned back to her. "Give me three hours, then tell Jack." He smiled. "I love you."

"Find him." Aimee's face was already streaming tears. "Do not stop, do not rest, do not let anything stand in your way until you do. Bring our son home." She clasped her hands together as if praying. "I love you too."

Her face was so ripped by fear that he felt a surge run through him. Without even knowing it, he crushed the round metal doorknob in his fist. He nodded to her, not trusting himself to speak right then, and headed out the door.

* * *

Alex drove like a madman to the underground bunker buried beneath the main USSTRATCOM building. It was these subterranean layers that housed everything from their biological research, containment, and specialized surgery, as well as what the HAWCs called the 'Toy Box' – the weapons development level.

He went through the secured gate, and on arrival leaped from the car and left it where it was. He saluted the two guards and in seconds was heading down in the fortified elevator.

The doors slid open, and as expected he saw that his descent had alerted the head of research, Doctor Andrew Quartermain. The thin, bespectacled, and young-looking man's eyes were wide when the lift doors opened and Alex stepped out.

"Captain Hunter, I wasn't expecting you. *Um*, at all." His lips pressed together for a moment. "This visit isn't on our schedule, is it?"

"No, this is personal," Alex said. "Something critical just came up." He had no time for explanations, challenges, or authorization paperwork. But he knew he couldn't do everything alone. Alex put his hand on Quartermain's shoulder. "I need your help."

The scientist immediately brightened. "Yes, sure, of course. What can I do for you?"

"My son has gone missing in the Middle East. He was on a plane that's gone down. I've arranged to be on a high-speed jet to get there, but it can't land. Do you understand?"

Quartermain's knitted brows smoothed and he began to nod. "Yes, I do ... you'll need to leave the plane at altitude and land under your own power." He lifted his chin. "How high?"

"High enough to avoid most ground detection and weapons systems – possibly 35,000 to 40,000 feet. And it'll be at significant velocity."

"I'll bet." Quartermain smiled. "And it'll be cold, freezing. Plus, way too high for a chute." He scratched his chin and then looked up. "One last question: which part of the Middle East?"

"Yemen," Alex replied.

Quartermain whistled. "A war zone." He lifted a hand and began to count things off on his fingers. "You'll need a pressurized suit with significant armor. For Yemen, I suggest desert battle armor. And for the arrival I think an EAM. Are you familiar with the Ejectable Aerial Mobility kit?"

"I am." Alex knew them well. "The angel wings. Perfect."

"Angel indeed," Quartermain scoffed.

The scientist then went and typed instructions into a console. He entered Alex's profile so the suit kit returned would be a perfect fit for the six-foot-two, heavily muscled soldier.

Quartermain included some standard weaponry before turning back to Alex. "I assume you haven't had time to draw together a team."

Alex shook his head.

"You'll need backup."

"I don't have time for that—" Alex began.

"At least a single team member watching your six." Quartermain waited.

"My six?" Alex lifted an eyebrow.

"Yeah, you know, your back." Quartermain grinned sheepishly. "See, I can speak the lingo."

Alex half-smiled, knowing the young scientist just wanted to be part of the gang. "Sure, I get it. But what I really need is to be there, now."

Quartermain held up a finger. "Wait." He raced to a wall, withdrew a keyboard from a slot and began to furiously enter commands. Another door opened and a large solid suitcase rolled out on a moving ramp.

Alex recognized it and his eyebrows shot up. "Is that a Defensive Operational Ground vehicle?"

"Yep." Quartermain nodded. "And upgraded."

"Okay." Alex nodded. "I've changed my mind about that backup."

"Knew you would." Quartermain continued to type instructions.

Alex had worked with one of the Defensive Operational Ground vehicles, or DOGs, before. But that had been years ago in Chechnya, and back then it had just been a series of armored boxes linked together, with a machine gun at one end and enough software to make it responsive to the HAWCs. Now he was looking forward to seeing what improvements the tech guys had made to the combat support units.

Quartermain crossed to it and pressed a button near the handle. A small stick like a thumb drive ejected from it. He lifted it to his lips and spoke a long string of numbers. Lights came on over the case. He handed the small item to Alex.

"You know what to do."

Alex smiled and lifted the stick to his mouth. "Captain Alex Hunter."

"*Captain Alex Hunter,*" came the mechanized reply from the solid box case. And then: "*Orders, terrain, lethality?*"

Alex's eyes were dead level as he stared straight ahead. "Orders are: guard, protect, defend. Independent action when required. Desert terrain. Maximum lethality, full combat mode."

His orders were repeated, and then: "*Alex Hunter voice imprinted. Command structure acknowledged. Orders received and awaiting initiation.*" The box's lights went out.

Alex turned to the scientist. "Thank you."

He stuck out one large hand, and Quartermain shook it.

The scientist shrugged. "Anytime, sir. But, Captain Hunter, you know I can't lie to the colonel when he asks about this." He turned away to rummage on his shelves for a moment. "He'd tear my ears off."

Alex nodded. "I know. Tell him. I want them to follow me. I just can't wait for them now."

"Good." Quartermain finished his search and turned back. He was holding two gauntlets which he handed to Alex. "They're compatible with the suit – offense and defense, and have enough capability to do what you need to do. It'll allow the team to find and communicate with you when they arrive. Also, you'll be able to track the downed craft's black box."

Alex took the armored sleeves which were covered in electronics. "Heavier. Hey, these are omni gauntlets – I thought they were still in testing?"

"They are. You're my first field-of-fire test. If they explode and take your arms off, I'll mark it down as a fail." Quartermain grinned. "Joking ... I hope." He then stood back and gave Alex an awkward salute. "Godspeed and good hunting, sir."

Alex returned the salute, grabbed the cases, and headed for the secure elevator.

CHAPTER 26

Today – Russian Ministry of Defense, Khamovniki District, Moscow

Major Nikolas Belakov sat at his desk reviewing the latest field information. His large body made the metal chair squeal in distress beneath his bulk.

He read the short paragraph again – another village had been emptied, this time in Belarus, following similar events there in 1984 and 2002. And for all he knew, many more times stretching back before their records had even begun. He carefully added the information into his database, his big, blunt fingers delicately tapping the keys.

He then ran an extrapolation on a computer program he had created that plotted all the vanishings across Europe, both east and west. He was aware of the basic details of those in the west, but he was more focused on the ones closer to home. The ones he might be able to get to.

The pattern was always the same – the pyramid or pyramids would arrive, or appear, then within a few days the locals would begin to be taken. Usually, but not always, it was the young men who disappeared first, possibly preferred due to their size or strength. He remembered the abomination he had seen in the Caucasus all those years ago, so he could guess what they were being taken for. Belakov quickly shut down that train of thought as his father had been taken during that mission, and the suspicion of what that meant made him feel physically ill. And ferociously angry.

The Russian sat back as the new data was uploaded into the plot point analysis, and while the program did its work, he couldn't help but let his mind wander again.

It had been twenty years since he had walked out of the Caucasus, alone. He had waited by the trucks for two days for his father, Uri Churnov, or anyone else from his team to come out. But no one ever did. There had only been the strange Englishmen who had stolen the nightmarish body, his only hard evidence.

Young Belakov had alerted his superiors but by the time they got there, listened with disbelief to his story, then trekked up into the mountains, it was all over. His father was gone, Tanya Kolsov was gone, and every single person in the squad was gone. There was nothing left and no clues except a lot of tracks – bare hand- and footprints – and all human. But Belakov knew that just because they were human did not mean they were normal.

Of course, no one believed him. He couldn't even show them the thing in the shed that the villagers had caught because it was gone. Even the villagers became mute and refused to speak. But their eyes told the then young Belakov that they were scared. To this day, he could find no record of any military or police operation to extract the strange sample. Someone had it, somewhere, and he doubted it was the Americans.

His thoughts returned to this Englishman, Saunders; was he the same secret financier of the initial trip in the Caucasus that had managed to claim their prize? Belakov knew that next time he needed to be smarter.

The rescue teams had combed the mountaintops and valleys for weeks after the strange events without finding anything. Eventually they gave up. But not Belakov. He would never give up. Not while there was breath in his body.

Belakov exhaled and sat back. It had taken him years, collecting evidence, and his superiors now appreciated the threat, and now he had his own team of highly trained specialists. And he now knew that the Americans seemed to be on the same trail.

The Russian rubbed his stubbled jaw. Maybe he could work with them. After all, they both faced the same foe.

He wondered what clues they had uncovered or samples they possessed. He would love to have combined information, but politics meant that could never happen. At least via formal channels.

His computer pinged, breaking his reverie, as it finished updating the plot points. He was now able to predict where the pyramid would arrive next and when.

Every eighteen years the visitors returned and became active, as if they had their favorite hunting ground and only waited for it to restock before coming back to harvest the new growth.

Borneo had been the test. He had guessed the next disappearance event would be there, but his timing had been off by either days or hours and he had missed it. But after using the new data, his computer had given him a new data point. It was out of his jurisdiction, but maybe he would have a chance to avenge his father after all.

Belakov stood and pulled his phone from his pocket. "Bruchev, assemble the team. We leave in one hour. For Yemen."

CHAPTER 27

On his way down the corridor, Jack Hammerson was stopped by an aide who saluted then handed him a small tech pellet. Hammerson quickly plugged it into his reader – it was the report on the anonymous helicopter seen leaving the scene in Australia.

They had tracked it to an air pad in Australia's far north, and then the passengers, six of them, had all boarded a private flight to Hong Kong. There they had refueled before the surveillance satellite had continued to track the plane to the United Kingdom. On landing there, the passengers were picked up in two dark-colored Range Rovers and ferried to the same destination – a huge property in Covington, Cambridgeshire called the Saunders Estate.

There was supplementary analysis of the estate's owner, Bradley Phillip Saunders, a retired tech billionaire who had a hand in several activist organizations, which the idle rich often funded to stroke their own vanity or wash their moral consciences.

"Why do you have a private army, Mr. Saunders, interfering in foreign countries?" Hammerson's eyes narrowed. "What are you up to?"

He'd soon find out.

* * *

Minutes later, Hammerson shot to his feet and slammed both fists down on the desktop. "What do you mean Joshua isn't on the plane?" His eyes near bulged as he yelled into the phone. "*You had one job, soldier.*"

Hammerson then paced as he listened to Klara Müller report over the speaker. She explained in a professional and clear account that she hadn't let Joshua Hunter out of her sight for a second. But somehow the boy had switched places with another kid.

Hammerson grunted; he could imagine how Joshua had somehow deceived the HAWC who was sent to look over him. He probably made her think he was there when he was already miles away. The kid could do that.

Hammerson knew Klara was an experienced HAWC; it was he who had underestimated the boy. He dialed it back a notch. "So where is he?" he asked.

"He didn't leave the airport, so we assume he took another flight," Klara replied.

The colonel shut his eyes for a moment. "Do you have any idea what Alex Hunter will do when—" His eyes shot open. "Oh shit; the plane that went down in Yemen with the senator on board. Please tell me Joshua wasn't on that one."

"Not that we know of. But ... we now know his friend was on it," she replied.

"Then so was Joshua. That's why he gave us the slip. Because he knew we were watching him." Hammerson tilted his head back and exhaled. "Damn shit show. Hold the line."

He picked up another phone and speed-dialed Alex's house. Aimee answered on the first ring.

He began. "Aimee, I don't want you to worry, but—"

She cut across him. "Joshua was on the flight that crashed in Yemen."

Hammerson almost staggered. His head dropped – he didn't need to know how she knew. "Does Alex—"

"He's already on his way there," she snapped back.

Hammerson nodded. "Yeah, of course he is."

"If he's alive, Alex will find him." She exhaled, sounding exhausted. "You were supposed to be watching him."

"Aimee, you know what sort of kid he is. He's different; if he didn't want to be seen, he wouldn't be seen. He eluded one of my best people – made her think he was somewhere else, *someone* else." While he was speaking Hammerson began to plan ahead – he knew Yemen was a freaking kill-box right now. "When did Alex leave?"

"He's probably already halfway there by now. I suggest you get after him with support. You know what it's like in there." She drew a breath. "If anything has happened to Joshua, I don't know what Alex will do. What he will become. He's only just rebuilding himself." Her voice became soft. "I could lose them both."

"I understand. A team will be in the air within the hour," Hammerson replied.

"Find them, Jack, bring them both home. Please." She hung up before he could say another word.

Hammerson exhaled as he slowly put the phone down. He had a million things to do, and he needed to be sharp. But then something else intruded on his thinking – Yemen and its potential to be the next abduction site.

Hammerson accessed the computer program that held all the information on the strange global events linked to the abomination that had come ashore in Miami. He opened the report on the hotspots where the disappearance events appeared to recur, and found where Doctor Linley and his team had been able to provide even more accuracy about the destinations' locations.

He opened the Yemen link and saw the drill-down – it was to a place far out in the desert called The Well of Barhout.

Hammerson sat down and used the powerful Military Universal Search Engine, or MUSE, to break into the flight plan of the Felix Air flight that had gone down, seeking its last known position. When he saw it, he groaned, long and loud – the plane had crashed on the edge of the desert, just a few dozen miles from the anomaly site. "Yeah, why not, what else could go wrong?" he muttered.

Colonel Jack Hammerson sat for a few seconds as his mind worked to draw some positives from the fiasco. This might turn out to be an opportunity to kill two birds with one stone, he concluded.

He then picked up the phone where his HAWC Klara Müller was still standing by. "Listen up, new orders: get to Yemen, now. Find out about the downed plane. Joshua was on it. I'll have a team join you." He hung up and began the HAWC call-up. He needed a small team, but the best. And people that Alex had worked with. If Joshua was involved, then volatile emotions would make for a combustible mix. He needed people Alex knew and trusted.

Colonel Jack Hammerson finalized his plan, and in a few more minutes his rescue team had been called up and the armory was awaiting their arrival. He paused; there was one more thing they needed. He couldn't send his team in without all the intel they had.

He didn't expect them to try to absorb the enormous amount of data they had collected and assimilated, and they didn't have time anyway – so Plan B was to send the guy who'd collated it.

Hammerson picked up the phone and dialed the secure USSTRATCOM laboratory.

"Alfred ..." He half-smiled. "Remember how you told me you'd like the opportunity to see one of those weird pyramids, and their owners, in person?"

His smile broke into a grin. "Get to the armory, like five minutes ago, and be prepared to be on a chopper in half an hour."

INCIDENT 05

I, bringer of death and destruction.

CHAPTER 28

Alex got to his feet in the back of the Rockwell B-1 Lancer, a supersonic variable-sweep wing, heavy bomber, sometimes called "*the Bone*".

In the huge bay area in the rear of the aircraft Alex paced like a caged lion, impatience boiling within him.

The Bone had a top speed of Mach 2.2 at high altitude, and the capability of flying for long distances at Mach 0.85 at very low altitudes. It could reach full-capability heights of 70,000 feet and was a technological marvel capable of carrying more than two school buses' worth of ordnance faster than the speed of sound. Plus, it was near invisible, occupying less than one percent of the space on an enemy's radar compared to the B-52 Stratofortress.

Today the Bone was just on a "flex" run over the Middle East, designed to test out adversary capability, and unbeknown to the senior officers back at base, Alex Hunter had pulled strings and called in markers to be able to tag along.

Alex had kitted up in the bay area and checked the gauntlets that Quartermain had provided – their small screens told him that all offensive and defensive capabilities were online and fully charged, and he spent several minutes going through the list. There was everything he needed, and more.

He opened the tracking screen feed and it showed him the location of the downed Felix Airways plane – they were still hundreds of miles from the black box's ping, but it was as close as the pilot could get without performing an obvious deviation and drawing unwarranted scrutiny. It'd be up to Alex to do the rest.

"Five minutes," the pilot intoned. "Gonna bring us down to 35,000 feet and ease back on the gas. Still gonna beat the crap out of you and be one cold day in hell out there, sir."

"That's all I need. Appreciate it. I owe you one, Bill." Alex slid the visor down over his face. "See you when I get back."

"Hope so," The pilot was unable to mask his skepticism.

The clay-colored suit Alex wore was insulated and heavily armored, but still light enough to not restrict his movement. He knew it'd be cold – in fact lethal at around minus 74 degrees – at 35,000 feet. He'd be moving fast in the thin atmosphere so any damage he sustained should only be for a short duration. He would have to rely on his boosted metabolism to repair him before he hit the ground.

He opened the first case and shrugged on the heavy flight pack, securing it tightly across his chest, stomach, and shoulders. He switched it on and found the device fully operational – just as well, as without it he wasn't getting to ground.

Alex's final task was lifting the dark, heavy suitcase – DOG – his guardian. He smiled. "Just you and me, buddy."

"*Go time*," the pilot said, and the bomb doors whined open.

Alex quickly gripped the inside cargo bay wall as a maelstrom of freezing air blasted in at him. This wasn't a jump craft, and so there was no rear platform to leap from. There was just a long oblong hole in the floor, and even with the Rockwell Lancer slowing, the wind speed rushing past outside was around 700 miles per hour.

His first task was to exit the craft without being smashed to pieces along the undercarriage. And not just him – Alex lifted the heavy, dark box.

"DOG."

"*Online,*" came the response.

"Find me on landing."

"*Find Captain Alex Hunter on landing – acknowledged,*" the box replied.

Alex then threw the box out through the open bomb doors with all the strength he could muster, and it vanished into the ink-black night air.

The pilot came online again. "Putting her in a slow dive on, five, four, three, two … *go.*"

Alex flexed his thighs and then sprang forward headfirst as the pilot used the motion of the forward aircraft dive to try to give him a little extra wind-shadow room from the undercarriage.

It worked.

Alex was out of the doors and half a mile behind the plane before he knew what was happening. The cold instantly bit right through his suit, and he tried to ignore it as he pushed his body into an arrow shape. The thin air meant there was little resistance and he was immediately traveling at just over 300 miles per hour.

At that height and velocity, he was covering hundreds of miles every few thousand feet he dropped. At night and without illumination or landmarks below him, everything was just black on black. But the digital readout on the inside visor of his helmet told him he was heading in the right direction – right toward the plane's black box.

At 25,000 feet, he felt his fingers and toes begin to freeze up. He flexed them, and the agony shot up through his arms and legs. He couldn't allow his hands to become immobile, not now, not when he'd soon need them.

At 10,000 feet the air was becoming thicker, and he slowed to around 200 miles per hour. It was also warmer, so his extremities thawed. They throbbed mercilessly, but he knew they'd fully repair soon enough.

He was getting lower, but was still hundreds of miles from his destination, and there was no way he wanted to trek across miles of desert – he couldn't afford the time or energy.

At 5000 feet he decided it was time. He reached up to the panel on the harness on his chest, pulling down a lever. Wings deployed on either side of his shoulders – the 'angel wings' of the EAM kit Quartermain had given him.

Alex went into a glide. Then he pressed a recessed button on the panel, and the air intakes at the front sucked in the rushing air and expelled it as super-fast compressed jets from the rear of the suit. Alex was blasted forward, but now rather than gravity being in control, he was.

He quickly accelerated back to 300 miles per hour and came in fast toward the position where his locater was telling him the plane had gone down.

The reason he liked the angel wings was that there was no fuel burn – they were near silent – and to anyone watching from below he was invisible. In minutes he began to be able to make out the shapes of hills, claypan flats, and dunes in the starlight.

He was now only a few hundred feet above ground but still traveling at close to 300 miles per hour. He needed to slow and the simplest way to do that was to swivel in the air, then reduce exhaust flow.

With the air jets reducing their blast, he gradually de-scended. Lower still, then he cut off all power and dropped the last ten feet to the ground to land on his feet. The soft whine of the engines died away and there was silence around him.

Alex turned slowly and reached out with his senses. He heard nothing, and only sensed the tiny heartbeats of small animals, perhaps a desert rat, or a snake, within 100 feet of him.

He quickly shucked off the EAM kit and let it fall to the ground. He then reached into a slot on his belt for a hockey puck–sized, dark object, and swiveled the top half. A ring of tiny lights came on around the rim, and each started to blink off.

Alex then tossed the melt-disk onto the EAM where it stuck. He watched as the lights counted down to zero, and then the object initiated. After a few seconds, the EAM glowed, softened, turned to sludge, and then melted and sank into the sand.

Alex checked his gauntlet – the black box was just half a mile away now over a range of small hills. He set off immediately.

***

Approximately fifty-five miles to the south of Alex there was an impact crater in the sand dune. At the top edge the grains of sand began to tremble, then collapse inwards as something at the bottom of the crater began to move.

A few seconds later there came an eruption from the crater's depths as something dark, smooth, and metallic with four legs exploded from the earth. It quickly accelerated to close to eighty miles an hour, kicking up sand behind it as it moved in a blur.

Its one and only priority now was to join its designated mission leader – Alex Hunter. Its instructions were already locked in: *Guard, protect, defend – maximum lethality, full combat mode.*

Nothing would slow or deter it.

CHAPTER 29

Alex crested the hill of sand and sunblasted rock to finally catch sight of the plane wreckage in the distance. It was in a slight depression between several hills, sitting in the center of a huge impact crater. He crouched to watch as sporadic gunfire rang out.

There was a group around the wreckage trading fire with another group spread out on a rise. He concentrated and saw that those on the hill had the mustard-colored desert camouflage uniforms of the Yemeni government. Which meant the group at the wreck were probably Houthis.

He knew that the Houthis were a band of lawless terrorists and opportunists, and would scavenge, murder, ransom, and kill their way to what they wanted. Also, he had no doubt that it was they who had brought the plane down and were now picking over its carcass for what tidbits they could salvage. He had heard from others in the field that they would even pull the gold wedding bands from the fingers of severed hands – they lived by the law of the jungle, and that was all.

Alex sensed that Joshua wasn't in the wreckage – or was that just because he couldn't sense if there was a *living* Joshua

214

in the wreckage? The fear of what that might mean made his head swim momentarily. He needed to get down there – and the Houthis were in the way.

He stood and jogged to the rear of the Yemeni forces. As he approached, bullets flew from the Houthis and went overhead, past him, and spattered into the sand all around him. The Yemeni government forces probably had similar aim, and he guessed that unless one side retreated or surrendered, the gunfight could go on for days. Or until the government forces or Houthis brought in heavy weapons and destroyed everything.

When he neared them, one of the government fighters in the rear of a truck turned to see him. Even though Alex had his visor up and off his face, the man immediately swung his rifle around to fire several rounds. As damned luck would have it, Alex was probably the first person he'd managed to hit in his entire life.

Two of his rounds hit Alex dead center in the chest. The impacts were painful, but the armored suit took the hits with little damage, and only caused Alex to falter a step from the projectiles' velocity.

He held his hand up. *"American, American, don't shoot."*

Unfortunately, the bullet impacts activated the self-defense protocol of the suit, and the visor came down automatically over his face and the more muscular combat armor slid into place.

The man's eyes filled with panic as he witnessed the bulking up of the robotic form and lifted his gun again. This time Alex accelerated, moving so fast the man couldn't track him. Alex leaped up onto the back of the truck and easily ripped the gun from the man's grip.

The terrified soldier held his hands in front of his face as the huge being dressed in the clay-colored armor with the helmet's featureless, full-face shield towered over him.

With the threat disarmed, Alex was able to retract the face shield. "I'm American, a friend." Alex only knew a few words in Arabic, but at least one of them was 'friend': "*Sadiq, sadiq.*"

The man lowered his hands, but his eyes were still fearful.

"English?" Alex asked.

The man shook his head but kept his eyes on Alex as he half-turned to yell. "*Capitan Hadid!*"

Alex followed where he was looking and saw a senior soldier raise his head and stare at them for a moment.

Alex waved to the senior soldier, handed the man back his gun, and jumped down from the truck.

As he approached, this time, half a dozen of the soldiers turned to train their weapons on him. The Yemeni captain narrowed his eyes.

They stared at Alex, sizing him up. But then their eyes were drawn to something over his shoulder. Alex half-turned and saw that an object was coming at them at a blistering speed, kicking up sand in a rooster tail behind it.

Only seconds later it arrived and took up a defensive position in front of Alex. The soldier's eyes went wide. On detecting the weapons pointed at its ward, DOG immediately went into attack mode, deploying its heavy armor shielding as well as preparing several weapons – Alex saw the barrels emerging from under what he thought of as its chin. Alex noticed that some of them were more than just for bullets and were undoubtedly field lasers.

It was the first time Alex had seen the new-model combat guardian fully operational. This one was smoother than the one he'd worked with in the past, and the joins had more flexibility to allow more fluid movement, making it look even more like a real animal, if anything.

Maybe that was what the designers had intended, to instill a greater degree of familiarity and bonding between soldier and their personal guardian.

DOG began to advance, and Alex knew it had probably already calculated a defensive and offensive plan that would kill every man with a weapon in the next few seconds. If one more soldier fired, they'd all be dead.

"DOG, halt, desist," Alex said.

The metallic war device ceased advancing but didn't retract its weapons.

"Who are you?" Captain Hadid asked in English.

"Captain Alex Hunter, American, HAWC Special Forces." Alex glanced at the plane wreckage, where sporadic gunfire was still being traded. "The downed plane had our citizens on board. I need to examine it."

Hadid ignored the request and pointed. "What is that thing?"

Alex briefly glanced at DOG. "My bodyguard."

"*Pfft*, Americans. Unbelievable." Hadid shook his head and then turned. "The Houthis are dug in around the crash site. Our orders are to secure the plane, but as yet we can't even get close."

Alex stood. "I can."

"There's too many of them. And we can't use grenades or rockets as any survivors – and the aircraft – will suffer further damage." Hadid also stood but stayed behind a truck. "We've requested reinforcements, but …"

"But they'll be a while." Alex half-smiled. "Give me five minutes."

"Five minutes?" Hadid scoffed. "This will be interesting. We'll give you cover."

The last thing Alex wanted was a lot of undertrained bad shots flying past him as he went in. "No, hold your fire. The best thing you can do is try to stop any of the Houthi soldiers from getting away." He looked back down at the plane. He couldn't see exactly how many of the rebel fighters there were but guessed there must have been at least a dozen and probably more. Also, the debris from the plane was spread over 200 feet so there were lots of places for concealment. "Await my signal."

Hadid nodded and Alex faced DOG. Almost like a real animal it seemed to look up at him, awaiting its instructions.

"Right flank. Meet deadly force with deadly force. Execute."

Alex watched as DOG sped away and then he initiated the full-face visor in his helmet. The HAWC then sprinted out to the left flank, both he and the robotic animal moving at a speed that was beyond the compression of the Yemeni government soldiers watching, and undoubtedly the Houthi forces who now spotted them and tried to hit them.

Bullets flew past him, and in his peripheral vision he saw the four-legged DOG round the plane wreckage on the other side. Alex couldn't help but grin at what they'd make of the thing coming at them. Just before it killed them.

Alex rounded the collapsed nose section of the aircraft and came face to face with several of the Houthi warriors who were waiting for him. There were half a dozen of them, and they were ready, three down on one knee with guns to their shoulders, and three upright behind them like a disorganized firing squad.

They had the clarity of thought to begin firing, and Alex knew there was no way to avoid all the rounds, so he just headed into the storm of lead and relied on his momentum, the suit's armor plating, and his own rapid-healing metabolism to repair any damage.

Most of the men had AK-47s, as they were cheap, reliable, and fired a 7.62 × 39 mm cartridge with a muzzle velocity of 2350 feet per second.

The bullets were heavy and fast, and at the speed he was travelling most of the rounds missed him. But many didn't. And each hit felt like being punched with an iron fist.

Alex knew he could take it, but the continual impacts slowed him and knocked him off balance. Then he saw another man down on one knee with an anti-tank RPG tight at his shoulder and his eye down over the targeting system. In another blink the guy fired.

Shit, Alex thought.

The small, high-impact fragmentation grenade exited fast, and in just a few dozen feet had already accelerated to 600 miles per hour. Alex could move fast, but not that fast.

He was off-balance but had time for one thing: he engaged his wrist gauntlet defense system and a circular, three-foot shield made of super-hardened tungsten composite flared open.

Alex planted his legs and held it up. The RPG impacted and exploded, and as Alex hoped, all the flying debris, percussive force, and heat was thrown out to the sides. However, the massive explosive impact still blew him back ten feet and made his ears scream like sirens.

But even before the flames had died down and the sound had fallen away, he had retracted the shield and was accelerating forward once more.

Many of the Houthi warriors just stood there with mouths gaping in disbelief that the huge clay-colored being had just come through an explosion, unharmed. But by the time they commenced firing again Alex's mass combined with his velocity meant he was already in among them, and when he struck it was like a bowling ball hitting the pins. Bones broke like kindling, muscles were ripped, and heads caved in. Two of the men were flung twenty feet into the air.

When Alex slowed and reassessed his situation for a split second, he saw he'd been wrong; there were at least twenty fighters, all armed, and several had shoulder-mounted RPGs. Plus, these were not out-of-date anti-tank devices but the Iranian weapons with *nadar* rounds with depleted uranium tips – shield or no shield, suit or no suit, they'd blow him to pieces.

One was already sighting on him, and he knew he'd never get to the man in time to stop him. Alex dived toward a pile of plane debris, rolled, and when he came up, he had scooped up a sheet of metal debris two feet wide. Employing his entire shoulder strength, he flung it like a discus. His aim was good and it struck home, and from the nose up, the top of the man's head separated from his chin.

Although dead, the standing man's finger reflexively tightened on the trigger, but without a brain or eyes, the aim of the RPG that flew at Alex was off, and it rocketed right past him to explode out in the desert with a massive orange bloom.

Alex saw DOG engaging with his adversaries on the left flank. Several warriors fired, but the metallic hound with computer-assisted targeting put a round between each of their eyes, and its armor plating was more than a match for even the heavy machine guns they had employed.

Unfortunately, there was another RPG, and this guy got his rocket away. Alex marveled at the DOG's defenses. As soon as it detected the small missile, its head and legs retracted in a blink, leaving little more than a smooth armored box.

The grenade hit, detonated, and blew DOG fifty feet out into the sand dunes. But as soon as it hit the ground, DOG's legs and head reappeared, and like a motorbike kicking up dirt, it came back at the rocket firer far faster than he could get out of the way. Perhaps the RPG had caused it to reassess the threat potential and so upgrade its response, because the emitted light beam that shot out and went across the man's chest, from one side to the other, followed by a puff of smoke from the singed material and flesh, felled him instantly. The man's top half fell sideways to the left and the bottom half collapsed backwards. On the ground, the man's eyes were wide and his mouth worked and Alex bet he was asking what just happened.

On seeing this, it seemed the remaining Houthis had had enough and began sprinting away from the pair of demons who had attacked them. Unfortunately for the fleeing men, the Yemeni troops finally proved useful, picking off most of the running men once they were out in the open and easy targets. Many of the fleeing Houthis didn't get further than twenty feet, with only one or two vanishing over the rise.

Alex knew some would escape, but it didn't matter; the fight was over. DOG raced up to Alex and stopped in front of him. He looked down. "Good boy," he said without thinking, then laughed. Alex smiled down at the smooth metal face. "Well, I think you're a good boy. And I'd give you a treat, but ..." He was sure the lights in the creature's eyes glowed a little brighter with the compliment.

"I'm going mad, aren't I?"

DOG didn't respond.

"I'll take that as a yes." Alex chuckled and waved a hand to the government forces who came down from the hill and surrounded the plane.

The results of their investigation filled Alex with hope – it only took them minutes to ascertain that there were far fewer passenger bodies in the wreckage than there should have been. And then they found the tracks leading off into the desert.

Alex went down on one knee to examine them and saw the familiar tread of Joshua's cross-trainer shoes, his favorites. He was walking beside another pair of smaller shoes – it seemed Armina, the senator's daughter, had survived as well.

He put his hand flat on Joshua's footprint and closed his eyes. After another moment he breathed a sigh of relief, as he could sense his son was unhurt.

He then opened his eyes and looked at the ground around the crash site – he didn't see any stretcher drag marks so, assuming there were no injured to care for and the survivors had come to a decision quickly, he guessed they would have been on the move for at least eight hours. Big head start, but they'd be moving slowly.

Alex stood and looked back at the section of the fuselage that was intact, while the front and rear were totally obliterated. He bet somehow Joshua shielded and saved them in that section of cabin space.

He checked his gauntlet and called up a map of the region. It showed the closest towns and villages. There were several.

He called Hadid over and showed the man the map. "These tracks are heading east. If you were them, what would be your plan?"

Captain Hadid nodded. "They need to escape, get home. Best to do this from an airport." He glanced at the map again. "The closest is Al Mukalla. But it is too far to walk, so I would try and get to the coast. Maybe buy or steal a boat there."

"Makes sense," Alex replied.

Hadid then grimaced. "Lots of Houthis, though. This is their territory. Your countrymen have embarked on a very dangerous journey."

Alex pointed at the small tracks. "They've got kids with them. They have no choice." Alex looked out over the desert.

Hadid pointed at the hard-packed earth. "I also see that some Houthi fighters went after them. A small band, maybe just ten, but enough to give them trouble."

"I expected that," Alex replied.

"There's one more thing," Hadid said. "That area ..." He bobbed his head. "Very bad. Everyone avoids it."

"I don't care." Alex turned. "If they've gone there, I'm going there."

"Do you expect us to follow?" Hadid asked.

"I could use the support and advice; this is your land. But you have to do what you think is right." Alex looked at the captain. "I have no choice; my son is with them."

"Your son?" Hadid sighed. "I too have a son." He looked out to the desert claypan then back to Alex. "There is an old Arabic saying: *If you see the tracks of a wolf, better carry a stick.*" Hadid's mouth was turned down. "And today, I see the tracks of a wolf."

Alex nodded and smiled. "I see them too."

"Then I will be your stick. I will take twenty men and accompany you. Let us see if we can bring back these children of America."

He called to select his men, and left a trusted lieutenant, Zabu Wardou, in charge of the wreck until reinforcements arrived. They were ready in short order.

"I'll be out front." Alex turned to the metal creature beside him. "DOG, let's go."

He began to run, fast, the metallic animal by his side.

CHAPTER 30

Abu ben Ghazi, the local Houthi commander, had received a communication from the small village of Ayuri to inform him there was just one survivor from his squad that had been dispatched to search the plane wreck.

He frowned as he remembered the garbled message. The men had been set upon by government forces, although that should have been nothing to be concerned about. But then the messenger had referred to a strange warrior that had appeared, accompanied by a metal demon. Together they had killed everyone in seconds.

It didn't make sense. Ghazi didn't believe the story, nor did he believe this survivor; he thought it more likely the man had deserted and ran for his life. How could he know his brothers had been wiped out if he wasn't there to witness it? He'd deal with the coward later.

For now, Ghazi knew he needed to reassert his dominance. He used the radio to call up most of the fighters and heavy weaponry he had in the area and deployed it all to the crash site. He needed to be seen as the strong horse, and therefore the Yemeni government forces needed to be reminded exactly who was the stallion and who was the donkey.

In another hour he had 200 men, rockets, and heavy artillery heading toward the downed airplane.

CHAPTER 31

Six hours after the crash – Somewhere in the open desert, Al Mahrah province, Yemen

Joshua's head still throbbed mercilessly after the plane crash and from overexerting himself to protect the cabin. At least his nose had stopped bleeding, which was a good thing seeing as how it had been draining him of precious fluid they didn't have in the oven-hot desert. He squinted into the scorching sunlight as he watched the men argue.

"So, we're lost?" Senator Mahdi Saeed, Armina's father, seethed at their predicament.

Josh looked around. The ground felt hot even through his shoes, and it was dusty and dry, a yellow ochre color that now stained the legs of his pants to the knee. Even the air seemed yellow, as well as Armina's hair.

Already it hurt to swallow. They still had water bottles, but there was probably only enough water for another day or so ... if they used it sparingly.

"Compass isn't working, and the GPS is out." The man who replied was a big guy named Brock, the head of the secret service contingent sent to protect the senator.

With him were five other team members who all looked formidable but disheveled after the crash. There were others who had survived – thanks to Joshua – two of the senator's administrative assistants, Iylah and Vince, plus an older couple who were on their way to Israel, named Mosh and Dalila.

And that was it, twelve survivors altogether. Everyone else had been outside of Joshua's protective bubble and had been lost. He didn't want to think that if he had been just a little bit stronger, maybe he could have saved them all.

It was no wonder that no one asked who he was other than his name, or wondered how he'd even got on the plane. There were much bigger issues now – they were low on food and water, and they were lost somewhere in the Houthi-controlled Yemeni desert. People would be after them, and most likely, it'd be the people who shot down the plane.

Even Josh knew that captured Americans either got ransomed or beheaded. That was bad, very bad, but right now what gave him a leaden feeling in his stomach was wondering what would happen when his mom and dad found out.

"We had just entered Yemeni air space when we were hit. That means we are probably still in the Al Mahrah province." Brock looked up at the sun and then pointed. "If we keep heading east, we can make it to one of the coastal villages."

The senator sighed. "The villages are all Houthi controlled, the district is Houthi controlled – basically the entire country in these parts, except for the cities, is Houthi controlled."

"We won't be staying," Brock replied calmly. "At the coast, we beg, steal, or borrow a boat and head down the coast to Al Mukalla. It's government controlled and they have an airport."

"Hundreds of miles," Saeed complained.

"We have no choice. We can do it, or die trying," Broke replied. "Think of the alternatives."

"There are no alternatives – if we surrender to these people, we will be dead. Most of us." The senator sighed and looked to Armina standing beside Joshua. "My daughter."

Brock nodded. "All the more reason to persist. We don't want her captured by the Houthis."

Mahdi Saeed stared at his daughter for a moment more as his mind worked. Joshua could see the realization of what capture would mean for Armina and the other women dawn on his face. "I'm sorry, you're right. We continue, day and night – we never give up."

Brock nodded. "We rest during the heat of the day, and travel by night when it's cool. If we can do twenty miles a night, we can be there in five days." He faced the group. "But right now, we need to get moving and put some distance between us and the crash site." He turned to face the desert, and Joshua followed his gaze east.

There seemed an endless land of hard-packed clay and ridged outcrops of darker stone that had been scoured by the heat and dryness for thousands of years – and it'd be like that for miles and miles. They'd need to cross it all before they got to the coast.

The senator called the group together and stood before them as they fell silent. "We need to cross the desert. It'll be an arduous trip. But we have to assume we're being followed by the very people who fired the missile," he said, looking at each of them. "We cannot let them catch up to us."

The group mumbled their agreement.

The older man, Mosh, raised a hand. "How did we survive?" he asked. "The plane was totally destroyed, except for our cabin area."

"Perhaps God wasn't ready to take us yet," Mosh's wife, Dalila, replied.

"If whichever god you pray to granted us this miracle, then let us also pray that he protects us for a little longer," Saeed replied.

The older woman looked to be in her sixties, and had a cut over one eye, but she smiled warmly and nodded. Mosh returned her smile and patted her hand. He then turned to the senator.

"We're ready."

Joshua looked back the way they had come. Brock was right; their assailants were coming after them, he could sense it. He then looked to the claypan desert before them and frowned as he concentrated. It was weird; for the first time in his life, he couldn't make out what was ahead. It was as if there was an oily curtain of confusion shrouding everything. The entire area just felt, *bad*.

It must be the heat, he told himself.

"Is everyone ready?" Brock asked.

A few nods, or silence.

Brock nodded. "Then let's go."

Armina glanced at her father and then turned back to Joshua. "I'm betting that right now, you wished you had gone to Egypt instead." She smiled.

He laughed softly. "Are you kidding? I wouldn't miss this for the world." He turned away. He felt good being with her. But the sense of something bad up ahead made his senses scream a warning. He knew he'd cop hell from his father, but right now, he really wished he was here.

CHAPTER 32

Right now, just on 10,000 feet overhead and invisible to the naked eye, three human beings bulleted toward the earth. The largest of them was holding tight to his body something that looked like a flat coffin.

The three HAWCs' communications systems were still being blocked from tracking down Alex or getting him to respond, but they could lock in on the high-strength transponder call of the aircraft's black box, which still pinged as strongly as ever.

Sam Reid knew the crash site was as good a place as any to start, as that's where Alex would be, or at least would have been. Whatever happened, they could pick up his tracks from there.

They were initially going to take a pass over the site and then corkscrew down, but Sam saw the flowering orange blooms of war way down below.

He had to adjust his dive as he carried the portable life-pod that contained Alfred Linley, their science advisor. The man didn't have the experience to jump from high altitude or operate a winged suit, so he was just along for the ride this time.

"All right in there, Doc?" Sam asked.

"No problem in here. I'm just hoping for a smooth landing. Anything interesting I should know about?" Linley asked.

"Just a war going on below us," Sam replied with a grin.

"I have complete confidence that you will avoid it, Lieutenant. Now, if you don't mind, I'll get back to saying a few prayers," Linley said, but there was a smile in his voice.

Sam chuckled – he liked the guy – and focused again on the explosions far below them. From the percussive size of the blasts he could tell there was some significant ordinance below.

"Looking red hot down there," Casey said. "We're coming down fast and we do not want to land in the middle of it."

"We won't." Sam used his helmet's vision amplification on the war zone. He picked up the Yemeni government army colors, plus the desert garb and some uniforms of the Houthi rebels. And it seemed the rebels had the numbers, a lot more numbers, *and* all the big guns.

"Initiate EAMs and we'll come down a few miles to the west," Sam said.

He deployed the suit's wings and they extended from his back out from each side of his shoulders. Casey and Klara did the same and immediately the trio went into a glide.

The HAWCs then started the boosters and the air intakes sucked in the rushing air and expelled it as super-fast compressed jets. They were then blasted forward and accelerated over the landscape and away from the conflict.

The HAWCs came down a couple of miles west of the fighting, executing spins in the air and using the thrusters to rapidly decelerate on touchdown. The wings folded back into their suits, and Sam eased the large pod to the ground and entered the code to open it. He then lifted his gauntlet to try his comms system.

"Dammit, still getting interference," he said.

The pod door slid back and Alfred Linley sat up, blinked, and looked around. "Nice landing, thank you."

"Don't thank us yet, Doc," Klara replied. "We're in a hot war zone."

Linley looked at the huge setting sun still throwing its blast furnace heat down on them. "Got that right." He stood and stepped out of the pod. He too was dressed in the HAWC armor.

Sam dragged the pod to the group and dropped his EAM into it. Klara and Casey threw theirs on top of it, making a pile. Klara pulled a thermal disk just like Alex had used and dropped it on the top. It counted down and then melted their suits and pod into the sand.

Casey checked her other instrumentation. "All green on sensors, weapons systems, and comms. Tech is all online and A-okay."

Klara held up her gauntlet and read data from the small screen. "Black box is loud and strong." She pointed east. "That way, three klicks."

"Come on in," Sam said, and the three HAWCs and scientist went into a huddle. "We need to get to that site, evaluate the situation and pick up Alex or Joshua's trail, ASAP," Sam said.

"Except there looked to be around 200 people in there blowing each other's brains out," Klara replied.

"I'm betting it's the Yemeni government up against the Houthi rebels," Casey said.

"You won that bet. We need to find out what the government guys know, and right now they're outgunned and outnumbered about four or five to one." Sam straightened. "Why don't we even the odds a little?"

"That's what I'm here for." Casey grinned. "No use going on a little overseas holiday if you can't enjoy yourself."

"We use the element of surprise, hit 'em hard. Unfortunately, we won't have time to announce ourselves to the Yemeni guys, so we might end up taking heat from both sides." Sam turned to the battlefield. "Time to go to work. Double time. And Doc? You gotta keep up."

"Don't worry about me." Linley expertly deployed the visor over his face.

Sam began to run with Klara and Casey at each of his shoulders keeping pace, and Linley right on their tail.

* * *

In thirty minutes, the sun had just set and the three HAWCs and scientist came to a rocky hill close to the crash site, beyond which they could hear the sounds of a battle raging. They belly-crawled to the top and looked over the ridge. It was like every other war zone they had seen in their lives; people killing, people dying – explosions, fire, screaming, chaos, and fear. If hell had a tune, this would be it.

As smoke drifted across the field, Sam saw that the Yemeni forces had been pushed back onto a few rocky slopes and into disorganized groups and were under siege by a huge number of rebels. They were dug in, but they wouldn't last long.

"We need to pick up Alex's trail from the downed plane site and interrogate the government forces. But we can't do that while they're getting the hell bombed out of them." He said.

"The Yemeni guys will fall in the next few hours." Casey said. "From what I know about Houthis, it'll be a massacre."

"It's a killing field; we can't get them out," Klara observed. "Too much heat with the big guns."

"Then we take those big guns out," Sam replied. "Casey, eleven o'clock, the HM-41 howitzer is all yours."

"Got it." She stared hard at the piece of equipment, assessing its pattern and time of loading and firing.

"Klara, there's a rocket truck at three o'clock. That's yours." Sam then turned to the center of the field where there were three big guns working together. "And I'll take out that nest of heavy field guns."

He turned to the scientist. "Stay here. You have one job: don't get captured, shot, or blown up."

Linley smiled and slapped the metallic holster at his hip. "I'm a trained shooter, don't worry about me, Lieutenant Reid."

Casey chuckled. "Yeah, Doc, hitting bullseyes is good practice. And even better when they don't shoot back." She winked. "But I like your spunk."

Sam saw the Houthi rebel forces gathering in preparation to advance. "Time's up. Go to war mode."

The three HAWCs set their armor for heavy combat mode – extra shielding came down over their faces and torsos, raised knobs lifted over their knuckles, and even an additional red lens came down over their eyes.

The suits were also hydraulically assisted which meant they boosted the wearer's speed, agility, and strength. Sam didn't even need that as his internal MECH infrastructure already made him a human tank, and with Klara and Casey's already honed physiques they were a formidable fighting force.

"On my three, two, one ..." Sam exploded forward.

Three high-speed human missiles came over the hill and then broke apart, each having their allotted targets in their sights.

* * *

Sam saw his first target, the truck turned sideways and on its rear the cannon, a huge Heidar-41, a 122-mm self-propelled artillery system. Iranian, of course; the Houthis' major sponsors. The mobile field cannon was designed for high accuracy and fast loading, and right now, he saw the next shell being slid in on its rail. They'd be ready to fire in the next few seconds.

Just fifty feet out, Sam accelerated and counted down his steps to arrival. The gun was recalibrated and then the Arabic word for *fire* was screamed.

At that point, Sam only had time to do one thing – he dropped his armored shoulder and slammed into the side of the truck just as it fired. The projectile was launched just as the side of the truck was lifted two feet up from the ground, so the shell missed its target and detonated out in the desert.

Before the Houthis could work out what had happened, Sam leaped up onto the back of the truck. The rebels went from confusion to shock as they saw the giant in a strange suit appear on the weapon's firing platform.

Sam rushed the two men at the loading station and backhanded one, causing his body to fly from the truck, cartwheeling in the air. The other he chest-punched with his armored gloves and felt the ribs crack beneath his blow.

He had to move quickly as there were other armaments to disable – the last thing he did was use his enormous strength to batter at the firing mechanism, bending the steel and crushing the loading chamber – nothing would be loaded or fired from that gun ever again. Sam then paused to turn and watch as the other two HAWCs arrived at their designated targets.

Klara's objective was a smaller artillery system, named 'Seraj', again, Iranian. It was a 35-mm cannon with a radar and advanced optical system. It was obvious that these desert fighters were being supported with a lot of money and tech, as each of these weapons cost tens of millions of dollars.

Klara smashed headfirst into the cannon team, knocking them down, and then she took over the trailer bay and spun the weapon around. She loaded a shell, targeted another heavy weapon among the small army and fired – blowing their own weapons to pieces.

Use their own tech against them, nice touch, Sam thought.

He then turned back to see Casey Franks leap up onto the back of another truck that contained a mounted Gatling gun. She didn't have to deal with the operator, for as soon as she appeared, he leaped from his seat, jumped down to the desert and ran for his life.

Casey followed Klara's lead and turned the heavy gun on the Houthi troops, firstly raking a line of fifty-cal gunners up on the ridge, and then ripping into a phalanx of RPG launchers.

The result was exactly as Sam hoped – chaos and confusion. Some of the Houthis fled, others turned to combat their new adversaries, and many just dropped either dead or injured from the HAWC onslaught.

A line of bullets raced up and across Sam's huge back and each felt like a horse kick. The armor absorbed or deflected their impact, but they still hurt like a bitch and reminded him he'd been in the same place for too long – time to get moving.

The huge HAWC leaped down into the melee and did his best to add to the chaos. He ran fast, smashing into soldiers, disarming others, and bending weapons' barrels. Only once did he have to deploy his gauntlet shield as a grenade was thrown his way.

Casey and Klara did the same, and in the next ten minutes they had left all the artillery vehicles and heavy weaponry in ruins and melted back into the cover of the night's darkness.

The sounds of battle had been replaced by soldiers screaming in pain and confusion, looking for an attacking army, or yelling about demons among them. Most had had enough and were on the run.

Sam spoke into his comms system. "Pull back to the ridge." And five minutes later he joined Klara and Casey, and the trio gazed down at the results of their attack – fires burned, equipment lay destroyed on the battlefield, and bodies lay everywhere. Further out, the last Houthis were retreating over the ridge, while the government forces could only stare silently in disbelief.

"Good night's work." Casey grinned.

"It's not over yet," Sam replied. "I want you to watch them for a little longer to make sure they don't regroup and double back. I'm going to take a trip over to meet with the Yemeni government forces and let them know we're the good guys."

He turned to focus in on the downed plane. "Then we can see what they know about the wreckage, Alex, and Joshua."

* * *

Sam approached the dug-in position of the Yemeni government forces. They had their heads down but every gun they possessed was pointed at the massive clay-colored being closing in on them.

He stopped at the base of the slope, noticing that he and the other HAWCs had arrived just in time as the hillside was cratered by shell blasts and there were many dead government men strewn on the rocky slope who hadn't managed to make it to adequate shelter.

"Friends," Sam yelled and held his hands up as he walked closer. "It's over."

A single soldier stood, but all their rifles remained trained on Sam. "Are you with the one called Hunter?"

"Yes, I'm his friend, and I'm looking for him," Sam said, and stared up at the man. He let his eyes travel over the other soldiers – there weren't many – and slowly let his hands drop.

The soldier then said something to his men, and the guns were lowered. He turned back to Sam. "I am Lieutenant Wardou. Thank you; we could not have held out much longer."

"Permission to bring my team in, Lieutenant?" Sam requested.

"Yes, permission granted." Wardou came down the slope.

Sam called Klara, Casey, and Linley in, and they retracted their helmet visors as they came across the bomb-cratered claypan.

"That is all?" Wardou asked. "Where are the rest?"

"That's it," Sam said.

"Such fighting and firepower." The man nodded. "We need to acquire this technology for our soldiers."

Many of the soldiers came down to walk around Sam. He was six-foot-five, but in the suit with the heavy armor, boots, and helmet, he was more than a head taller than their largest man.

The soldiers touched Sam's desert camouflage armor, rapping on the hard plates, and closely examining the scratches and burn marks where he had taken hits.

Casey and Klara joined him, and the two women in their suits also stood six feet tall.

"They're women," one of the men exclaimed. He came closer with a leery grin on his face and went to touch the chest of Casey's suit.

Casey grabbed his hand, squeezed, and twisted. The man screamed and went to his knees.

"Haven't met many American women, *huh*?" She tugged his hand higher as the man wailed and clutched his twisted elbow joint.

"At ease, Franks," Sam said.

Casey put her boot on the man's shoulder and pushed him. He fell back, holding his strained arm and shoulder. The other soldiers laughed but avoided Casey and Klara from then on.

"Tell me about Alex Hunter," Sam asked the lieutenant.

"He was like you; he fought like a demon. He took on all the Houthis by himself." Lieutenant Wardou seemed to think. "No, not by himself, he had a metal animal with him."

"He had a sentry DOG," Klara replied. "Seems Quartermain kitted him out."

"Good," Sam said.

"Yes, it looked a little like a dog – an iron soldier-dog." Wardou nodded. "There were survivors from the plane crash. Americans. He found their tracks, and then followed them. My captain, Captain Hadid, took some of our troops and went with him as support."

"That means Joshua must be alive. Thank God." Casey exhaled. 'Which way did they go?' she asked.

Lieutenant Wardou turned to point. "They headed into the forbidden desert."

"Forbidden desert?" Casey chuckled. "Yeah, sounds about right."

Sam turned to Linley and the pair of HAWCs. "Saddle up, folks, we have a destination."

CHAPTER 33

Colonel Jack Hammerson checked the satellite images from over Yemen one more time and saw that they were still grainy and indistinct. But only in one area ranging about twenty miles in diameter. And, no surprises, it was the area all his HAWCs had headed into. Someone or something down there was either interfering with the signal or creating a disturbance bubble over the lower atmosphere.

In addition, the comms were down. He had confidence that his HAWCs would find Alex, but he hated being in the dark. He tried a satellite with a different view aspect, but that twenty-mile area remained fried no matter which way he looked at it.

He had one last option. He opened an older system named the Global Plotting Network, which used thousands of hidden relay spikes around the planet that bounced a web of signals across states and countries. It was able to link to the HAWCs' unique comms systems and give an update of their position.

It was rarely used now that they had so many high-quality satellites. But when they didn't work, it was time to go old school.

Hammerson brought the system online and then focused it on the Middle East. He then coordinated the relay spikes and used those embedded in Yemen. Sure enough, he found Sam, Casey, and Klara, and then about twenty miles further west he saw Alex.

"Here we go." He sat forward.

He could also use the enormously powerful ground-level system to send data squirts. The message would be super compressed and sent directly to his HAWCs' comms devices. It could be sent and received through two feet of solid lead, so he knew it would arrive, but the odds of that happening were greatly improved if he knew exactly where his HAWCs were – and now he did.

Hammerson knew he had no chance of telling Alex to pull back. Until Joshua was found, the HAWC would be liked a guided missile that would never stop. But if he couldn't stop him, he could at least protect his people in the field by trying to get his best asset to wait while HAWC reinforcements came to assist him on his mission.

"Here goes nothing." Hammerson wrote the brief message, encrypted and compressed it, then sent it. The GPN blinked for a moment as hopefully the message was delivered.

Hammerson poured himself two fingers of bourbon and lifted the amber fluid in front of his face. He spoke to the glass: "Time for my dogs of war to become a pack."

CHAPTER 34

Alex held up a hand and Captain Ali Hadid stopped. Alex read the message that came in on his comms system – Sam, Casey, and Klara had arrived in the field. They were making their way to him, but he needed to wait for them as they had critical intel. Hammerson finished with: *That is an order.*

Alex bared his teeth and sharply exhaled. *A damn order.* When it came to his son, he only had one order – *Find him.*

But he trusted Jack Hammerson and knew he owed his superior officer everything. The guy had resurrected him and saved his life too many times to count. He was Alex's mentor and, in some ways, even a guiding father figure.

Alex turned back to the desert. He conceded he needed his fellow HAWCs; everything was easier when they were a team.

"What is the matter?" Hadid asked.

"I've been ordered to wait for my fellow soldiers to arrive. But time is against us." He shook his head. "I don't know if I can."

"Is this a good order, from a good leader?" the Yemeni Government captain asked.

Alex exhaled. "I trust the officer delivering it."

"Will you be stronger with this team with you?" Hadid lifted his chin.

Alex nodded once.

"Then you must wait." Hadid placed a hand on Alex's shoulder. "But *we* do not have to. We will continue, and if we find the survivors, we will keep them safe for you. When you meet up with your soldiers, you can catch up." He grinned. "I have seen the speed you and your little metal friend can conjure, and it should not be a problem." He glanced down at the metallic DOG, who seemed to look up with tilted head.

Alex began to nod and smile in return. "Yeah, we can catch up." He shook the man's hand. "Thank you."

Holding the Yemeni soldier's hand, he detected something – subterfuge, evasion, or at least something hidden. Alex released the man's hand and stepped back. It didn't matter, he guessed. After all, the entire region held secrets and it was no surprise the people in it did as well.

"I'll try and link back up with you by morning," Alex said.

"God's speed, Captain Hunter." The man saluted.

Alex turned back the way they had come and began to jog back to meet his team. The canine battle droid trotted beside him.

CHAPTER 35

Six hours later, Captain Ali Hadid of the Yemeni national armed forces stood at the edge of the forbidden zone, cradling his rifle. His men waited in the trucks, twenty of them in a convoy of seven vehicles – light utility vehicles, trucks, and an armored SUV with rooftop fifty-cal weapon. All awaited Hadid's next instruction.

Some of the men were seasoned fighters but some were raw recruits who, if not watched, would rip off their uniforms and flee as soon as the first bullets flew. But this was the material he had to work with, and he would do his job. Besides, he had shot deserters before, and after you shot the first few, the others thought twice about running.

Captain Hadid had another reason to forge on. A personal and lucrative one, and one he hadn't shared with the American soldier: an Englishman by the name of Saunders had hired him to seek answers about something out in the forbidden zone. And he had just needed an opportunity to break away from the main force to explore it.

Normally Hadid would have had sport with such adventurers or taken their money and ignored them, but as a sign of his intent, this Saunders had deposited US$10,000 in a

Swiss account for him, with the promise of $40,000 more when he reported what he found – and a $50,000 nest egg would set him up in a nice business, Hadid thought. And what if he found something worth ten times more? He had the feeling this rich Englishman would pay. Hadid smiled; he had worked hard all his life and had little to show for it. Finally, he believed he was going to get what he deserved.

The captain turned slowly; the night desert was dark and silent. There was no breeze and all he heard was the soft murmuring of some of his men and the tick of cooling truck engines.

They were now right on the boundary of the forbidden zone, and the land that stretched before him was much like all the unforgiving desert they had been crossing. He inhaled the cool, dry air and it was a relief from the day's singeing heat inside his nostrils. He could still smell the sunblasted rocks and the scorched-to-dust landscape. Not a single blade of grass or drop of water – at least above ground.

But Hadid knew there were water sources if you knew where to look. The one risk to him was the Houthi fighters who were undoubtedly out there somewhere, and he bet if they were going to be camped anywhere, it would be close to water.

He looked down; the plane crash survivors' tracks continued, but oddly, he now noticed there was a change in the color of the soil as they moved into the forbidden zone. It was darker on the side he stood on now, but it changed to a lighter, more arid and finer dust on the other side, as if the earth had been further dried or cooked. Which was strange, as the sun, wind, and air, were the same on both sides of the boundary.

So, what was different? Maybe it was just the supposed curse on the blighted land.

He'd soon find out. He climbed back into the lead vehicle. "Forward."

They headed in and the cool night breeze in his face was pleasant and unchanging with each mile they traveled. After three hours, he turned his collar up against the cold and sipped from a canteen, grimacing at the slimy and brackish taste of the water after the day's heat. He reached up to feel his jaw – he had a gold cap on a back molar, and it ached as though someone was continually tugging at it.

It took several more hours before they arrived at what they believed was the dead center of the zone. The plane crash survivors' tracks still drew them on, but so far, he had seen no sign of them – no smoke from fires or dust clouds signifying moving people or vehicles. By now the only thing really driving him forward was the payoff he would receive from the Englishman.

"*Halt*." Hadid began to get a disquieting feeling in his stomach. He stood in his seat and switched on the powerful rooftop lamp, swiveling it slowly over the desolate landscape. He doubted there could be Houthi fighters camped out there, as without vehicles even seasoned desert warriors would struggle to cross this accursed place. But for some reason he felt there was *something* out there.

Beside him a few of the other vehicles deployed their own search lights, moving their powerful beams over the land that was devoid of life.

Strange, he thought. The only thing he expected to find was the rapidly drying bodies of the American plane crash survivors. He squinted down at the ground. Though the hard-packed arid surface didn't show many marks, he could still make out the tracks of the survivors pressing on. How were they doing it? he wondered.

It was Jibril in the covered truck beside him who began to slowly drive forward without authorization.

"Halt," Hadid shouted to the man. He frowned when Private Jibril ignored him. The private was staring straight ahead as if in a trance, hands clenching the steering wheel, his lips pulled back showing grimacing teeth. And not only did the young soldier ignore the order, but he began to pick up speed.

Hadid contemplated having his tires shot out, but in the deep desert, trucks were the difference between life and death – he needed the truck more than Jibril. If they got close, he'd prefer to shoot the man than the vehicle.

Hadid looked down at his driver. "Get after that fool," he shouted.

His driver did as ordered and the entire convoy followed his lead, accelerating forward in pursuit of Jibril and his truck.

Thoughts of the man deserting, blind enthusiasm, or even heatstroke came to Hadid's mind. If Jibril was trying to defect and hand over the vehicle and its munitions to the enemy, he would be shot dead on the spot. If he had heatstroke, he may still be shot just for angering him.

The oddity was, none of the five men crammed in the back of Jibril's truck seemed to try to stop him – were they all in on it? Hadid wondered.

A sudden thought stabbed at him – was Jibril also being paid by the Englishman? Maybe this Saunders was hedging his bets, and Jibril wanted to be first to bring him answers. Not a chance, Hadid thought.

Jibril continued to drive at top speed, and Hadid knew they'd never overtake him. But as they came over the hill, he saw the man's destination – a massive hole in the ground as large as a Sanaa city block.

Hadid remembered the stories now – this must be the Well of Barhout, also known as the Well of Hell, where demons supposedly lived, and the insane man was driving straight for it.

A tingle of fear shot through the captain when he recalled that this was the reason the entire area was forbidden. With a shouted command, Hadid stopped the convoy.

But the tingle remained, and now not only did his teeth ache, but his entire body throbbed with pain, and his heart beat like he had just climbed the steepest of hills.

He quickly sent a message to Mr. Saunders' private satellite link about their progress, what he was observing, and their coordinates so he could take credit for any find. He then lifted his head to watch as Jibril and his truck kept driving toward the massive dark orifice in the ground as though he couldn't see it.

"What is wrong with that idiot?" Hadid seethed.

But then the man and his truck arrived at the rim of the well, and rather than stop or even slow, he simply drove over the edge and vanished.

Hadid's mouth dropped open. There was no sound; it was as if the truck and its occupants had simply ceased to exist.

"*Madness*," Hadid whispered.

The driver next to him turned and Hadid faced the man and saw that his eyes were red-rimmed and he was squinting as if he was in pain – perhaps the same pain Hadid was enduring.

Hadid's phone pinged with a message from the Englishman, and he quickly read it: *Investigate further. Tell me what you see.*

Hadid scoffed. He'd had enough of this accursed place. There was no sign of any Houthi fighters, or water, but the tracks of the plane survivors also headed straight for the dark void. But where were they? Had they suffered the same fate as Jibril? he wondered.

Something was very wrong here. Sometimes curses were real. He swallowed noisily, his throat dry. As far as he was concerned, his job was over. Or if this English pig wanted him to go further, then he would need to pay double.

Just as Hadid was about to give the order to turn around, his truck moved forward a few feet.

"Hold your position." Hadid frowned.

"I didn't ..." the driver objected.

The truck moved again. Hadid looked out over the side, and this time he noticed that the tires didn't turn, and there was a sliding rather than a driving sensation.

He stared hard at the wheels and saw the skids marks in the earth's dust-like surface. Were they on a slope? he wondered.

He continued to stare so hard his eyes burned, and sure enough the truck slid again, two inches. Then a foot. Then another three.

Hadid had had enough. "Turn around."

As soon as his driver put his hands on the wheel, the SUV slid, and slid faster. And not just their own vehicle. Beside him the other trucks and group transports were all sliding or rolling forward.

One of the men threw his truck into reverse and jammed his foot on the accelerator. But all this did was spray dust and grit out in front of the vehicle which only managed to fractionally slow its forward skid.

Inexorably, they were being dragged toward the edge of the accursed well, and Hadid wasn't going to sit here and wait to suffer the same fate as Jibril.

"Abandon vehicles." He jumped out.

Big mistake.

As soon as his feet hit the hard-packed claypan, he began to slide. The other men who had followed his lead faced the same predicament, and now free from the significant weight of the trucks, their lighter bodies were no match for whatever strange magnetism was drawing them toward the massive sinkhole.

Hadid fell to his belly and saw up close that the dirt was riven with scratches, as though people had raked at it with their fingernails. Forbidden zone or not, there should be

Houthis here; is this what had happened to them? Or was it the Americans who had been scrabbling in the dirt for ther lives?

It only took four more minutes for the first of the men to go over the edge into the well, screaming as he went. Then the other men followed, one by one, and the trucks, and finally Hadid dug clawed hands into the well's rim when his boots lost traction and dangled over nothing but dark air.

He fell into the void and, looking back up, he saw the massive hole as a circle above him getting smaller and smaller as he dropped away from the starlight.

Then came darkness, cold, but strangely, no impact. Was he still falling?

The pain in his head was now agony. Then everything went black.

* * *

Captain Ali Hadid blinked a few times and then opened his eyes wide. He had expected to be killed instantly from the fall, but his next thought, that perhaps he was in heaven, faltered when he saw he was floating upside down just above the ground.

Beside him Jibril and many of the men hung like they were driftwood in water, or maybe flies caught in a web. He saw that – insanely – he was trapped just a half-dozen feet above the floor of the cave, but nothing was holding him. He swung his arms and moved his legs but there was nothing to hold on to or push off from, so he just remained in the same place.

Hadid looked down his body and saw that high above them the massive well mouth was just a tiny halo of starlight, and the rest of the cavern was mostly lost in darkness. But it wasn't silent, as there was the gentle hum and thump of machines somewhere in the distance.

Maybe I am not in heaven, but hell? he wondered.

"Hey, hey, Jibril, *wake up*," Hadid hissed.

His soldier slowly opened his eyes. He looked dazed, almost drugged, but then he started to panic and swing his arms when he found he was suspended in the air.

"What is this?" he screamed.

"*Silence*," Hadid warned.

A look of fear ripped across Jibril's face, and Hadid could tell it was his will alone stopping the man from shrieking in mindless panic.

The other men were now beginning to stir. Hadid knew they needed to free themselves from whatever or whoever was holding them here. Perhaps it was some sort of American or Russian technology that was making them float? Maybe some sort of secret experiment they had stumbled upon?

"Someone is coming," Jibril squeaked.

Hadid tried to swivel in the air but found it near impossible. The direction in which he had been hung was the only way he could face. But he could see Jibril's expression contort in terror as he was first to see who or what it was that approached.

Then Hadid saw them. The tall beings that moved among the floating men were nearly eight feet tall, skinny, and their heads too high up to see clearly. One took hold of Hadid's ankle, and he saw that the arm and hand that held him had three long fingers that looked like old, gnarled wood. But, nightmarishly, there were scales upon the digits that ended in sharp, hooked talons.

Almost languidly the creatures took hold of the other soldiers like they were plucking fruit from trees and guided them along a path and then in through a doorway. Immediately their surroundings changed from a cave to some sort of smooth corridor.

They stopped from time to time, and some of the men were carried into one room or another before the procession continued. Hadid's men called to him, begged him, their captain, to help them. But he could only crush his eyes shut and turn away as he was as helpless as they were.

But at the door of one of the rooms, Hadid had a chance to glimpse inside, and he felt his blood freeze. There were bodies there, piled up like cordwood, and the ones facing him were naked.

Hadid's gorge rose when he saw that all their eyes had been removed. But not removed far, because on a long table were long lines of human eyes, with their retinal cords and optical nerves still attached. Some were bound together, creating clusters like bunches of grapes – the creatures were obviously experimenting or using them for some dark purpose he could never hope to understand. And would never want to.

Transfixed, Hadid couldn't be sure if it was just the moving shadows in the gloom or if those plucked eyes swiveled to stare at him. The Yemeni captain whimpered as they moved on.

His remaining men moaned and cried, and just in front of him Jibril's bladder voided and splashed down his body to the floor.

A calm resolve came over Hadid then. He used all his strength to reach for his pistol. If he could shoot one of the beings, they may scatter and give him enough time to get down from whatever bonds held him aloft.

It took him several minutes to slowly work his hand along his body to reach and carefully pull his revolver free. But try as he might he could not aim it out at the things.

In the next minute he was maneuvered away again, and he and Jibril were directed into their own room. The pair were floated inside, where two more of the creatures waited for them.

He knew then he had been right; they were in hell. This room had bodies slumped against a wall. But the tops of their heads had been removed and stacked next to them like eggshells. On a table, a line of human brains was awaiting some foul use, and with mad eyes Hadid saw that there were cords pressed into them. As he watched, one of the brains pulsated and shivered as if a current had run through the attachment.

Hadid realized they were keeping the brains alive for some reason, and he wondered if inside those gray-pink mounds, the minds of the men cried out in useless bondage, without the ability to do anything but submit to whatever fate the monsters had in store for them.

"Help me," Jibril whimpered.

"I cannot." Hadid replied in trembling voice and strained against his invisible bonds.

He then used all his remaining strength to slowly turn the revolver. His teeth were gritted and perspiration streamed down his face. He knew now that saving anyone was impossible. All Hadid could do was turn the gun around, and point it straight up along his body toward his own chin.

"I'm sorry," he whispered.

He pulled the trigger.

INCIDENT 06

All hail the new king.

CHAPTER 36

Al Olaya Hotel Penthouse, Riyadh, Saudi Arabia

Bradley Phillip Saunders read the message from his contact in Yemen. Then read it again. Captain Ali Hadid had found yet more activity at the Well of Barhout. It was becoming active again and as he suspected, it was ground zero in this region. This was looking *very* promising, he thought.

He tried calling the man directly to draw more details, but oddly, the bounce-back message told him the link had been severed. After several more attempts he gave up.

Saunders sat back with steepled fingers under his chin and thought through what that meant – perhaps the rebels had intercepted them and his team had been wiped out. Plausible, he thought. Also plausible was that the interference bubble had got stronger the closer he got to the well, and so Hadid was now 'whited out'.

But in the corner of his mind there was a whisper that Hadid and his men had been collected by the visitors, and right now he was suffering the same fate as all the others from over the countless millennia.

He chuckled softly. It would serve the greedy fool right, as he had been specifically told not to get too close. And if he had, well, it was no great loss to the human race.

But if any of the above were true it told Saunders one important thing, and that was that he had truly located a real-time event site, and importantly, after all this time, they were here when he was ready for them.

Saunders smiled; the one thing he was confident of was that he believed he was prepared. But if he was going to make contact with the creatures and be the ambassador for Earth, he needed to be there, in person, and that meant he needed to pull all the threads together that he had been organizing for years. All the decades of planning came down to this one chance.

He smiled, and then began to laugh softly. Were these the same beings that had contacted the Allonians over 7000 years ago? The scroll he had deciphered told how they had made Akmezdah the ruler of his entire kingdom and bestowed gifts of technology on him that were far advanced for his civilization. Would they do the same for him? he wondered.

Saunders tingled with the possibilities, and then lunged forward to pick up the hotel phone. First things first – he needed his team in there to secure the site. Then he would follow.

He also knew that there was a chance he might have to go to the visitors' world, so he and his team needed to be properly attired. The dissection analysis on the creature he had brought home from the Caucasus decades ago had shown them that these things were engineered to breathe gases that were extremely toxic to human beings. Plus, their muscular-skeletal framework had suggested a form powerful enough to counter a much higher gravity, and skin that had been blasted by significant heat radiation.

He had tried to develop self-contained vehicles and suits, although the technology was beyond him. But it wasn't for others.

"If I have seen further, it is by standing on the shoulders of giants." He smiled and then began to whistle a soft tune as he quickly put his plans in motion.

In just minutes he had organized a helicopter, had contacted his security team and had them en route to Yemen. The last call was to his secret contact inside the American USSTRATCOM facility who was to arrange some critical gear for him.

Saunders closed his eyes and gave free rein to the visions of himself in some sort of ceremonial robe introducing the visitors to the UN, and the British Queen, and maybe even the US President.

He lifted his head as his mind whirled. What if all this time he had been waiting for the world to change, when it was the world that was waiting for *him* to change it? After all, he'd always known he was destined to be more than just another rich and idle nobody.

"*King of the world,*" he whispered and then giggled. After another moment he stood, grabbed a prepacked bag, and headed for the private elevator.

He had a few things to pick up, but still knew he could be at the well within twenty-four hours. This time he was ready, and this time he had timed it perfectly.

* * *

Doctor Lee Huang took the call from Bradley Saunders and felt his heart rate kick up a notch. The button had been pressed – it was happening, it was *really* happening.

All the dreams, all the planning, had come down to this moment, right now. He knew that what he was about to do was extremely high risk, and if he was caught, he wouldn't need to worry about being fired; he'd be thrown into military prison for ten years.

He stood at his desk, mentally ticking off the things to be done. Timing was everything. He'd be found out for sure, because when he stole a couple of multi-million-dollar suits of hostile environment armor, he would have to enter his personal passcode and biometric print.

But Huang didn't care. By the time they discovered the theft he'd be far away – far, far away – maybe even in a different universe altogether. And by the time they returned, they could arrive as the new leaders, rulers, of the world. He almost swooned at the thought.

He checked his watch. The head of the weapons research division, Doctor Quartermain, always took his afternoon coffee break at 3.30 pm sharp and was gone for just fifteen minutes.

But that would be enough time for Huang to head down in the secure elevator and grab two enviro-suit cases – they'd be heavy, but he only had to get them onto a trolley and to the elevator.

On the helipad someone with his level of clearance could sign out a chopper without any problems. And he didn't even need a pilot as he was fully qualified. By the time anyone even noticed he was gone, he'd be out over the Atlantic. And then he just needed to leapfrog all the way to the Middle East to join Bradley Saunders, who had his connecting flight waiting for him.

That military idiot, Jack Hammerson, couldn't be bothered trying to communicate with the visitors. That's because the military only had one strategy, which basically boiled down to: *If a man had a hammer, then everything they saw was a nail.*

But not him. Or Mr. Saunders.

Huang checked his watch again – ten minutes to go. He worked to calm his breathing – he could do this. And he would make history.

* * *

Just two hours later a flustered Doctor Andrew Quartermain called Jack Hammerson and informed him that two heavily armored enviro-suits had been checked out by Doctor Lee Huang. And the man was also missing. Plus, he had personally taken a long-range helicopter.

After the call, Hammerson remembered the meeting he'd had with the scientist. He also recalled where the man's sympathies lay.

Hammerson's eyes narrowed. "I know where you're going, you little creep."

But why? What could he be planning? he wondered. Nothing good, he bet.

Stealing two enviro-suits and fleeing suggested Huang had an accomplice. But who was it?

He reached for the phone and called through to Rick Jones in one of the many USSTRATCOM tech centers. "Rick, it's Jack, I need a search, right now."

"What do you need?" Jones replied.

"Phone records of Doctor Lee Huang – personal and private – who has he been talking to in the last week? I'll wait." Hammerson sat, staring straight ahead.

It took Jones just three minutes to download the business and private call logs of the man. There were several to other technology departments, a few take-out joints, and then several overseas calls via his private line.

"There's plenty to some place in the United Kingdom." Jones said. "Covington, Cambridgeshire. Mean anything to you?"

"Yeah, a lot. Thanks Rick, owe you one." Hammerson rang off.

The Saunders' Estate. Hammerson scoffed.

That bastard. Guess there's someone else who had decided on aiding and abetting the creatures. Could they really be that crazy? He wondered.

Whatever Huang and Saunders had planned, Hammerson knew in his bones that somehow they were going to sell out the human race. He'd known megalomaniacs like this before and it was always the same; riches and power were an intoxicating drug to many people. And their vanity never allowed them to doubt their own nefarious motives. Or see the risks.

He sat back and drummed his fingers on the desk for a moment. Hammerson's plan was for someone to go through that pyramid portal and ensure the monsters never came back. Had Huang somehow known that was on the cards?

Jack Hammerson continued to stare off into the distance. What if Huang or Saunders *did* suspect it, and somehow managed to tell these creatures what was going to happen? And the monsters then changed their mode of operation and moved elsewhere, or used some sort of technology to make it harder or even impossible to find them?

He stopped his drumming. He had no choice – he had to move it up and make the plan happen, now.

Jack Hammerson lunged for the phone and called Quartermain back. The young scientist picked up on the first ring.

"Prepare five heavy enviro-suits. I'll send down the profiles. One more thing: prepare an MSB, Presidential Order 38175." Hammerson drew in a deep breath at the implications of what he was doing as Quartermain acknowledged the highest-level authorization in the country.

Hammerson's eyes were dead. "Have them all on a high-speed plane within twenty minutes. Stand by for details."

CHAPTER 37

Alex crested the hill and looked back out over a night-dark landscape hard-baked by the relentless sun. Bursting from the sea of sand and gravel were dark ridges of rock like a school of massive craggy leviathans breaching the surface.

The land was ancient, lonely, and remorseless. His son was lost out there somewhere, and he felt a pain stick hard in his chest when he thought about him.

He felt a wave of fury surge through him at the thought that someone or something might harm his son. But it was accompanied by a sense of powerlessness and guilt at leaving both Josh and Aimee by themselves so much. Joshua probably only lied to him because he felt he couldn't be open with him.

What if he lost his son forever? The dark thoughts gathered like storm clouds in his mind. What if he never had the chance to see him again, talk to him again?

Alex dragged a forearm across watering eyes as he remembered throwing a ball, wrestling with him when he was a little boy and letting him win. He even remembered the tiny things like teaching him how to drink from a soda bottle and not letting the backwash go back in.

And if anything did happen to him, that would be it; Aimee would blame him and never forgive him. She'd then also be gone. He would be nothing without them. He would have no purpose and would, essentially, cease to exist. Alex tilted his head back and screwed his eyes shut.

"Please let me find him. Please," he prayed.

He kept his eyes closed for several seconds as he felt a dark pressure build in his chest. His jaws clamped tight, but he couldn't help himself and let out a roar of agony that rolled across the endless desert.

Beside him DOG pinged.

Alex lowered his head and sucked in a few deep breaths to center himself. He turned back the way he had come.

"Yeah, I can see 'em," he said. In the distance he saw four dust trails and knew exactly who three of them belonged to – he'd know soon enough who the fourth was. He sat down, and the metallic sentry turned to stand guard over him by watching back out over the dry sea of desert behind him.

He turned to stare at the canine robot for a moment.

"I envy you," he said. "A simple existence – fight, reset, fight again." He snorted softly. "Like me, I guess, except you don't have to carry the ghosts of the dead with you."

DOG turned its head, perhaps sensing Alex's inner turmoil as he had been tuned to Alex's brain wave signature. Any change would be noted by the war machine.

It took a step closer, and instinctively Alex put a hand on its head. "Don't worry, I'm okay. Sort of." Alex continued to stare at the metallic animal. "I served with another android before. She was called Sophia. Only problem was, she thought she was human." He shrugged. "And maybe in her mind she was." Alex sighed. "Didn't work out too well, though." He nodded. "But she gave her life for us in the end. So, I guess she did her job."

He sighed and pulled out his water bottle, sipped, and waited. In the desert the heat of the sun leaked away quickly after it went down, to be replaced with a bone-numbing cold at night. It was a place of extremes, and though he was fine in his insulated suit, he just prayed Joshua had at least found shelter somewhere.

It would be good to see his team. A single HAWC was the most lethal human being on the planet. But he knew HAWCs together were an unstoppable force, and what he was heading toward might just need that level of firepower.

He squinted, watching the group dip behind the last hill and then rise over it, at which point the huge figure in the middle paused, scanned the horizon and then stopped to stare in Alex's direction. After a moment, he raised one huge log-like arm and waved.

Alex returned the greeting and got to his feet, and the four figures sprinted down the slope toward him. In minutes they were in front of him.

They retracted their visors and Alex saw Casey sneer-grin at him, the familiar scar pulling her cheek up on one side. He knew she had 101 quips to unload on him, but kept them behind her teeth, as she knew why he was here.

Klara smiled. "Beats the moon." She looked around. "But then again, this place looks like Mars."

"You've been to Mars?" Alex asked.

Klara grinned. "Not yet, but I'm still young."

"Sorry to slow you up, boss," Sam said. "We had orders."

Alex nodded. "If it was anyone else, I would have kept going. But you guys are worth waiting for. Glad you made it." He then bumped armored fists with each of them, then turned to the fourth man.

Alex recognized the tall scientist from the research labs. "Doctor Linley, right?"

The man strode forward and stuck out his hand. Alex shook it. "Good to be here, Captain. I'm here to—"

"Offer expertise and assistance, I hope," Alex cut in. He still held the man's hand and pulled him a little closer. "This is not going to be a holiday, Doctor. We may be called on to fight to survive."

"Don't worry, I know," the scientist replied. "I'll do what is asked of me."

"Good man." Alex let his hand go.

The scientist turned to nod toward DOG, which was standing just behind Alex. "How is the field unit? Performing to expectations?"

Alex smiled. "Yeah, I don't have to feed him, and his kill count is better than mine."

"Performing to specs then. Perfect." Linley nodded.

"I've got a trail on the plane crash survivors, and a squad of Yemeni government forces with vehicles who went on ahead," Alex said. "I promised to catch them up, so hope you all kept some breath in those lungs."

Sam thumbed over his shoulder. "We just helped their buddies out a few miles back."

"This place is crawling with Houthis, and they're armed to the teeth," Casey added.

"This is their territory. Will they follow us?" Alex asked.

"Not a chance." Klara grinned. "We messed them up pretty bad."

"Good. Okay, suck it up, people, and let's go." Alex began to jog across the sun-scorched earth, taking the HAWCs and the scientist with him.

CHAPTER 38

The six dots in the Yemeni night sky were invisible to the naked eye, and further, had no signature on radar or other devices used for scanning the atmosphere.

They were totally silent, and each was around six-and-a-half feet long with small rigid glider-wings out to their sides and traveling at around 300 miles per hour.

They could have been HAWCs. But they weren't.

When they were just 500 feet from the ground the wings folded back and midnight-black parachutes were deployed – it was a standard infiltration drop and was executed with practiced precision.

Nikolas Belakov landed easily, ejected the parachute and walked a few paces forward. From a pouch he drew out his plotter and checked their position in relation to their objectives: the first being the Well of Barhout, and then in turn where the HAWCs were, and then where the English mercenaries were.

Russia had sophisticated interception software, and the antiquated system the HAWCs used, via a land spike system, was easily picked up and decoded. The English mercenary was even sloppier, just using standard signal-boosted information blips.

Belakov lifted his head to scan the desert. He wasn't sure yet why or how the HAWCs had got here so quickly, as when he had last encountered the American Special Forces soldiers in Borneo, he felt he had been in front of them. Now they had accelerated.

It didn't matter; he sought the pyramid and its monstrous owners. His mission was simply to seek and destroy. If the HAWCs were on the same path, then he could potentially work with them. If they sought any type of partnership or relationship with the creatures, or got in his way, then they would need to be swept aside so he could successfully complete his job.

But the English mercenaries had been a thorn in his side for years. His tracking of the strange pyramid sightings had shown evidence that they seemed to already be working with and covering for the pyramid's nightmarish denizens. And right now, he had a score to settle with Bradley Phillip Saunders, and as the English were his proxies, then they were his initial target – they had information. And Belakov wanted it.

The English were closest and tracking toward the Well of Barhout. He intended to intersect with them before they got there.

Belakov's team joined him, and he pointed at the small screen. "Target one is two miles west of us. We need to get in front of them and interrogate them." He lifted his head. "This way. Double time."

He began to jog, and the other five huge men, all wearing armor-plated desert tactical gear, kept pace with him.

* * *

Dave 'Winter' Winterson led the four mercenaries across the unforgiving landscape. Even though they traveled by the cool of night, the men were still hot, pissed off, and grumbling.

And he could understand why – each wore about thirty pounds of tactical gear, plus they had to lug their weapons.

And Winterson agreed with them. *Just as well we're all being paid a small fortune,* he thought. Otherwise he'd start flapping his arms and fly home himself.

Besides, as soon as they confirmed that an occupied pyramid was there, Saunders' 'management team' would drop in, and then they only needed to babysit Saunders himself for a day while he tried to make friends with those weird freaks who had been stealing people since long before any of them were even born.

Winterson felt no twinge of conscience; as far as he was concerned, the people they took didn't matter to him, and as long as the monstrosities stayed away from him and his, and Saunders continued to pay up big, he'd do his job and look the other way.

He lifted a hand to halt his team and Bo Hoskins, Steve "Arty" Artwell, Phil "Guv" Guvens, and the Irishman, Fergal O'Shea, came to a stop while all wearing their usual sullen expressions.

Winterson checked his position and then nodded with satisfaction. "Four more miles, give or take."

"Just as fucking well." Artwell wiped his face with the scarf looped around his neck. "This shithole is either freezing or cooking me alive."

"Whatsa matter, Art? Did you wear your wife's woolen underwear again?" Fergal brayed.

Artwell rounded on him. "Shut it, you Irish turd."

"All of you shut up. Let's just get this done, and then we can get back home to drink booze and count our money." Winterson glared. "Besides, we're not far from our objective so we're nearly all squared."

The men grunted their displeasure, but Winterson knew they begrudgingly agreed. He waved them on, and they climbed to the top of a hill of dry black rock that still radiated the day's heat back at them like the surface of a hot skillet. At the top Winterson saw that saw Phil Guvens had stopped to stare out over the landscape.

He pulled his night vision goggles down over his eyes and turned slowly – there were more rocks, hard-packed orange-yellow clay, and zero vegetation. There was another hill in the far distance, and he bet their objective was beyond that.

Nearly there, he thought. *Thank God*. Winterson was about to wave the team on when a soldier's intuition made him pause. He had done two tours in Afghanistan and sometimes the only thing that kept you alive was that feeling in your gut about which house to charge into and which one to toss a grenade in first.

Phil Guvens must have felt the same, and the pair stared out into the dark desert for a moment.

Finally, Winterson turned to him. "What do you think, Guv?"

After a moment Guvens half-turned. "What do you see out there, Winter?"

Winterson let his eyes move over the desert landscape for a few seconds more. "About 100 places to hide. And twice as many to die."

"We're being watched," Guv said. "I can feel it in my bones."

"Maybe." Winterson watched for a moment more. "Let's just get this done, and then fuck off home."

Guvens shook his head. "Nah, I dunno. I just have this feeling we're not going home from this one."

Winterson snorted. "How many missions we been on together, Guv?"

"Too many," the man replied.

"I always got you home before, didn't I?" Winterson half-smiled.

"Yeah. Yeah, you did." Guvens nodded.

"Then put a sock in it, and let's go earn our money." Winterson waved him and the team on.

The men headed down the slope and were only 100 feet onto the plain when spider holes erupted all around them. Huge, armor-plated men launched themselves from within them.

"Engage," Winterson yelled.

His men were quick, but whoever these guys were they were quicker: ballistic armored, and better trained.

Guv went first and took a bullet between the eyes. Fergal gagged loudly as a large blade was thrust into the side of his neck, and Hoskins took a round in the thigh.

"Drop them." Their six attackers had them dead to rights and the biggest guy had a gun barrel pointed right between Winterson's eyes.

He was paid a lot, but not enough to die in some shitty desert.

"Lay 'em down, boys." Winterson let his rifle drop. He knew he'd said *boys*, but in reality, it was just him, Artwell, and the wounded Hoskins remaining.

They were quickly disarmed, hands pulled behind their backs and plastic ties looped around their wrists. In minutes Winterson, the still bleeding Hoskins, and Artwell, were seated facing each other.

The huge soldiers stood behind them. Winterson saw that Hoskins' wound pulsed dark blood and knew his man would bleed out soon. No one moved to treat the injury.

Winterson looked up at what he thought was the group's leader, and the biggest guy there. "You need to put a patch on that wound, or he'll bleed out."

The big man just stared for a moment. He lifted his face shield. "Do you remember me?"

Winterson narrowed his eyes as he looked at the man, and he clearly detected the Russian accent this time.

After a moment he shook his head. "Nuh."

"I remember you." The Russian smiled, but there was no warmth in it. "Twenty years ago in the Caucasus. I was there. Just a boy." His smile widened. "You took the strange body away in the helicopter. Left me with no proof of what killed my unit. And my father."

"I don't remember." Winterson shook his head. "Anyway, fuck that. You need to treat this man."

"Okay." The Russian pulled his gun, put the barrel to Hoskins' temple and pulled the trigger. Blood and brains blew in a funnel shape out over the dry sand, and Hoskins fell to the side.

"Problem solved," the man said.

Winterson swallowed dryly. He suddenly had a shitty feeling that Guvens was right, and he might not be sipping drinks and counting money back home any time soon.

"What do you want?" He asked.

"Good, now we are getting down to it." The man squatted in front of him and smiled, but his eyes were dead. "I am Major Nikolas Belakov, Russian Special Forces, and I have been looking for you for a long time."

Belakov stared hard into the Englishman's face. "My group has been tasked with finding out about these pyramid people." His brow furrowed, and he wagged a finger in Winterson's face. "And you will tell me – what they are, where they come from, why you are helping them, and also who is paying you."

The remaining mercenary, Artwell, turned from the Russian to watch Winterson. His English partner just shrugged. "We don't know that much. We're just soldiers doing a job."

Belakov's mouth turned down. "You are not soldiers, not anymore. Now you are men paid for service and without loyalty. So, I think I only need one of you." The grin returned. "In the next thirty seconds I will shoot one of you. Who will decide to talk? And who will live?"

"Me," Winterson said quickly.

Artwell's eyes went wide. "You fucking pri—"

Belakov shot Artwell between the eyes. The Russian leader holstered his weapon and then briefly checked his watch. He lowered his gun-barrel gaze to Winterson. "Begin."

* * *

Belakov listened as the man told him everything – the English mercenary spoke fast, and it only took half an hour – he started with the contract initiation with the billionaire Bradley Saunders decades ago, and how they had been gathering intel, assisting, and covering up for the visitors for years while Saunders studied them, helped them gather people, and worked on ways to communicate with them. And this time, he felt he could.

It seemed to the billionaire the people being abducted were just incidental collateral loss. Belakov worked to keep his expression emotionless, as he remembered what this pig and his master Saunders had done in the Caucasus just on twenty years ago – then, it was his father who had been 'just incidental collateral loss'.

This man was just a pawn to be moved around the chessboard. It was the Englishman Saunders Belakov really wanted. He dreamed of strangling him with his bare hands. But first he wanted to make sure their precious visitors and their abominable pets were all turned to ash.

Belakov paused to ask a question now and then, but the ex-soldier Winterson knew that his choices were to talk or die, and Belakov had already proved that the Russians were playing for keeps.

Finally, Belakov got to his feet. "Good." He circled a finger in the air, and the other Russians slotted away water bottles and checked their weapons.

"I've done my bit. Now you do yours. Untie me," Winterson said. He was still sitting on the ground, hands tied behind bis back.

"I said if you talk, you live." Belakov shrugged. "You talked, so you live. I never said I'd untie you."

Winterson glared. "You've taken my weapons, ammunition, and comms—"

"Oh yes, I forgot." Belakov reached down, took the man's canteen, and unscrewed it. He upended it and let the water empty onto the sand and grit. He had promised not to kill him, and he was a man of his word. But that didn't mean he didn't hope Winterson died slowly.

"How am I supposed to survive?" Winterson yelled.

Belakov chuckled. "You are a tough man. You will find a way." He went to lead his men away but paused. "One more thing, Englishman; if I see you again, I will kill you. And I promise I will make it painful."

Winterson glared, but after a moment, he nodded once.

Belakov checked his position plotter and saw that the other group, probably the HAWCs, were converging just to the east of them.

He had questions for them as well. If they were friends, then maybe they could work together. If not, he was happy to leave more dead bodies to the desert.

* * *

Winterson watched the departing Russians. They'd stripped him of his weapons, water, and comms devices. But frankly, he was still surprised that they'd let him live, because he knew if their positions were reversed, those fuckers would all be corpses, every single damn one of them.

He gave them a few more minutes and then he strained to reach his bound hands down behind him to his left boot, where he pressed a stud on the heel that ejected a small blade. He cut himself free in seconds.

Winterson rubbed his wrists and then reached into his right boot for a small messaging device that Bradley Saunders had had specially made for them. He opened it and began to send a message, along with his coordinates.

In a few minutes he got a response – they were on their way.

CHAPTER 39

Alex received the ping notification in his ear comms system notifying him that a compressed high-priority information squirt had been sent.

He raised a hand and the three HAWCs and scientist caught up to him as he stopped.

"What is it, boss?" Casey asked.

"Hammerson." Alex read the message on his gauntlet and grunted softly. "New directives incoming, as well as updated kit."

"Cool, weapons tech?" Casey asked.

"Yes, but the priority is new suits – hostile environment suits – super hardened and sealed. With MECH assist." He looked up at Sam. "Even for us."

Sam's huge forehead creased. "That makes no sense. I've already got …" His forehead smoothed and his deep chuckle began. "They want us to go through."

"Yeah, that's what I think," Alex replied.

"Oh my God," Linley said, and walked forward. "We talked about it, but …"

"Through the portal?" Klara asked. "We're taking the war to these things?"

"Hold; more instructions coming in." Alex looked up. "Drop has been effected and will be coming down right here ..." He pointed at a dot in the sky. "... right now."

They all watched the dot get bigger and then the multi-parachutes deploy to slow the object's descent when it was just 1000 feet up.

They headed to the item's touchdown point, and in a few minutes found the huge ten-foot by ten-foot crate that had sunk into the desert ground.

Alex used his bare hands to rip the lid from the crate and saw the individual boxes for the new enviro-suits and racks of weapons. He pulled one free and nodded.

"Yeah, what I expected – lasers – the only thing that won't be affected by a change in gravity like a projectile or compressed air pulse would be."

Sam used his huge frame to lift the boxes out. Each one was as long as a coffin and had a name label.

"Doctor Linley, your new robes await," Sam said, and laid the box in front of the scientist.

"This is a dream come true," Linley said as he opened the box.

"Yeah, sure, Doc," Casey sneered. "If your dream is to go and fight monsters in hell."

DOG stood watching silently, and Sam turned. "Nothing for you, fella. You're armored up enough." He then used his blade to prize the lid from his own box and stared down at the suit within.

He grunted. "This is top-of-the-line heavy impact armor – it'll take a cannon blast." He lifted one of the gauntlets and saw the built-in hydraulics. "We're gonna be strong and well defended. I'm guessing they expect we're about to walk into some heavy weather."

"More like heavy gravity, with over 300-degree heat and a toxic atmosphere." Linley pulled the arm section of the suit out and turned over one of the gauntlets, examining it.

"You need a hand, Doc?" Casey asked.

He turned to her and smiled. "I helped design them."

She chuckled. "Great, then you can give *me* a hand." Casey was already pulling off her existing armored suit.

Linley stopped to stare at Casey, seeming unable to look away. Alex chuckled. Casey was around five-ten and had muscles on muscles. She was powerful, flat-chested, and ripped by scars, some old, some still flaring pink. She probably had more, but her body was also covered in vivid, angry tattoos of fighting dragons, skulls, women's names, and daggers dripping blood.

She caught Linley looking. "You keep staring, Doc, you're not gonna be able to pull those pants on."

Sam roared with laughter as Linley's face reddened and he then focused on climbing into his own kit.

Casey started to flex the armored gloves. "I can't wait to see what these babies can do."

Klara did the same, and Alex found a small data stick and pressed it into his gauntlet. Information scrolled down the screen. He quickly read the update from the HAWC commander.

"Confirmed – from the Commander in Chief, highest-level order. We shut the doorway, for good." He looked up. "This can only be achieved by destruction of the opposite side portal."

"Then that's it; opposite means off-world." Casey grinned. "One thing I love about this job is that I get to travel." She raised a hand. "Question. These suits are designed to make war at their end. We go there and destroy the portal; but just how do we get home?"

"And how will we know if we've really stopped them?" Klara asked. "And how do we stop a planet?"

Alex read down the information a little more. Then he reached inside the crate for another box, roughly three feet by one in length. He opened it and stared down at the silver cylinder.

"This is how: we use an MSB-136 – a planet killer." He nodded and smiled. "And it's got a timer. We take it through, secure the site, plant the MSB, and then evac."

Sam joined him and looked down at the brushed silver cylinder, which was scuba-tank size but without any markings apart from smaller pipes and dials running over it.

"I've never seen one before." Sam looked up. "But then, I've never needed to blow up a planet before."

"So small for so much power." Linley looked down at the device almost lovingly. "Anti-matter detonation. The initial plasma blast disperses antimatter particles." He looked up. "On contact with matter, the resulting detonation would be a white-hot cancellation event. Nothing will remain."

Sam whistled.

"The knockout punch." Klara grunted with a nod. "Works for me."

Alex looked at each of his team members. "First prize, we destroy the portal, for good, and all make it home. But we acknowledge that destroying the portal is the priority."

"*HUA*," the HAWCs replied.

Alex spoke the words – the rallying cry – which possibly meant that they might need to make the ultimate sacrifice. But he knew he didn't mean them this time. Destroying the portal or the alien world was not his priority. Finding Joshua was. Once the boy had been recovered or was safe, then everything else could fall into place.

Alex stared down at the powerful device, the planet buster, and wondered just how any of them were supposed to make it back. This smacked of just another suicide mission that soldiers had been sent on for as long as war had existed.

It didn't matter. He didn't matter. Because Joshua was his immortality. If the boy lived and the world and its people were safe, then he knew he would have fulfilled the purpose for which he was put on Earth. He blinked a couple of times to refocus.

"Okay," Alex said, and reached in for his suit. "Let's get to work."

The group had removed their desert suits and dropped them all in the crate. When they were done, they'd deploy a melt-disk as they had before, which would turn everything to sludge and prevent anyone else getting their hands on the technology.

Alex climbed into the suit, which needed to be assembled around the wearer. This time all the parts of the body would need to be shielded as they were expecting to encounter more than just higher gravity and heat but a toxic and slightly radioactive atmosphere as well.

The soldiers needed to be powerful enough to be able to fight in the heavy gravity without any loss of speed or maneuverability. All with the fully sealed protection of full shielding against weapons they knew little about as yet. The suits were a similar design to the ones recently worn for the Dark Side mission on the moon, except the armor was reinforced and the hydraulics had been boosted.

"Field test on boost power." Casey slid back the small panel on her chest and pressed the button there. She then reached into the crate for her old helmet and swung it upwards. The helmet headed up into the night sky and kept going. The group stared upward for several moments.

"How high you think that went?" Casey grinned.

Sam sighed. "You do know our instructions are to melt our old kit? All of it."

Casey grimaced. "Oh yeah. Sorry." She found a melt-disk and tossed it onto the pile of old armor. "Fire in the hole."

In just a few minutes the experienced soldiers were ready, and each took turns checking the seals on their suits, and that their weapons systems were all online and functional. They spent a little extra time on Linley. Even though he knew everything about the technology, it was obvious he had never worn the suit before.

The scientist flexed an armored gloved hand. "I feel I could tear steel with these."

"You probably could," Sam replied.

Casey slapped his armored shoulder. "That's the spirit, Doc, because where we're going, we do *not* come in peace."

Alex checked his shields, weapons systems, and then checked their position. His last task was to place the MSB-136 in its harness and strap it to the small of his back.

"Let's go, we've got a planet to save."

"And one to destroy," Casey finished.

From somewhere far out in the dark desert they all heard the sound of a helmet striking the hard-packed ground.

CHAPTER 40

Joshua slowly came awake. And then the pain hit him.

"Ou-*ccccch*."

He put a hand to his head and blinked open bloodshot eyes. He immediately felt the pressure of his pulse pounding in his ears. His face felt hot and puffy, and his eyes were swollen. Then he saw why – *I'm upside down*, he realized.

He looked up, or rather down, and saw that he was about three feet from the ground.

"What the …?" He turned one way then the other. Beside him hung Armina, and about fifty feet away were the two women who had also came down in the plane, also out cold. But that was it; all the others were missing.

"Hey." He reached out an arm but was just a little short of Armina, who dangled unconscious with her mouth open and a line of drool reaching all the way to the ground.

The two women a little further out hung corpse-like, but he knew they weren't dead. He guessed that maybe his rapid metabolism had allowed him to shake off whatever had rendered them unconscious a little more quickly than the others.

But shake what off, and where were they? He looked at his feet and saw they were stuck in some sort of glue at the ceiling. He turned as best he could in the darkened space. He could see that there were other marks on the ceiling between him and the women, as if more people had been there before who were now gone – all the men maybe?

He quickly examined the rest of the room and saw that the walls looked a little organic; however, there was a definite paneling effect, and the panels seemed to be made of something akin to honeycomb sheets, but he guessed something stronger. And it was hot in here, really hot. Not like the desert heat, but more humid.

Joshua pulled his body up and reached his shoes, undoing the laces. He dropped to the ground, spinning in the air to land lightly on his feet, and took in more of his surroundings as the blood settled in his body and his mind cleared.

Sniffing, he smelled odd scents that were animal-like, and something like almonds and vinegar that reminded him of the reptile cage at the local zoo his dad had taken him to when he was younger. But there was also the slight hint of engine oil and perhaps ozone, as if electronics were overheating.

Joshua began to recall the last thing he remembered: he and the group had been walking across the desert when the men in the lead had broken into a run, moving faster and faster, and then, weirdly, had started sliding. Those further behind had called to them to stop, but then they were all grabbed by some sort of force, and as if a table was tipping and crumbs sliding across its surface, they had all been drawn toward a massive hole in the ground.

He remembered everyone panicking, screaming, then falling into darkness. But he didn't remember hitting the bottom; just a nothingness from then on.

Until now. Joshua reached out with his mind, trying to sense where the others were. Beyond the room there were faint sounds, and beyond that, he came across the men he had been with – Armina's father, Vince, the remaining security people, and even old Mosh.

But they were strange; their thinking was different, simpler, and it was as if they were somehow constrained – no, that wasn't quite right – it was as if they were pacified, or slumbering and dreaming. But they weren't pleasant dreams; they were ones of torment and anguish.

Then he found other thought patterns, and these were more complex, guarded, and entirely different from anything Joshua recognized. He realized they were not human minds – to them, the people they had captured were nothing more than products, things they used like tools or lumber to be crafted and altered to be useful to them.

He'd learned enough to know he just needed to get the hell out of there. Joshua turned, reached for Armina and shook her gently.

"Hey," he whispered. But there wasn't even a flicker of her eyelids or a groan. "Hey, Armina, wake up." Nothing, she was out cold.

He then quickly crossed to the two women and tried to wake them, but they were the same. Whatever had happened to them had put them into a deep slumber or even a coma.

Joshua then went back to Armina. He couldn't reach her feet from the floor but he gently pulled until her feet slid from her cross trainers. She fell into his arms, and he carried her to one of the walls and eased her into a sitting position with her back against it. He rubbed her hand, then her cheek, and then sat next to her, frowning. He didn't know what else to do.

"Stay here," he said redundantly, then crossed to the doorway and peered out. The corridor was dark but he could see it was made of the same material as the room. He tried to see, hear, or sense any danger nearby, and this time, he felt the alien minds approaching.

"Ah, crap." He stepped back into the room.

He looked for another exit but found none, then his eyes went to the pair of still hanging women, wondering if he could tug them down in time, and quickly realized he couldn't. He had to hide, but there was nowhere to go, so he hurried back to Armina against the wall just as huge shadows filled the doorway.

His mind working furiously, Joshua remembered that he had been able to shield them when they had been in the plane. So why not now? Maybe this time, instead of trying to protect them against the force of impact, he could try shielding them against light waves. If the creatures had vision that was not too dissimilar to his, then it might just work.

He flexed just as the two beings entered the room.

Joshua looked up at them, grimacing as a shock of terror ran through him, and the fear made him feel like he badly needed to piss.

Monsters, he thought.

They were taller than the tallest basketballer he had ever seen and covered in slimy-looking scales. They had more than two arms, ending in long, clawed hands. But it was their heads that made him feel sick with fear – the grotesque beings had faces like reptiles with needle-like teeth set in powerful jaws that looked like they could crush your bones and flesh with ease. The creatures looked vaguely familiar, and then Joshua realized he'd seen something similar before in the drawings of Egyptian gods he had seen at school.

He also saw that they had too many red eyes that burned with intelligence, and on top of their heads, instead of hair there were worm-like growths that were never still. Joshua quickly looked away lest he cry out, squeezed his eyes shut, and silently prayed that he and Armina were invisible to them.

After a few moments of silence, he couldn't help but open one eye. He saw that the massive creatures had crossed directly to the hanging women, walking right past Josh and Armina as if they didn't exist.

Joshua breathed a sigh of relief, but then watched in horror as the creatures reached for the women, who simply fell from the ceiling and were grabbed like sacks of meat and held up. The monsters' sharp claws shredded their clothing, stripping it from them. Then with no dignity at all the two women were grabbed, one by her long hair and the other by her arm and dragged out as if they weighed nothing.

Just then Armina murmured in her slumber, and at the door one of the creatures turned back. Joshua saw the multiple lines of blood-red eyes on the snout move slowly over the room, each one moving independently like some sort of bobble-eyed gecko. He held his breath and waited, trying hard to keep his fear and revulsion at bay.

Seconds seemed an eternity, and he could sense the indecision and confusion in the creature's mind. But after a moment it turned and headed down the corridor, and Joshua let his breath out with a whoosh. His heart was beating a mile a minute, both from holding the air in and from what he had seen.

He now knew he had been captured by something that was not from this Earth. Joshua closed his eyes and concentrated on his father, but still couldn't get a clear sense of him. At least this time there was a faint ghost of feeling, as if Alex was nearer. But wherever he was, something was stopping him from making full contact.

So Joshua needed to work out what to do on his own. He needed to get out, and then, like finding higher ground to get better radio signals, he knew they'd be able to "see" each other.

Joshua was also determined to save Armina. But he knew she would be devastated if he got her out without at least trying to find her father.

He sighed. He had to at least see what had happened to the others, and a good place to start was to find out where the monsters had taken the two women.

CHAPTER 41

Belakov checked his position plotter and saw the five bodies coming at them. There was also a smaller signature with a metallic trace; what that was he could not yet determine. But he knew they were the HAWCs. He also knew he needed to take more care with this group.

His team and theirs were more likely to share common goals, but he judged it best to deal with them from a position of power. The HAWCs were both physical and high-tech warriors who had a fearsome reputation. But so did his Russian wolf warriors.

Just as he had done successfully with the English mercenaries, he'd wait and ambush them, and disarm them. Then they could talk. He turned to his team. "Dig in. I want them disarmed and disabled, but not dead." He turned back to the inky-black desert. "Unless they force our hand."

The group of huge men spread out, switching their armor to thermal concealment, and the suits' exterior began to cool, rendering them invisible to heat-seeking optics. Then they began to conceal themselves in the path of the oncoming HAWCs.

* * *

Alex, Sam, Casey and Klara ran in single file over the deathly dry terrain. Nearly fifty yards further back came Alfred Linley, who was struggling a little. DOG trotted beside the scientist as Alex had ordered it to ensure the man didn't get into trouble.

Alex had been in deserts before – rocky, sandy, or frozen – and they usually had some life in them, whether it was a stunted shrub, small thorny lizard, or beetle that hid under the sand during the day. But here, there was nothing.

He understood now why the locals avoided this particular part of the desert and thought the place was cursed. Having a race of beings that had been using this area for millennia to trap and mutilate people didn't help, he bet.

For maybe the hundredth time Alex reached out to try to find his son. He strained, pushing out his senses further and further until his head throbbed, but still nothing came back. His gut told him Joshua was there, somewhere, but somehow just outside of his reach, as though he was being kept behind some sort of veil.

More likely it was the entire site that had been cloaked – the creatures now knew humans were better equipped technologically to find them, so they in turn might be trying to obscure their presence.

Alex focused hard as he tried one last time to locate Joshua, and while his mind was distracted, the ambush was sprung. Huge men literally rose from the desert around them.

Dammit, he thought. *I walked us right into it.*

It was six on five, with Sam Reid attracting two men because of his size. They were quick and professional and the guy behind Alex looped an arm around his neck and tried to wrench him backwards.

The first thing Alex noticed was that none of their assailants held weapons. As the log-like arm clamped down harder on his neck, Alex grabbed it and used it to pull the man over his shoulder so he was in front of him. The HAWC leader then punched him in his armored face, the blow so hard he cracked the bulletproof visor and the man's head snapped back on his neck. He then grabbed his attacker's chest harness and flung the guy twenty feet out into the dark desert, where he rolled several times and lay still.

DOG's combat armor automatically deployed, and its mouth opened, displaying multiple barrels. It began to charge, but Alex threw out a hand. "DOG, stand down!" The canine robot froze.

Even though Linley also wore a high-powered suit he was knocked down, and it was obvious the scientist wasn't an expert in knowing how to fight in one. Or fight at all.

Casey launched into a side kick and her armored boot struck a significant layer of shielding over her attacker's torso. The man was half a head taller and never budged, but his return kick smashed into Casey's gut.

A blow like that must have hurt, but the tough HAWC didn't flinch and instead grabbed the boot, lifted the leg, and flipped the man backwards.

Klara traded blows with her adversary, and her strength-assisted suit made her punches like a jackhammer into his chest and face shielding. The sound was like someone beating a steel drum, and she knocked her opponent back a step while making a dent in his armor. She went to finish him, and her hand went to her holster.

"No weapons," Alex shouted, and headed to cover the scientist.

One of the attackers had Linley on the ground and had placed a boot on his chest – big mistake, as his eyes were diverted from the battlefield for a second or two. It was enough.

Alex dropped a shoulder and struck him in the mid-section. The impact was brutal, and the guy flew backwards and stayed down on his back, arms flung wide.

After a few more moments Sam slammed his two attackers together with enough force to dent some of their armor plates and daze the pair of them. He then lifted both, one in each hand.

With their superior training plus heavy combat enviro-suits, the HAWCs easily outmatched their opponents, and they hadn't even needed to put their suits into boost mode. Sam held up the two struggling men, looking like he was about to smash them together once more for good luck.

"*Stop.*" This came from the guy Alex had initially thrown out into the desert.

He held up a hand and walked slowly back toward them, holding his ribs. "Sam Reid, we meet again."

Sam turned, still holding the two soldiers. He waited. The man slid his face shielding up. Sam snorted and threw the men to the ground.

"Who are you?" Alex demanded.

"Major Nikolas Belakov, Russian Special Forces," he replied, and then tilted his head. "And I think I finally meet the Arcadian, yes?"

"You're lucky you're not all dead. If one of you had drawn a weapon, then this guy …" Alex thumbed over his shoulder at the metal attack droid. "… would have put holes in all of you."

"I like it." Belakov eyed DOG. "We have similar. But bigger."

"Borneo, right?" Casey said.

He nodded. "I'm sorry about this, but these are strange times. I made a mistake, thinking I could overpower you, and then force you to listen to me."

"Let 'em up," Alex said. And then, "I'm only listening now because you didn't use weapons. But I still may kill you for pissing me off."

"If we'd used weapons, perhaps some of your soldiers might be dead too," Belakov replied. His men gathered behind him. "You seek the ones stealing people. We do also." He pointed out to the dark desert. "A few hours back we caught up with the band of English mercenaries that had been assisting them. They were commissioned by an Englishman by the name of Bradley Saunders. He is what we would call an oligarch, and he is coming here, maybe to talk to these things, maybe to see if he can help them further."

"What are your plans?" Alex asked.

"To destroy or disrupt." Belakov looked away momentarily and then back. "Revenge." His expression was deadpan. "In 2002, my father led a squad into the Caucasus mountains to investigate abductions of villagers. He was taken, along with his entire squad. I was the only survivor. Someone helped the pyramid creatures. I now know it was a young Bradley Saunders. This is personal to me."

Alex nodded and then exhaled. "And my son is in there somewhere right now." He turned back. "Our plans are the same as yours. Work with us."

Belakov seemed to think about it, and then nodded. "Agreed, but not under your command. As an alliance."

"Good enough," Alex said, and then suddenly spun back to the desert. He tilted his head as he sensed something. "I ... see him ..." It was like a jolt of electricity ran right through his body. "He's there. He's alive."

Alex walked a few paces toward the Well of Hell, and then turned back. "Hurry, we don't have much time."

CHAPTER 42

"*We need to move,*" Joshua whispered.

He lifted Armina under his arm. She was slowly rousing, but it was like she was coming to after anesthetic and staggered with her eyes closed. Whatever narcotic or force had been applied to them, only Joshua's system had been able to shake it off quickly.

He dragged Armina to the doorway and paused. It was easy to determine which way the things had gone because of their odious lingering smell. When he was satisfied there were no sounds he snuck out, and Armina shuffled beside him, her head resting on his shoulder.

He went past several more rooms or cells and saw that these, too, had the sticky substance on the ceiling, which meant they had once held captives or were perhaps expecting more. He squinted into the darkness – there were piles of clothing heaped against the walls – but there was something strange about what he was seeing.

Then it clicked: he saw that this wasn't all modern clothing. Some of it looked old, very old, as in ancient desert garb, and there were curved daggers in sheaths, gold bracelets, and even an old sword as long as he was. It all made him wonder how long this place had been here.

Armina murmured and then groaned, but her eyes stayed closed. Joshua froze as she made the noises. He had to scout ahead for a way out but hoped she could remain silent.

"Armina," he whispered.

"I'm ... hot," she breathed.

He smiled. "Yeah, me too." He used his sleeve to absorb the sweat from her damp forehead.

"Where ...?" Her eyes blinked open groggily. And then she focused. "*Where are we?*"

"I don't know exactly. But ..." He steeled himself. "I think we've been taken by something, *um*, something not human."

She glared at him. "*What?*"

"*Shusssh.*" He pressed a hand over her mouth. "They're not friendly."

She knocked his hand away. "Where's my father? Where are the others?"

"I don't know. But we need to get out," he whispered.

"Not without my father." She went to pull away from him, but he held her. She continued to struggle.

Joshua grabbed her in both hands and looked deep into her eyes. "Okay, we'll look. But we need to be real quiet. No matter what you see. Can you do that?"

Her mouth turned down and her lip trembled, but she managed to nod. "I think so. But I'm scared."

"I know, me too. It's okay." He took her hand, peered around the corner, and then tugged. "Let's go."

Joshua followed the path, or rather the smell, of the two creatures that had taken the women. The pair stayed close to the wall, and thankfully other rooms they passed were all empty. But up ahead they were coming to an area that was lit by a soft red glow, and there were odd sounds that could have been water dripping, or something draining with a sucking sound.

Joshua slowed and peered into the room.

In just seconds he took it in. And it was hell on Earth.

He immediately spun away to swallow down some rising bile. He held Armina back a few steps. "Just wait here. Please."

He sucked in a breath of the hot, fetid air and crept forward. He slowly peered around the corner again and just stared. There were long benches and the huge lizard-like beings had the two women up on the top, who now squirmed in a semi-awake state.

One of the creatures held something to the dark-haired woman's neck and she shuddered for a moment, and then lay still.

Joshua frowned, trying to understand what he was seeing. The woman relaxed, and relaxed more, and then her whole body seemed to *soften*. In the next instant the creature began to disassemble her like a child's doll.

Insanely, the thing pulled her arms and legs from the torso. There was no blood or wrenching or tearing of tendons, bones, or muscles, but instead, everything just slipped apart like it was never really held together. It also stripped her long hair from her scalp and tossed it aside like a wig.

The near eight-foot-tall creature briefly examined the woman's slim arms, and then turned to place them and the torso into a huge vat of glutinous red liquid, where they floated for a moment and then slowly sank. Joshua guessed they were being dissolved or rendered down.

The legs were then examined and set aside, and the creatures turned their attention to the blonde woman. Joshua felt his stomach threaten to void as he watched in shock as they worked on her head, lifting away the top of the skull to remove her brain. This was placed on another benchtop where there were, Joshua saw, lines of other human brains – removed but not dead. Because the most horrifying thing was, they were still functioning; Joshua could sense consciousness in them, they were aware, their owners crying out on some level, trapped in a limbo of helplessness, wondering what had happened to them. It made tears of fear and futility run down Joshua's face.

The brains were then worked on, manipulated, and smoothed into a single long gray sheet. But they weren't destroyed, as he could still see veins running through them, pumping a fluid that wasn't blood, but instead something else that would feed the organs and keep them alive.

The final task of the lizard-like creatures was to place the legs on a stack of other limbs, piled like logs waiting to be used for firewood. There were men's brawny arms and legs, and the smoother ones of women. Some were then collected up and taken to a separate platform. Human torsos, four of them, were lined up beside each other, with a single empty neck left at one end. Then, ten of the arms and legs were organized outside of the torso center mass. Some of the brain matter sheet was included on the surface of the torsos, and finally a glass-like dark bulb was embedded into the flesh over the brain matter sheet.

The creatures then stepped back to work at a control panel. Red light bathed the masses of mutilated humanity. As the light cascaded down onto the flesh, Joshua picked up the screams in his head. It was the people, the remnants of their minds in the brain matter, their voices not making sense. But one thing was clear to Joshua: some part of their consciousness remained and was trapped in this new monstrosity, and they knew it.

As he watched, the flesh of the different bodies somehow melted together. The multiple torsos became one central mass, the brain matter was absorbed into the thing's back, and the multiple limbs all attached. The torso showed lumps where some form of thick ribbing structure was developing.

But the horrors weren't finished, because in the next few seconds the thing twitched.

Joshua felt he was in a trance as he watched. Under the glow of the red light, the new abomination began to shudder. The neck with the single pipe at its center had closed over and drawn back into the frame, and for a moment the glass bulb on its back glowed as the creature at the control panel worked at some nightmarish machine.

The red light went off. And then, horrifyingly, the merged being rose on its legs. It crawled down off the benchtop like a massive pink and brown spider, with the sets of arms at the front extended, their fingers grasping at the air.

One of the reptilian beings led it to the massive vat of steaming reddish-brown liquid that contained the rendered-down rejected limbs and pieces of flesh, and the lizard creature pulled a nozzle from the side of the vat. As if in anticipation, the neck extended a cartridge pipe with a sucking mouth-part on one end. The nozzle was then stuck in the neck hole, and the liquid was pumped into it as the obscenity sucked it down – its first meal.

Joshua felt his legs go weak and he looked away to stop himself from vomiting. When he looked back, the creature who had destroyed the women began to assemble another pile of limbs and torsos as the process started all over again.

Joshua felt lightheaded and held on to the wall. He now knew what had happened to the rest of the people on the plane. And what would happen to them if they were caught.

He began to ease back, just as a gut-wrenchingly loud scream from behind him made him start in fright. He spun to see that Armina had crept up to stare into the room.

She stood, her hands in front of her, jabbering in fear. Then she backed up and spun around to sprint blindly away from him.

"*Wait*, Armina, *wait!*"

Joshua set off after her, just as the lizard creatures screeched a sound that made his hair stand on end. Joshua put his head down and kept going.

From behind he heard the thumping of feet – too many feet – and he knew that one of the newly created abominations had been sent in pursuit. In the dimness he couldn't see where Armina had gone, so he turned a hard left at the first corner, but in seconds hit a dead end. And she wasn't there. He spun back – the thing was coming fast, and he had nowhere to go.

CHAPTER 43

David 'Winter' Winterson stood on the top of a hill of dark, sunblasted rock and waited. On the horizon there was just a faint blush of orange as the giant sun was lifting itself toward sunrise.

He kept watching it, and after another few minutes a dot appeared within that stripe of color as the high-speed chopper came in low and fast. He initiated an electronic blip-flare that was like a strobing light for them to home in on.

The craft slowed, and then came down quickly – and he knew why. Around these parts there could be any one of a dozen groups with shoulder-mounted RPGs just itching to let one fly at an unidentified helicopter. Plus, those Russian assholes were still lurking somewhere.

The chopper settled but its blades kept up a rotation. Their ride would not be hanging around for them, and he bet the pilot was already impatient to get the hell out.

The door slid back and two men jumped out.

"What the fuck is this?" Winterson laughed as he shook his head.

Both men were in huge suits that looked like a cross between a suit of armor and a deep-sea diving kit. They had their visors retracted, and he could see that one was Bradley Saunders and the other some Asian guy.

They grabbed bags from the back of the chopper, waved, and the machine dusted off and veered away as if the pilot had a hot date back at the base.

Winterson turned off the blip-flare and walked toward his paymaster. He gave a small salute, more to stroke the billionaire's ego, and grinned.

"Welcome to Yemen," he said.

"Thank you." Saunders nodded to his colleague. "This is Doctor Huang."

"Wang." Winterson nodded.

"*Huang*." Huang glared.

"Whatever." Winterson yawned.

Saunders looked around. "Where's the rest of your men?"

"Dead. All dead," Winterson replied testily. "Killed by a small squad of Russians. Probably special forces. Seems we're not the only ones on the ground right now."

"Rules of the game." Saunders shrugged. "How far advanced are they?"

Prick, Winterson thought. "I think they're headed toward the eastern mouth of the well. But according to your notes it's the western side that has the entry and no force field. We can beat them to the bottom if we head in now."

Saunders nodded and smiled, looking almost giddy with excitement. He turned to Huang. "Ready to meet a god?"

"More than anything in my life, sir," Huang replied overenthusiastically.

CHAPTER 44

Alex was first to climb to the top of the hill and stare down onto the plain below them. The other HAWCs joined him, then Linley and DOG, as well as the five Russians.

"Hole-*eeey* shit," Casey said.

"From what I hear, not so holy," Sam replied.

Below them was the massive hole known as the Well of Hell. It was hundreds of feet across, and much deeper again. It was an eerie, impenetrably black crater in the orange-brown landscape.

"Doctor, your opinion?" Alex asked.

Linley joined him. "It's what we suspected. These visitors have been coming for countless millennia. Maybe even before humans evolved. But now that we have the ability to see them, they've needed to draw back to remote sites, like jungles, deserts, mountaintops, or down in giant sinkholes. They're hiding in there from us."

"Well, we've found 'em now," Casey said.

"I got movement, western rim," Klara said – she had switched her helmet vision to amplify, and the others turned and changed up their own.

Sure enough, they saw three men vanishing into the pit via a narrow ledge trail.

"The English mercenary, Winterson," Belakov said bitterly. "I let him live. But I warned him that if I saw him again, I would kill him."

"Who's with him?" Alex turned.

"I would say one of the men is their benefactor, the billionaire Bradley Saunders." Belakov nodded slowly. "As I said, I have a score to settle with him."

"Not till we've questioned him," Alex said.

Belakov's gaze was flat, and he didn't acknowledge the statement.

"What are they doing here?" Sam asked.

"According to the mercenary, the rich man wants to try and communicate with the creatures," Belakov replied. "He has been helping them for years – covering for them, assisting them, and cleaning up after them. I would say he is a man in love."

"Betraying his own species. I would say he's an asshole," Casey growled.

"He thinks he is above his own species, so betrayal is no problem for him," Belakov replied.

"We can run him down," Klara said.

Alex would normally have sprinted around the rim with the team and caught the Englishman to learn what he knew. His information might have been critical to their mission. But his impatience gnawed at him. He knew in his gut Joshua was down there and still alive.

He shook his head. "Take too long to get down there and then get around the rim. We just peg and drop from our side. Intersect with him at the bottom."

"You have climbing gear?" Sam asked the Russian.

"No, but you do," Belakov replied.

Alex walked a few paces forward and the Russian then narrowed his eyes as he stared at the HAWC captain's back.

"Excuse me, Captain Hunter – that thing strapped to your back. It looks a little like an MSB-136. Some call it a planet killer bomb. Am I wrong?" Belakov asked.

Alex half-turned. "Let's just say, when we're finished here, we won't be seeing these monsters again."

Belakov smiled. "Yes, good, I want them all to burn in hell." He waggled one big blunt finger. "Just make sure your little bomb goes off and does its job. On their side of the fence."

Alex nodded grimly. "It'll do what it's supposed to do."

"Hey, Boris, let me guess; you have a bigger bomb?" Casey scoffed.

Belakov shrugged. "We have the Stalin-211 – can blow up two planets."

Casey laughed out loud. "I love this guy."

"That's enough." Alex turned away again. "Okay, listen up people. Remember what happened when we got close to the pyramid in Australia. They sent out those creatures to attack us. Also, there was the force field that drew us in." He looked across each of their faces. "We drop in, and find Joshua, and then shut the door for good. These are the priorities."

Sam and Casey glanced at one another, and Alex went on. "If time permits, we search for any other survivors and extract them. Then we deliver the package, on the other side of the portal. If it is closed, then we trust our scientific expert to open it."

Linley nodded. "I think I can do it."

"Think you can?" Belakov chuckled. "Please don't arm bomb until doorway is open."

Alex smiled. "Hopefully we're all heading home with a smile real soon." He faced Belakov. "Are you and your team ready for this?"

The Russian nodded slowly. "I've been tracking these things for more than twenty years. My team and I are ready for anything."

Alex then looked down at the canine-looking android that was looking up at him. "What about you?"

"*Guard, protect, defend – maximum lethality, full combat mode,*" DOG replied.

"Works for me. Let's do this." Alex began to run down the slope toward the edge of the well.

CHAPTER 45

The nine-strong group sprinted down the hill. The power-boosted suits the HAWCs wore meant they took the lead with the Russians close behind. As they neared the sinkhole's rim, Alex still didn't feel any of the attractive force he had encountered before and wondered whether they might have caught a break.

As they neared the edge, he knew he needed a rear guard to keep their exit open, and also to ensure no one got past them. He looked down at the running metallic animal beside him. "DOG – *halt* – sentinel duties."

Alex also stopped in front of the android as the guardian DOG halted and tilted its head toward him. It was probably only his imagination but he was sure he heard a small sound emanate from within it that might have been confusion or maybe simple disappointment over the order.

"Alert on plane survivors. Alert on Joshua Hunter," Alex said. He held up a hand. "Stay." And repeated the order. "*Sentinel duties.* Acknowledge."

"*Sentinel duties. Acknowledged.*" The DOG then seemed to freeze, but Alex knew that its sensors would be scanning the rim and wider surface around the massive pit. Plus, its multiple cameras and movement sensors would now be engaged. He needed eyes on the rim in case Joshua managed to climb out without him knowing it.

Alex and the HAWCs then charged forward, and as they got to the edge of the well they barely slowed. They each pulled something like a fat handgun from their belts and aimed it at the hard stone of the well's edge. It fired a bolt into the rock that had a line attached. The HAWCs attached the guns to the back of their belts and literally ran over the edge as the wire line unrolled with enough tension to let them travel down at speed without falling.

High above them the Russians waited.

Alex dropped and felt the density of the air change. His scanners told him there was still breathable oxygen outside of his suit, but it was thicker somehow. For now, they had the ring of morning sunshine above to light the way, but once they moved outside of that, there would be complete darkness.

After dropping around 400 feet he saw the floor of the well approaching and slowed his descent to touch down lightly. Casey, Sam, and Klara did the same.

Alex then unhitched his wire and attached it to the rock floor. The other HAWCs did the same, and Alex tugged on the wire twice to signal for the Russians to come down.

They didn't need any encouragement, and in seconds the Russian team was traveling down the wire at speed.

Alex watched, impressed with their skill. He didn't have to wait long before all nine of them were present and ready to continue. He turned slowly. The cave floor was damp which was surprising after the bone-dry surface above them. But the old Arabic saying was true: the desert has plenty of water; you just have to know where to look.

"There." Casey pointed her wrist light.

Only fifty feet from them were piles of weapons and some clothing scattered on the cave floor. She walked a few paces and picked up one of the guns. "Hey, this is a World War 2 infantry rifle." She pulled back the bolt and ejected a round. "Still works." She looked down. "Daggers, ammo belts, and check this out…" she held up a rusted Roman sword.

"I'm guessing people have been dropping in, or being pulled in here, for a long time," Alex said. "We make sure it stops today."

"*HUA*," the HAWCs replied.

Belakov held up a thermal reader. "There's a heat signature on the western wall where Saunders would have scaled down."

Alex nodded. "We head over, everyone keeps their eyes open. These things have probably got tech we've never encountered before."

"Also, this Saunders and his mercenaries are not on the side of the human race. They will be unpredictable," Belakov added.

"So are we," Casey said, and followed Alex Hunter in.

* * *

Alex held up a hand and stopped the group. They were in a tunnel, not a cave. He ran a hand down one of the walls – it looked smooth and more organic than stone or some form of metal.

"Somewhere along the way, we crossed from the sinkhole into the pyramid," he said quietly, and stood silently for a moment, listening. He then pushed out his senses, primarily looking for Joshua, but also scanning for any danger up ahead.

"Anything, boss?" Sam asked.

"A lot of life emanations, but I can't see Josh." He turned, and noted that the Russians had loaded grenades in the undercarriage of their guns.

"You're not firing grenades in here. Not until my son is out," he warned.

One of the Russians snorted, and Alex allowed his helmet visor to slide back. He glared at the huge man, his eyes shining silver in the darkness. He pointed at his chest. "Put it away, or I will kill you right here with my bare hands."

The man stared for a moment.

"Do it." Casey said low and mean.

The Russian slotted the rifle and launcher over his shoulder.

Belakov raised a hand. "We understand." He growled something at his men, and all of them drew out sidearms. Belakov turned back. "But we know that our small arms are ineffective against the many-legged things. So, you must understand, if we are in a fight to the death, we will fight to ensure it is our adversaries' death and not ours."

"Fine. But follow our lead." Alex turned away again. "Because we brought lasers. HAWCs, lock and load."

The HAWCs took out the field lasers, extended the barrel and switched them on. A line of red lights ran up the tubular barrel of the weapons as they charged up.

Alex waved them on, and the group moved further into the tunnel system. After several minutes Alex stopped them at another side cave or room. This time, he sensed an impression of his son.

"Franks, Linley." He went inside, and waved Casey and Linley in with him. The room was empty apart from piles of clothes and other detritus on the floor.

"Look," Casey said after a moment.

Alex looked up at where she was indicating to see shoes stuck to a substance on the ceiling. "Doctor, what do you think?"

Linley looked up for a moment. "Reid, give me a hand."

Sam grabbed the scientist around the waist and lifted him. Linley reached up and dragged one down, and Sam lowered him.

Linley then felt the shoe bottom and looked at his hands. "Something adhesive. Looks biological." He handed it to Alex. "I guess they've got to store their stock somewhere until they're ready to process it."

"Fuck, I want to kill these things." Casey bared her teeth. "Then bring 'em back to life and kill them again."

Alex examined the shoe. "A woman's, modern design. Could have come from the downed flight crew." He let it drop, then scanned the ceiling again and stopped to stare. He then leapt up to grab a sneaker from the biological glue. He held it in his hands, his fingers gripping it tight.

"Joshua," he said softly.

He closed his eyes, concentrating and trying to pick up any new information, but he got nothing. He then reached up to drag down the sneaker's partner and put them both in a thigh container on his heavy armor.

He slowly turned to look into each of the corners of the room. "They were here, Joshua was here; we're not far behind them."

Alex headed out, picking up speed. And then they came to a split in the tunnel – both options looked viable.

"Dammit; we don't have time for this." Alex seethed but couldn't pick up which tunnel was his best choice.

He turned. "Casey, you get the Russians on door number two."

"You got it, boss." She turned to Belakov. "Okay, Boris, we're up."

Belakov shook his head. "No, we should not split up."

"No choice; these things may decide to leave soon, and we've got more work to do, and little time." Alex looked from Casey to Belakov. "Follow her lead. Meet back here in fifteen." He faced Casey again. "If you find Joshua, don't wait for us. You get him out. Understood?"

"Count on it." She turned. "Tight and close, comrades. Let's go."

She vanished into the gloom of the right-side tunnel. Belakov gave Alex a small salute, and then motioned for his men to follow.

Alex then turned to the dark interior of the left-side tunnel. "Double time." He headed in, taking Sam, Klara, and Linley with him.

CHAPTER 46

Saunders and Huang followed Winterson along the strange corridor that seemed to be built from a mix of organic growth and synthetic materials.

The mercenary half-turned. "Getting hot in here. Real hot."

"Like their home world, I imagine." Saunders didn't feel the heat and humidity in his temperature-controlled suit. "Undoubtedly makes them more comfortable. It's not a problem."

"Well, I'm not wearing one of those insulated tin cans, so I ain't comfortable." The mercenary spat. "Plus, I've seen the weird bastards that come out of these pyramids, so I really hope you know how to talk to them."

"I believe I can now communicate with them," Saunders replied imperiously, but he knew that until he tried, it was all guesswork. "You just concentrate on doing the job you're paid to do, Mr. Winterson, and I'll concentrate on doing mine."

Winterson stopped and turned "Hey, I don't remember agreeing to getting my entire squad killed, or saying I'd join you in trying to make friends with some giant lizards." He exhaled through bared teeth. "No money worth that."

Saunders noticed the man sweated profusely now and his face was pale as a sheet. Fear, no doubt, he thought. The man had worked for him for decades, and he had thought he was fearless. Obviously, everyone had their limits, he surmised.

"Please take a deep breath, calm down, and continue, sir." Saunders said forcefully.

"You do know I have no gun, right?" Winterson walked closer to the pair of men. "If we get attacked, we're sitting ducks. And don't forget, those fuckers are experimenting on people. You've seen those leg-arm monsters, right?"

"*Pfft.*" Huang waved it away. "We also study species and experiment on them. Only a few years ago we were putting acid drops in bunnies' eyes, flu virus into beagle puppies, and do you not remember that picture of the human ear sewn to a mouse's back?"

"Yeah, no doubt about you fucking scientists." Winterson turned to glare at the scientist. "And by the way, notice how all those cases you mention involve pissant little animals? For all you know, that's the way these things might see us."

Saunders met the mercenary's gaze. "Listen, Mr. Winterson; there were five of you, now there is one. That means you get to collect all their payments and bonuses as well as your own. A good and profitable outcome for you. Probably enough to retire on. Don't you agree, *sir*?"

Winterson seemed to think on it and then turned. "Yeah, fine, but money's only good if you get to spend it."

"Which of course you will, Mr. Winterson. So please, lead us on."

Winterson turned with brows knitted. "And why am I leading? You guys are the ones wearing all the fucking armor," he grumbled, but he faced forward again and continued anyway.

The trio passed several of the rooms that contained empty clothing, some new and some little more than moldering rags. The air got thicker and hotter, the atmosphere more claustrophobic, and also it seemed to become oppressively dark in the corridors or tunnels. Winterson slowed and then after a while stopped. "Can you guys keep it down?" he hissed.

The two men who weren't used to the bulk of the enviro-suits weren't navigating the spaces so well and their armor scraped the walls.

After another few minutes, Huang lifted a hand. "Hey, the suit's sensors are telling me there's something moving up ahead."

"Mine too," Saunders agreed, and checked the other sensors. "Brilliant technology. I commend the US military's research teams."

"No charge," Huang sneered.

"I've got lifeform readings. Non-human," Saunders intoned. "At last."

"Shut up." Winterson turned again, grimacing. "This is starting to freak me out. And all I've got is a knife." He turned back for a moment before facing Saunders again. "You know what? I've changed my mind; you can keep your money. I didn't sign up for this shit."

The pair of men said nothing.

"Well?" Winterson asked.

The mercenary then noticed that the pair of men were staring. Not at him, but right past him.

Finally, Saunders spoke. "It seems ... our arrival has been noticed."

Winterson spun around in the dark corridor as Huang backed up a step to get behind Saunders.

The corridor was narrow, only about four feet wide, but if there was a ceiling in the area they were in, it was lost in darkness. Standing up ahead of them in the gloom was a being standing roughly eight feet tall. Two rows of eyes glinted redly, reflecting their lights like some sort of nocturnal animal.

"Oh, God." Winterson gulped.

Crowded in beside the huge being was something straight out of a Lovecraftian nightmare – a creature that was like a large brown and pink centipede, but smooth, with many legs at its back end, but rows of human arms and hands at its front. It had no eyes or even a head that they could discern, but it seemed to wait on some dark command from its master.

Winterson spoke out of the side of his mouth. "Hey, listen, if you can speak to these things, now would be a really good time."

Saunders felt perspiration running down his sides in rivulets even though the suit had an internal cooling system. He swallowed down his nervousness, and tried to recall the words generated by a team of theoretical linguists created from the scroll language. He cleared his throat, and then vocalized what he understood to be a greeting.

"Salutations, oh great one."

He had no idea if what he was saying was being pronounced correctly, or even what the cultural rules were on a first meeting with these creatures, but he got a response.

The huge being craned forward. As it came nearer the men held their breath. They now saw up close the tooth-lined, lizard-like snout, but that was where the resemblance to any earthly creature finished.

"A god. Sobek," Huang whispered.

There were two rows of three red eyes that were like glistening blood-red rubies up each side of a long face that shone wetly, as though the interlocking scales were covered in some sort of secreted mucus or oil.

Saunders theorized that as their own world was so dry, this would assist in helping them retain moisture.

There were long arms at the shoulders, and then another smaller pair of arms extending from its sides – all four ended in wicked claws. The body itself was a dark, mottled green-black color, and Saunders couldn't tell if it was an armor-plated skin, or if it wore some sort of suit.

It loomed closer to Saunders and Winterson stepped out of the way, keeping his back to the wall.

The creature towered over them, and Saunders tried again, using different words and language patterns he had learned from the tomb scroll. He was desperate to introduce himself, and he wanted to let them know he was here to help. The words he chose next described them as being a helper, friend, or maybe even servant.

This one elicited a response, as the thing's mouth opened, and it spoke in a hissing sibilant tone. It repeated the words Saunders had used.

"I knew it." Huang clasped his hands together as if in prayer. "Ladies and gentlemen, we now have open dialogue."

Then the thing reached out a long arm and its hand touched Saunders' armor, feeling it, pulling and pressing at different places. Saunders lifted his visor and allowed it to roll all the way back, exposing his face.

The creature raised a long bony hand and almost gently caressed Saunders' flesh, feeling his cheek and then pulling his chin down to open his lips.

Saunders half-turned to speak out of the corner of his mouth. "Open yours too," he said to Huang. "Let them see you."

The scientist baulked for a moment, but then allowed his visor to be retracted. He gulped. "I am on your side," Huang breathed.

"Yeah, fuck that," Winterson said softly, and began backing away from the other two men.

The thing turned to briefly examine the Asian scientist, and then it turned to Winterson, who pushed himself back even harder against the wall of the tunnel. The creature reached out to grasp him and feel his arms, pressing the muscles.

"That's enough." Winterson knocked the long, bony hand or claw away.

The creature turned away briefly without saying a word, but the many-armed thing moved forward, silently and with a degree of agility that belied its large size.

"Oh, fuck no." Winterson went to back up further, but Saunders got behind him, blocking him.

"Stay calm, we're all friends here," Saunders said.

Then the many-armed and -legged thing grabbed at Winterson, holding his arms and clothing in many of its hands, and began to tug him toward it.

"Get it the fuck off me," Winterson screamed.

"Let it happen," Saunders urged. "We're friends now."

"Bullshit we are." Winterson's voice was high. "*Help ...*"

The man tried to stab at it with his blade but couldn't even cut the toughened skin. He was then dragged further by the centipede being, and Saunders nodded and then pointed to his own chest. "*Friend, servant, slave,*" he said in what he hoped was their language. He pointed at Huang, and then repeated the words.

"*Fucking help me.*" Winterson dug his heels in, but he was no match for the thing's titanic strength.

Finally, Saunders pointed at the retreating Winterson. "Not friend." He shook his head. "Not friend."

"You fucking ..." Winterson struggled, but he had no chance. "... *assho-ooole!*" he screamed as he vanished into the gloom.

"Yes, we are your friends." Saunders nodded vigorously.

The creature seemed to think on it for a moment, before stepping forward to take Saunders by the hand. He also grabbed Huang's hand with one of his mid arms.

"He understood you," Huang said. "He's taking us with him."

"We've been chosen," Saunders said almost dreamily.

The creature led them away, like a parent might lead their children.

CHAPTER 47

Joshua was making his way forward blindly now – he crawled on his hands and knees along the dark tunnel. He couldn't hear the thing that had been chasing him anymore. But he also couldn't find Armina and had no idea which direction to even look.

He got the feeling his father was close now, and that gave him a sense of relief. But he didn't know if that was a true indication or not as it was all still somehow blurry and obscured in his mind. For one stupid moment he worried about what his father would say about all the ways Joshua had let him down. Joshua exhaled; he didn't care, he'd take any punishment just to see him again and get home.

Suddenly, thoughts of his home, his mom and dad and his big dog clouded his mind, and he sniffed back wet tears. He swallowed the lump in his throat and tried to refocus.

Joshua continued crawling until he came to an entrance from which emanated a soft light. He eased his head around the corner to peek inside – and saw that the light was coming from around the edges of some sort of large oval door. But he couldn't tell if it was open or not because at its center it was nothing but pure blackness, and that blackness rippled slightly like liquid.

While he crouched there, trying to see inside the open door to judge if it was a way out, he felt something soft alight on his shoulder just where it met his neck – something soft and slightly moist.

At first, he thought it might be Armina finding him, and for some reason kissing him. He turned. And then felt like an electric shock ran right through his body – it was one of the many-legged things, and what had touched him was the feeding tube that had extended like a trunk made of pink flesh and ribbed cartilage. Its end was puckering open and closed against his sweaty skin and he didn't know if it was tasting him or trying to communicate.

Instinctively he knocked it away, and then one of the thing's hands shot out to grab onto his forearm. Joshua pulled back, but he found the thing was immensely strong, and hot, and in that moment of agitated contact he saw inside its mind, or rather its many minds, and found a layer of simple thoughts of a desire for obedience, hard work, and food. But below that layer was something else. Joshua then saw flashes of men in uniforms, fighting in the desert, and driving trucks.

"That was you. All of you," Joshua whispered.

But then the visions vanished as the creature's orders or objective crystallized in its simple layer of brain cells and it tried to yank him backwards down the corridor.

Joshua was extremely strong, but this thing was beyond him, and when a second hand grabbed at him, he began to panic.

Not going, he thought, and this time he flexed, and the arm that held him broke in several places, the sound of thick snapping bones like new kindling breaking. But if the thing felt the damage, it never showed it, as it simply reached out with another set of arms.

This time hands covered his face, grabbed at his collar, and he felt his legs begin to slip on the ground. The beast outweighed him by hundreds of pounds, and in seconds he was being dragged backwards.

Joshua had time to suck in a deep breath and let out one screamed word: "*Dad!*"

***

Sam saw Alex jerk upright, stagger momentarily, and then turn.

"Got something?" Sam asked.

"Yes, I think ..." Alex closed his eyes for a moment. "*Got him.* It's Joshua, this way." He pushed past Sam, Klara, and Linley, and began to sprint.

"Ah, shit," Sam exhaled, knowing they'd struggle to keep up with him. "Let's go, Doc. Klara, see that he keeps up."

The trio sprinted after Alex Hunter.

CHAPTER 48

Casey held up her hand and the Russians stopped behind her.

"Something just up ahead," she whispered.

She remained motionless for several moments, using her scanners, and then eventually lifted the visor off her face and sniffed. "Smells like someone's burning fresh shit in here."

She waved them on. A moment later they entered a larger space and she stopped them again and held up her motion tracker. "Movement." She moved the tracker slowly around, and then pointed it at the far side of the room.

"I think we have company," Belakov said softly. He turned to murmur something to his men, who then pulled their heavier weapons from over their shoulders.

A shadow within the shadows materialized out of the gloom, revealing itself to be one of the huge reptilian beings. Right behind it crawled one of the many-legged obscenities, acting like its attack dog.

"Holy fuck," Casey whispered as she replaced her visor. "A controller and its pet."

The muscular snout of the alligator-headed creature pointed at Casey and the multiple red eyes almost seemed to burn in its face. It raised one long arm.

"Here we go." Casey went to pull up her laser, but as she did, she was bumped to the side by the six huge Russians who fully entered the room and fanned out, firing as they went.

Casey spun back in time to see their rounds strike the thing but bounce off. And just then, the spider-like being shot forward in a blur of motion.

"It's fucking armored, you morons," she yelled, and was then overwhelmed by the brawny, many-limbed creature. It enveloped her, gripped one of her arms, both legs, and even in her power suit it was able to use its bulk to begin to press her to the floor. With her single free arm, she reached into her belt for the only thing she could get hold of – a melt-disk.

Casey pulled out the metallic puck-sized disk, initiated it, and then swung it up at the creature's torso, slamming it into its underside where it stuck.

"Eat that, you mother." She grinned as the disk reached the end of its countdown and began its burn.

Just as the abomination gripped Casey's other arm and began to drag her, the disk glowed white-hot and then its searing heat spread to whatever it was attached to – the torso of the creature also glowed, smoke rose, and in seconds a bike tire–sized hole opened on the thing, obliterating its internal muscle and skeletal structure.

It collapsed, but Casey saw that it wasn't dead and was still trying to reach for her even though its bone and muscle framework was gone.

Finish this, she thought, and pulled her laser, aimed, and fired a thin beam at the small, glassine bulb on the creature's back. The bulb shattered and the abomination collapsed.

Casey was still down and lifted her weapon to then target the tall reptilian creature, whose attention was still on the Russians, and struck its shoulder. The laser passed right through the flesh and bone.

There was an unholy screech, and the thing held up a small object, pointed at them – *a weapon*. Casey rolled across the floor and came to her feet, but behind her it struck two of the Russians who simply ceased to exist – one second they were there giving it all they had, and the next there was just a cloud of gray sparkling dust floating to the ground. Even the men's weapons had been totally disintegrated.

Another of the Russians charged the being, his fury roared in some sort of war cry. He had his gun in one hand and a long blade in the other. From six feet out he dived.

Brave fool, Casey thought, although she had to work hard to resist charging in herself. *Fight smart*, she cautioned herself as she tried to get a clear shot at the monstrosity.

But the Russian quickly found that just as his bullets were useless, his blade snapped against the tough body. The thing then grabbed the Russian in four arms and lifted him. Across the room Belakov got to his feet, yelling and pointing his gun, but there was no shot as his soldier was lifted higher in front of them, shielding the tall creature.

The dagger-like fingers dug in, penetrating the armored suit the Russian wore. And then they pulled apart, ripping the man in half – blood and entrails sprayed. Belakov yelled at his remaining men to take cover. They did, but they loaded their RPG launchers – Alex's orders or not, surviving took priority.

Casey fired her laser again and again, but despite its size the thing was fast and had clearly learned to stay out of the laser beam's path. It turned and shot its energy beam at her, and once again she had to run, duck, dive to the ground and roll. But now down, she was slower, and the creature sighted on her. It fired, the beam began to trace a line across the ground toward her body.

Casey leapt out of the beam's way just as a rocket tail left the RPG launcher of one of the Russians and sped across the small room. "*Shit*!" She yelled, and punched her visor button. Instantly it telescoped up over her face.

The explosion was near deafening in the small space, and debris blew back at them. Casey's suit easily protected her. But as she got to one knee, she saw that all the surviving Russians were down and moving groggily. She spun back to locate the creature, but it was gone.

"Where'd it go?" She leaped to her feet and searched the room. She saw no body fragments – they'd missed it. "Damn it." She turned, knowing they'd fucked up. "Element of surprise is now gone."

Casey Franks lifted her comms and tried to contact Alex. But the system delivered nothing but crackling white noise inside the heart of the pyramid.

CHAPTER 49

The many-armed creature dragged Joshua along the corridor and then began to speed up. He punched at it, trying to destroy more limbs, and even though he succeeded in damaging several, the thing was far more powerful than him and seemingly immune to pain, and simply continued its course to whatever destination it was being drawn to.

After a few seconds he found himself being hauled into a larger room and there, standing beside one wall, was one of the horrifying alligator-headed beings.

Joshua continued to wrestle with the many-armed thing holding him, panicking a little, trying to get away from the reptilian thing because he felt an impression of malevolence from it that he had never felt in a sentient being before.

Then the spider creature stopped and held Joshua out like an offering.

"Get away from me," he said as the reptile creature bent forward.

It turned one of its rows of red, bead-like eyes on him with little interest. It reached out one long, taloned arm, and Joshua flexed, determined to bend or break the fingers off.

The thing looked like it was momentarily in a high wind and a nictating membrane slid over all six eyes as its movement slowed. But this lasted only a few seconds, and there was no damage to the creature.

However, it did seem to spark the thing's interest. It reached out to grab Joshua with its pair of smaller mid-torso arms, and then lifted him to hold him in front of its face so it could examine him in detail.

Then the long mouth opened and Joshua thought he was about to be eaten. So, he flexed again, causing the thing to shut its mouth with a wet *snap*. It hissed and made some sort of clicking-grunting noise deep in its throat. Joshua thought he must have intrigued it, as it continued to stare at him.

"Let me go," Joshua demanded.

The creature turned back to the entrance and stared for a moment as though listening. Then, it put him down onto the ground, while still holding on to him, and began to move off into the corridor, pulling Joshua with it.

He beat it with his small fists but it was too strong; he couldn't seem to make any impression on it, let alone slow it down. A few moments later he found himself back in the room with the dark, liquid-looking doorway. And the thing was pulling him toward it.

Joshua could then sense the alienness of what lay beyond that dark portal, and he jerked and tugged hard, but the tall creature continued to walk toward it, dragging a struggling Joshua with it.

The doorway rippled like black water and Joshua flexed, and flexed again, but this time the creature ignored its effects. Joshua then reached across to grab its hand, hoping to at least bend back the iron-like grip of its fingers. But as soon as he laid hands on it, his mind exploded with images – he saw then their world, their plans, and worse, what this thing had in store for him.

He was an oddity it had found among the human race, and therefore one it wanted to analyze. He saw himself stretched out on a benchtop, his arms and legs tied down. His body was surgically opened, and his organs lay piled beside him on the bench. His entire head and face were gone, the brain dissected and pulverized, even his eyes, tongue and ears, all segmented and scrutinized to try to establish what made him different from all the countless others.

Joshua screamed and yanked his arm again and again, until he felt his shoulder pop with pain. But the thing just gripped him harder and began to step through the black, bottomless-looking portal.

Joshua's eyes went wide. "*No, no, no ...*"

And then they were gone.

INCIDENT 07

One step, and a million miles from home.

CHAPTER 50

Alex heard the RPG detonation as he ran, and guessed the Russians must have been under attack, otherwise Casey would have kicked their asses for using their explosives against his orders.

He came to a juncture and paused. He still couldn't sense exactly where Joshua was but this time he had a clue – on the ground at the mouth of the left-side tunnel there was a scraped mark in the damp sludge on the floor, and he was sure it belonged to a kid's bare foot that would fit the sneakers he had with him.

Good enough. He turned as he heard Sam coming at him, fast. He waved him on. "This way."

Alex accelerated down the tunnel and soon picked up his son's trail – it wasn't a set of footprints but more a stream of images, scents, and echoes, and all of them carried a perception of distress and fear.

He sprinted hard and got to the dim, vault-like room with the familiar dark portal in it just seconds later. He stopped and turned slowly, looking for any sign of his son.

"No," he whispered. "Please no."

Alex saw the swirling doorway, which looked like someone had disturbed a pool of black oil, exactly like the one in the pyramid in Australia. He walked toward it, already knowing what had happened.

He slumped. He'd just missed him.

Alex paced before the portal just as Sam arrived, followed by Klara and an out-of-breath Linley. Moments later, Casey and the remaining Russians joined them.

"They must have gone through," Linley said. "They're getting ready to leave."

Sam looked from the doorway to Alex. "Joshua?"

"They've taken him. Through there." Alex stared into the dark void.

"Without a suit." Linley exhaled.

"Orders?" Sam asked.

Alex turned. "I go get him."

"*We* go get him," Casey corrected.

"We need to shut the door," Linley said. "For good. If not, they'll be back again next Saros moon cycle. And perhaps next time, with better defenses."

"This is why we are here." Alex turned to his team, his face furious and eyes like silver lights in the dark room, and one of the Russians cursed softly.

"HAWCs, muscle up. We take the war to them," Alex said.

"*HUA*." Sam, Casey, and Klara never questioned or hesitated and quickly began checking their weapons.

Alex took the MSB-136 from his back and checked it over for a few moments. He handed it to Linley. "I'm going to give us thirty minutes to find and retrieve my son. Inside that portal, you plant the bomb on the doorway, and then evac. If possible."

Linley nodded and held out his hands. He took the device and then looked up. "I assume this means you want me with you?"

Alex nodded. "Yeah, I want you with us. To use your big brain to help close that portal in case we can't. I won't make you come, but I need you." Alex waited.

Linley nodded and returned a half-smile. "I wouldn't miss this for the world." He held up an arm. "Besides, I've been dying to see what these suits can do in boost mode."

To the side, Belakov was talking to his remaining men, who also checked their weapons as they prepared. He then turned. "I'm coming."

"No," Alex said. "You'll just get in the way."

Belakov shook his head. "I have waited twenty years for this. To avenge my father. I will not be denied. My men will stay here as sentinels."

Alex stared for a moment, contemplating it, and finally Linley broke the silence.

"Your projectile weapons will be useless. The gravity will also distort their trajectory, and it will also drag you down. You'll feel like you are wearing lead weights."

Belakov nodded. "Just me. My suit will give me some protection – I only need minutes."

"Okay, you're right, I need your men as sentinels. If anything gets past us, you cannot let them back through. And if it's my son; take care of him." Alex then turned to the scientist. "Linley, give him your laser. Your priority is the bomb placement."

"Thank you." Belakov smiled. "I promise to try and return it in one piece."

"*Ha!*" Casey exclaimed. "I love you, Boris, but I think you should focus on *you* coming back in one piece."

Alex looked back at the portal and spoke while staring into it. "Doctor, arm the bomb."

Linley worked the dials, and then lashed it to his back. "Done, thirty minutes and counting down."

Alex sucked in a deep breath. "On my three, two, one ..."

He, Sam, Casey, Klara, Linley, and the huge Russian ran at the dark portal and vanished.

CHAPTER 51

Colonel Jack Hammerson sprang forward.

He had been sitting in the darkened room, staring into the distance. One entire wall of his office was a bank of screens: some of them had landscape-level views of the Yemeni desert, but most of the satellite images were still nothing but confused static.

However, one of the screens had the five lifelines showing for the four HAWCs and the scientist, Linley, and they all suddenly went into flatline.

"Whoa." He exhaled loudly. *They've gone through*, he thought.

He continued to stare at the screen showing the five lines, and a terrible suspicion crept in: but what if they hadn't? What if the flatlining meant they were all dead? Vaporized.

He sat thinking for several seconds – there was always a Plan B, and that was to drop an EPW, an earth-penetrating weapon, commonly known as a nuclear bunker buster. The weapon was designed to penetrate soil, rock, or concrete to deliver a nuclear warhead to an underground target and could obliterate deep below-ground facilities.

The resultant underground explosion also released significantly more detonation energy into the ground compared to a surface burst or air burst explosion. Anything and every-thing down there would be burned to hell.

The plan was that if they caught them at the right time the portal would be open and deliver a vent of super-heated gases, radiation, and a percussive blast that might destroy the opposite end doorway.

Might.

The HAWC commander reached for the phone. But then he paused, his hand hanging in the air.

He also knew that if the doorway to their home world was closed, then they'd only be giving themselves a black eye. And if his HAWCs weren't dead already, they certainly would be after that.

Hammerson slowly lowered his hand.

He had no choice but to wait. For now.

* * *

DOG came back online.

It had been on guard duty at the rim of the well, ensuring nothing non-human breached the surface. But the moment Alex's thought patterns vanished from its sensors, its guardian protocols activated.

Guard, protect, defend. Independent action when required. Desert terrain. Full combat mode. Maximum lethality.

Shielding came up over the metallic canine's face and body, and in a blur of heavily armored steel-titanium composite, it launched itself toward Alex Hunter's last known position.

CHAPTER 52

Just as if plunging into water, Joshua sucked in a deep breath and then held it. But the sudden blast of furious heat burned his skin, and a fierce weight meant his joints ached from the strain.

He remembered what he had done with the plane and flexed to create a gravity and atmospheric bubble around himself that was like a tiny sphere of home while he was in ... where?

He kept his eyes closed to just slits as he looked around. He was in a blood-red world. He glanced up and saw that in the sky above him there were two suns, giant boiling fireballs, and all around him the sand dunes seem to extend forever.

They were on a path of stones that looked older than time itself, and behind him was the doorway, exactly like the one he had been dragged through, but now seeming to be nothing more than a two-dimensional portal at the end of the path. Its surface still swirled like dark liquid, as if their passing through it had left ongoing ripples.

He was in a procession of nightmarish beings. There were two of the alligator-head creatures, and dozens of the things like giant spiders, which he now knew were made up of people, parts of people. They were all a little different; some were long like centipedes, with long pads of muscles with arms and legs protruding from each side, and some were rounded pillows of human torsos melted together and surrounded by limbs.

Further out there were other oddities – perhaps a human head on top of one, and he was sure there were animal limbs and heads on a few others as well.

The creature who had dragged him through the portal still held Joshua's arm, and he grabbed it now, knowing he could not escape its grip, but knowing he needed to find out more.

He reached inside its complex mind and drew forth its thoughts, memories, and plans. With a shudder he saw that these beings had been plundering our world, and countless other worlds, for millions of years. They had no respect for the beings they took as they saw them as nothing more than donkeys harvested to do their hard labor.

He also saw that the ruined remnants of humanity that shuffled along the path would live for many centuries, until they literally rotted and fell apart. Their final reward was to be liquified and then fed to the others.

They were heading toward what looked like a city in the distance, and Joshua could see that some of the massive structures were pyramids that scraped the sky, with many more under construction. He could just make out that countless many-armed things were climbing up their gleaming sides, doing the building or repair work.

From the eight-foot-tall creature that held him, its talon-like hands digging in, he sensed elation – perhaps at being home, or perhaps because its slave-raiding visit had yielded more stock, more slave workers for its buildings.

Help me.

Who'd said that? Joshua spun around. "Armina?"

He frowned as he searched for her. It sounded like her voice in his head, but ...

Suddenly there came a deep, blaring horn sound, like a warning or distress alarm. The bass-deep sound rolled across the arid landscape, and he looked up at the creature holding him and saw confusion in its face, and perhaps what might have been fear.

It spun, looking back the way they had come, toward the now distant portal, just as something else began to come through.

CHAPTER 53

Alex was the first to land. He fell to his knees as the new gravitational pull took hold and made the weight of his own body feel colossal. Sam came through next, then Casey, Klara, Linley, and finally Belakov.

Alex lifted his head and turned it slowly. Around him was a red hell of sand and gravel, and there were oily distortion waves in the air from the atmospheric heat. He sucked in a breath. Even in the mechanized suit he felt his body being punished.

Something wormlike burrowed toward him and surfaced to fix a head like a remora on his glove, but it had no hope of penetrating the armor.

Looking for fluids, Alex bet. He punched down on the revolting thing, crushing it to spill a sticky tar-like liquid onto the sand. Around him more burrow tunnels started to appear.

"Get up," he yelled to his team, and then struggled to his feet using his own enhanced strength. Sam did the same, but he drew on his internal MECH structure to combat the enormous gravity. But Casey, Klara, and Belakov stayed down.

"Go to boost," Alex said.

Each HAWC punched the button in the center of their chest, and immediately felt the armored suit's technology compensate for the gravity to give them increased strength and mobility. Only Belakov struggled, but he made it to his feet, his shoulders slumped.

"Is heavy," he said. "And hot."

"I warned you," Alex said. "You either stay with us and keep up or head back through. No passengers; there's too much at stake."

"I keep up." The Russian sucked in a huge breath. "I only need to raise my gun arm, yes?"

"It's 312 hundred degrees," Linley said as he read off more data from his forearm gauntlet. "And the atmosphere is as we expected – a mix of carbon monoxide, sulfur, methane, hydrogen, and only fifteen percent oxygen – not primordial, more ... industrialized ... poisoned."

"There are our targets," Sam said, pointing.

In the distance, there was a caravan with several of the tall lizard-like people among it, as well as dozens and dozens of the decrepit souls in spider form, now altered to suit the alien environment. They were heading toward a skyscraper city.

"We can't let them get closer to the city; they'll likely have reinforcements." Alex said.

Linley looked like he was struggling even in his armored power suit. He turned to face the portal door, and broke into a smile. "Yes, yes, as we suspected, it *is* a two-way gate. And look, it has many destinations for planet Earth." He stepped closer. "But I'm sure these strange constellation maps are for other destinations, non-Earthly." He turned. "I'll bet these things have been poaching lifeforms from all across the universe."

"If we destroy the portal, will that stop them?" Alex asked.

"I think so. If this is the only portal." Linley turned to him. "Or until they can build another one."

"Then we close the portal and degrade their capability as well," Alex replied.

At that moment a pulse of pure energy came flying back to strike the ground between them. The red sand melted into a five-foot round pool of dark, molten glass as the group hit the ground.

"Seems the welcoming committee has noticed us," Sam said.

The group saw that the creatures from the caravan had been turned on them. They began to pick up speed.

"And here they come." Klara looked up. "Lot of bodies coming this way."

"Good. More to kill," Casey replied.

CHAPTER 54

The crawling horde rumbled toward them, falling over each other in their rush to get at the human beings. The only upside was that the gravity slowed them a little from the frantic, blistering speed they had had on Earth, but it still reminded Alex of when you poked an ants' nest and the insects came boiling out to attack the intruder.

"Use the lasers to hit the bulbs on their backs; it's their command center," Linley said.

"I'm good, but not that good," Klara replied.

Alex agreed; the things were still too far out to try to hit accurately, let alone hit something the size of a thumb on their back.

Klara fired anyway, and the laser's beam was a red-hot line of death, severing the legs on one side of her target creature and rendering it unable to balance or right itself. However, it still tried to drag itself toward them.

"That'll do in the meantime," Linley announced.

"Get behind us, Doc, you got some precious cargo there," Alex yelled. He aimed his weapon. "Free fire; give 'em hell."

Casey fired again and again, her beam reaching out to touch on and sever multiple limbs. She lowered her weapon. "Holy crap; you guys seeing this?"

In among the human spiders were larger creatures, some the size of elephants, and some even bigger. They had shaggy-haired bodies and limbs, and some had armored shingles as though they had once been monstrous armadillos.

"The results of their foraging on other worlds besides our own, I'll wager," Linley said.

The HAWCs were staying down as more and more of the creatures came at them. For every single one they hobbled, another two took their place.

"They're just going to keep us bogged down here until their reinforcements arrive," Alex said. "Sam, we go for the command structure. Let's take out the gator-heads."

"On it," Sam said, and rose to move up on the left flank. Alex did the same on the right. Both men began to run, as both had the benefit of the boost from their suits, but their own underlying power made them extremely formidable beings to begin with.

Casey, Klara, and Belakov kept firing continual beams into the horde and gave cover for Linley who stayed behind them but looked to be in awe of the red world and its denizens.

As Alex got closer, he saw something that filled him with hope – there was a sphere of swirling energy in among the group being led by one of the tall reptilian creatures, and he bet he knew what, and who, was causing it.

"*Joshua.*" He began to run even harder toward the oncoming mass of creatures, with Sam trying to keep pace but inevitably falling behind without Alex's blistering enhanced speed.

Alex dodged the pulses of energy flying past him, knowing that a direct hit would vaporize him and doom Joshua to whatever fate they had in store for him. But then he was fifty feet out, twenty, then ten, and then he leaped at the seething mass of many-armed and -legged creatures.

When Alex landed it was literally upon them, since so many of them were massed together that they were jammed in tight against each other's bodies. So he simply ran across their backs, and as he did so he pointed his laser at the beasts and held the trigger down so the beam cut a deadly line right through their thickened flesh and bone. Even the toughened skin and heavier internal structures were no match for the condensed light beam that sliced away limbs and cut some of the creatures completely in half.

Beneath him, the spider beings threw up dozens of arms, but Alex was too fast, and no matter how strong they were the higher gravity had slowed even these abominations down.

Alex then leaped from their backs to the planet's surface and in seconds had closed in on the main group, keeping his eyes on the ball of energy he prayed had his son cocooned within it.

"*Dad.*"

The single word, said by his son, generated a feeling of elation and fury within Alex that he had never felt before. His teeth clenched hard and tears of rage came to his eyes as his feet pounded down in a blur on the hard-packed red surface.

He glanced up to see a pulse of energy coming at him from the creature that held on to his son, and he dived to the side, allowing it to pass by him.

"Kill it, Dad, kill them all."

Alex dived, opening his arms wide, and then he was on it. He caught the thing in the mid-section where the small set of arms immediately gripped him.

He felt the talons scrabbling against the heavy armor he wore, and the alien was strong, but not strong enough to breach the special plating. At the same time it used its powerful upper arms to try and tear the helmet from his head. But Alex had a furious power beyond that of any other human being it had ever encountered, and that must have confused it. Each of Alex's blows cracked bones and ruptured skin, and after just a few moments, the reptilian being's movements got weaker.

As he began to overpower the creature, Alex saw that in one of its hands was a rounded object he assumed was the device that sent out the deadly energy pulses. He grabbed the wrist that held it and exerted all his strength on it. Satisfyingly, he heard the bones break, and the object fell to the ground.

The reptilian monster tried to strike him, rake at him, but Alex tightened a fist and clubbed at its head, smashing it, as the thing hissed and even resorted to trying to use its long-toothed snout to bite at his head and arms.

It finally went down with Alex on top of it, and its movements slowed. Never had Alex wanted to destroy something as he did now. And finally, when the thing lay back, defeated, there was one more thing he wanted to do. Alex retracted his face shield as he stared into its face. He held his breath and felt his skin burning as his eyes were being seared. But he wanted it to see him, wanted it to know.

"You picked the wrong world." He punched down with all his power into the chest, breaking through the alien's ribcage, and his hand reached the soft heart within. He grabbed it, and felt it beating in his hand, before he brought his fingers together, crushing the organ.

The monster fell back but kept moving, and Alex wondered whether it may have more hearts, or if the organ he destroyed wasn't a heart at all.

Alex then replaced his visor and closed his seared eyes, and waited as the blistered skin on his face repaired. But a thought intruded: *Finish it.*

Was it his own inner voice or Joshua demanding it? It didn't matter. He opened his healed eyes and looked down into the six red eyes of the beast. Then, grabbing both sides of the monster's head, he placed one heavy boot on its chest and wrenched with all his strength. With a tearing of flesh and snapping of bone he ripped the head completely from the body. Ochre blood spattered the red sand, where the small grub-like burrowers immediately appeared to suck it down.

He stood breathing heavily, dark blood covering his body and one arm to the elbow, and he held the ripped-free head by the worm-like protuberances on the top that had all now stopped their wriggling movement.

The others in the caravan were frozen in place as they watched, and after seeing what had happened they didn't stay to help but simply sped up their journey toward the city.

Alex reached down to pick up the thing's round pulser and jammed it in behind one of his chest plates. He looked up to see that the last retreating reptilian creatures were still firing pulses, but they weren't aimed at him but at his team.

"*Dad, Dad.*" Beside him Joshua's protective sphere began to wane and shrink, and Alex threw an arm out. "No, Josh, keep it up." Alex reached in to carefully pierce the cloud with one arm and grasped his son's hand.

Sam sprinted up to the pair. "Clock's ticking, boss. We got twelve minutes until the doc gives us boom time." He looked into the cloud and lowered his head toward it. "Hey, Josh, how's your day been?"

"*Very bad,*" the boy replied, but managed a weak smile.

Alex checked his gauntlet and saw the minutes ticking down way too fast. "Go, go, go," he yelled. He grabbed Joshua and lifted him, and then looked down at the monster's head lying on the red soil. He snatched it up in his other hand and looked to the retreating creatures. "Now for the rest of you."

The pair of HAWCs stood, with Alex holding Joshua's hand to guide him. A few pulses still passed over their heads from the creatures who were now rapidly vanishing in the distance.

The pair looked back to their group to see Doctor Linley standing by the portal still holding the MSB-136. When he met their gaze, the scientist urgently waved them over.

In the next second a single pulse from the Sobek creatures went past Alex and Sam and touched the scientist. One instant he was there, and the next, he and the bomb had both vanished into a cloud of glittering gray powder.

* * *

Back on the Earth side of the portal, the Russians spun away from the liquid-looking doorway to face the dark interior of the pyramid and raised their weapons at the sound of something coming at them at top speed.

Only seconds later, the canine droid raced into the room, and one of the men fired instinctively, but the bullets glanced off the dog's hardened armor.

DOG ignored them, and without slowing it headed straight for the portal, toward the last traces it could detect of Alex Hunter. In a blink it launched itself at the dark doorway and was gone.

One of the Russians straightened and half-turned to his colleague. "I don't know if that is a good thing or bad."

CHAPTER 55

Alex and Sam stared at each other for a moment after Doctor Linley had been vaporized. With their bomb.

"Well, shit. Now what?" Sam asked.

"We do it the hard way," Alex replied. "Just got to send someone home first."

Alex lifted Joshua and sprinted back to where Casey, Klara, and Belakov stood.

"He's gone," Casey yelled. "Those sons of bi—"

"Forget it," Alex said and pointed to the open portal. "You have new orders, Lieutenant."

Casey came to attention and Alex led Josh to her. "Get Joshua back through the portal, ASAP."

For a split second, Casey looked crestfallen that she wasn't going to be able to fight. But she threw it off as she realized the importance of her task. "You got it, boss." She looked at Joshua. "Hey, kid – time to go home."

"Armina," Joshua said, and turned to look around. "I sensed her. I think she's here."

"If she's here, I'll find her," Alex said. He looked Casey dead in the eyes. "I'm betting the Russians have plenty of F1 grenades. That right, Captain?" he asked Belakov.

"Yes, plenty," the Russian replied.

"Good." He checked the time, then faced Casey again. "If we're not back in twenty minutes, rig a single device with all of them and you use it to shut the portal – on the non-Earth side – you got it?"

She stared back for a moment, before nodding once. "*Sir.*"

Alex pointed at Belakov's chest. "Make it happen. Your work here is done." He then tossed Belakov the creature's head he was carrying. "For your father." Belakov caught it.

The big Russian nodded as he stared into its rapidly dimming eyes. "*Mudak.*" He then tucked the head under his arm like a football. He reached out to knock fists with Alex, then handed over his laser. "A pleasure to have met the Arcadian."

He went to turn away but paused. "You live up to the stories, Captain Alex Hunter. The man who cannot be killed will surely return." He saluted and turned away.

Maybe, Alex thought, and just as Casey went to head home, he yelled to them.

"*Joshua.*"

Casey paused and turned, while holding the boy.

Alex couldn't bring himself to say anything else, so he just raised a hand.

Joshua did the same.

Alex swallowed down a huge lump in his throat. "Franks." He said, and Casey nodded and begin to sprint back to the dark portal.

Alex watched the trio head toward the doorway – he knew they would make it and he felt a huge weight lift from his shoulders as his son would be safe. He wanted to wait until they passed through, but seconds mattered now.

Alex then turned to hand Sam the extra laser. "You get two. Make it count."

Sam took the weapon, holding one in each hand. "Just let me at them."

"What's the plan, boss?" Klara asked.

"We run 'em down. Try and avoid the spider bodies, and just take out the lizards. They're the threats. We take them down; we win the day." He handed Klara his laser. "You also get two."

She took it but looked up. "What about you?"

Alex reached behind his chest plate and retrieved the alien pulser he had taken from the creature. "Don't worry, I'll be taking more heads as well." He looked toward the towering city. "There must be a command center in there. We find it, and destroy it, and the threat to Earth is over."

As he lowered his hand he felt an odd grinding drag on the arm of his suit's armor. And then he knew. The heat was degrading their suits' electronics. They were designed for a burst of power, not continual combat mode.

"Our time's running out," he said.

"We'll never make it to the city, find the command center and be back at the portal before Casey blows it," Klara said.

"Maybe not," Alex replied. "But I meant the suits are wearing out. If they stop working, we'll be marooned in them."

Sam groaned. "This day sure ain't getting any better."

Alex turned back. "Then let's get this done."

They ran, hard, the suits doing most of the work, and they ate up the ground quickly. As they raced to the gleaming city of towering pyramids, Alex saw that the few remaining many-legged things moved out of their way and seemed only interested in stalking machine-like back to their city.

He thought he saw that one of the multi-armed and -legged things had something attached or growing from its back that could have been a human head, but he couldn't quite make out what it was. Nevertheless, he sensed something from it, something familiar. But Alex ignored it as they had more important priorities.

"Boss," Klara yelled. "Getting real hard to move back here."

Alex nodded. "It's the atmosphere. The sulfur and the heat; they must be eating the electronics."

He and Sam began to outpace Klara, but they still had a mile to go to catch up to the caravan. And then miles more to the city. Even Alex knew it was going to be impossible to return before Casey blew the portal.

And there was something else. "Sam, Klara, tell me what you think that is." He pointed to the sky ahead of them.

The female HAWC engaged her helmet's vision amplification. Over the city a shimmering dome was beginning to form. "I know what I think it is; we've spooked 'em enough that they're dropping a force field over the city – they're shutting the door on us."

"Yeah, that's what I thought." Alex squinted into the distance. "They've kept a small section open for the caravan to enter. I'm betting once they're through the entire thing will seal, with us on the outside."

"Something else," Sam said. "I see a line of spiders pouring from the city. It seems we're about to face their major response. They want to slow us down; keep us away from their home base."

"Those bastards use those slave things as their attack dog army as well," Klara spat.

Alex turned slowly. "Hey, something's happening."

Around them the ground began to rumble. Alex held his arms out to keep balance but sensed something was coming. Something really big.

"Incoming," Sam yelled and dived to the ground.

Then the behemoth arrived.

The hard-packed red earth exploded around them as something emerged that was like a massive whale breaching the ocean surface. Except this beast had long, scaled legs.

On the end of each were several curved talons. It seemed to be based on the same morphology as the human derivatives. However, as this thing dragged itself to the surface, they saw that its body was bigger than a school bus.

"A giant," Sam yelled.

"Like Linley told us." Alex began to back up. "This must be an amalgamation of beings from another world."

The creature was heavily armored and looked more like a crab as it shook itself free from the red dust. But it seemed the reptile creatures hadn't finished sending in their shock troops because further out another monster breached the sand's surface. The new monstrosity was a similar design of multiple arms or legs, but was covered in thick, wiry fur. And where the armored creature was big, this one was a land leviathan, and the size of a city block.

"Holy shit." Klara lifted her two laser rifles. "Cutting time." She fired a double beam at the thing.

The beams struck, burned, and punched through, but they were pinholes to the gargantuan. It must have felt them, though, because Klara got a response. It leaned around toward her, and from the front end they could see another of those retractable mouths. They soon learned this one had another use.

The beast aimed itself at Klara, who stood with legs planted, still firing her condensed light into the massive mountain of hair and flesh. Then the creature suddenly vomited or spat a stream of green-hued slime that struck Klara and about twenty feet of ground around her. Immediately smoke began to rise from the red sand. And then her armored suit.

It was like a sticky glue and it clung to her frame, and she wiped at it. Then more frantically.

"Boss. Got a problem here," she said quickly.

Oh shit, Alex thought. He could see one of the plates on her arm begin to soften as though it was made of wax left out in the hot sun, and then some sort of gas started rising from it.

More alarmingly, her helmet began to do the same. Without her armor she'd be dead in minutes if not seconds.

Sam was the first to reach her, and held her as she threw her head back in pain. The armored plates began to open holes that allowed in the planet's furious heat and toxic gases.

Above them, the colossal beings hadn't finished, and the one that had spat its acid onto Klara began to ready itself again, this time probably hoping to cover Sam as well.

Alex lifted the Sobek creature's pulser and fired it. A ball of energy shot from the puck-like thing and struck the side of the furred creature. Flames rose from the impact site, and he saw a red-raw manhole-sized cavity had been excavated into its skin.

A whining scream of pain filled the air, and the monster shuddered a little as though preparing to move off, but then began to swing back as if it had changed its mind. Alex wondered if perhaps it, too, had a glass bulb pressed into its surface that commanded it to continue its attack no matter how much pain and damage it absorbed.

Alex looked down at the puck weapon and saw on the side a dial with a row of small lights above it – an energy calibration? he wondered. He'd soon find out. He pushed it up to the maximum setting, aimed and fired again.

A pulse left the tiny device and grew larger in the air. By the time it had traveled the distance to the creature it was roughly the size of a truck wheel. It struck the side of the shaggy colossus just as it was lowering its front end toward Sam and Klara, and there was a blast of flesh and burned fur. Then the thing staggered to the side, revealing a gaping hole in its body easily twenty feet across. The red and dripping meat inside the gigantic wound sparkled as it continued to burn away, but it soon turned black as it dried.

That'll do, Alex thought, and immediately swung the pulser to the other creature, which was smaller and which so far had been constrained by the size of the bigger beast leading the attack.

Alex fired again, and this time when the ball of energy struck, the entire mid-section of the armor-plated creature was vaporized, leaving just a lot of light pole–sized hard-shelled legs standing that collapsed inwards like a forest.

Alex ran to Klara, who lay moaning on the ground. Already other holes were opening on her chest armor and helmet, and the hellish atmosphere and heat were reaching her body.

Sam quickly stuck magnetic patches on the largest holes, but more of the suit was beginning to soften. He turned. "Gotta evac her, boss." He then faced the alien city, which was still half a mile away.

Alex turned to see the last of the many-legged creatures streaming through the remaining hole in the force field. It was now only about twenty feet wide, and he knew that even if he sprinted, he'd be lucky to make it through.

"Take her." Alex stood, judging the distance.

"What? Boss, come on. This is futile." Sam lifted Klara in his arms.

Alex looked at the timer on his gauntlet – there was just on eleven minutes until Casey blew the gateway. Enough time for Sam and Klara to get out, but not enough for him to make it to the force field, and then back.

What damage could he do to them? He had no planet-busting bomb, and only a single pulser. But maybe he could cause them enough damage that they might think twice about coming back.

Alex tried to think of other options, but there were none.

"Gotta go, boss." Sam stepped closer. "Come on."

"Dammit. I need more—" Alex frowned. "What the Hell …?"

Sam turned. Sprinting across the red sand was an object that became more familiar the closer it came.

Alex grinned. "DOG."

In seconds the droid skidded to a halt in front of him and sat looking up, waiting for his command. Alex bet that if it had had a tail, it'd be wagging it.

He remembered how the droid he'd worked with before, Sophia, had ended her artificial life, and an idea came to him.

"DOG. Critical mission."

The droid stood to attention on its four legs. Alex couched, looking into its armored face. For some reason he felt the need to put a hand on its head as he spoke to it.

"Go through the opening in the force field, maximum speed. Enter city." He drew in a deep breath, feeling a pang of loss already. "Find the energy center, and then detonate internal fusion reactor."

DOG looked back at him, its eyes glowing. There was no regret, or challenge, just a desire to follow Alex's orders.

Alex got to his feet and pointed to the city. "Engage order."

The little droid sprinted away in a blur.

"Hell yeah." Sam still cradled an unconscious Klara. "Eat that behind your force field, you bastards."

Alex watched the DOG sprint toward the closing hole in the force field for a moment more. He then glanced at his timer. "Six minutes, Sam. Let's leave nothing in the tank or we're here for good."

"Not even a nice place to visit," Sam said, and began to run, carrying the female HAWC in his arms.

As the pair of HAWCs ran, Alex could hear Sam's armor begin to grind and complain. He felt his own doing the same. It'd be a race, not just between them and Casey's orders to blow the red planet's portal, but between them and their suit armor's integrity.

Every step they took brought them closer. But every time Alex looked, it seemed their escape route through the dark oval portal was going to be a hundred steps too far.

CHAPTER 56

Belakov dived through the gateway, followed by Casey Franks, who dragged Joshua with her. The glowing sphere around the boy immediately dissipated, and he lay on his back, sucking in huge breaths and with blood streaming from his nose. The skin on his face was red, blistered, and peeling.

"You're okay, kid." Casey pushed herself to a sitting position. Smoke rose from her armored exoskeleton. She watched the boy as the blisters on his face popped, dried, and then vanished.

Just like his father, she thought.

"Dad." Joshua got to his feet but he looked hunched and weak. He stood in front of the portal's seemingly bottomless, dark void.

"He'll be fine," Casey said, but she doubted that was going to be the reality. She checked her gauntlet; time was fast running out until she was due to blow the portal.

Belakov got to his feet and held up the still dripping reptilian head in front of his remaining team. The other Russians cheered the trophy and Belakov shook it. "Don't fuck with Mother Russia," he yelled, and shook the still bleeding body part again.

"Hey, stop patting yourself on the back, Boris. We ain't done yet," Casey said. "Everyone give me their grenades, right now. I need to splice them into a single detonation device, and then blow it on the far side of the portal – destroy it from their end."

She walked up to the dark portal, remembering what Linley had told her about closing it. It needed to be closed before she detonated the device, or the blowback would come right back into their faces.

Still doable, she thought.

The men began pulling out their reserves of the powerful Russian F1 grenades, which were silver canisters about half the size of soda cans. Belakov helped Casey quickly bind and wire them together, and then he placed a single timer on top.

"Time?" Belakov asked.

Casey checked her gauntlet timer and then cursed softly. "Three minutes." She sighed. "And Sam and the boss have got to be back in two minutes, fifty-nine seconds."

The Russian set it. "Done." He handed the loaf of bread–sized kit to her. "It is all in God's hands now."

Casey nodded and took the package. She turned it over. "There's no clamp or magnetic pad." She tilted her head back on her shoulders. "I'm gonna have to hold this mother in place as I shut the portal."

Belakov turned to her and smiled. "I think that might sting a little."

* * *

DOG moved at a blistering speed, avoiding being blasted, and making it through the hole in the force field with inches to spare. It then used its sensors to find the area within the city that was generating the greatest form of energy.

The powerful, canine-shaped android used its lasers to cut through walls, doors, and to slice in half any lifeform that got in its way.

When it found the generator room, it stopped and faced the machines. Behind it there was the pounding of running feet from all manner of grotesque creatures.

DOG repeated its very first underlying protocol: *Protect. Defend. Destroy.* It became motionless, but then all its armor peeled back to reveal a glowing heart, its fusion reactor, at its center. The heart glowed, hotter and brighter, and then, detonated.

Everything inside the dome force field was vaporized in a blast that was hotter than the sun – the skyscraping pyramids, the thousands of alligator-headed beings, as well as the countless multiple-limbed creatures created to be their eternal slaves. They all ceased to exist.

The force field contained the blast and magnified it internally. When the mist of chemicals and heat finally dissipated, all that remained was a giant lake of molten slag, which would one day cool to a smooth sheen of nothingness.

Out on the blood-red plain there was still an army of the many-legged creatures. They froze in place as their orders stopped being received.

CHAPTER 57

Alex and Sam ran, but they were slowing. Even the enormous strength of both men had finally been worn down, exactly like their suits, which began to change from lifeboats of super-powered armor and a life-sustaining atmosphere to cumbersome anchors. It was a race now to beat them becoming their coffins.

Alex looked at his gauntlet. "Two minutes. Let's lift it, Reid."

Both men put everything in as they closed the gap: 100 yards, eighty, fifty – the legs of Alex's suit stiffened up and he had to fight them to keep them moving – thirty yards, twenty, ten …

"Go!" Alex yelled as Sam dived, still holding the unconscious form of Klara. Both of them vanished through the oval gate.

Alex turned briefly and saw the massive pyramid city within the dome of its force field glow like the center of a sun. "Good boy," he said, knowing DOG had done its job.

Then the force field over the doomed city vanished, and a shock wave erupted toward him in a wall of explosive power. Alex turned and dived through the portal.

Alex hit the ground and felt instant relief as he went from burning red heat to darkness and cool. His armor popped and creaked from the change in temperature.

He turned. "*Close it!*" he yelled.

"On five, four ..." Casey yelled. She sucked in a huge breath, steeling herself, and then put her hand through the portal, clamping the suit's armored glove onto the red world's side of the portal frame, with the bomb held in it.

She shut her eyes and spoke through gritted teeth. "Three ... two ..."

"*What the hell are you doing?*" Alex jerked forward.

"*One!*" Casey yelled.

The portal center swirled, and then solidified to become a hard surface, taking Casey's arm with it. Casey fell back, her bleeding stump spurting blood in an arc in the air. Her eyes bulged as she held her cleanly severed forearm and made a hissing sound from between her bared teeth.

She held the stump out. "Sam."

Casey turned away as Sam Reid immediately pointed his laser at the spurting half-limb and fired a thin beam, cauterizing the massive wound.

"Goddamn it, Franks." But Alex knew what she had done and why. He hated to see it but understood she wouldn't have done it if it wasn't necessary – and any one of them would have done the same.

"You know me," she said through a pain-racked grimace. "Always wanting to be the center of attention."

Alex searched for Joshua, and saw the boy slumped against one wall. His son gave Alex a weak thumbs-up, and Alex rushed to him, lifting him and hugging him.

"You made it," Joshua said.

Alex put his son down and looked into his face. "You know I would cross worlds to keep you safe. And I did." He smiled and Joshua burst into tears and held on to his father.

"Hey." Alex held him at arm's length and then reached into the pocket on his thigh to draw forth Joshua's shoes. "You forgot these."

Joshua took them. And then they both saw that the soles were melted. "They're still good," he said, and sat to put them on.

Alex looked to Sam who was leaning over Klara. "How is she?"

Sam had pulled the helmet from the female HAWC's head, and she murmured but remained unconscious. "Burns to her exposed skin, and she sucked in a lot of the toxic gas, so I'm betting she has some lung damage." He nodded to Alex. "But I think she'll make it."

The three remaining Russians and the wounded Casey looked from the gateway to Alex.

"Did it work?" Casey asked.

"Did we blow the portal and close it?" Alex exhaled. "Probably, but with the portal closed, for all we know that detonation occurred a trillion light years away from us." He walked forward to lay a gloved hand against the now hard door. "We won't know for sure for another eighteen years when the next Saros eclipse cycle occurs." He turned back to them with a grim smile. "But I saw their city burn. There's nothing left."

"*HUA!*" Casey and Sam said.

Alex leaned over and helped Casey up. She stood, her face drained of color. "Alright, soldier?" he asked.

She gave him one of her smiles that with the scar on her cheek looked like a sneer. "How do I look?"

Alex put a hand on her shoulder. "Like someone who just saved our world."

"Boss." She straightened. "I feel better already."

Alex stared at the dark portal. "The city is gone, and all those souls trapped as slaves are now free. But if, somehow, they return, then we'd better be ready for them. Because next time they'll come back pissed off as all hell."

"We'll be ready." Belakov held up the severed head. "By the time they return, we will know a hundred ways to kill them."

"Keep us informed." Alex looked hard at the Russian, who nodded.

Joshua stood and came and put an arm around his dad's waist, and Alex looped an arm over the boy's shoulder.

Joshua looked up at him and his mouth turned down. "I still can't find Armina."

"We'll do a last sweep to clean up. If she's here, we'll get her," Alex said, but then shook his head. "But if she isn't ..."

"I know." Joshua turned away. "And no, we won't find her. I think she's gone."

Alex nodded, and just hoped that if she wasn't here, then she was dead.

CHAPTER 58

I can't see, Phillip Huang said. Or thought he said. *Can anyone hear me?*

Yes. No. Bradley Saunders felt the hot sand beneath his hands and feet. He felt strange; strong, but somehow bound and so crowded in it made him feel claustrophobic. It was like being stuck in an overcrowded car where he controlled some of the parts, but not all of them. And he was hungry. All the time.

Where are we? Huang asked.

Don't you know? Saunders thought as his reply. He began to laugh, but only in his mind. And maybe he would have cried as well if he'd had eyes. *We got our wish.*

What? Please tell me, Huang begged. *I feel strange. Am I dreaming?*

No dream. We wanted to help the Sobek people. The gods. Saunders giggled. *And now we can. Forever.*

You mean …? Oh no, not that, Huang begged.

You wanted to know if these many-armed constructs could think and retained any of their memories, Saunders replied. *Now you know the answer to those questions.*

More voices chimed in, some speaking Arabic, some English, and all were a confused babble.

Huang began to weep as another voice wafted across their collective consciousness.

Is my father there? the small voice asked. *I'm scared. I can't see anything.* She started to wail.

It's best you can't, Saunders replied softly.

I want to go home, the girl's voice begged.

You are home, Saunders replied.

Obey, came the command.

All the voices were immediately silenced, as the glassine orb pressed into their flesh sent a pulse of pain through the heavily muscled back and along the cranial mass.

After the city was destroyed, other cities across the planet took control of them. Commands were received and all the drones complied, turning to the western horizon and the location of the next great city.

The many-legged and -armed creature turned to follow the herd to the horizon, to the centuries of slavery ahead of them.

CHAPTER 59

One month later – Russian Ministry of Defense, Khamovniki District, Moscow

Belakov crossed to the special freezer he had installed in his office and opened the door. He smiled in at the alien head before lifting it out. He then carried it to a table and set it on a wooden block on top that he'd had specially made.

The Russian sat down in the soft, brown leather chair he had pulled up in front of it, and stared at his trophy for a long moment, noting its long reptilian form, the teeth a little more needle-like than a normal alligator's, and the rows of eyes, two rows, running up each side of its snout.

The eyes were dull now, but there was still a pink blush just retreating from the red glow they'd had when the creature was alive. On the top of the head were the worm-like growths – some form of hair? he wondered. Or feelers? He had no idea.

The Russian reached out to touch the skin. It was hard and cold, but he felt the bumps of the tiny scales and the bones beneath the skin. He knew he needed to hand it over to the science division so they could understand exactly what the thing was, how it had evolved, and also what its genetic, physical, and cellular processes were. Basically, if these accursed creatures ever returned, they needed to know how to kill them faster.

All in good time, though, because there was one important thing he needed to do first. Major Nikolas Belakov, Russian Special Forces, rose from his chair, grabbed a bottle of vodka from his shelf and poured two double shots. He then pulled the leather chair up even closer to the decapitated head and sat, staring at it for a few moments longer.

Belakov placed one shot glass in front of a photograph of his father, and the other he raised high.

"For my father, Uri Churnov, and all those lost in the Caucasus that day." He skolled the glass's contents, and then slowly lowered it.

His face became serious as he stared hard into the monster's milky eyes. "You fucked with the wrong world this time." He leaned forward to smile cruelly into the beast's lifeless face. "I hope you do come back. Because I'll be waiting."

CHAPTER 60

Buchanan Road, Boston, Massachusetts

Alex saw her through the window – Aimee was pacing on the front porch and stopped as their black SUV pulled up.

"There she is, *go*," he said.

Behind him the rear door was kicked open, and Joshua exploded from inside.

"*Mom.*"

Aimee burst into tears and sprinted toward him across the front lawn, arms outstretched. Though the boy was nearly as tall as she was, she managed to catch him in a bear hug and spin him around. Alex felt a lump come to his throat.

She kissed his head, ruffled his hair, and then held his cheeks as she looked deep into his face to examine every tiny scratch, abrasion, or bruise, as only mothers can.

Alex turned to shake the hand of his senior officer. "Thank you, Jack," he said.

"No, thank you, Arcadian." Colonel Jack Hammerson hung on to his hand. "Because of you, once again our world rests easy." He glanced out at Aimee. "And no one will ever know what you sacrifice."

Alex smiled flatly. "That is our way."

Alex then stepped out and watched Aimee and Josh a moment more. Then, from inside the house there came a noise like thunder, as if everything was being knocked over and smashed, and the screen door was blown off its hinges as the huge animal came off the deck like a 250-pound missile.

"*Incoming,*" Josh yelled as he let go of Aimee and the dog crashed into him, knocking him flat. Tor then lay on top of him, licking his face to the sound of Josh's wild laughter.

Aimee turned to Alex then, her cheeks still wet. She smiled, ran toward him and grabbed him, and kissed him hard on the mouth.

She pulled back. "I knew you'd get him. Only you could." She grabbed his hand and dragged him closer to Josh and Tor.

She pointed. "Don't let him grow up without you. Don't miss the best years of your – and his – life." She looked up at Alex and squeezed his hand, hard. "And mine."

Alex understood at that moment. That this was his life, and his world, and nothing was more important.

"I'm never going away again," he said.

"What?" Her brows shot up. "You promise?"

He nodded. "I'm resigning. I'm done."

She squealed and hugged him, covering his neck in kisses. "I love, I love, I love you." She then pushed him back a step and lifted her arms in the air. "Okay, everybody in the house," she yelled. "It's party time."

"C'mon, Dad." Josh ran to the house, followed by the huge animal.

Alex jogged behind him, and when he was on the porch, he turned to see Aimee facing the dark SUV.

Inside Hammerson saluted her. But she just stared, her expression like stone, and she slowly turned away without acknowledging him.

All things change, Alex thought as he watched the SUV drive off.

Aimee came and looped an arm around his waist and beamed up at him.

He held her face. "Nothing in this world could make me leave you and Josh ever again." He kissed her and then took her hand and together they headed inside their house.

EPILOGUE

Edge of Sabine-D crater, southwestern part of Mare Tranquillitatis – the moon

The Chinese lander slowed as it approached the lunar surface. Commander Yin Jiang commanded the ship himself, assisted by copilot Zhang Jun.

They counted down as the ship approached the glittering purple-gray surface, which now swirled below them as the thrusters worked hard to allow them to gently lower the heavy lander.

Zhang Jun counted down. "Five meters, four, three, two ..."

The struts kissed the lunar surface, and then the hydraulics compressed to take the weight. The engines cut off, and once again there was stillness on the tiny, gray astral body.

The pair of men turned to high-five each other and then quickly sent a message back to the Chinese National Space Administration in Haidian District, Beijing.

Commander Yin Jiang and Zhang Jun sat staring out at the eerie silence, and simply moved their eyes over the craggy surface with its sharp ridged craters and almost liquid-looking flat surfaces that sparkled with different mineral dusts.

"We're really here," Zhang Jun said.

The commander nodded. "Better late than never." He peered out at the surface again. "But since the Russians and Americans have abandoned the moon, then it is only right that we should stake a territorial claim over it." He turned, grinning. "He who has the high ground, has the advantage."

The men high-fived again, and Yin Jiang uncoupled his harness. "Retrieve the flag, I'm going to plant it."

"I should come. Second man out, of course," Zhang Jun said hopefully.

Yin Jiang thought for a moment and decided it couldn't hurt. "Yes, you can take my photograph. But you are not to be in the picture."

* * *

At the edge of the crater, a brushed-silver metallic body remained totally immobile while watching the lander with a focused intensity. It had picked up the Chinese communications from the lander when they were still in orbit; the language was just one of the many stored in its linguistic database. It could even tell from the dialect which province the men came from.

It watched as the hatch opened and the two men came down the ladder with the usual slowness brought on by the lower gravity and cumbersome suits. The pair headed toward a crater rim, where the light was best. One of them carried a Chinese flag and the other a camera.

Sophia judged the distance and then got to her feet to move quickly to the lander. She went up the ladder like a spider, and once inside she had a few minutes to find something of near comparable weight and eject it, and then fold herself into the small space left behind.

Then she had to do nothing but wait.

She was an android, but inside her chassis she felt a burst of something she hadn't felt in years – excitement – and she wondered if Alex Hunter on Earth missed her as much as she missed him.

AUTHOR'S NOTES

Many readers ask me about the background of my novels – is the science real or imagined? Where do I get the situations, equipment, characters, and their expertise from, and just how much of it has a basis in fact?

As a fiction writer I certainly create things to support my stories. But mostly, I'll do extensive research on the science behind my tale, and nearly always find something that fits!

Regarding my novel *The Well of Hell*, I begin my tale in ancient Yemen because it is one of the oldest places in the world, with archeological evidence of megalithic structures dating back to the Neolithic (20,000 years ago). It is also the home of the eerie Well of Hell, a real site in the Al-Mahara desert that is many millions of years old and a place of countless legends.

The city of Allonia, the great king Akmezdah and his son, and their ancient pyramids, were all constructs from my own imagination. However, in relation to pyramids, even though the Egyptians claim theirs are the oldest, especially the pyramid of Djoser which dates back more than 5000 years, there are far older ones – and it is the architecture of the mega-structure that is seen in many places all around the world – and all seeming to be of a similar design. It is almost as if someone taught these ancient people(s) how to build them!

Read on for more interesting facts that came out of my research.

Regards, *Greig Beck*

Where are the oldest pyramids in the world?

Just a few years ago, the Sudanese minister of information, Ahmed Bilal Othman, claimed that the Meroë Pyramids of Sudan are 2000 years older than Egypt's pyramids. Naturally, these claims stirred up outrage among Egyptians, particularly history experts.

Zahi Hawas, the Egyptian former minister of antiquities, countered by asserting that their pyramids are the oldest, especially the pyramid of Djoser, and Egypt has 132 pyramids which are considered to be among the oldest in the history of mankind.

Of course, there are other ancient pyramids, such as the beautiful Mayan pyramids in Mexico, and those megalithic structures were built 4500 years ago, according to archaeological consensus.

However, it might surprise you to learn that the oldest discovered pyramid in the world might have been constructed over 20,000 years ago. On the Indonesian island of Java there is the Gunung Padang recently discovered by a team of independent international researchers led by Indonesian geologist Doctor Hilman Natawidjaja.

Many dispute this 20,000-year estimation date, but the growing consensus is that the base layer of the pyramid (layer three) is *at least* 10,000 years old and possibly much older. If the researchers are indeed correct, Gunung Padang would be the most ancient man-made mega-structure on Earth.

Those civilizations that vanished

Civilization has a life-span – great races and their cities rise, flourish, and then wane and vanish completely, or are absorbed into other greater civilizations.

There are tales dating back centuries of intrepid explorers trekking across inhospitable deserts or hacking through jungles to discover massive crumbling temples or buried chambers full of treasure that were once the royal vault, or burial chamber of a king or queen.

Some of the more famous and well-known vanishing civilizations are: the Mayan, the Indus Valley civilization, Easter Island, Catalhöyük, Cahokia, Göbekli Tepe, Angkor, Neya, Nabta Playa, and the Turquoise Mountain in Afghanistan.

Why did people abandon these once-thriving cities? What brought them down? Sometimes the answer is known, in other cases it is a mystery. But the Indus civilization was a model for parts of my story and is a good example of the rise and mysterious fall of a great civilization.

The Indus, also known as the Harappan civilization, was one of the largest in ancient history, covering parts of India, Pakistan, and Afghanistan and containing as many as five million people. At its height, the Indus civilization boasted some of the world's most impressive architecture, among other achievements in science and the arts. But it disappeared approximately 3000 years ago, almost overnight, for reasons not fully known.

Like most of these fallen civilizations, all that remains is a few tumbled stones, broken pottery, and roads that only ghosts now travel upon.

The SAROS period – predictor of eclipses

The Saros is a period of 223 synodic months, or just on eighteen years, that can be used to predict eclipses of the sun and moon.

After an eclipse, the sun, Earth, and moon return to approximately the same relative geometry – a near straight line – and a nearly identical eclipse will occur, in what is referred to as a Saros eclipse cycle. In this time, gravitational forces are exerted and extreme tidal effects are observed.

The earliest discovered historical record of what is known as the Saros is by Babylonian astronomers. But it wasn't until 1686 that the name "saros" was applied to the eclipse cycle by Edmond Halley, the English astronomer and mathematician who was the first to calculate the orbit of a comet later named after him.

Interestingly, the Saros period of 223 lunar months was found hard-coded into the *Antikythera Mechanism,* described as the oldest example of an analogue computer used to predict astronomical positions and eclipses decades in advance, and was made around 150 to 100 BC in Greece. This Saros period number is one of a few inscriptions of the mechanism that are visible with an unaided eye.

The planet killer bomb

In my story I refer to the HAWCs using a "planet killer bomb", called an MSB-136. This is a made-up device and my MSB stands for "Murder-Suicide Bomb" because that's what it would be – after all, why would you blow up the planet when it's the only one you've got?

But there was a time when there was a push to develop bigger and bigger city killers, and the largest bomb detonated to date was on 30 October 1961. At that time, the biggest nuclear weapon ever constructed was set off over Novaya Zemlya Island in the Russian Arctic Sea. The Soviet "Tsar Bomba" had a yield of fifty megatons, or the power of around 3800 Hiroshima bombs all detonated simultaneously.

Although the Tsar Bomba was detonated two miles above ground, a seismic shock wave equivalent to an earthquake of over 5.0 on the Richter Scale was measured around the world. The mushroom cloud reached a height of thirty miles, and third-degree burns were possible at a distance of a hundred miles.

Thankfully, due to its immense size (the casing was as big as a Buick) it meant it could not be delivered via ballistic missile. It was therefore impractical for use as a military weapon, and, thankfully, the project was mothballed.

CPSIA information can be obtained
at www.ICGtesting.com
Printed in the USA
BVHW042131051022
648810BV00002B/15

9 781761 263941